Wolf Pack chronicles Standalone
BOX SET
Wolf Shifter Paranormal Romance

Amelia Wilson

Seeking the Alpha

Wolf Pack chronicles Series

Amelia Wilson

Contents

PROLOGUE:

You can never, truly, know when the worst day of your life is coming. It's always waiting for the perfect moment to spring out, to become an unexpected bump in the tracks that derails your entire life. Of course, Mia couldn't have known that she was living in the worst day of her life. She had pancakes for breakfast. A boy told a great joke in her science class. She even finished her homework early. How could she have ever have believed her worst day had finally arrived; looming over her like a dark shadow?

According to Mia, the woods were the soundest place to be. They were a secret haven, nestled in between her backyard and the middle school she walked to each day. The towering trees burst from the ground, sheltering her with their colorful leaves. They were mighty towers that she pretended were part of her own fortress, a powerful force that sheltered her from the troubles of her everyday life. She could close her eyes, and breathe in the delicious concoction of crisp autumn air, and tangy pine and leaves, still wet from a recent downpour.

Mia flourished here, and she walked home from the school one afternoon with an extra spring in her step, the keychains on her backpack jangling as she hopped carefully from stone to stone across the bubbling creek. She hummed to herself – a new song she'd learned in chorus class that day – relishing this tiny place of freedom. She passed a bulky tree, smiling up at its branches, blissfully unaware of the figure hiding behind it waiting to spring out at her.

Mia tumbled to the ground with a hard thud, and her backpack slid up her back as her legs flew back over her head and she rolled over. Another body collided into her, arms clutching round her waist as it dragged her down into a swooping ditch in between the trees. Mia cried out, trying desperately to untangle her arms from the knot of limbs, but she couldn't. The knot separated as they crashed into a pile of leaves. Mia felt the weight leave her and her eyes fluttered open, suddenly blinded by the blank slate of the grey sky above her. She could hear the leaves next to her shuffling wildly, and soon her attacker was standing right over her, his shadowy frame filling her vision.

"Rowan!" Mia shouted as she sprang up from the ground, still covered in a layer of crumpled leaves. She punched the shaggy-haired boy in the shoulder.

Rowan laughed, revealing the gap between his two front teeth. "You should've seen your face," Rowan said, clutching his stomach in the hope of containing his laughter.

"I already knew you were there," Mia said defensively.

"Yeah right," Rowan said, brushing his hair out of his face.

His locks were dark-chestnut; often unkempt and just covered his deep-hazel eyes. Mia stared a little too long at him and was startled as his hand reached out to help brush the leaves from her clothes. She felt a tiny spark, almost like the minuscule zap one gets from a wool sweater, as Rowan picked a bright-orange leaf from her jacket sleeve. Mia often felt this way when Rowan was around. He was almost like lightning to her, though she couldn't quite sum up this feeling into perfect words.

"Oh, I missed one," Mia said, but Rowan beat her to the leaf still burrowed in her amber hair.

"Your hair is soft," Rowan said nonchalantly. Even with his indifferent tone, Mia still took it to heart, as a compliment. At fourteen she was not really starting to think about boys, but whenever she was with Rowan she felt different.

"Race you to the rock!" She said, as she took off. She was already halfway to her favorite spot. Rowan groaned, shuffling awkwardly through the piles of leaves, kicking them up into the air.

They sat on their rock, looking out at their neighborhood nestled safely below. Mia took out a thick marker, coloring a new drawing wherever she could find space.

"You shouldn't draw on it, Mia," Rowan said. Mia shrugged.

"It's a little late for that," she said, gesturing to the dozens of faded drawings she had already completed during their times at the rock. She expected Rowan to laugh, but as she looked up at him she was immediately concerned at his firm expression. He gazed sadly out into the neighborhood.

"Mom's packed up the last few boxes already," Rowan said quietly.

Mia capped her marker, her heart sinking a bit. "You're not going too far, right?" She asked.

Rowan shrugged. "We'll be on the other side of town now," he said. "I don't think we'll be in the same high school next year." Mia looked down at her boots. Rowan had been her best friend since they were very small and they lived just a few steps down the road from each other. She liked how close he was to her all of the time, as if he could always be there for her whenever she needed him. However, looking at Rowan, now, she knew that she'd have to put her own feelings aside.

She dug into her backpack, pulling out a small object wrapped in paper. "Here," she said. "I was going to wait, but I thought you'd want it now."

Rowan opened the paper, his thumb running over an ornament made of clay, filled with dents from fingers trying to make it into a perfect shape. It was broken into two even pieces. His said, "Be, Bud."

"Oh, I have the other half," Mia said, holding up her clay ornament. Together, they spelled 'Best Buddies.'

"It's great," Rowan said as he carefully put it in his pocket.

"It's our promise," Mia said seriously. "Even though you're moving, we can still come here whenever you want. I'll even ride my bike to your new house on weekends."

Rowan slipped off of the rock, heading for the path towards home. "That sounds dangerous," he said.

"Not if I wear a helmet," Mia said with a smile as she followed after him.

"That's not what I meant, dummy," Rowan said.

"Excuse me?" Mia said. She was about to nudge him again, when Rowan froze in his tracks. Mia crashed into the puff of his jacket.

"Don't move," Rowan whispered; his breath harsh and as cold as the air around them. Mia felt the warmth drain from her skin as she glanced over his shoulder.

Just ahead, a dark cluster moved in front of them, barely making a sound. Mia hid behind Rowan without getting another look.

"What is it?" She whispered, but Rowan shushed her. Then, she could hear them. A low collection of growls and heavy sniffs. In all their trips to the woods, it had never crossed Mia's mind that there would be wolves lurking in the trees. There wasn't supposed to be any evil here, not out in these beautiful woods, and she had taken this blissful ignorance for granted.

The sound was getting closer now. Mia reached out for Rowan's hand, terrified. It was warm and comforting, even in the moment that might be their last. Rowan held on to her fingers tightly as he tried to take another step towards the trail, back to the safety of the neighborhood. It wasn't far, but the wolves became more uneasy with each step they took. Mia risked another peek, and could see them more clearly now. They were large. Their dark coats, of various browns and greys, were matted with dirt and – what looked like – blood. Their lips curled dangerously around their razor-like teeth in cruel sneers.

"What do we do?" Mia said, hot tears now welling in her eyes. She looked at her hand in Rowan's, startled to find that he was just as scared as she was. He was trembling as he dared another step. But the wolves wouldn't let him this time. They inched closer, growling louder now in warning...or was it hunger?

After what felt like hours, Rowan's voice cracked as he told Mia, "You have to run."

"Me? Why just me?" Mia whispered in a panic. "We can both go."

Rowan's shaggy hair shook back and forth. "We won't make it. Run and get my parents. Okay?"

Mia shook her head, though Rowan couldn't see.

Rowan clutched her fingers tighter. "Mia, I'm going to be okay, but you need to go," he said, eyeing their death about to circle them. "I'm going to count to three," Rowan said. "You run for the trail." Another snarl interrupted him. Mia jumped at the sound.

"One..." Mia leaned her cheek against Rowan's back, feeling the roughness of his jacket on her skin. She could swear she could hear his heart pounding. It could have been her own.

"Two..." Rowan said. He sounded as if he were going to cry.

"Rowan..." Mia started.

"Three-"

The world became a blur as Rowan left her. Mia ran, almost floated, towards the trail. She couldn't even feel her feet pounding on the ground, just the cold air and the hammering of her heartbeat in her ears as she sprinted for her life, for Rowan's life. She only looked back once, and she wished that she hadn't. All she saw was a wild flurry of dark fur and a sliver of Rowan's blue jacket as he disappeared into the trees with the wolves. Panic swallowed Mia whole, propelling her forward as her feet somehow found the pavement...

Hours went by as she sat in front of the door to her backyard. She watched the trees, waiting, trying not to cry. Finally, she pulled open the door and ran outside as a figure clumsily emerged from the trees. Rowan's father slid down the hill from the forest and bounded towards the street.

"I need to get to a hospital!" He cried out in terror. Others arrived, neighbors that had heard; Rowan's mother too. Mia went as white as a sheet at the sight of the mangled figure passing by. Rowan was pale, a ghost of a boy, his head lolled back across his father's arms. There was so much blood, seeping into his shredded clothes, and dripping onto the grass.

"Rowan!" Mia called, but Rowan didn't even stir. She chased after his father, seeing only the tuft of chestnut hair, now matted with blood.

It happened so fast. Rowan was thrown into his family's car. Mia ran for the side door of the car, pulling at the handle.

"I want to go with him!" She cried, but her own mother held her back. Mia choked on her tears as she watched the car pass under the streetlights that were just flickering on. It turned a corner and disappeared.

Mia didn't know that she would not see him again...not for another fifteen years.

CHAPTER 1: RUNAWAY

Mia tiptoed through a dingy apartment, frantically gathering up her clothes. Her things were buried under piles of beer cans, empty pill bottles, and unrecognizable trash. Her hands were shaking. Her whole body was shaking. She had been waiting for this moment for a long time, and there was no better time than now to run.

She scurried into the living room, her hands piled up with her belongings and she reached under the beat-up couch. Everything reeked of old cigarette smoke and the stale stench of weeks-old beer stained into the carpets. She didn't know what could be lurking under the couch, but her hands found the thick strap of her duffle bag. She pulled it out, dumping the contents of her arms into it. She sifted through the bundles of clothes, extra shoes and a tiny tube of toothpaste. She had forgotten the most important thing of all, though, and her stomach twisted at the thought.

She inched toward her bedroom door. It had a habit of creaking, but she knew the man sleeping in her bed had drunk enough to sleep through the entire afternoon. It was still early morning, but Mia didn't want to take any chances. She crossed over to her side of the bed, gently sliding her hand under the mattress on the floor. She watched the sleeping man carefully. His name was Grey, and even when he slept he looked like a menace. He breathed heavily through his thick red beard, his eyes knitted into a deep dreamlike anger.

If he woke up, Mia knew she'd end up dead. That's what he would tell her at least, especially if she ever tried to run away again. Mia was out of chances now, but she knew she'd finally get away this time. Her fingers brushed against a papery bundle. She pulled it out in one quick motion and grabbed her jacket from the floor as she headed out of the room. Something made her pause, though. She looked at Grey blissfully unaware of her plan. She almost wanted to laugh, but she felt too sick.

Why don't you just kill him? She thought, although she knew that was impossible. She wouldn't fight violence with more violence, even though she had dreamed about it for a while. She studied Grey: his hulking muscles, hairy chest heaving in and out, and the overpowering tattoo that covered his arm. It was a ferocious wolf emerging from the mouth of a skull. It looked like it could swallow Mia up right there. She hated the sight of it. To her, it was a reminder of what she had lost so long ago...

She sifted through the paper bundle. She only had a few hundred dollars at most. It was enough to get her where she wanted to go. After searching out countless mountain towns, she had decided Birchton was suitable. She kept telling herself that this was the only reason she had chosen it. It was far enough from Grey. She made sure she convinced herself there was nothing else special about Birchton.

As she looked out of the rumbling taxi, she could see the mountains and forests again. She rolled down the window, smelling that sweet familiar odor of nature that used to be so healing for her. Being in the city had definitely taken a toll on her. Nothing grew there, only more and more buildings. Mia hid her money back in her bag. Her fingers brushed up against something smooth hidden under her t-shirts. She reached for it, turning the old ornament over in her hands.

'st, dies' – a strange message if you didn't have the other half. Mia smirked as she looked at it. Her fourteen-year-old self didn't think the message through very well. She placed her thumb in one of the uneven prints, thinking of all the other messages she wished she could have written instead. She had had fifteen years to think about it, but she refrained from letting her mind wander any further. She placed the ornament back into her bag, along with the memories of the boy to whom she had given the other half.

No, she told herself, there's nothing special about Birchton.

Birchton was almost like a town you'd see on an old postcard. There was a main street with hardly any patrons crossing it. It was almost as if the town had been asleep for many years. There was a run-down theater, an auto-repair shop, and several antique stores with their windows stuffed full of treasures from the past. Mia's taxi stopped in front of The Petunia, a greasy-spoon diner with a loft above it. Home, at least for now.

Mia's chunky leather boots felt out of place on the pavement. Everyone around her was dressed in mountain garb, comfortable scarves, thick flannels, denim vests, and hunting pants. Just the sight of Mia's ripped dark jeans and oversized hoodie, and her amber hair now tinged with dark-low-lights, would've pinned her as a city-slicker for sure. Mia told herself that everything was temporary, even though she didn't know what would come after this place.

"You must be Mia," A woman's voice called out. Mia turned to see an old woman dressed in an apron and a plaid shirt walking out of the diner. She had a cigarette hanging out of her mouth, and a nametag that read 'Louise'.

"That's me," Mia said awkwardly, holding out her hand. Louise resorted to patting her firmly on the shoulder, a very masculine form of greeting that she wasn't used to.

"Glad you've decided to take up the old place," Louise said. "Though I gotta warn you, most people don't make it that long, here."

"That's fine," Mia said. "I don't plan on staying that long."

"Now for this first month you've got to put down a deposit, just in case you break anything," Louise said. "So it'll bring ya to four-seventeen."

Mia was confused at first, then realized that Louise meant the place would be four hundred and seventeen dollars.

"Of course," Mia said, digging for her money. She counted it out, instantly worried. She was a hundred dollars short. "I, uh," Mia started, already trying to think of some kind of excuse. Louise eyed the money, taking it from her hands and counting it in front of her.

"Hmm," she said, which added to Mia's worry. This was the only place where she could stay, and there was no way in hell she would turn around and go back to square one.

"Tell you what," Louise said as she pocketed the money. She pointed to a paper sign taped to the door of the diner: 'Help wanted.'

"You work for me a few days these next couple weeks and we can call the rest paid," Louise proposed. Mia scanned the inside of the diner, filled with stubbly-chinned men who were eyeing her cautiously. She had never felt so much like an outsider before, but she didn't have a choice.

"Sounds good," Mia said, and soon she was following Louise up a set of crooked splintered stairs.

After Louise left, it was the first time Mia had truly been alone in a while. She could feel a strange air around her, a deafening silence that lingered in every corner of the loft. The place was just as bad as her old home, in terms of looks. There was a beat-up single mattress on an old frame against the back wall that squealed as soon as she sat on it. She studied the rest of the room. Paintings of deer and other wildlife covered the walls. There was an old fridge, a small camping stove, a tiny counter space, and a small bathroom area the size of a closet. It was almost like a hotel room, Mia thought, but an ugly and overpriced one.

She paced around, the floor creaking under her weight. It felt as though it could give up any second and she'd fall right through, into the diner below. She carefully unpacked her belongings, hoping to make the space more personal. Only the ornament rested on the bottom of the duffel bag, but Mia decided to leave it, and pushed the bag under the bed. There should have been more money in there too, but this secret deposit had squeezed her funds dry.

She instantly regretted living above a diner. The smells of the kitchen wafted up from the floorboards, filling up the attic-sized room. There was some classic country cooking being made right under her feet, potatoes and meatloaf, country-fried steak and gravy, and the mouth-watering oily scent of chicken being fried. Mia clutched at her aching stomach, growling at her in anger. She hadn't eaten a single thing that day.

She wandered the streets. Everything was closing down right about now, except for the diner. Mia knew she couldn't expect a handout from Louise, not after agreeing to work for her and everything. She walked a little further up the street, where a convenience store was still open.

The glow of the light from the store lit up her face as she stepped inside. The bell rung as the door swung open. There was a little old lady perched at the counter, her face buried in a gossip magazine. Country music rambled on a creaky radio. The old woman smiled at Mia as she sauntered casually around the store, eyeing the colorful boxes of packaged snacks and fridges full of cold drinks that all promised her a full belly. The chips and candies were beckoning her, as were the packets of instant ramen noodles that she was so accustomed to.

Mia hated this act, and this wasn't her first performance. First, she'd do a lap around the store, watching the woman at the front. She scoped out for cameras. Lucky for her, the only ones were pointed at the door and the counter. Without thinking, Mia's hands grabbed for multiple snacks, whatever she could get her hands on. She was glad she doubled up on her sweater and jacket as she quietly tucked everything into them.

She got to the counter holding just a few candy bars. The old woman put down her magazine.

"Hungry, huh?" She joked.

Mia's knees were shaking under the counter. She knew it was better to steal and get away with it than try to take things by force. Not that she was the type to hold someone up, but many people in Grey's circle of friends weren't strangers to putting guns in people's faces. Mia's finale consisted of her patting her pockets, frantically apologizing that she didn't have her wallet, and making her swift getaway with her new treasures.

She hated living this way, it only reminded her of what it was like being in the city and of all the horrible things she had to learn just to survive. But she knew that tonight she didn't have a choice. As she lay in bed, her stomach sated, for now, she looked up at the dingy ceiling and wondered if maybe there would ever be a day where she didn't feel like she was running. After that horrible, horrible day, she would always find herself running...

CHAPTER 2: LONER

To anyone else, the woods would have seemed as dead as a crypt, with only the sound of the slight rustling of old leaves shaking from their branches. But to the large crouching wolf hiding behind the branches, the entire forest was a hive buzzing with activity. Scents of the blood, fur, and urine of other animals were in the air, flooding the wolf's nose. He was hungry he decided, his instincts roaming free out in his element. His wild-hazel eyes darted across the dark shadows of the trees, searching for something to sink his teeth into. It had been a while since he had hunted, and he was craving the visceral activity of chasing after another living creature.

At long last, the branches in the distance parted, the rustling leaves echoing in the wolf's ears. He could sense everything out here, even the pounding heart of the young doe stepping quietly into the clearing. The smell of its flesh was driving the wolf wild. Soon, the forest would provide him with a bountiful feast. He inched closer, keeping his sights on the peaceful deer. It was blissfully unaware of his presence, mindlessly chewing on a blade of grass.

The wolf stepped closer, dreaming of the taste of the deer's sinuous flesh against his tongue. Its blood would be sweet, and still warm from the kill. He could already feel his mouth watering. He was ready to leap from his hiding place, ready to chase his prey all the way down the mountain if he had to. He took a chance with a great leap as he soared off the ground. But just before his paws could touch down on the leaves again, he froze. The deer did the same, and for one second their instincts were matched. Danger was near. Wolves' howls filled the forest. The wolf shrunk back from his prey. Not here, he thought. Not again.

He let it get away. The white rear of the deer bounced back into the trees, never to be seen again. It would soon find a place to hide unless another wolf got lucky and made it its meal. The wolf knew he should hide as well, but not here in the middle of the forest.

He sprinted towards home, still hearing the chorus of wolf howls in the distance. He could tell the pack was far enough away not to catch onto his scent, but he was still worried. In all of his time living out here, he had never encountered other wolves before, and he didn't want to stay and find out who they were, even though he might have a clue.

The wolf's feet bounded towards a soft glow peeking out through a cluster of trees. Leaves swept up from under his feet as he ran, faster and faster, trying to escape the rallying cry of the wolves behind him. They must be hunting or marking their territory. This wolf hadn't quite done that yet, though he was itching to keep tabs on what was rightfully his. This was his forest, and he hated the idea of intruders encroaching on it, but if they knew he was here, they could capture him as they once did long ago.

The glow grew brighter, and soon he could see light seeping from the windows of a small cabin. The wolf stopped at the door, pacing back and forth. Now would be the hardest part of his night. His entire body shook as he felt a swollen shadow pulsing through his intestines. He hunched up, jaws agape as he gagged as if trying to vomit out the curse that was plaguing him. Muscles contracted, tearing from bone as his veins stretched into grotesque shapes inside of him. The wolf whined in agony as he rolled into the dirt, furiously convulsing as his legs spread out behind him. The bones began to shift into place, rearranging themselves until they were straightened. This change inched up the rest of his body, straightening his spine, twisting his neck, and finally his arms.

With a sharp gasp that filled his lungs, he was alive again. Human again. The man, naked and shivering in the dirt, stood up on his wobbling legs. He braced himself against a pile of wood, coughing violently. It was always strange to shift back, and even after years of being a shifter, he still wasn't quite used to it. There was a strange feeling whenever he turned, as if his very soul was also split in two.

To him it was a curse, living as both man and animal. Sometimes the soul would remain as one, a human's tainted with the dark desires that the wolf constantly barraged him with. It wasn't a voice that spoke to him, or for which he was grateful. But it was always there, this shadowy urge that was hard to fight. It almost consumed him sometimes, the constant demand to run and to hunt. And then there was the most frustrating urge of all, one that often kept him up at night for hours. He needed a mate. He'd ignored this want for so long, but it was unbearably painful to live a life of solitude.

The cabin was cozy, and warm as always. It was a safe place, the man thought; the perfect place to spend the rest of your life, even though he was only twenty-nine. He walked through the entryway and straight for the bathroom. He needed a shower, bad. The stench of an entire days' worth of running through the forest was radiating from him. He stepped into the shower, letting everything wash off him. The water steamed over him, relaxing his aching muscles as it dripped over his firm chest. Whatever the wolf did, he would have to pay for it later as a human.

He leaned his head back, letting the showerhead pour over his face. He closed his eyes, nearly drowning, although he didn't care. He'd been tempted in the beginning, and often since. He used to wonder if a life like this was worth living. But he found himself holding on for something he wasn't quite sure of yet. He knew that there was something waiting for him, it was a strange feeling. Incomplete.

He watched the black dirt swirl down the drain. He tried not to think about that day again. Not now. He turned off the water and dried himself off in the steamy mirror. Wiping away the grey fog, he looked at himself, as he had already done, dozens of times in this lonely cabin. He brushed his wet tousled hair back with his fingers. His dark-chestnut hair sat just below his ears.

Still Rowan, he reassured himself.

Rowan said this often. It was his reminder that there was still a piece of him inside of this monster that he always carried with him. Somehow, it made him feel more human; a form he wished he could have taken for life. Rowan knew there were others like him. After all, he had seen them for himself, albeit briefly. He looked at his rippling stomach in the mirror. His muscles were incredibly toned, from years of running and hunting in the woods. His eyes trailed over his body, inspecting himself.

He was covered in scars, thick webs of ruined tissue that stretched from his stomach to his throat. They were a reminder of the other monsters that had given them to him, along with this curse, all from that same horrible day. He hadn't seen her since. He pulled on his knit sweater and once again pushed it from his mind.

A warm stew simmered on the stove in the tiny glowing kitchen. The smell of earthy spices filled the room. Rowan stirred the pot of root vegetables. Soft potatoes, carrots, and parsnips from his weekly grocery run, plus the fresh herbs he had found out in the woods himself. Absolutely no meat. He'd lost the taste for it after he had become a shifter. But the wolf craved flesh blood, almost every day; another urge he'd have to stifle later.

Rowan ladled his dinner into a bowl and sat in his usual corner at the table. He looked across at the empty chair in front of him. It was almost like a joke to him that he should even have two chairs. It wasn't as if he was expecting anyone to come here, was he? He shrugged, eyeing the layer of dust gathered on the empty chair, wondering.

The second worst part of his night would always be sleep. He hated to sleep, even though he could only procure so much of it, because it meant nightmares. He relived that horrible day over and over again, feeling the teeth of those monsters ripping him apart. He saw her there too, but in every dream, she could never save him and only watched with horror. Rowan tossed and turned on his bed, which was too big and empty for one person. Before drifting into his nightmare state, he was startled to hear an incessant howling nearby. They wouldn't find his cabin tonight, they were still too far away. For a moment he wondered if they had finally found him and were on their way to try to bring him back into the wild.

Rowan buried his face in his pillow, listening to the sound of his steady breathing. If he started on this train of thought again he would never sleep. It was the usual lineup: the worst day of his life, the first time he'd shifted, and the frightened young face of Mia as she looked over her shoulder at him, the last time he had seen her.

And there was a fourth fear which shook Rowan to his core. The big accident, the one that had caused him to disappear in the first place. The sight of that girl's eyes as he lunged for her. He was a monster, he thought, and he truly believed it...

CHAPTER 3: FAMILIAR FACE

Louise hadn't said anything about being a busgirl in the job description. Dishes were Mia's least favorite thing to deal with, and there she was piling up the greasy plates and silverware into a grey bin. She hated the idea that she was doing this just so she could stay in that run-down loft. Her first night had been hard for her, especially when she tried to sleep. There were so many fears running through her head, most of them about Grey.

Throughout the morning, she had scanned the tired faces of the diner's patrons. She hoped that one of Grey's friends wasn't lurking around anywhere. She had only met a handful of them, but she knew Grey had a lot of connections. After all, he was a smart drug dealer and was bound to have his thick fingers dipped in other towns near the city.

Mia focused on the plates piling up in the bin, blocking out the harsh memories that were trying to flood back into her mind. She had never gotten into drugs, but she wondered that if she had stayed with Grey long enough they would have been the glue that kept her from running.

"Mia, another table," Louise said for about the tenth time that morning. Mia seated customers, filled their coffee, the usual tasks that went along with waitressing. She was used to jobs like these. They helped her get to this town in the first place.

She poured fresh coffee into the mugs of a line of police officers filling up the seats at the counter. They watched her carefully, which made her uneasy. They were a bunch of burly men, their uniforms appearing almost too tight on them. Mia caught one of them staring at her over the rim of his mug. He had black hair and a thick mustache that was bound to be soaked with coffee. Mia felt a small shudder run down her back.

There was something about him that made her feel unsafe, despite the sight of the police uniform he wore. They stood up and left without another word, and barely a tip. Mia cursed under her breath as she tucked the few bills into her apron. Maybe they were just acting strangely because she was new in town. Just by being here, she was disrupting their daily rhythm of life. That seemed to be the theme of the day, as the customers gave her curious glances, looking up from their menus. Mia knew she was out of place here, but she reminded herself of just how temporary everything could be.

As she finished rolling up napkins and silverware during her break, she noticed a lone customer sitting in a torn-up booth near the window. He wore a ball cap over his dark, messy hair. His canvas jacket made Mia think he could be one of the local farmers or one of the many men that worked in the nearby steel mill. He was handsome, Mia thought. He had a firm jaw-line and a trace of stubble on his face. He seemed deep in thought about something, or deeply troubled. Mia wondered what he could be thinking about, but she knew that maybe she'd be thinking about him after he'd left.

Mia picked up her bin and bussed the table behind the man. He seemed to stand out from the other people that she had seen throughout the morning. She glanced at the back of his coat. For some reason, her mind took her to a darker place and a sadder time. She remembered her face pressed up against a young Rowan's coat a final time on that terrifying day that she had lost him. From the back, this man almost gave her the same feeling, the same image. She felt drawn to him.

She knew she couldn't linger around him forever and took her bin back towards the kitchen. As she passed by the man's booth, she was almost startled at the faintest voice saying

"Excuse me?" It was deep and soothing, the kind of voice that belonged to someone that didn't like to speak much.

Mia turned to face him, almost dropping the dirty dishes on the checkered floor as she felt time slowing around her. She was staring right into a pair of beautiful hazel eyes. They locked onto hers, and for a second Mia could swear that they widened just a little at the sight of her. Mia's heartbeat quickened as she pieced together the rest of him. Shaggy chestnut hair, just barely over his ears.

Rowan?

She could sense him studying her as well, his eyebrows knitted together in concentration. It had been such a long time, and Mia had always wondered what he would look like, now that they were twenty-nine. She worried that he wouldn't be able to recognize her.

"I'd like to pay," the man said as he held out a card. Mia nodded, reaching for it, their fingers nearly brushing against each other. She steadied her breath, trying not to think about holding Rowan's hand that day in the woods, her fingers slipping from his as she ran from him. She could have held onto that card forever if it meant keeping this man here in front of her.

But she couldn't and instead took the card to the register. She didn't like being nosy, but she had to know for sure that it was Rowan. After his father had found him out in the woods, he had been rushed to the hospital. Mia wasn't even allowed to visit him. Only family members could see a patient that was in critical condition. And after those countless weeks of waiting for him to recover, Mia waited even longer for Rowan to come back to the neighborhood. He never did.

Weeks turned into months, with no sign of her best friend. She took it upon herself one weekend to ride her bike to where his new house would have been, only to find that there was a for sale sign still staked into the dirt, swinging in the lonely breeze. With no number left behind to call, and no word from the school of his whereabouts, Rowan soon became a ghost to Mia. The more time passed, the more he felt like an imaginary friend in Mia's memories. For years she wondered what had happened to that boy in the blue coat. Mia couldn't believe that he could possibly be the one sitting in the booth just a few feet from her.

She took a risk and looked at his card. She instantly regretted it. Printed in raised letters was the name, Frank Richards. Mia's heart sank as she ran the transaction, just looking at the man out of the corner of her eye. She brought him back the card, tossing aside any hope of even starting a conversation with him. Like all her thoughts of Rowan, this one was just another dream, though she had thought for sure that this time he would be real again.

The man took his card and gave her a small nod as he stepped out of the booth. Mia felt him almost brush against her as he walked towards the door. She could feel her face growing hot. How could she have been so foolish even to think that Rowan would be all the way out here? They were miles from their hometown. After his recovery, Rowan could have been taken anywhere. That was the curse of being a child, never truly having a say in where you ended up until you were much older.

Mia's shift finally ended. Louise let her keep the tips she made, which wasn't much. Still, it was maybe enough to buy dinner. Mia stepped into the chilly air, realizing that she wasn't that hungry. She kept thinking about Frank Richards and knew there was something strange about him that she just couldn't shake. He had looked so much like Rowan, and as she wandered down the sidewalk she looked at everyone who passed by, hoping that she could get just another glimpse of him. He was already looking foggy in her memory, and she was worried that she would lose him forever, once again.

As the sidewalk turned into a corner, Mia stood and watched the other side of the street. She recognized someone, but it wasn't Rowan. Her feet turned into concrete as a tall, burly, bearded man walked angrily down the other side of the street. Grey.

Mia's heart raced. How the hell did he find her there? And so soon? She knew she had to get back to her place. She needed to get her things so she could leave again. Without another thought, she rushed across the street, opposite to where she had seen Grey. She was so caught up in her thoughts, that she didn't see the large logging truck approaching her from the left. Mia's eyes widened. She wouldn't make it. She'd die here in the middle of this strange town on a strange street.

But something grabbed her, and pulled her back. A firm hand gripped her arm, and for a second Mia was weightless as she was brought back effortlessly to the sidewalk. The truck blared its horn as it disappeared down the street. Mia caught her breath, still feeling the warm touch of the hand clutching her. She looked up at her savior, worried that she'd be staring at Grey's face. But it wasn't Grey at all. It was Frank Richards, watching her with those sad hazel eyes.

"Thank you," Mia said. The sound of her voice seemed to transform Frank somehow. His expression softened, and became more compassionate, with a twinge of sadness. It was as if he had been waiting to hear her voice for a very long time. With a sudden jolt, however, he tore away from her, thrusting his hands into his pockets.

"Of course," he said quietly, his words rushed as he bounded across the street.

"Wait!" Mia called out to him. She just had to know the truth or it would torment her for the rest of the night.

But he didn't come back. Mia watched as he kept his hands in his pockets while he stepped into the nearby woods. For one moment, he turned to look at her over his shoulder. It had to be Rowan, she thought. It had to be.

The she remembered that she had seen Grey; the reason she had run in the first place. She looked only to find that he had also disappeared. Mia dismissed it as an illusion, though the vision of him still haunted her.

Mia threw her apron over the small counter space. She felt strange, an odd disturbance joining her in the room, almost like a shadow. Looking around her loft space, it was easy to feel creeped out. Wandering to the two windows near the entrance, she pulled apart the ragged curtains to stare out into the street. What am I even looking for? She asked herself, even though she knew that deep down there was an answer. Her eyes were searching for a handsome, muscular man, with chestnut hair. She could still feel the imprint of his hand on her arm, his grip carrying a sense of urgency. He was only trying to save her, but Mia thought for a moment he had touched her as if he had been waiting to do so for a long time.

Okay, definitely overthinking this, Mia, she thought as she tore away from the window. The curtains were promptly pulled shut as if it would help cover up her desires, or her hidden fears about Grey lurking in the streets.

The camp stove wasn't much, but it was better than having a hotel room with barely anything in it. Mia stirred a packet of instant noodles, watching the boiling water bubble up around them. Her mind was elsewhere, focusing on the man that she had seen; replaying an imaginary conversation with him over and over.

In her mind, Mia would have taken Frank Richard's card. She would have run it and wandered back to his table. Of course, instead of being awkward, he would have looked right at her and stared at her as if he was too afraid to look away.

"You're very familiar," Mia would have said.

"I thought you would have recognized an old friend," he would say with a charming smirk.

"I'm sorry," Mia would have said. "I don't have any friends named Frank Richards."

She imagined the man offering to walk with her; waiting for her until her shift was done so they could finally sit down and catch up on everything. Perhaps the man had gone on many exciting adventures and had seen some amazing things, and that's why he had never found his way back home. Mia wanted to ask him everything. Of course, none of this would ever be possible if the man wasn't Rowan. She stepped back, startled by the water from her noodles bubbling over the pot, spilling boiling water on the counter space.

As she wiped down the splintered floor, she knew how foolish she was being. All of her daydreams were based around Rowan, and she often found herself drifting towards thoughts of him, only to dismiss them as what they really were. Just hopeless daydreams.

Mia tossed and turned in her sleep, the mattress creaking up a storm as she struggled to find unconsciousness. Her eyes drifted up to the shadows dancing around on her angled ceiling, light coming in from the streetlights and the few cars that passed by. It sounded as if there was rain outside and Mia tried to tune into it to settle her nerves.

Just when she felt as if she was finally about to fall sleep, there was a knock on the door. Mia jolted up, pulling her scratchy sheets higher over her. Had she actually heard that sound? Was her mind playing tricks on her in the dark? It wasn't until she heard the second knock that she knew it was real, and the next question was whether or not she should answer it.

She draped her blanket over her shoulders, her bare feet carefully treading over the floor to avoid splinters. The knocking continued, and soon the rhythm of it matched up with Mia's frantic heartbeat as she crept closer towards the door. The stairs creaked under her as she walked down them. She instantly regretted not grabbing anything with which to defend herself, before opening the door. After all, there could be something evil waiting for her on the other side, and she wouldn't know until it was too late.

Her hand stretched out toward the knob. For a moment she had hesitated. It was safer to fake being out of the house rather than revealing herself here. But who knew what hour it was? Mia clutched the knob, and the knocking still hammering in her ears. It seemed much more terrifying now that she was closer to it. She resisted the urge to close her eyes, as she finally opened the door.

Rain poured from outside, dripping off of the small awning over the doorway. Crouched under it, buried in the collar of a coat; was Frank Richards himself. He smiled meekly as rainwater dripped from the ends of his hair. He used his hand to smooth it back, a gesture that Mia was all too familiar with.

"I hope it's not too late," Frank said. "I just...I needed to come by."

Mia stepped aside without hesitation. She was relieved that it wasn't Grey or any of his friends.

"What are you doing here?" Mia asked as she led him up the stairs. "God, you're soaked. Let me take your coat." Frank shed his wet coat and handed it to Mia. He wore a warm-looking sweater underneath. Mia hung his coat up on the railing near the stairs. She felt an odd sense of familiarity with him as if he had visited many times before.

They stood in the middle of the loft. Mia hadn't even thought to turn the lights on, and they were looking at each other in the soft yellow glow of the streetlights pouring in from the windows. His presence felt so comforting to Mia, despite the fact that she hardly knew who this man was.

Mia barely knew what she was supposed to say. Should she make him tea? Ask him to sit down on the bed – the only real place for anyone to sit down? She suddenly wasn't sure what to do with herself, and instead pulled the sleeves of her sweater helplessly over her hands. Then, she remembered. She knew what she was supposed to say.

"You're very familiar," she said quietly. Frank smiled, and it was eerie to Mia how similar his smile was to her fantasy from earlier. He even had the faintest and most charming gap between his two front teeth.

Frank moved closer to her, his boots creaking softly against the wooden floor. Mia almost felt uneasy. Was it because she was afraid to be alone in the dark with a stranger? Or was she afraid that he wasn't the man she had thought he was?

Then, he said something that almost made Mia think it was all a dream.

"I thought you would have recognized an old friend," Frank said.

Mia could feel all of her nerves vibrating inside of her. They prickled around the skin on the back of her neck, creating a strange tingle down her spine and towards her fingers gripping tighter on the cuffs of her sleeves.

"I'm sorry," Mia said. "I don't have any friends named Frank Richards." She waited with a phantom anxiety for what he was about to say.

"Well, it's a good thing my name isn't Frank Richards," the man said. Mia felt a jump in her heartbeat.

"I knew it," she whispered. She stared at him a moment longer, taking him in. All of her memories fast-forwarding through her mind in a flash. Not knowing what else to say, she instinctively held out her arms and was almost knocked down as her friend crashed into her, holding so tightly to her that she thought he would break her ribs.

Rowan's nose buried into her hair, smelling her, cherishing her. It had been such a long time.

"I knew I'd find you, Mia," he said.

She smiled at the sound of her name. "What took you so long?" Mia asked. She breathed in his scent. He was musky, mixed with a fresh hint of earthy soap that emanated from the fibers of his wooly sweater.

"I wanted to come back to you," Rowan said. "I tried so hard, but I couldn't find you."

"I tried to find you too," Mia said, her voice cracking. She hadn't realized how emotional this moment would be between them after being apart for so long. "But Rowan...listen, I've been through a lot since you've been gone—" before she could finish, Rowan gently shushed her, his arms tightening around her still. He pulled away, just enough so that he could look at her.

"We'll have plenty of time to talk about everything," Rowan said. "I'm not going anywhere."

"Please don't," Mia found herself saying. She had never thought this way about Rowan before, but now that they were older, she wasn't going to let these feelings get pushed to the side, especially since she finally had him in front of her.

Mia felt herself growing unsteady at his touch, realizing how close his face was to hers. She could feel his breath on her forehead and noticed his lips parted just slightly in invitation. She reached up and touched the stubble on his face.

"You have a beard now," she said, giggling playfully.

"You're still as beautiful as ever," Rowan said. Mia still couldn't believe this was happening to her. Just moments before she wasn't sure if it was her childhood friend that had saved her from that truck.

There was something strange in all of this. Rowan had never spoken to her this way before. And yet, Mia wanted to cling to every word, not worrying about what they meant later. They mattered now, and she wanted him now. Mia looked into Rowan's eyes. He leaned in closer, his nose just touching hers.

"I've been thinking of this moment for a long, long time," he whispered to her.

"Me too," Mia said. "More times than I can count, honestly."

"No more counting, then," he said as his hand cupped around her cheek. Mia closed her eyes, feeling his thumb gently brushing back and forth along her skin. It was electrifying, and for a split second, she pictured herself sitting once again on her and Rowan's favorite rock.

But they were all grown up now, and time had manifested a strong desire in Mia. Before she knew it Rowan was kissing her, his lips soft and delicate against hers, but also hungry. Mia collapsed into his arms, forgetting Grey and the years of time that separated her from Rowan. All that mattered was that he was there.

Mia was losing herself to him, completely wound up in his massive arms.

"Rowan is this—" she wanted to ask if it was strange. After all, it was so sudden how he had grabbed for her and was kissing her this way. But Rowan ignored her, bringing her towards the nearest wall by the bed, kissing her neck. Mia was floored. She could barely process how quickly things were happening. This has to be a dream, she thought, but she didn't want to wake up.

Rowan was pressing himself further into her, his pelvis making contact with the front of her sweatpants. Mia was nearly shaking at this moment, but she longed to embrace everything that was going to happen between the two of them. His body was so warm against hers; his breath heavy as he kept his lips trailing along her neck, planting sweet kisses on her skin. Mia wrapped her arms around him as his hands started searching the rest of her body.

Once again, she felt strange. All of this was so sudden. But Rowan kept pulling at her clothes, tasting her skin, and it had made her feel so alive and full of a new fire. The room spun around her as she reached for Rowan's pants, fumbling with the button and the zipper. Rowan's hands slid from her waist up towards her ribcage, his thumbs digging into her skin as he worked his way to the bare breasts that were hiding under her thin t-shirt.

Mia was excited now. She could feel herself getting wetter just from Rowan's touch. Throwing caution to the wind, Mia spread her fingers further down into his pants, her fingertips caressing the thick hardness that Rowan's boxers were holding back. Rowan gave a soft moan at the touch of her hand, which prompted Mia even further. She trailed along the fabric until her fingers could reach his warm bare skin.

Her heart was pounding now as she sighed, getting a firm grip around Rowan's shaft. Rowan's head tilted back as Mia worked with her hands up and down along his smooth, veiny skin, caressing his tip until she could feel just a hint of wet emerging from him.

She suddenly longed for more of him. She wanted to taste him, and to feel him inside of her. A new book of possibilities lay before her, and Mia was determined to flip through every page as long as it would satisfy her new craving.

"Let's get you on the bed," Rowan said, suddenly pulling Mia away so that he could lift her. She was weightless in his arms, and when Rowan laid her down, she didn't even hear the mattress make a single sound. She could only see him hovering over her, and as he lifted his shirt she could see every muscle bulging from his shoulders down to his rippling stomach.

"What are we doing?" Mia asked, breathless as Rowan lifted her leg over his shoulder, slowly prying the sweatpants from her body.

"Something I've wanted to do for a long time," he said. Without another word, Mia let him in between her legs. He brushed his lips against her, gently caressing her inner thighs, the stubble on his face prickling her. Mia stifled her giggles but stopped laughing as soon as Rowan pulled her panties to the side.

She nearly gasped in surprise once his tongue found her vulva, and moaned as he licked inside and out, his lips working around her. He was so passionate, and so gentle with her that it was hard for Mia not to come.

When she could feel herself getting close, she reached her hand out and placed it on top of his messy hair.

"Let's take this another step further," she said. Rowan lifted his head from in between her legs. Suddenly, Mia was horrified at the monster in front of her. From the shadows and the light casting an odd glow over his face, Mia discovered that it wasn't Rowan at all.

It was Grey, smiling devilishly as he reached up to grab her by the throat. Mia screamed, but it was silenced by her sputtering and choking as Grey clenched his fist harder around her. He laughed, like an insane criminal as he shook her furiously. "You thought you'd get away so easily?" He said, his voice practically inhuman.

Mia flailed her arms, now finding herself alone in her bed. She tore the sheets from her, throwing them onto the floor as she nearly tumbled from the mattress. The bed shrieked in protest as her weight left it. Mia paced wildly back and forth. The sun was just peeking in through her window, filling the room with a soft blue glow. It had been a dream after all, at least half of it was. The other was a complete nightmare. Mia wiped the cold sweat from her brow as she took up her blanket, and wrapped it around herself. She walked towards the stairs, looking down at her door waiting below. It was shut tight, and silent. Once again, Rowan was just a ghost to her.

CHAPTER 4: THE PAST

"How do you know it was her?" Brian asked as Rowan chopped a piece of wood on a stump. Brian was the only friend that Rowan had dared to make in Birchton, but only because he had a secret just as Rowan did. Rowan had just moved into town when he had been confronted at a bar by a biker passing through. A roaring bar fight would have taken place if Brian hadn't been there to step in. He had short blonde hair and was a mountain of a man, all muscle, though you couldn't tell from his round appearance. He had had the strength of a bear as he had helped Rowan get the biker off of his back. It wasn't long until Rowan found out that Brian actually was a bear; a shifter like he was.

Shifters were common around the mountain towns, mainly because they could live a life of solitude. It was easier to go off into the woods and shift freely than to struggle with the weight of a career and a stressful life in the city. Depending on the shifter, certain levels of stress were known to trigger one's abilities. Rowan had learned that he would shift whenever he felt overwhelmed by his anger, or when he thought too much about the past. That was why he was always trying to suppress it. He always felt as if he was running from something, but he was mainly just running from the wolf.

He kept himself busy, and chopping wood for his cabin was one of those tasks where he could safely release some of the tension he felt.

Brian gulped down a beer almost in a single swig, waiting for an answer.

"I just knew it was her," Rowan said. "I recognized her immediately. Even though she's changed so much."

Brian shrugged. "Yeah that's usually what time does to people," he joked.

Rowan didn't respond, which was strange to Brian. Rowan was always somewhat down, but never this low.

"Did you say anything to her?" Brian asked.

Rowan raised his ax, eyeing the log in front of him. He dropped his hands with a single breath, and the wood was splintered in half as the ax came down.

"I blew it," he said. "I couldn't even think of anything to say to her. She probably just thinks I'm a random creep. She even saw my fake name."

"But you said you think she recognized you. Isn't that enough to start a conversation?"

"I know, but people change, Brian. Besides, how weird would that have been for me just to call her by her name after fifteen years? She doesn't even know where I have been during that time. You think she'd be a little weirded out don't you think?"

Rowan began to struggle with the ax. It slid clumsily from under his hands. Brian put down his beer bottle and held out his hand.

"You're going to chop your hand off," he said. "Take a seat while I show you how a bear does it."

Rowan watched as Brian effortlessly swung the ax into the wood as if it were cardboard.

"I think there's something you're not really wanting to say here, Rowie," Brian said in between chops. Rowan looked at the ground. Brian always joked that Rowan wore his heart on his sleeve, and it really got on Rowan's nerves how well he could read him. Maybe it was a strange sense that shifters shared, the gift to be in tune with other creatures in nature.

"I'm scared, man," Rowan said as he took a swig of his own beer. He liked to drink every now and then, especially when the nights were at their worst. He hated the times where he couldn't get himself under control, and when he'd have to spend the night out in the woods, fearing that if he stayed in his cabin the wolf would destroy every inch of it.

"What do you have to be scared of?" Brian asked, his brows sweaty.

"Mia was my best friend," Rowan said quietly. "I'd give anything to spend another day with her, to try to piece together everything that happened with us."

"That sounds like a reasonably healthy friendship," Brian shrugged. "What's there to lose?"

Rowan hated thinking about this. He always fantasized what it would be like to meet Mia again. With those fantasies came the harsh reality. He was carrying this curse with him, and if he ever wanted to be that close to Mia again, he would have to tell her about it. Who knows how she would react to that news? Rowan thought of the moment over and over in his head like a horrible loop.

"I could lose everything," Rowan said. "What am I supposed to say? 'Hey, surprise! It's your best friend Rowan. Remember when I got attacked by wolves? Well do I have some news for you...'"

"You don't have to make it so dramatic," Brian said. "From everything you've told me, this girl sounds like she used to be everything to you. It shouldn't be that hard to tell her the truth. But you have to start small. Take it in steps."

"I don't think it'll ever be how it used to be," Rowan said, leaning far back into his seat. He looked up at the clouds. The sky was blood-red as the sun sank below the horizon. The sight of it was haunting, almost reminiscent of the sky he had looked up at when he was lying on the cold forest floor, the blood spilling out from the deep gashes in his stomach. He was just fourteen. He'd only seen that kind of gore in the movies his parents didn't let him watch, at the time. He wasn't prepared for the cruel reality that was in front of him. When the wolves had finally left him, he looked up at that blood-red sky, waiting for death. He cried when he thought he would never see Mia again.

There he was, thinking about the past again. He could feel his body shaking, but a firm hand rested on his shoulder.

"Hey don't you go wolf on me now, buddy," Brian said.

Rowan patted his hand in appreciation. It was good to have someone like him around, someone that could understand the pain that goes along with being a shifter. It made him feel less alone, but Brian's presence certainly couldn't relieve the awful tension that came with the wolf's need to mate.

For a second, Rowan pictured Mia in that diner. She had changed so much, but she looked even more beautiful than Rowan remembered. He knew that deep down he had always cared for Mia, ever since they were children. But he could feel a strange transformation of his feelings, from innocent youthful daydreams to desires of a far more mature nature.

"Thanks for listening," Rowan said to Brian. Brian sat on the ground next to him, getting back to his beer, his forehead glistening with sweat now.

"Always here, friend," Brian said.

"Do you think she would talk to me?" Rowan asked. "Even after all this time?"

Brian shrugged. "That's something you're going to have to find out for yourself," he said firmly. "I think your problem is that you're looking at this through the same thirteen-year-old lens."

"What do you mean?" Rowan asked.

"I mean, that people are always changing, which means things are going to be different. But it's an easy fix, Rowan." He tapped his temple with a large finger and winked. "All you have to do is change what's up here."

Rowan was surprised at Brian's solid advice. Most of the time he would get distracted talking about his hunting stories. But something about his words stuck in Rowan's head.

He went for a run with his friend. Sometimes a good sprint through the forest did wonders for his body, and helped subdue the wolf inside. Brian bounded next to him, a giant brown bear who's incredible mass shuddered with each step. They ran to a nearby waterfall, where they could shift and jump into the cold rush of the flowing water. There was a sort of calmness to this routine, and as Rowan watched Brian perched at the top of the waterfall, swinging his enormous paw into the river to catch fish, he wondered if it would be all too much for someone like Mia to comprehend.

He hated to think of it, but maybe he was content here after all. He hated being a wolf, but suffering as a lone wolf was much easier than having someone else have to worry about him. Rowan dipped his feet into the cold water, naked and free. But what good was his freedom if he could never connect with Mia again? Would it haunt him just as worse if he knew he had another chance that he didn't take? Rowan pondered this as the water numbed his toes.

He knew his sense of content was false. Otherwise, he wouldn't have this nagging buzz in his chest, whenever he thought of Mia and of her beautiful, wide eyes as she looked at him when he had saved her once again.

CHAPTER 5: REFUGE

Music was blaring as the townspeople came alive after their working hours. They made the pilgrimage to the closest bar, nestled at the farthest corner of the town. Mia was among the worn-out group, but decided to take her place at the end of the bar. She quietly shifted her glass of rum and Coke from one hand to the other. Mingling wasn't on her mind, even though Birchton was basically her new home. Instead, her mind wandered, with thoughts of Rowan and the strange new feelings that her dream had brought her. If that really was him, who had saved her the other day, why did he run off like that?

Mia felt so conflicted. Dare she take the risk to find Frank Richards, or Rowan, again? For the past few days, she had wondered if she would run in-to him, just casually on the streets. She walked around town after her shifts, looking for any sign of the man with the messy dark hair. Soon, she was occupied with other fantasies. What do you say to someone who's been a ghost for fifteen years? Would she embrace him; something she had longed to do since the day he disappeared? She imagined these make-believe sce-narios, just small flashes of hope in her mind when she might possibly have Rowan back in her life.

The room had filled up now. It was a Friday night, and everyone was looking to let loose after their week of hard labor. Mia was certainly feeling exhausted from working again, but she knew that she needed to keep her funds up, in case she needed to run. That near-sighting of Grey, if it even was Grey, bothered her. She had gone straight home to lock her doors and waited for the worst, but he had never come to get her. He only terrorized her in her dreams. He didn't bust through the door, and grab her by the arm as he had done that night she had first tried to run.

She was hiding in a motel that night, but she stayed too close to home. Grey knew everybody, especially the prostitutes and drug dealers that also frequented the same motel. Within moments they had found Mia, and soon Grey appeared, his face twisted and red with rage. It took a few weeks for all of her bruises to heal. That's when Mia really started to plan, but it would be several months until she gained the courage to run again.

Grey was charming at first. There were dinner dates and nights out dancing, not to mention the sex had been great. But it wasn't long until Grey had completely transformed into a true monster. He would disappear late at night, and come home with stacks of cash, never saying where he got it from. Then Mia found the drugs. They were hidden in a stash jar made to look like a soda can. When she brought it up, Grey showed her the true nature that he'd been hiding the entire time they'd been together. Soon Mia became a prisoner in their apartment.

Mia drank quickly. She needed to stop thinking about him. She didn't come out, all this way, only to get caught again. Rowan could help me, she thought. If only Rowan knew what was going on, then maybe he could do something about it. He always had a solution for everything. Then again, was that man even Rowan? She jumped at the sound of a beer bottle smashing. Laughter surrounded her, coming from tables of regulars that often shot her a glance. Everywhere she went, she was reminded that she was an outsider.

It was almost like being in school again, finding somewhere to sit at the lunch table. But Mia didn't feel like making friends. So when the same dark-haired, thick-mustached cop from the diner walked over to her, she found herself completely unprepared and a little uneasy.

"How's it going?" He asked smoothly as he took a seat on the empty stool next to hers. Mia nodded, firmly clutching her empty glass. The cop, dressed in casual clothes this time, noticed it. "Can I get you another one?" He asked. Mia kept her eyes on the counter, only letting them slip to the side every now and then. She didn't want this guy getting a good look at her face.

"I'm fine, thanks," Mia said. Typically she would have let any man buy her a drink. She was used to partying and hanging around in bars, drinking until the sun came up. But this one felt different. Everything is different when you're on the run. The cop turned his whole body towards her, filling up her peripheral.

"You're new around here, huh? Saw you were working for Louise."

Mia had prepared for everything; even a phony story in case someone asked her too many questions. "Just passing through," she said. "Saving money to help my mom." She'd leave it at that, but this guy wouldn't stop.

"My name's Craig," Craig said, holding out his hand. Mia looked at it, unsure, but eventually reached out and shook it. When she let go she felt a twinge of regret, as if she had slipped up in her false narrative.

"Jamie," she said.

"Nice to meet you, Jamie. You like it out here in Birchton?"

"So far."

"You looked like you could use some company," Craig said. "If you don't mind having me?"

He looked at her with steely eyes, as if he were trying to read her mind. It was all getting to be too much for Mia. She was used to guys wanting to sit with her in places like this, but Craig was studying her. She could have sworn that his dark eyes were almost hungry.

"I was actually on my way out," Mia said as she slid off of her bar stool. As she passed by Craig, she felt a hand snatch at her wrist, pulling her backward. It felt nothing like the careful grasp of her rescuer's hand the other day. This was far more menacing. Mia gave Craig a nervous smile, as she gently tried to tug her hand away. But Craig held firm. Mia's heart began to pound as she looked around the bar, nervous. Did anyone else notice how strange this was?

Craig kept a calm demeanor, his eyes flashing from overly-friendly to more sinister. "Careful walking around at night," he said in a taunting voice. "You never know what's running around out there."

Mia stared into those dark eyes for what felt like hours until he finally released her hand.

"Are you a cop even when you're not on duty?" She said to him and instantly regretted it. Craig grabbed his beer bottle without a word, just a sly half-smile as he walked past her.

"I'm a lot of things," he said quietly. "With a mouth like that, you might just find out what they are."

Mia's feet pounded against the sidewalk. She bunched her coat closer to her, trying to keep the icy winds of an oncoming storm from piercing through her clothes. She needed to get back to her loft, before she got drenched. But she could hardly think about that. Her mind was on fire with thoughts of Grey, and the way Craig had stared her down. It almost felt as if it was Grey himself watching her. She racked her brain for any sort of backup plan. But there wasn't any, just the hope of her tiny loft waiting for her above the glowing diner. She looked around her, the memory of Craig's ominous words echoing in her ears, pouring from the dark, surrounding her as she realized she was truly alone on the streets.

Then the rain came. First it was a light spritz, then a torrential downpour that soaked into Mia's shoes. She cursed under her breath as she finally saw her loft just several steps away. Instinctively she looked behind her only to find that nobody was there, though she could somehow feel a strange warm breath on the back of her neck. She broke into a run, bounding up the creaking rotting steps to her loft.

She was relieved that she had made it unscathed and longed for the warmth of the room to wash over her. When she opened the door though, she was met with the horrible sight of more water, gushing from the ceiling and coating the floor. A surprised Louise was already there, holding her jacket over her head in a poor attempt to stay dry. Next to her was a repairman, staring at the burst pipe in the corner of the room that soaking Mia's mattress and he seemed just as baffled as Louise did.

"What happened?" Mia asked. Louise shook her head, annoyed at the incompetent repairman trying to shut off the water.

"Pipes burst," Louise said. "Seeped right into the kitchen, too. Jesus, I need a cigarette." Mia almost followed her out but she stared at her belongings, realizing in horror that everything was about to be ruined. Especially her most important possession. She dove for the mattress, despite the repairman's warnings. With the water flooding over her, she grabbed her duffle bag and threw her nearly wet clothes into it.

"Won't be completely dry until Wednesday or so," Louise said as she took a drag from her cigarette. Mia's stomach dropped. There was nowhere else for her to go. She looked at the rainy streets, now empty. Everyone was safe in their homes. "Is there anywhere else to stay until then?" Mia asked, already feeling hopeless with her duffle bag in tow.

Louise shook her head. "I'm sorry, Hun. The closest place is the motel, but it's about a half hour by car," she said. "I'd let you stay with me but my husband's not too keen on strangers." Mia nodded, still studying the street. Without another thought, she pulled her hood over her head. "It's alright," she said. "I think I know a place."

It was a huge risk, but she waited until Louise was gone before she stepped into the woods. She didn't know where he'd be, but this was the last place she had seen him go. He couldn't be too far out. This is stupid, she thought to herself as she stepped over rotted tree trunks. The smell of the woods filled her nose, and she noticed that it had been the first time she'd been in a forest since that fateful day.

She heard something crashing through the leaves nearby. So many phantoms invaded her mind of what it could be. It was Grey. It was Craig, with his sinister smile. As she ducked under a thick branch she eventually found the truth.

It was a wolf, and it watched her with bright eyes. Before Mia could tell if it was her imagination, her foot had already slipped from the ledge. And then she fell, sliding and tumbling down the steep hill without a sound.

CHAPTER 6: FRIENDS

Mia awoke to the sound of pipes creaking, and for a moment she thought she was back in her soaking wet loft. She sat up, only to find that her entire body felt like it was on fire. Her muscles ached with horrible tension as she adjusted herself to a seated position. What had happened out there in the woods? She felt the scratchy touch of a wool blanket against her hand and ran her hand along the flowery pattern. She recognized it almost immediately. Now she really felt like she was in a dream. What was Rowan's mother's blanket doing on this bed? She had seen it dozens of times on the family's couch whenever she visited.

And there it was right in front of her again, still as colorful and flowery as it had always been. She smiled faintly, still feeling a little strange. That had to mean that the commotion coming from the bathroom was someone she knew. Rowan.

Gathering her strength, she inched herself off of the bed. Her legs were freezing, as were her toes when they touched the wooden floor. She was wearing her t-shirt, but where were her pants? Looking down at her bare legs, she noticed they were covered in cuts and scrapes; presumably from her fall in the woods. The last thing she remembered was that wolf, or had it even been a wolf? She remembered falling, tumbling violently against the ground before landing hard on her back. The wind was knocked from her chest, and she stared up at the blackness surrounding her while she felt the rain pelt her face.

Her pants were neatly folded on a small stool near a closet. She looked around the room. It was small, the walls made of thick wooden logs and not even decorated. The only sign of décor was a picture frame laid flat on a dresser. Mia walked over to it, looking towards the door to see if her captor, or Rowan, would come back. She turned up the frame and saw the smiling faces of Rowan's parents staring right back at her. It was extremely outdated, one of those photos from an old photography studio, but Mia knew it was Rowan's parents.

Another loud noise, followed by a harsh curse came from outside of the room. Mia followed it, her heart pounding, and cut up knees aching with each step. She had waited years for this moment but never thought it happen like this. She shuffled to the doorway, barely containing her breath as she reached for the doorknob. All it took was one little turn of it to see Rowan again.

With her eyes closed, Mia worried this was still a dream and that she'd see her best friend, fourteen years old, standing in front of her. She pictured the blood seeping from his torn clothes, pouring onto the floor and from his mouth. She had to force her eyes open in fear that it would be the truth. Finally, she yanked open the door as if she were ripping off a Band-Aid.

The hallway was empty, but she could see that one door was open to her right, the sound of creaking pipes and rushing water faintly coming from it. Mia crept towards it. I'm in the wrong house, she thought, this is all just my imagination. But she thought of the quilt and the picture and knew that it just had to be the truth. She stood in the doorway, shocked at the sight of him staring at himself in the mirror, studying his own face.

She couldn't feel the words rising up in her throat. They stayed put, forming a lump that she wouldn't be able to swallow. She didn't have to say anything. Rowan noticed her in the doorway and gave a sharp startled cry at the sight of her.

"Mia!" the name sounded almost foreign from his mouth, but it was still familiar as it hung in the thick steamy air around them. Mia stood like a statue, her arms firm at her sides, as she took in the sight of him. He had just taken a shower and was half dressed. His skin was still dewy from the steam that lingered over his tight chest. Water drizzled over his glossy abs and his bulging arms. Rowan tousled his still-wet hair as he stared into Mia's eyes. The gesture alone was enough to bring Mia back to that place in the past. Rowan had certainly grown over the past fifteen years, and time had certainly been in his favor. The only things that stood out were the thick scars that covered his body. A flash of the horrible attack pierced through her mind like a sharp pinprick, but she shook it off.

The moment lingered between them. What was she supposed to say after all this time apart? Rowan used to be a phantom, always floating in the background of her thoughts and her dreams. And yet, here he was in the flesh, living and breathing in front of her. She realized she didn't have any words, even though she had had so much time to plan them. Warm tears welled up in her eyes and she figured she wouldn't say anything. Instead, she walked towards him, wrapping her arms around his sturdy waist.

It took Rowan by surprise. He was as stiff as an arrow as she held tightly to him. He was still wet, but Mia didn't care. She was with her best friend once again and closed her eyes in a strange feeling of relief. He was alive, and he was back in her life again. She felt his large hands reaching around her, clutching the small of her back so lightly as if he was afraid of touching her. It was a strange embrace, in which Mia realized that she had never seen Rowan this way before, and it gave her a strange prickling feeling in her chest, almost like lightning.

"I missed you," she whispered. "I missed you so much..."

She pulled away, beaming. She expected him to do the same, but to her dismay his face was gravely serious now, studying her, not sure if she was real. She waited to hear him say the same words, but instead, he let go of her as he awkwardly took a few steps back, as if it weren't appropriate for them to be touching.

"You, um, your pants..." Rowan said as he looked down at her lacy underwear, almost covered up by her t-shirt. Mia's face grew hot as she pulled her shirt down further over them. Rowan averted his gaze to the floor, finding his t-shirt and covering up his rippling abs and jagged scars.

She wasn't expecting a reaction like that from him and had only pictured the Rowan from her dreams. Then again Rowan had never seen her like that before, with so few clothes.

"Sorry," Mia said. "It's just, it's been a long time, hasn't it? You look good." A thick awkwardness stood like a wall in between them, and Mia's first reaction was to get out of the bathroom.

"Have, uh, have you eaten yet?" Rowan asked. His voice was cool and quiet as if he wasn't used to speaking. Mia shook her head as she stepped out of the room, feeling a strange pang of what felt like guilt or embarrassment she couldn't tell. She'd pictured meeting Rowan over and over again in her mind, and this moment was nothing like any of those encounters.

Mia watched Rowan, sitting in the dusty chair as he stirred a pot on his outdated stove.

"These are just leftovers," he said. "I hope you don't mind."

Mia shook her head. "Are you seriously asking if I mind, after all those times I've been to your house on leftovers night?" She joked. Surprisingly, Rowan almost chuckled, a small crack in the corner of his mouth almost turning into a smile. Mia was slightly relieved now. The same Rowan was still in there somewhere.

He stood stiffly by the bubbling soup.

"It's ready," he said and waited. Mia stood, about to serve herself, but Rowan stepped forward. "Wait," he said. "Sorry, how rude of me." He reached into a small cupboard and carefully ladled a serving of steaming vegetable soup before bringing it to the table. The rest of the table was set as if he had been expecting her for a visit. There was fresh bread in a basket and a glass of water from a speckled tin cup.

"You have a nice place out here," Mia said. "Very...secluded." She gazed around at the bare walls. "I don't really get guests," he said as he sat in the chair in front of her. The word 'guest' made Mia feel strange as if she were just passing through in his life instead of being his former best friend.

The food smelled delicious, but Mia wasn't hungry. She kept eyeing Rowan as he ate quietly.

"How did you find me?" She asked.

Rowan looked up from his food and calculated his answer carefully. "I was coming back from town," he said. "I saw you in the ditch and pulled you out." Mia didn't believe him. She hadn't seen a single soul on the streets earlier, and she had fallen too far down the ditch for Rowan just to see her casually.

"You found me all the way down there?" She prodded. His eyes darted away from her again as if he were afraid to look for too long. Mia decided to go right for it, the question she'd been longing to ask for fifteen years. "Rowan...where did you go?" She hadn't spoken his name for a while. It lingered on her lips, tingling over the tip of her tongue like it was a magic word.

Rowan tore into a piece of bread. Mia noticed his hands were shaking slightly. He winced as he took a bite, tucking the food into his cheek.

"Well, there was the accident," he said plainly. "I remember being in the hospital for a few days, and then we moved to another state." It sounded so rehearsed as if he had told everyone this. But Mia wasn't everyone else, or so she had thought.

"I went to your new house," she said sadly. "I couldn't call you. I didn't even get a letter or anything. I didn't even get to say goodbye...I thought something terrible had happened to you."

"I didn't have a phone," Rowan said, and Mia wondered if he had heard any of her words.

Another painful silence hovered in front of them, Rowan putting up an invisible wall. He sighed deeply, and Mia noticed his foot was bouncing up and down, something he often did when he was nervous.

"I mean, I had tried to reach you," he said, his voice slightly shaking. "There were a lot of things that got in the way." Mia realized something was terribly wrong.

"Like what?" She asked. Rowan jerked his head up, visibly distressed.

"I'm sorry," he said. "I think I just need a second."

Mia wanted to ask where he was going, but he was too quick. The wooden chair squealed against the floor as he stood up and walked outside into the pouring rain.

Mia stared at her food, desperately wanting to cry, though she didn't know what for. She had been woven so tightly into his life. Now she felt like a loose thread waiting to be pulled out and tossed aside. He's not the same, Mia thought. He's just a shell of what he used to be.

CHAPTER 7: THE PAST

He told her she could stay, but he wasn't sure if she did. Rowan woke up on the floor of the bathroom, as he sometimes did when he shifted through the night. He was cold against the linoleum, but he felt the warm fibers of a knitted blanket over his naked body. Pulling it closer, he recognized it was the one his mother had made that was draped over his bed. Rowan looked down at his hands, covered in mud and shredded bits of leaves. He sat up to pull the blanket from his feet. They were also caked with a crusted layer of dirt. Rowan sighed, his lungs aching from the cold air of his nightly run through the woods.

He cursed at his mistake of the previous night. It all had gone as horribly as he always feared it would. Brian had been wrong about everything. He stood to get into the shower, which was almost his second home at that point. He really needed to get the wolf under control. He knew shifters had their triggers, and Rowan struggled with the possibility that Mia just might be his after all. Either that or the overwhelming stress that swallowed over him as soon as he saw her. Rowan had always felt like he wanted to protect Mia, and it crushed him when he realized he was only pushing her away when she was trying to get closer.

Something skittered on the floor as he picked up the blanket. He bent down and his heart thundered in his chest as he held it in his hands. He ran in thumb in the small dents of the half circle made of clay. 'st, dies' was clumsily painted on the ornament, and he held tightly to it. His throat tightened as he flipped it over. Mia's name was written in pen, along with the date the ornament was made. Just a few days before he had been attacked.

Rowan pictured fourteen-year-old Mia at the art table, concentrating as her hands pinched carefully at the lump of clay. Of all the things she could have made, she decided to make something for both of them. Rowan clutched tightly to it, wishing for some kind of power to come from it. But he needed the other half for his wish to come true. He could have told Mia everything last night when he had the chance, but the wolf inside was screaming to get out again.

He had to apologize to her somehow. After all, she had been so excited to see him. Why hadn't he felt the same? Especially when he had held her. It had all felt so strange to him, as if he wasn't supposed to be a part of her life anymore. He walked towards his bedroom, reaching for the doorknob. He pictured her sound asleep, wrapped comfortably in his sheets. He'd make her breakfast, maybe try all of this again. Maybe then he could answer all of her questions.

But she wasn't there. The sheets lay twisted into crooked layers on an empty bed. Rowan felt hurt now. He had ruined everything, and all it was all the monster's fault. He pulled at the empty covers. The bed was cold. It must have been hours since she had left him. Rowan felt himself shaking again, but he wasn't about to let himself shift again. He wouldn't give the wolf the satisfaction of coming out, not after what he had done the night before.

Instead, he grabbed the alarm clock on his nightstand and hurled it across the room. It crashed against his closet door and burst into pieces. He shook his head, trying to regain his composure as he picked up the clock regretfully and tried to put it together. He looked up at the closet, full of secrets and things that weren't supposed to be looked at ever again. But he felt the need this one time just to look. It would only be for a second. There was only one thing he needed.

There was a box with a few things from when he ran away. He sifted through a handful of action figures, old notes and addresses from his time away, and a folded up picture that was slightly ripped at the edges. He didn't even want to look at the letter, the one that said 'Mia' on the front in crooked letters. His hands brushed against something smooth. He lifted out the other half of the clay ornament and frantically shut everything back into the closet.

Rowan stared down at the two halves in each of his hands. One was certainly not like the other. No matter how hard he had tried, he couldn't remove all of the blood from his half. The stain had lingered, seeped into the clay permanently. It had been in his pocket after all, while the monsters tore away at his limbs, sinking their teeth into his side. He could feel the sting of them on him now, their breath hot against his face as they growled in fury at him, hiding his terrified screams.

He pieced them together, scowling when they didn't quite fit the same. Each half was chipped in some way, preventing them from completely touching, though the message was still clear, '*Best Buddies*.' Rowan placed them carefully on the bed. He wondered if he should find her, but something clawed at the back of his mind that Mia didn't want to be found.

He went to the coffee shop instead of the diner that day. He figured she'd be working with Louise. Even though he'd said she could stay, he still felt guilty about what had happened between them. And then there was this other horrible nagging thought, this need to mate that was growing stronger each day. The wolf wouldn't give up until he was satisfied. His mind presented him with flashes of how Mia had looked, standing in front of him. She was so vulnerable, so delicate in that pair of underwear. Rowan clenched his teeth as he grabbed his black coffee from the counter and found a seat. How could he possibly think of that at a time like this?

An old man offered him a seat.

"You the guy that lives out in the woods?" He asked casually. Rowan nodded. The rest of the town knew about him. They whispered strange ideas about him at first, that maybe he could be a killer out in hiding. They weren't completely wrong. He was hiding from something, the darkness that chased him everywhere, though he had told everyone a carefully innocent narrative. The old man tossed down a floppy newspaper onto the table. "Hope you got yourself a gun out there." He tipped his baseball cap as he left.

Rowan took a seat and stared down at the newspaper. The headline glared up at him: 'Teen Girl fully Recovered after Wolf Attack.' Rowan's stomach gurgled inside of him. He skipped over the written interview with the victim. The rest of the article went on about the local hunting groups, spreading out and hunting wolves to protect the nearby towns. He stared down at the picture of the girl, so young. She was smiling, but her eyes looked tired and sunken in.

They were so wide with terror when he had attacked her so long ago.

Rowan tossed the paper over to the other table. Somehow it had found him again, even after running for so long. He had forgotten that face; had forced it from his mind. He could still see it in his nightmares though; her screams flooding his ears while his teeth sunk into her shoulder. No, he couldn't think of that here. His legs were shaking and he pressed them hard against the tiled floor, otherwise, he'd take off again, shift again, and cause even more havoc and suffering. He thought of the wolves howling the other night, the sound spreading through the forest like thin fingers, ready to pluck him out from his solitude. They were looking for him. They wanted to bring him back to them, but Rowan couldn't bear to face them after what had happened.

He had wanted to tell Mia about this monster inside of him last night, so badly, just to feel close to her again. When they were younger, she always had a way of comforting him, as if she could read his mind and know just the right thing to say. But what would she say if he told her how he had attacked that girl? How she had screamed and tripped over a fallen branch, the keychains on her backpack jangling onto the dirt as he jumped on her. It was all an accident. He knew it was because his abilities weren't under control.

And as the vision of that young girl shifted into that of Mia in his mind, Rowan feared they never would be.

CHAPTER 8: CONNECTIONS

Mia carried her duffel bag with her as she finished her very last shift at the diner. It was the shortest amount of time she had ever worked anywhere, with her past record being about two weeks. It was all because she had made the mistake of asking Louise about the loft, only to be told that the repairs were going to take about a week to complete.

Mia wasn't used to letting her emotions get the best of her. Because of Grey, she was more prone to hide her anger and her outbursts, in fear that he would do something horrible to her. But Grey wasn't here anymore, at least that's what she had hoped. She hadn't meant to make a scene, but her painfully awkward reunion with Rowan combined with the fact her home was basically a huge question mark was enough for her to explode. Louise stared at her in shock, and in an instant, Mia wished that she could take it back, somehow. But it had was already too late. The entire diner had heard, not to mention the kitchen staff, their mouths agape.

It was possibly the worst impression she could have left in Birchton, but Mia didn't care. She was used to moving around, ever since she had left home after high-school. One could only listen to talk being a disappointment to their family for so long. Mia went from party-hopping to couch-hopping in a matter of weeks, until she ended up on Grey's couch, or his bed to be exact. Sure, she had friends, but even in those rough times, they didn't understand the pain that she carried, and that there was this strange gaping hole that had stuck with her since she was younger.

Mia scraped her boots along the pavement. Her knees were still sore from falling down the ditch. She still wondered how the hell Rowan had found her out there, let alone in the darkness and the pouring rain. She secretly hoped that he could find her again out here. But after their failed conversation, she thought that maybe there wasn't any point in trying to find out what happened to her friend.

Rowan wasn't budging, and he was being incredibly secretive, which was so strange for him. Mia knew she should blame it on time, but she couldn't help but blame herself. She felt as if she had intruded on Rowan's new life, even though it was cold and lonely out in the middle of the woods. He seemed to be comfortable there.

The day turned into evening, and Mia could only think that maybe the motel had some vacancies. She had managed to get some money from Louise after all, though it took several moments of shouting. She sunk herself further into her large hoodie, wanting to hide from everything in the world. Her outburst had made her feel horrible. It wasn't Louise's fault that the pipes had burst, but she had been too upset even to think about that. Maybe after some time away from Birchton, she could come back and muster an apology, though she doubted if it would be accepted.

Mia hated hitchhiking. She had done it several times growing up, and there was never a time when she felt remotely safe or comfortable. The first time she had attempted it was when she went looking for Rowan. For some reason, her childish brain told her that maybe Rowan was just in the next town over. She had climbed quickly into a strange man's truck, only for a neighbor to see her at a stoplight and to call the police. Mia thought about that moment often. Her parents held her so tightly and thought she was sobbing because she was scared, not because she had failed to find her best friend.

The man that picked her up now, reminded her of the same man from so many years ago. He was large and hairy, with a thick, bushy grey beard that dragged over his dirty button-down shirt. He smelled like sweat and meat and hoarsely coughed up phlegm every so often. He agreed to drive her to the motel, from where Mia could hastily plan where she was going next. He kept looking over at her like all the creepy people would whenever they picked her up off the street. Even women seemed menacing to her if they agreed to give her a ride. Mia believed everyone had secret intentions lurking in their hearts.

She looked at the window as the beat-up pickup passed by a string of houses.

"Yer prettier up close," the driver said through his beard, his country accent thick like sausage gravy. "You meetin' anybody special at this motel?"

"Just a friend," Mia said. She knew what she had to say to stay alive. There always had to be the illusion of someone waiting for her somewhere. She pictured Rowan alone in his cabin, still lying on the bathroom floor, strangely covered in mud and leaves. Mia didn't understand where he had gone, or why he was naked from head to toe when he got back.

Even Rowan had intentions, though she couldn't pinpoint what they were exactly. He lingered in the back of her mind as he always did. Suddenly, Mia felt strange. She had tried so hard to find him, only to run away again in the wrong direction. She gazed out at the houses, and as her eyes fell on a 'For Sale' sign, swinging in the breeze, she knew what she had to do. She had told herself there wasn't a reason to come to Birchton, but now that she had seen Rowan, it had shifted something inside of her. She had been so upset with him, but maybe if she could go back and understand his intentions she could fix this.

The truck was driving faster now, the house flashing by.

"Stop, please," Mia said sternly.

"What?" The driver asked, his thick eyebrows knitted in confusion.

"I forgot something important," Mia hastily explained. "I have to get out right now." The truck slammed to a halt and Mia bolted from the passenger door. The truck squealed off down the street, and she watched in relief. It might have been a death sentence for her if she had stayed, but it was the fact that she would never truly know that haunted her.

The house had been abandoned for a while. The paint was peeling on the siding, and the screen door was wrecked, with countless holes. Mia trudged towards the back door, careful not to be seen. She had done a lot of dangerous things growing up, but breaking into a house was definitely a first for her. However, desperate times called for desperate measures. She'd have to stay out here and try to find Rowan tomorrow. In the meantime, she could work out an apology or a question of some kind to tell him.

The door was locked; shut tight with a special lock reserved for realtors to open for anyone who was interested in the phantom-like house. Mia sighed, regretting her decision to try to get in here. But anything was better than the 'what-ifs' that came from hitchhiking across town. Mia reached into her duffel bag, and wound a t-shirt around her hand. She'd seen this done in movies and hoped that this would be one of those rare moments where something actually worked. She closed her eyes and punched her covered fist through a small decorative glass window beside the back door.

It shattered, but not as loudly as she had thought it would. She unwrapped her hand, wincing at the sight of a single shard jabbed into her finger.

It wasn't that bad, but a droplet of blood dripped from her small wound onto the concrete steps of the back stairway. After a few moments of reaching clumsily for the door lock, she was able to get in safely. The entire house was empty, and her footsteps echoed across the creaking wooden floors. It was only one story, with a small cleared-out living room. At least, there was carpet, so it would be slightly warmer than when had Rowan slept on the freezing bathroom floor.

Mia curled up in her hoodie, resting her head on her duffel bag. The carpet smelled like mildew and the shady chemicals that were probably used to try to mask the damage that time had done to it. She rolled onto her back, eyeing the darkness that was swallowing up the house. It made her think of Rowan's house when his parents had packed up all of their things and left. Where had they gone? She asked herself. She never really knew, and had only the fragments of speculation that she'd picked up while she was running errands in town with her mom. Her mind drifted to thoughts of sitting with Rowan in their favorite spot in the woods. As her eyes fluttered closed, she wondered if he had found the ornament she had left behind.

Lost in tired confusion, she didn't realize someone was shouting at her until she felt large hands grabbing for her arms. Mia panicked, her mind finally cooperating as she struggled under the weight of the man as he rolled her onto her stomach. It was Rowan, but he'd never treat her this way, would he? Or it was Grey. He had found her after all.

"What the hell do you want from me?" she shouted, writhing under the iron-like grip. To her horror, a light from outside was cutting through the darkness of the living room. Multiple lights. Blue and red. Mia's head felt heavy as she began to realize she was being arrested.

"What were you thinking little lady?" A familiar voice said. "That you can just stroll up to any house you want and stay there? We got laws against that if you didn't know." She knew exactly who it was, but was terrified to even get a glimpse.

"Get your hands off of me!" Mia shouted, but Craig kept a firm hold on her.

"You'll save yourself a lot of trouble if you stop struggling," the cop said through his teeth as a cold pair of handcuffs clasped against her wrists. This wasn't happening, Mia thought. But as she was pulled to her feet she realized it was all very, very real.

"I can explain," Mia tried to say. "I wasn't going to tear the place down or anything!"

The cop turned her around, and she found herself face-to-face with possibly the second worst person who could have found her out here. Craig nudged her roughly.

"Get walkin'," he said. "We got a comfy place you can stay, trust me." Mia didn't trust him at all. If he weren't a cop, she would have spat in Craig's face, and made another scene, as she had done earlier that day.

As his hand reached around to guide her from the house, Mia noticed his shirt sleeve was pulled up. Her eyes widened and her heart sank eighty stories towards the ground in a cruel realization. There, imprinted in his skin, in thick black ink, was a tattoo of a wolf head emerging from the gaping mouth of a skull.

CHAPTER 9: INTENTIONS

'Consequence' was the word that trailed through Mia's mind as she stared down at the scuffed tiled floor of the minuscule prison cell. She never had to factor in consequence before, mainly because she has never been caught, if she did something illegal. She was tired and furious.

"Hello? Is anyone getting me the hell out of here?" She shouted through the thick bars of her cage. Craig was nowhere to be seen, since he had chucked her into the cell. Mia looked at the deep impressions the hand-cuffs had left behind, and cursed Craig for being so rough with her.

How did they even find me? She thought to herself as she studied the rest of the room. It seemed to be a small office area, with only two other cells in the room, both of them empty. Birchton wasn't a town for trouble-makers like her. There was a desk with a swivel chair in front of her. Her first thought was to look for the keys, though she suspected somebody was carrying them. But who?

Soon the doors opened, and Craig waltzed into the room, trailed by two other men in police uniforms that seemed too tight on them. Mia recognized them as the same officers who had sat with Craig in the diner. One of them had thick red hair and an unfortunate under bite. He leaned up against her cell, his massive stomach pressing into the metal bars.

"Brought you something," he said with a sly crooked grin as he reached through the bars, his thick fist clutching a candy bar.

Mia didn't want to take it. She glared daggers at him until he dismissed her with a "Fine, more for me."

The other officer sat in the rolling chair, digging through Mia's duffle bag.

"Hey!" She shouted, clutching at the bars again. "Get your hands off my stuff!"

The skinny officer, who had tanned skin and a shaved head, looked up from her bag. "Why don't you chill out for a second?" He said in a patron-izing tone.

Mia watched in horror as they pulled out her clothes one piece at a time. They paused as the skinny officer pulled out one of her bras. They "oohed" and "aahed" at it, tossing it back and forth and laughing. What kind of officers were these guys? Mia thought. She certainly knew that this wasn't common police behavior. "Stop it!" She shouted over them. They silenced, stifling their laughter.

Craig stepped in, grabbing the bra from the large officer and throwing it back in the bag. "Alright, alright," he said holding his hands up. "You guys have had your fun, but I think it's time we ask the lady if she knows anything about this." Mia's forehead wrinkled as she saw that Craig was holding something small and blue in his hand. Her wallet!

Craig raised an eyebrow as he opened it up in front of her, showing her the driver's license shoved inside. "Last time we talked," Craig said with his classic smirk. "You told me your name was Jamie." He looked back and forth from the wallet to Mia. "According to this right here, it says your name is Mia Hudgens, correct? Can you read that or am I crazy?" He shoved his arm into the cell, holding the wallet right in front of Mia's face.

Mia didn't have the time for any of this. She reached for her wallet like an angry viper, ripping it straight out of Craig's hand. Craig shrank back, startled, but then he laughed with his police buddies at Mia's demonstration of spirit.

"She's a little firecracker ain't she?" He said as he slapped his knee. "I can see what he likes about you."

Mia didn't like where this was going. She had been brought here because she had been sleeping in that abandoned house. Now Craig was talking about another 'he.' Did he mean Rowan? Or somebody else?

"She also smells amazing," the large cop said as he inched closer to the cell again. The skinny cop hit him in the stomach.

"Shut your damned mouth, Trent," he said through his teeth.

"What?" Trent said holding up his hands. He lowered his voice, though Mia could still catch what he was saying. "She doesn't know I mean it that way."

There was something definitely strange about these cops. "How did you find me?" Mia asked. Craig was sorting through a cellphone now.

"We're the police, honey," Craig said nonchalantly. "We got eyes and ears everywhere." He held the cell-phone further out in front of him, pointing it right at Mia. "Smile for me," he said, and Mia heard a shutter click as he took a picture.

"What was that for?" She asked as she watched Craig walk towards the desk with the cell phone.

"Just for a report," Craig said. "We're on a very special case, a missing person's case if you want to call it that." His eyes narrowed at her, and Mia felt as if she was going to be sick as she slowly began to realize.

"I'm not missing," Mia said, her voice barely a whisper. She sat on the bed, the springs squealing under her weight as she brought her knees to her chest. If you had asked a certain someone, they would have definitely said that Mia was missing. And Mia knew just who that was. She had to think quickly, or things were bound to get much, much worse.

She looked up at the cops. "I want to make a phone call," she said. They looked at her as if she were asking to be released. "Please," she added, hoping it would add to her request somehow. Suddenly, to her dismay, they all started laughing.

"She wants to make a phone call!" The skinny cop cried. Craig nudged him with his elbow.

"Well hold on now, Rico," he said calmly. "She's a prisoner, after all. The least we can do is grant her this one favor. As long as she doesn't have any tricks up her sleeve."

Surprisingly, he reached into his pocket, producing a gleaming set of jangling keys. Freedom, Mia thought as she eyed them hungrily. Her legs were shaking as she watched Craig open the door. She was startled by the sharp click of handcuffs around her wrist as the door opened.

"For safety," Trent scoffed. Mia was brought to the desk, where a corded telephone sat next to a computer. Craig shoved her into an empty chair, clasping the other cuff on the arm. Mia used her free hand to grab the phone, holding it up to her ear as she tried to think. Her heart sank as she realized that she would have called Rowan, if only he had owned a telephone. He didn't even leave her a cell-phone number to call. That sounded all too familiar.

Mia shuddered as the dial-tone flooded her eardrum, a low dull hum that droned constantly, waiting for her to press the little square buttons that could maybe get her out of there. Mia realized that she couldn't call anyone, not even her parents. She could have tried Louise, but she was pretty much a dead end at this point.

The cops waited quietly for her to dial the phone, but she could only look at her hand cuffed to the chair. Maybe if she was careful enough...but that was incredibly risky, and risk was what got her into this mess in the first place. But somewhere in her mind, she believed that it could maybe help her out.

It happened in a flash. Mia swung the phone at Trent. He yelped as it hit him in the eye and swung clumsily over the desk. The chair was next. Mia swiped it from under her, awkwardly flailing it in the direction of Rico and Craig. They stepped back, and soon the room was in chaos. Shouting echoed through the tiny office holding area as Mia kicked and swung wildly, knocking over papers, files, and mugs with cold coffee in them.

However, it wasn't long before she felt the iron grip of Rico and Craig around her. Mia screamed as she tried to fight, but there was no way she could have taken them all at once. Still, out of desperation, she knew she had to try. These men were planning something evil. They could see why he liked her.

Mia's head hit the wall as she crashed onto the bed in the cell. The metal feet screeched across the tiles, followed by the slam of the cell door clanging behind her. Mia reached up, touching warm, ruby-red blood dripping from her forehead.

She looked up at the three men, all of them cursing her wildly.

"The fuck is wrong with you trying a thing like that?" Craig hollered, his face turning a sickening purple.

"Craig, help me out here, man!" Rico shouted over him. Craig settled, his eyes widening at Trent as he collapsed on the floor. Mia crept further back into her cell as Trent looked up at her. Something about him had changed now. His eyes were darker, colder, and more sinister than they had been. He licked his lips as his entire body began to shudder.

"Get him cooled down!" Craig yelled to Rico. "We can't do this shit here!"

Mia watched in horror as Rico rolled up his sleeves and went for Trent, who was convulsing on the floor.

"Trent, you gotta calm down! Trent!" Rico struggled to keep him tethered to reality. Trent broke from his grasp, rushing towards the cell. His body collided violently with the bars. Mia jumped at the sickening clang, and her eyes locked with Trent's as he clawed at the metal in between them.

"Just want a taste!" Trent cried, his voice gravelly, and almost like a growl. Craig and Rico locked their arms around him. Trent fought them off, still clinging to the bars as if he was going to rip them straight from the wall. He was trying to get to Mia.

His shirt was pulled from around him, tearing the buttons as Rico and Craig held him long enough for him to settle. Rico grabbed a water bottle from the floor, splashing it on Trent's face. Trent seemed to awaken from a trance as he gazed around the room, regaining his bearings.

"What happened?" he asked as he tugged the fragments of his shirt off.

"It's okay," Craig said quietly. His demeanor had certainly changed dramatically, from cool and collected to terrified.

Mia crossed back over to the bed, evaluating the situation. Something had caught her eye, two things in fact. One of them was peeking from under Rico's rolled up sleeve, just barely the bottom of a wolf's jaw. Her eyes flitted to Trent, picking up his shirt. His white undershirt had exposed his arms, and when he turned around, Mia realized a true horror.

All of them had the same mark, the same gaping jaws of a skeleton revealing a wolf's head, ready to swallow her up. *They aren't here to arrest me*, Mia realized. *They're going to take me back to Grey...*

CHAPTER 10: BREAKOUT

Rowan could see everything, and feel the natural wave of energy of all the living things in the forest. He kept to the edge of the woods that bordered Birchton, his head low as he searched with his nose. The leaves still felt wet from the night before and gave off an earthy pungent scent. His thoughts were animal-like, and reduced to sensations. Find her. Hunt. Mate. He tried to push the last urge from his mind, but it lingered there. He was connected to her, and this desire propelled him through the trees. He picked up a sound, a strange babble of two men standing behind the police building. Rowan inched closer. Danger. He picked up their scent, and he couldn't help but growl a bit.

He wound down the hill from the woods, staying out of sight. He crouched behind a dumpster and waited. The two men were deep in conversation. A skinny man had his hand on the larger one and seemed to be consoling him somehow. Though they were human, Rowan could tell they had a secret, like him. Wolves, he thought. The larger man patted his head with a cloth and nodded to the skinny one. The skinny man reached for the door and opened it. Rowan felt a tug in his chest, as a new smell wafted towards him from the breeze of the door. Mia.

Without another thought, he took off in a sprint towards the door. His claws skittered across the concrete as he shot through the doorway. The men screamed at him, though he couldn't tell what they were saying. Rowan didn't care. He knew he had a mission to fulfill and he had to find his mate. Her scent was growing stronger now. It was sweet, with a slight tang, almost like wine. The lights inside were blinding, and the floor cold under his paws. He slipped a bit, lacking solid ground to keep his feet on.

He felt the heavy bodies as they landed on him. It was the men, trying to hook their arms around his waist. Rowan growled loudly, his hackles raised as he wiggled free of their clutches. He skidded clumsily into a wall, but regained his footing and followed the scent. The building was a maze of office rooms and hallways, but he finally found a cracked door. He slid again when he heard piercing gunshots explode near him. He could smell the smoke from the gun and heard the skittering pieces of concrete wall fall to the floor where the bullets had missed.

Another gunshot echoed through the hall, but Rowan hurried on. Mia. Danger. Wolves. But he couldn't see any wolves on the other side of the door, just another human with a wretched scent. He stared at Rowan with wide eyes, holding a heavy baton in one of his hands. He shouted something that Rowan didn't understand, holding the baton out in a threatening way. Rowan shrunk down, growling at the man in rage. There was a startled cry that distracted him, a female. Rowan saw the girl with the amber hair tucked into the corner of her cell. Mia.

She was terrified. After all, she had no idea that it was him. Rowan shouldn't have risked the look and was struck hard in his side with a crack of the baton. The man shouted into the hallway, where the others were. Rowan knew he didn't have much time. He snapped his jaws around the baton and swung with all his might, knocking the man off of his feet as he swung towards a desk.

He heard something rattle to the floor, a metallic jangling flooded his ears. Keys. Rowan watched the eyes of the man on the floor, darting from the keys to the cell. Rowan growled as he cornered him. To his surprise, the man tried to growl back, struggling on the floor, a stance that Rowan instantly recognized. Wolf, he thought.

Rowan bounded for him as the man tried to grab the keys. They slid across the tiled floor towards the cell. The man shuddered as teeth sunk into his arm. He cried out in agony, but Rowan held firm, wanting to crunch right into his bones. Painful memories flashed in his mind. He had done this before. That girl had screamed the same way. Flesh and blood, he thought. He shook his head roughly from side to side, tasting the metallic tang of blood as it seeped into his mouth.

The other two men had caught up, and were pointing their guns towards Rowan. Rowan let go of the arm, not sure where to turn now. He could risk running, but he would get a bullet put in him the second he moved. The guards moved closer to him, all of them shouting at each other now about what they should do. He was surrounded, but not for long.

Suddenly, the room went black. The shouting ceased, turning to harsh whispers as the men tried to find their way around the room. But Rowan could still see them crystal clear, not with his eyes, but with his nose and his ears. He could sense movement around him, and heard the jangling of keys from nearby. A desperate flash of a gun went off nearby him, followed by more shouting. Apparently one of them was still trying to kill him. Rowan could smell each of them and tackled the closest one into the nearby desk. It screeched as the man fell, and Rowan jumped away as another gunshot blasted throughout the room.

He could feel the bodies around them, but not the warm comforting one of Mia nearby. He heard a door open, and a crack of light seeped into the room. A shadow lingered in front of it, and soon it was swung open as the men realized what was happening. As they struggled to their feet, Rowan ducked under the desk and slipped through the crack, following after the girl in the bright prison uniform as she nearly tripped around the corner. Rowan ran for her, and she turned and cried out at the sight of him. But he wasn't going to hurt her. He saw she was going the wrong way, and he nudged at her thigh, pushing her to go towards the back door.

She seemed to understand, and through this archaic method of communication, they scurried out from the back door and towards the woods. The men's shouting disappeared, even though they appeared shortly after Rowan and Mia had escaped. They cursed out into the trees, unaware that Mia and Rowan were already headed for home.

Mia leaned against a tree, catching her breath. They had been running for what felt like hours, but the soft glow of the cabin was in the distance now, waiting for them. Rowan sat in front of Mia and he could tell that she felt uneasy around him. She leaned down and grabbed a stick, holding it out towards his face. Rowan growled at the gesture but felt it catch in his throat as his muscles began to twitch. He had to get away from her. The wolf was tired, ready to become human again. Of all the times to shift. He shuffled towards a thick cluster of trees, hoping to hide behind one of the trunks, while he completed his horrific transformation, but he didn't make it. He rolled in the dirt and leaves as he shook frantically against the forest floor. His thoughts became clearer and to his horror he realized that he was out in plain sight, revealing his dark secret to the only person he cared about.

His limbs stretched out, completing the shift as the fur was shed around them and turned back into muscle and skin. Rowan struggled to his feet, leaning up against a tree as he took in a sharp breath of cold air.

"Oh my God..." a quiet voice said into the wind. Rowan turned, clutching at his aching chest as he looked at Mia. She took a few steps back, stumbling as she stared at him in horror. This is what Rowan had feared the most. He had saved Mia but somehow he had still managed to look like a monster, standing naked and wild in front of her.

"Mia, I really need to explain," he said as he took a step closer. He placed his hand in front of his crotch, attempting to hide from her. Mia shook her head, clasping her hands over her mouth.

"Please, Mia, "Rowan's voice was desperate as her name left his lips. "I wanted to tell you." He realized at that moment that he couldn't lose her again, although he was certainly very close to.

"Rowan...what are you?" Her voice cracked as tears welled up in her eyes. Rowan held out his hands, helpless. Where could he even start? Especially after the horrific scene that Mia had just witnessed.

"I'm sorry," he said, his voice breaking. "I've been trying to figure that out..." A sharp pain travelled through his chest. It hurt to breathe. It hurt to be there. He lowered himself to his knees, the cold finally getting to him, prickling at his human skin.

He wanted to cry. It was as if every pain in his life had collided together, forming another cruel beast inside of him. He had never been so afraid. He steadied his breath as he held his face in his hands. Leaves crunched around him. Rowan knew she would leave. He would have thought about it too if the roles had been reversed, though he knew in his heart he would have stayed. Maybe for a second, he had believed that she would, which only hurt him more.

But to his surprise, the leaves crunched closer to him. Warmth radiated from nearby. A faint whisper called to him through his stream of painful thoughts.

"Let me help you." He felt the rough fabric of her uniform brush against his skin, as her comforting arm found its way around his bare shoulder. When she touched him, it was as if the rest of the world had disappeared with the wind.

It was just him and Mia. He felt her fingers thread through his, and this time he held on to them tightly. It made him think of the last time they had touched, on the day he was attacked. She only ran after that, far into the woods. But he she stayed, and it caused a spark to flicker inside of his empty chest.

As Rowan pieced together the events of Mia's rescue though, he realized their nightmarish reality. They couldn't sit like this forever. This time, they both would have to run.

CHAPTER 11: IN HIDING

Mia's eyes were heavy, and she longed to sleep as she propped her head on the arm of an old couch in Rowan's cabin. To the right of the kitchen was a small sitting room, with a couch, a fireplace, and several shelves lining the walls, each of them filled with books and other oddities. Mia could see a bird skull propped carefully on one of the shelves, next to a stack of books that appeared to have been read. Rowan was always an avid reader, hungrily devouring information whenever he could.

Rowan emerged from the kitchen, and placed a steaming mug of tea in front of her. He continued to watch her out of the corner of his eye as if he were unsure of whether or not she should be there. It made Mia feel uneasy, especially after what she had witnessed out in the woods, just a while ago.

She stared awkwardly at her friend as he poked carefully at a fire that was growing larger under the mantle, her prison uniform burning up into ash inside. How calmly he handled himself, despite the growling fierce creature he had revealed himself to be.

"How long?" Mia asked as she watched the embers swirl up into the chimney. Rowan ran his hand through his hair and scratched at the stubble on his cheek.

"Since the attack," he said, not taking his eyes from the fire. Though she was exhausted, Mia still felt a chill come over her. She would finally know the truth.

"Do your parent's know?" She asked. Rowan stared straight ahead, silent as his mind wandered back in time. Mia adjusted, sighing heavily. "Look, I've waited long enough just to find you again. I think the least you can do is answer my questions," She didn't realize how harsh her voice sounded until the words hovered in front of her. But they seemed to snap Rowan out of whatever state he was in. He put down the fireplace poker and took a seat next to Mia. He turned his body towards her, his eyes glancing at her every so often.

"It really messed me up," Rowan said. "I stayed in the hospital for a while. I was crushed when they said you couldn't see me. As I was recovering, though, I started to feel really strange. I could hear things, and see things much better than I ever could before the attack."

Mia watched his chest rise and fall with each nervous breath. His skin gleamed through the gap in his shirt where he was too lazy to button it up all the way.

"Then, one night it got much stranger," he said. "I shifted for the first time in my hospital bed. It was the worst pain I had ever felt; even worse than when I was attacked. It was very brief, and I thought it was just a nightmare and I shifted back. But then my parents visited during the day."

He picked at the fabric of the couch. Mia wondered how long it had been since he had told someone this. The thought of Rowan, so young and scared shifting into a wolf had frightened her.

"So they knew?" Mia asked.

Rowan nodded reluctantly. "I was so scared, I just felt it come over me, and they saw what was going on. It was a family secret from then on," he said. "We had already packed up the house, but my parents knew they couldn't keep me in town. I could have hurt someone. It wasn't long before I actually did, despite all of their efforts."

"What do you mean?"

"My parents found a place, far outside of town. We stayed there a while, but I knew they looked at me like I was some kind of monster. It hurts, feeling as if you're a burden on the people you love the most." When he said that he looked at Mia, and she felt her heart beat a little faster. For a glimmer of a second, she thought he could have been talking about her. "I found some people," Rowan continued. "They were like me, I guess, but they knew how to control their shifting. They offered to help me, and I took them up on their offer for a while. But I was too stubborn."

He stood up and walked over to the window to peek through the blinds.

"There was an accident after that," he said sadly. "I was still too new to my shifting. I was—," he hesitated.

Mia didn't want to press him any further, though she knew more questions burned inside of her. She stood up from the couch, placing her mug on the coffee table. She went to Rowan's side and tenderly touched his shoulder. He felt warm under her touch, almost feverish.

"You don't have to say anything," she said quietly. "Can you just tell me, why? Why you didn't even try to talk to me after what happened? I was your best friend, Rowan. We told each other everything."

Rowan turned over his shoulder to look at her. The glow of the fire spread over his face, making him look dark and ominous as he stood tall over her. Mia wasn't afraid, though. There were worse things out there, one of them being the fear that she'd lose Rowan again. From the way he was looking down at her, she thought he could have been feeling the same way.

"I wanted to tell you," he said somberly. "I just didn't know how."

He stared into her eyes, and Mia wanted so badly to comfort him. However, she was scared to hold him again, scared of her arms feeling empty like when she had embraced him the other night. She was so close to him, and she could feel the warmth radiating from his sturdy body. There was a faintly familiar smell to him that made her ache strangely.

"I wish we could have found each other sooner," Mia said out of impulse. "Then maybe we wouldn't have to be in this mess."

"What do you mean?" Rowan asked.

Mia sighed, not even knowing where to start. She realized Rowan must have felt this way too as he had bared his soul to her.

"I've made some mistakes myself," Mia said as she looked down at her hands. "And I think it's caught up with me now. Those guys back there, the policemen..." She almost didn't want to finish. What would Rowan think of her if he knew what she had gotten herself into? The idea of even bringing up her past relationship also made her feel strange, maybe because she wanted to protect Rowan somehow, to preserve this image he may have had of her in his mind.

"Listen, I didn't even know that shifters were a thing until you told me," she said. "But now that I know, I think it's helped me to figure something out. Those policemen; I think they may be shifters too."

"Hmm," Rowan said, his brow furrowed. He suddenly became too aware of the window, and Mia felt his firm hand reach around for the small of her back. His fingers pressed into her as he gently guided her back towards the couch. It almost took her breath away. But why? She thought. Rowan had touched her plenty of times. But not like this.

"I could smell something on them," Rowan said. "Back in the office. They had the sharp smell of wolf."

"Not only that," Mia said, still hesitating. But looking into Rowan's light eyes, she knew she had to tell the whole truth. "They have the same tattoo as...my ex. His name is Grey."

Rowan's attention was caught by the word 'ex' and Mia watched as disapproval flickered across his face.

"Your ex," he said, pondering. Mia adjusted nervously on the couch. The way his jaw was clenched made her nervous. Was he just as aggressive as Grey had been?

"I left him just last week," Mia said quietly. "He...he was abusive towards me."

"He...what?" Rowan said, his voice a little harsh.

Mia saw his knuckles turn white as he balled his hands into fists on his lap.

"How long?" Rowan asked.

"A couple of years," Mia said, slightly ashamed. She knew it had been a mistake, but she was so terrified of Grey, and of being alone, she found it hard to leave.

"Great..."

She couldn't translate the tone of his voice. She tried to get Rowan to look at her again, to gaze into her eyes so she could at least gauge if he was alright. But he kept his eyes locked on the coffee table. He was upset with her, she figured. Who wouldn't be? She knew she was stupid to get wrapped up in a horrifying relationship. Mia suddenly felt guilt washing over her, transforming into anger.

"I shouldn't have told you," she said dismissively as she stood up from the couch. "I knew it would make you upset." Her feet carried her towards the bedroom.

"Wait," Rowan called out. Within seconds he was back at her side, his hand shooting out to grab her arm. Mia caught her breath as she felt herself being pulled in closer to Rowan's chest. She shuddered at his touch, as his hands enveloped her, resting softly on her back. She felt the soft caress of his thumb against her, through the t-shirt he had given her to wear. Her cheek pressed against him and she could hear his heart thundering in his chest. She wrapped her arms around him, accepting his embrace. She was surprised how comforting he was. She could feel Rowan's warm breath as he buried his face in her hair. For a brief moment, Mia felt whole again, as if a fraction of her life was back in its place.

"I'm sorry," Rowan whispered. "I should have been there." He pulled away just as quickly as he had grabbed her. Their faces were so close, nearly touching. In a wild flash of a fantasy, Mia could have kissed him at that moment, as she had in her dream. But she wasn't sure of what would happen after that.

"You can still be here," Mia said calmly. "Those policemen - they were going to take me back to Grey."

Rowan calculated, looking towards the window again as if the wolf pack would jump in at any second.

"We can hide out here," Rowan said. "Until we can figure out how to get out of here, you should stay with me." Mia was dizzy, and she couldn't tell if it was because she was tired or if those last few words Rowan said were doing something strange to her. She should stay with him, she thought. She nodded at him without another word.

She was surprised that he embraced her again, but this time she looked into the crackling fire, thinking of how the shadows had danced over Rowan's face. She hoped that for once she was making the right choice.

CHAPTER 12: TRUE NATURE

Rowan was grateful for the passing days, though they seemed to go by like water rushing along a creek. The exchanges between him and Mia started short; basically brief awkward exchanges in passing. But as the days went on, Rowan started to notice Mia growing warmer towards him as if she had gotten used to being in the cabin. He no longer felt like a ghost to her and it was making him more relieved.

He watched as she fell asleep reading on the couch, lost in one of his books from the shelf. They had dinner together and Rowan had surprised her by bringing home a container of their favorite cookies that they had both enjoyed when they were younger. The nights were even longer, and they would stay up by the fire for hours, lost in their memories of the past, and catching each other up on the events in their lives that the other had not witnessed. But, at the end of each night, Rowan found himself left with a strange and empty void after Mia said goodnight, only to close herself off in his room until morning.

The wolf was growing hungrier now, and it didn't help that Mia was around him all of the time. Just little touches, a small brush of the hand here and a casual bump of the leg there, was enough to send him reeling into thoughts that he didn't dare confide in Mia, at least not right now. His urge to mate would nag at him throughout the days, and Rowan would have to shift outside for a moment, blowing off his energy in the long nights.

But not a single one of these touches or nights in deep conversation or a bite of their favorite childhood treat could make them forget the horror that lingered just several miles away. Grey was on the hunt, and so was his pack. Rowan struggled for so long to come up with an escape plan, only to be distracted by his need to be around Mia.

"What's wrong?" He asked her after about a week of confinement in the cabin. Mia hung over the edge of the couch, staring up at the ceiling.

"I haven't been outside in forever," Mia grumbled.

"Mia, you know you have to stay inside," Rowan consoled. "It's too dangerous for you to go out into town."

"I don't even want to go into town," she said. "I just need to get out of here. Just for a moment." It was hard for Rowan not to be offended. He had hoped that he could have given Mia everything she needed. Apparently, it just wasn't enough.

However, Rowan knew a place that might be safe enough. It wasn't too far from the cabin, and he figured it would be far enough away so that Grey and the pack couldn't get to them. The pleading look in her eyes made it hard for him to resist.

"Come with me," he told her, reaching out his hand. "There's a place I'd like you to see."

Rowan could feel the strange pains in his chest, as he led Mia through the woods. The wolf inside was begging for him to shift, but Rowan stayed as a human, though it took a tremendous amount of energy. He had kept his ability hidden for hours at a time, and it would be a while before it was dark again.

Rowan looked at the crushed branches around him. He had met Brian out here and had told him that Mia was hiding out in the cabin. Brian agreed to mark his scent around the perimeter of the cabin, creating almost a safety circle to keep the wolf pack off of Mia's scent. It wasn't much, but it would have to be enough. They would know Rowan's scent, for sure, which made him almost regret bringing Mia all the way out into the woods, and out of their circle.

They came to a cluster of branches. Rowan was already excited by the sound of rushing water and could tell Mia was feeling the same.

"Okay, remember our rock?" Rowan said as he clutched one of the thin branches. The leaves rustled under his touch.

"Oh, you mean the one we'd meet by, every single day after school?" Mia said as she cocked her head to the side. "No, I don't think I know what you're talking about," Rowan smirked as he nudged her shoulder. He pulled back the branches and Mia was suddenly not in the joking mood.

Her eyes lit up at the sight of the water as it toppled over the edge of the waterfall and fell into cascading layers of foam in the river.

"A much bigger rock than I had anticipated," Mia joked as she ducked through the branches and started to run towards the river.

"Careful!" Rowan called out to her as he weaved his way towards her. He paused to listen to the roar of the falls. Sometimes it helped him drown out the sounds of the wolf inside, just for a few blissful moments of silence.

Mia tip-toed over rocks, relishing her precious break from the cabin. Rowan stayed close behind; watching as she looked playfully over her shoulder at him. Her hair seemed to shimmer in the fiery-yellow of the late afternoon sun.

"Wow, what a slowpoke," she yelled to him over the roar of the water. Rowan was distracted. It was something about the way Mia's hips swung from side to side as she stepped over the rocks. He watched her body maneuver up the side of the rocks, her legs long and powerful, her back arching delicately behind her as she climbed. It was doing something to Rowan, and at that moment he realized just how much Mia had changed since he had last seen her.

She let out a small cry, disrupting his thoughts. Mia's foot had slid down the rock, and she nearly fell falling towards the jagged stones that waited at the stream's bottom. Rowan was quick, and he lunged across the water for her, catching her by the waist so she landed clumsily in his arms. Rowan checked her for injuries, but to his surprise, she was laughing, a sound he hadn't heard in years. He held onto her, gently carrying her towards a small cavern overlooking the waterfall. She smiled up at him as her hands locked around his neck.

"Aren't you going to put me down?" She asked slyly.

Rowan couldn't help but stare at Mia, how adorable she looked while wearing one of his large t-shirts and an old pair of shorts. He could feel something stirring inside of him and for once he discovered that it wasn't the wolf. It was his own flicker of desire. He still felt the weight of her body in his hands, as if they left a ghostly imprint, and longed to be able to touch her again.

"Are we safe out here?" Mia asked as she stared down at the flowing river. Gentle bursts of mist clouded around them, cold but refreshing.

"I think so," Rowan said. "But I'd protect you if we weren't." Mia looked at him, flashing a sarcastic grin.

"Oh wow, how strong and brave of you," she said in a low mocking tone.

"You don't believe me?" Rowan asked. "Even after you'd seen me shift? I can tear someone up if I have to."

He knew he shouldn't have said it, and after he had his stomach tightened. He ran his hand through his hair. Unfortunately, the waterfall's roar couldn't block out the grim visions he often saw; the grisly moments from his past.

Something pulled him out of it, a hand reaching over and clasping his cold fingers.

"Hey," Mia said calmly. "Thanks for this."

"Yeah," Rowan said. He could have told her the truth, but he was worried the stress would trigger him and unleash the wolf.

"You seem tense," Mia said. "Everything okay?"

Rowan put on a confident façade. He couldn't let her know he was in pain.

"This is the longest I've gone without shifting," he said. "Most people are good at fighting it, but I didn't train myself long enough to get the hang of it. The more you practice, the more you understand your triggers."

"And what kind do you have?" Mia asked, nudging him slightly.

Rowan would have said that it was her, in that instant. Just the simplest touch made his chest flutter. It felt almost silly, child-like. Then again he had never gotten the chance to experience these moments.

"I can't say," Rowan said with a smirk. "Maybe just stress I guess? Everyone is different. It could be an emotion, or even an object, anything really."

Mia kicked her feet along the edge of the rocks, contemplating. She looked up and stared into his eyes, studying the traces of time.

"I know what you're thinking," Rowan said.

"What am I thinking?"

"That you're stressing me out by staying with me," he said. He waited for the worst.

"Wrong," Mia said. "Try again."

"I'm stressing you out with my insane wolf abilities," he said. Again, the worst hovered between them. But, instead of confiding her thoughts, Mia's hand left his fingers and came up to his face. He closed his eyes at the warmth emanating from her touch as her hand clasped around his cheek.

"I'll give you a hint," she whispered softly. He felt her breathe just as her lips touched against his. Rowan never thought he would have something like this, but in that brief moment, it was so tangible.

It was his own voice telling him to pull her closer, to take up her beautiful body in his sturdy arms. She was on his lap now, as time sped up between them. Rowan wasn't ready for anything like this. Mia kissed him with such ferocity, as if she had been carrying this kiss as a burden for ages. Her legs wrapped tightly around him as her breasts pressed further against his chest, wanting to get closer. Rowan felt her heart beating along with his, as his hands searched up her back, his fingers tangling in her hair. Hers did the same, memorizing him.

This was all so foreign to him, but he was willing just to get a taste of everything that she had to offer. He felt something though, a hardness between his legs pressing against Mia as well. Mia gasped slightly, pulling away from him, just to get another look at his face. He was worried something was wrong but was relieved to see that she was smiling the faintest and most satisfied smile. He kissed her again, arms wrapping around her perfect waist as his hands barely lifted up her shirt.

And then he saw it. Crystal-clear, and shattering through their perfect moment. Out in the middle of the woods, staring right at him, was a lone wolf. His fur was as black as midnight.

CHAPTER 13: TOGETHER

Mia flipped a fluffy yellow omelet gracefully in the pan and smiled faintly at Rowan. He watched from over her shoulder as he turned over a thick steaming layer of shredded hash browns, beside her.

"Good form," he said with a smile.

"Thanks," Mia said. "Too bad I didn't work in the kitchen at the diner instead. Probably would've lasted longer." She felt an ache of guilt, the image of her screaming at Louise imprinted into her mind.

"What happened?" Rowan asked.

"My attitude happened," Mia said, already feeling her attitude on shaky ground just thinking about it. "Sometimes I just snap. And then it's like I can't even see clearly anymore. And usually after that is when a dumb decision is made."

"Decisions...like Grey?"

Mia sighed, putting the pan on the stove a little too harshly. She hated that Grey was back in her life and more importantly, that he was planting himself right in the middle of her reunion with Rowan.

"Grey was a mistake," Mia said firmly. "And I didn't see it until it was too late. He said he would kill me if I tried to leave again!" She could feel her body shaking, her knees feeling weak at the thought of Grey's face right in front of hers.

"Hey," Rowan's calm voice brought her back to reality. She felt his solid arms wrap around her from behind, and his lips brushed against her ear. This had all felt so strange to her. Their kiss at the waterfall had shifted their friendship into another direction, one that Mia wanted to follow, just to see where it led.

She had just started to kindle these feelings for Rowan before he disappeared. Now that they were older, Mia's thoughts were starting to mature. The thrill of being on top of him had made her dizzy, and she wondered how long it would be before she would be able to touch him like that again.

"That wolf we saw," she began, her voice wavering.

Rowan's arms pulled her in, tighter, safe and secure. "It wasn't Grey," he said quietly.

"How can you be so sure?" She asked as she turned around to face him. She could always tell when Rowan was lying, and he was certainly telling the truth, despite her own suspicions.

"I know him," Rowan said, his arms leaving her sides and turning off the stove.

Mia felt cold again, a strange emptiness as soon as he let go of her. "Another shifter?" She asked. She was so caught up in finding Rowan that she barely knew about his strange abilities and the separate world that revolved around them.

Rowan nodded, pursing his lips. "He's trying to get me back," he said somberly. Mia pieced it together. "From that group, you were telling me about," she said. "Why didn't you stay with them?"

Rowan wouldn't look at her. Clearly, there was a dark space between them. She knew he had kept a secret, one far worse than him being a shifter, but would he be willing to share it with her? Mia felt a slight emptiness when Rowan suddenly walked away.

"Where are you going?" She asked with concern in her voice. She felt as if whenever it came to his wolf abilities, she could only helplessly watch. She watched as the omelet in the pan sizzled, burning slightly around the edges. Grabbing a plate from one of the long, makeshift cupboards, she carefully transferred the omelet, figuring that she would just have to eat by herself.

Before she could even lift the first bite to her lips, Rowan returned, taking his seat at the table. He had a small piece of paper in his hands that he kept turning over and over.

"I don't know if you've already heard about the attacks," Rowan said, his eyes staring miles and miles away in another place, somewhere that Mia couldn't see.

"What are you talking about?" Mia asked, suddenly feeling an ominous darkness wavering over her.

Rowan handed her the piece of paper silently. It was an envelope, worn with age and from being handled so much. On one crinkled side, Mia's name stared back up at her, the writing in sprawling hasty letters.

"Rowan, I don't get what this is," she said. But Rowan gestured with a slight nod for her to open it and find out.

Mia's fingers trembled as her thumb ripped at the envelope sealed carefully by Rowan's tongue. She almost didn't want to open it, for fear of what awful secret she would uncover inside. Pulling out the contents she found a letter addressed to her, written in the same hasty letters on the envelope. The work of a younger Rowan:

"Mia,

I've tried to write this to you thousands of times, but I can never seem to get this on paper without having to tell you the truth. We've always said that we would always be best buddies...no matter what. And now by writing this, I'm worried that it might make you change your mind. But we swore once that we would always tell each other everything. I've become a monster, and what's even worse is what I've done as this monster. I hurt someone, badly.

She was a young girl; maybe as old as we were. I wasn't under control. I was still reckless and wild. I attacked her, the same way that I was attacked. I'm not sure if she's going to be okay, but I've been haunted by what I've done ever since. There are others like me. I'm living with them. They're teaching me, wanting me to get this under control, but I've messed up too much. I don't think anyone can fix what I've done. So I'm leaving this letter behind, hoping that one day you'll learn the one true thing I've been afraid of, other than myself. Losing you. I'm hiding somewhere, and I know you don't understand all of this, but I hope that one day we can meet again so that I have the chance to try to tell you—"

Mia's heart pounded in her chest as she read it. But she couldn't finish it, not because she was afraid, but because the bottom of the letter had been purposely ripped off. Her thumb brushed along the rough edges as reality sunk in. Rowan had attacked a girl while he was shifted.

"Is she alive?" Mia asked. "The girl you attacked?"

Rowan nodded. "She's okay," he said. "But they've been hunting wolves in that area, wolves that I know weren't responsible for this. I just know that it's all my fault."

"I see," Mia said quietly. She looked up at him. He was staring at her with pleading eyes. "What kept you from leaving this behind?" She asked, folding the letter back into the envelope. She didn't want to see it. It only made her feel horrible about what Rowan had done.

"I was afraid," Rowan said. "I thought that if I had left it for you, you would be so upset that you wouldn't even try to find me. It all sounds so crazy to believe. So I kept it hidden, figuring that maybe if you ever found out I could tell you."

"Rowan," Mia said, reaching out to touch his hand. His fingers clasped around them, like that day in the forest so long ago. "I've been trying to find you my whole life," Mia said. "You've made a mistake. It was horrible, yes, but I've messed up too. It's just what happens over time."

"I know," Rowan said. "It's just that I've missed so much of your life. I thought that maybe if this never happened to me, then things could have been, well...different."

"What do you mean?" Mia asked.

Rowan shrugged, running a hand through his hair. "So that I have the chance to tell you...that I've loved you for all of my life," He said. The words hung in front of them, and Mia wished she could just reach out and grab them. Rowan looked down at the envelope. "That's what the end of the letter said," he whispered.

They sat quietly for a moment, as Mia felt her emotions swirling inside of her.

Suddenly, it was as if everything had faded away and a door had opened in front of her. She needed Rowan in her life. He was always the one who was there to save her. And here he was just trying to save her again, from another heartbreak.

"I've loved you for all of my life," Mia said, the words flowing softly from her mouth like sweet honey. It was as if an enormous brick had been lifted from her back.

Rowan looked up at her from behind his messy hair. His lips turned up into a smile, and he clutched so tightly to Mia's hand that Mia thought he would break it. In a flash, he pushed the table away. The scraping of wood against the floor and the clinking dishes of their uneaten dinner filled the room as he pulled Mia right out of her seat.

Mia closed her eyes, the blood rushing through her veins as Rowan kissed her. He was firm and demanding, more so than their encounter at the waterfall. Mia took him in, letting go of everything she was so afraid of. She felt his arms tightly around her waist as he grabbed her, pulling her close into his rock-solid body. She reached around his neck, feeling his soft hair trailing against her hands. Rowan leaned down, planting kiss after kiss on her neck.

"I want you," he whispered sharply into her ear. "I've wanted you for a long time."

"Is that you or the wolf talking?" Mia dared to ask. She couldn't feel her breath, just her heart pumping against his chest.

"Both," Rowan said with a sly grin. "I always thought you'd be my mate." Mia's eyes widened. His mate? She felt a strange tingle over her legs and most sensitive places. She suddenly longed to fulfill his wish.

"Take me, then," she said with a smirk.

Rowan, was now fueled with his animalistic urges, and he slammed Mia against the wall of the kitchen. Pans clattered around them. Mia's hands searched under his shirt, feeling those warm sturdy abs against her fingertips, and touching his firm chest muscles. She gently traced the outlines of his scars. She wanted to be on top of him again, but this time with no restrictions. This time it wouldn't be just a dream. Rowan was clawing at her clothes, grabbing at the small of her back as he kissed her again, feverishly. He wanted the same. Mia's head spun as if the air had left the room. She fumbled with his belt as she unbuttoned his pants. Rowan moaned with anticipation as soon as the fabric hit the floor. Mia gasped again as she felt something long and hard brush against her hand. She clutched for it, realizing just how enormous he was.

"Holy shit," she breathed. "You're massive."

Without another thought, she bent down and pulled Rowan's cock, veiny and pulsing, from underneath his briefs.

She was a little intimidated. How was she going to fit all of it in her mouth? Her eyes went up to Rowan as he waited for her. Mia wrapped her lips around him, her tongue barely brushing against his tip as she inched him further into her mouth. Rowan sighed deeply as she gracefully slid over his shaft, up and down, until she could feel his veins pulsing against her lips. She could feel his fingers weaving through her hair, and clutching at the back of her skull as she moved back and forth.

"I can't wait anymore," Rowan said through his teeth as he took himself out of her mouth. In one swoop, he lifted her up. "Where are we going?" Mia asked as he bounded down the cramped hall.

"Somewhere I can do this properly," Rowan said hungrily as he kicked open the door to his bedroom. He threw her on the bed, promptly lifting his shirt over his head. Mia had him completely naked now, and he was an absolute god in front of her, rippling with muscles built up from being in the wild. She was willing to see just how wild he would get.

Rowan climbed over her, bringing her up on her knees as he lifted up her shirt. Mia kissed his warm neck, feeling the adrenaline pulsing through his veins as he felt for her soft, supple breasts. Clothes flew across the room in a flurry as Rowan ripped at her shorts, pulled off her bra until there was nothing left in between them but a lacy black pair of panties.

Rowan stared up and down at her body, lit up by the moonlight seeping through the curtains.

"What's wrong?" Mia asked.

But Rowan was smiling. "You're gorgeous," he said.

Mia sighed at the touch of his hands running up her thighs and reaching around for her buttocks. He grabbed them, kneading them firmly in his hands, until he slid his hands under the fabric, touching her bare skin. Mia admired the healed skin over his chest. Rowan seemed slightly ashamed, but Mia leaned down to kiss them softly, erasing the pain. Rowan laid her down, gently sucking on her breasts, his breath heavy with want. His fingers lingered down in between her legs, just barely moving away Mia's underwear as he slipped his fingers inside of her. Mia gasped at how easily they went in. She was warm and ready for him.

But first, Rowan wanted a taste. With a devilish grin, he bent down, pulling her underwear to the side again and this time searching her with his tongue. Mia moaned as his warm lips puckered around her vulva. He tasted every part of her, the tip of his tongue swirling around her clit.

Then she was completely naked as he pulled off the only fabric in between them. But Mia wanted to do this right. She was the one longing to be on top. She sat up and pushed Rowan onto his back on the bed.

"Excuse you," Rowan said, and Mia shushed him harshly as she strad-dled him. Her breasts hovered over his face as she lowered herself slowly over his erection.

She moaned as she felt him slide inside of her. She had never known whether this moment would ever come to pass in her life, and she loved Rowan's face as he fully entered her. Mia was grinding against him, gently riding him as her ass bounced against Rowan's thighs. Rowan reached for it again, pulling her in to get himself deeper. He was so thick and long as he slid inside and out of her.

Mia looked into his eyes as she thrust, her breasts bouncing in between them.

Something on Rowan's face began to change. He was no longer sweet as he had been when he had touched her before. He looked more intimidating now, and Mia found the word...Animalistic. A shudder overcame her entire body, and soon she found herself thrown onto her back by Rowan's massive arms.

"I've been waiting so long for you, my mate," Rowan said. The word 'mate' lingered in Mia's ears, and just the sound of it made her want to come for him. She'd be a good mate, she decided, let him do whatever he wanted. And Rowan did just that, as he spread Mia's legs further apart before he en-tered her again. Mia could feel warmth seeping from her as she swallowed him up. He was almost too much to take in, but she wanted all of it.

Rowan thrust, slowly and gently at first. But then the animal overcame him, and soon he had turned completely wild on Mia. He picked her up with inhuman strength, slamming her against the closet door as he took her with such ferocity. Mia moaned, her legs wrapping around him as he wildly bounced her up and down over his cock.

"What next?" Mia said in between thrusts.

Rowan smirked as he threw her back onto the bed. Mia had never real-ized that she liked it so rough.

She was bent over the bed, soaking wet with anticipation as Rowan guided himself in between her lips.

"You like this cock?" He growled as Mia's ass slapped against his waist. Mia moaned in response, shocked at how rough he was with her. But she'd hear all of his dirty words as long as it meant she got to feel his thick hard cock inside of her.

Mia arched her back as Rowan took her from behind. He grabbed for her ass again, pulling himself deeper and deeper until Mia cried out.

"Did I hurt you?" Rowan asked.

"No," Mia said. "Give me more." This was all she needed to say to unlock Rowan's full potential. He growled fiercely through his teeth as he pounded faster and faster, his cock spreading her lips apart as they slid over him.

He was hitting all the right spots, enough to make the room spin around Mia. She felt Rowan's hand reach around, sliding down her stomach and heading straight for her clit as he rubbed it in between his fingers.

"You're soaking wet," he moaned as he kept thrusting. Mia could feel the sweat dripping from his body onto hers. He touched her so carefully, but with such purpose that she could feel herself about to go over the edge.

"Don't stop!" She cried out as she clutched at the wrinkled bed sheets. Her knuckles turned white as she buried her face in the bed while Rowan thrust. An overwhelming wave of pleasure washed over Mia, making her toes curl with delight as she screamed out Rowan's name in the seclusion of the cabin. She felt herself contract around him as she came, warmth pouring from her and dripping down her legs.

It wasn't long before Rowan had flipped her onto her back. He closed his eyes. Mia felt him pulsing inside of her. She could feel his seed emanating from him as he softly moaned her name while he climaxed. He brought himself back down, and they laid still for a while, with Rowan breathing heavily over her, sweat dripping from his brow.

Mia smiled at him with satisfaction. In all of her life, she had never dreamed that this moment with come, and she was perfectly content to have shared this with Rowan.

"That was perfect," Mia breathed as she looked up at the moon, her tired and naked body wrapped in one of Rowan's blankets. She felt his hand on her shoulder, followed by his soft lips as he gently kissed her neck.

"Thank you," he whispered.

He left her side, wandering to the other side of the room, but Mia kept her gaze on the white glaring moon in the sky. It wasn't full, but Mia had a strange prick on the back of her neck as she remembered what Rowan was.

"You were really an animal," she said with a small laugh. But when she turned around, she realized Rowan wasn't laughing.

He sat on the floor, his legs crossed, as he breathed heavily. Mia was instantly concerned at how fast and ragged his breaths were.

"Rowan, what's wrong?" She asked. "What's going on?"

But Rowan couldn't answer. His neck muscles tightened as if he was under a spell that wouldn't let him speak. His body shook, but he was paralyzed, confined to the floor as he tried to hold on. Mia realized that his body was trying to shift. "Oh God, let's get you outside," Mia said.

"Mia, I can't hold on," Rowan said through his teeth. His jaw clenched. Mia grabbed for his arm, trying to calm him down. She couldn't let him loose again, she wanted to stay to try to help him overcome this monstrous urge. "Just breathe," she said quietly. "Please don't go..."

"Sorry —" Rowan tried to say, but his voice was growing harsher, more like a growl.

It was too late. He had held on all day, but the wolf was longing to shift. Mia had indulged it just a bit too much, and she realized that she was triggering the shift.

"Mia...I'm so sorry...I'm trying..." Rowan choked as he fell onto his side. "It's really bad this time..." Mia felt warm tears in her eyes and a wild panic throughout her whole body. She shushed him, trying to stay calm. "It's okay. It's okay," she kept saying, but she could only watch in horror as Rowan contorted back into a wolf, his limbs stretching and pulling until they were formed into paws. Soon, he was on his four legs, growling up at her.

"Rowan," she said calmly, but the fur rose up on the back of Rowan's neck. She knew he couldn't control this, but maybe she could try. She reached out her hand as she tiptoed towards him, but the wolf was angry for some reason. She thought maybe because he was so worked up from before.

"It's just me," she said softly, getting closer now. But Rowan's jaws snapped at her as he barked sharply at her. His lips curled around his sharp set of teeth, and for a second Mia could picture that poor young girl that he had attacked. The horrible truth was settling in.

"Rowan, please come back!" Mia pleaded desperately, but Rowan was more agitated. He snapped at her hand again, this time his teeth grazed against her skin. Mia let out a sharp startled cry, which silenced the wolf.

He looked at her strangely, as if it suddenly realized what it had done to her. In a mad dash, it sprinted through the hallway, clattering against the table. Dishes crashed to the floor as he clumsily tumbled over the furniture of the cabin. Mia rushed towards the back door, trying to avoid the growling animal that was once Rowan.

In a swift motion, she opened the door in the sitting room and stepped to the side as the wolf disappeared into the night. Mia slid her back down the wall, her head in her hands as she cried. She cried for the both of them because she knew Rowan couldn't. She looked at the blood dripping from her hand. Rowan would never hurt her, she knew that, but this animal was something different, and she could only hope that there was a way to get Rowan back...

CHAPTER 14: OPEN SEASON

Rowan didn't know where he was going, but he had to get as far away as he could from the cabin, for fear of what harm he might do to Mia. The wolf was satisfied after the tensions he had been feeling for so long, and yet he was still irritable for some reason. He paws thudded against the dirt, kicking up rotted leaves as he sprinted further into the night. Run, the voice kept saying to him. Hide.

He realized that he had run far, past the waterfall, and he no longer could catch the scent of his home or any of Brian's markings that might help him find his way back. The wolf looked around at the forest, suddenly lost amongst the towering trees and the sounds of the night. Rowan didn't mind the woods, but he briefly remembered a fragment from his human memory, of the lone wolf he had seen watching him from the waterfall. It made him uneasy. Enemy, echoed in his mind.

Rowan sniffed around a cluster of shrubs, picking up the sweet scent of berries struggling to grow in the cold. He figured he had come far enough, and rested, placing his head on his two front paws. His ears lowered, as he felt a strange pang of loneliness creep over him. He could feel a slight shudder, possibly from the cold, but most likely from the man inside that wanted to come back out. He wouldn't let him. The wolf was upset and wanted to be alone. He couldn't come back and face the struggles of being a human once again. It was too strenuous for an animal.

He was tired and could feel sleep pulling on his eyes. But there was strange activity nearby that captured his attention. His ears perked up at the sound of something trudging through the forest. He raised his nose to the air. It wasn't another animal and not those wolves that he had sniffed out when he had rescued Mia. He stood, crouching among the shrubs as he continued to listen. There were hushed voices, and a light passing through the trees, searching back and forth.

Humans, Rowan thought, and an image of Mia flashed in his mind. It wasn't her out there, but the thought of her back in the cabin, by herself.

He wouldn't want anyone to stumble upon his home and possibly take Mia back into town where the policemen would find her.

He sprung from the bushes, lurking around the trees as he tried to avoid the ominous light searching through the woods. But he wasn't sure where it would land next, until it passed right over him. The light blared into the corner of his eye, and he instinctively turned towards it. The voices grew louder, men's voices. Rowan caught a glimpse of a reflective vest on one of them. They didn't smell familiar, but before Rowan could tell they were hunters he was already startled by the deafening pop of a gunshot.

Rowan took off running, with only the thought of survival in his animal mind. The hunters were following him now, their boots crushing the leaves as they fired off another shot. There were two of them, but Rowan knew he couldn't take them both. His ears tucked back, feeling the icy wind against his fur as he ran, not looking back. Mia, he thought. Danger.

He ducked and squeezed his way under a fallen tree trunk, hoping the men couldn't get to him there. He came out from the other side, relieved for only a second until he heard another gunshot, followed by a sharp sting that pierced his shoulder. He yelped and tried to keep running, his nose finding the edge of Brian's vast safety circle. But it was too late. He collapsed on the forest floor, whimpering in pain from the bullet that had entered his body. The voices were getting closer, and soon they would finish him off and throw his body in the back of their truck. He'd be a trophy to them, and they wouldn't have any idea that he had been a human just moments before. The lights shone over the tree trunk. Rowan could almost feel it burning into his back.

But another sound cut through the hunter's voices. A low deep-throated growl that didn't sound anything like a wolf's. Rowan froze, as another gunshot went off. But the growling continued until it was a harsh breathy roar that echoed through the trees. The men sounded frightened now, their voices more distant as they ran in the other direction. Rowan closed his eyes, but before darkness washed over him he could make out a familiar scent. Bear, he thought. Friend.

Mia pulled on one of Rowan's thick sweaters over her head. The wool was a little itchy, but it was warm enough. They hadn't made a fire that night, and Mia wasn't sure how to get one going until Rowan came back.

She picked up the furniture that Rowan had knocked over when he had shifted. She tilted one of the kitchen chairs back into place and grabbed a broom to clean up the mess from their untouched food that was now spilled all over the floor.

Mia winced as she clutched the broom handle, looking at the fresh bandage around her wound from Rowan's teeth. He hadn't gotten her that badly, but just the fact that he would still bite her made her feel a little sick to her stomach. She wondered, only for a second, about whether she would end up like him because of it. She realized that she didn't know what she was getting herself into when she found out about Rowan's abilities. As she dumped the remnants of her crispy and cold omelet in the trash, she wondered if there really was any way for him to get his shifting under control.

She cleaned up the cabin as best that she could, and then sat on the worn couch while she decided what to do. She could wait for Rowan, but for some reason, she felt a strange emptiness tugging at her. Maybe he wouldn't come back. Maybe he was too ashamed about what had happened between them; especially since it had happened after their blissful moment together. She suddenly felt upset. How could he not have known it was her and that she was just trying to calm him down? Wasn't he less aggressive the night he had saved her from her prison cell?

She walked over to Rowan's bookshelf. She had already been working her way through some of them but figured she would try something else for tonight. As she gripped at the hard spine of the book, her hand brushed against something cold. She gasped as it slid over the edge of the bookshelf and towards the floor. Mia's hand automatically shot out towards it, just barely grabbing the object in time before it crashed onto the hardwood.

She sighed with relief and opened up her palm. She stared intently down at it, and she felt as if she were going to cry all over again. It was half of a circle, but the clay had been smoothed out from someone scrubbing it furiously. Seeped into some of the cracks were veins of dark red, which Mia realized might have been blood.

Suddenly, she felt herself being transported back into that time. She saw Rowan's body dangling from his father's arms, the blood soaked through his clothes as he was rushed towards a car in the street. It would have been in his pocket. Mia eyed the blood stains forever stuck in the clay, unable to be scrubbed out no matter how hard Rowan had tried. But Mia was more surprised that he had kept it, after all of this time. She looked back at the shelf to find her own half of the ornament there. She grabbed it, and knowingly placed the two halves next to each other. They were uneven from age, the clay rugged on either side, preventing them from touching all the way.

Mia crossed over to the couch, staring down at the words *'Best Buddies,'* painted clumsily on the clay. She wished Rowan could be here now, and maybe they could make the pieces fit together. She thought that had been the case earlier that night when they had shared themselves with one another. But Mia thought of the empty spaces in the cracks of the ornament. No matter how hard she had tried to make them fit, they couldn't.

She placed them on the coffee table in front of her. Suddenly she didn't feel like looking at them anymore, or else she would feel sick. Just seconds later, she heard a sharp crash, followed by a loud thud that almost made her jump right out of her skin. The wind howled louder now, and Mia clutched a blanket from the couch to block out the cold as her feet took her towards the source of the sound. She ducked behind the wall of the sitting room.

It could be Rowan, she thought. But then again, Rowan would always go for the bathroom after he had shifted back. She would know. After all, she was the one who had found him naked and muddy on the floor the first night she had stayed over. She inched closer to the kitchen. The moonlight appeared much more sinister now that it was glowing through a gaping hole in one of the windows.

As she stood in the kitchen, she felt the blood drain from her face as she looked down at what had flown into the cabin. On the floor, covered in shards of gleaming glass, was a large brick. Mia's feet turned to lead. There weren't any bricks around here, just stones and chopped wood surrounding the house.

An unsettling wave of dread settled over her. Rowan wasn't coming back. But something else, someone else, had.

Mia could only think of one other person that could have discovered her out here.

Grey.

She thought she should wait for another sound, just to confirm that someone else was here trying to get her to come out, but she was completely helpless out in the cabin by herself. She realized that she needed to find Rowan right away, even if it meant risking her life to run out into the woods to find him. She picked up the brick and thought long and hard about what to do.

Mia was shaking so much that she was afraid she wouldn't even be able to run. But she could at least try to divert whatever this threat was long enough for her to gain some distance from them. She dropped the blanket from her shoulders and crept back into the living room, grabbing the fireplace poker.

She tiptoed back through the kitchen and down the long hallway back to Rowan's room. If it was Grey, or Craig and one of the other police officers, they would surely be able to smell her in the cabin.

There was the t-shirt that she had been wearing earlier that day. She kept her body low to the ground and hid next to the bed, worried that if she walked around openly, she would be attacked right there and then. She figured that whoever was out there was calculating their next move just as she was.

She grabbed the shirt, wrapping it around the brick. It would smell enough like her, at least she had hoped it would. Just before she was about to step back out into the hallway, she froze and held her breath as a shadow passed over the floor. The outstretched crude shadow of a man lingered in the beam of moonlight in front of her. A pair of arms reached up, trying to get a better look inside. Mia shrunk herself further against the bed.

How much time would she have until Grey and the others broke in? She waited for what felt like hours before the shadow decided to leave. Mia rushed into the hallway, keeping her head down low as she cradled the brick in her arms. She stood by the front door for a moment. She could hear voices, multiple ones, speaking in hushed tones. For a second she worried that they could hear her breathing.

Then, the doorknob wiggled sharply back and forth as someone tried to open it from the other side. Mia waited, and then there was a thud, and another as someone lunged their entire body into the wood. Mia panicked. She had the shirt and the brick, but would it be enough? She remembered something, though, when she was in prison. Trent, that large officer, had tried to shift after Mia hit her head. He wanted her blood.

She knew what she had to do. Slipping back into the kitchen, she grabbed a shard of glass and headed for the back door of the cabin, near the other side of the fireplace in the living room. It would have to be her only way out, and she desperately hoped that Grey and the others wouldn't be there on the other side when she opened it.

Mia closed her eyes as she held the window shard to the palm of her hand, wincing as she felt the slight burn of the glass sliding against her skin. She stared down at the ruby-red blood seeping from the fresh cut, and immediately tried to cover the t-shirt with it. "Sorry, Rowan," Mia said under her breath, though she figured he would understand.

She readied herself, knowing she had no time left to spare. With a quick flash, she opened the back door, where she had previously let Rowan out. Her feet left the solid footing of the wooden floor, and out into the cold forest. She could hear the voices clearly now, deep and menacing. She looked to her right. There was a ditch there, sloping down into a deeper part of the woods.

Mia held her breath again and held the brick high over her head. With one swift motion, she flung it as far as she could. It soared beyond the cabin, towards the ditch. It tumbled loudly as it slid through the rustling dead leaves. The voices grew louder as they ran towards the sound. It wouldn't be long before they knew it was a trick.

Mia's feet carried her as fast as the day she ran from the other wolves, but this time she didn't look back. She knew that Rowan wouldn't be there, only something horrible, and this fueled her to run as fast as she could. The freezing air stung her eyes, making them tear up. Each breath was sharp and frigid, painful. But not nearly as painful as it would be to be captured by Grey.

She could hear something now, large and rustling. She finally dared to look back, unable even to see the cabin. If they had shifted, there was no way she could outrun them. They've caught up to me, she thought. But her legs carried her over another steep hill. She was getting tired now, her thighs burning with each step.

The sound was louder now, made by something large. Mia thought of Grey, his massive form now pictured as a wolf as he sunk his jaws into her. She needed to keep running. She needed to find Rowan. As she reached the top of the hill, her ankle gave out from under her and she slipped, tumbling further and further down the other side. She landed hard against the ground, realizing now that the sound was right next to her.

"Shit…" she said, and scrambled to her feet, searching for anything to use as a weapon. If she was going to die, she would do it here, fighting while trying to find the man she loved.

But it wasn't a wolf. Instead, Mia was face-to-face with a massive brown bear. It moaned at her, almost as if he were the one afraid of her. Mia froze in her tracks. Wolves were one thing, but she knew she would die instantly in the claws of a bear. She stood perfectly still, staring into the bear's eyes. It came closer to her, and she remembered all those things about pretending to be dead. She almost fell onto her side, but the bear was inches from her now, sniffing her carefully.

Then, in a second he was twitching, its incredibly large body shuddering as it transformed smoothly into a large mountain of a man. He was naked, but he covered himself at the sight of Mia, slightly embarrassed. Mia's mouth fell open as she looked at the bearded man in front of her. Another shifter.

"Uh, hi," the man said awkwardly. "Wow, I wasn't expecting to meet you like this, but…I'm Brian."

CHAPTER 15: SURROUNDED

Mia watched curiously as Brian carried on ahead of her. She tried not to look at his large toned backside as he walked, his muscles gleaming in the moonlight.

"Sorry you have to see me, you know, naked," he said casually. "Let me just take care of that." He strode over to a tree trunk and reached into an opening near the roots. There was a thick package, wrapped in plastic. Brian unwrapped it, pulling out a pair of pants and a thick flannel shirt. "Got a few stashed out here, in case of emergencies," he explained as he dressed on the other side of a tree trunk.

"Were you out here looking for me?" Mia asked. She knew that other shifters existed, but she wasn't expecting to see a bear shifter on this night. Brian buttoned up his shirt, nodding at her.

"Of course," Brian said. "My question is, what were you looking for?"

Mia crossed her arms, trying to keep out the cold. "I'm trying to find Rowan," she said. "There were wolf shifters, trying to break into his cabin."

"Oh yeah," Brian said. "He told me about those. Sounds like you've got a crazy ex on your hands."

Mia refused to laugh, and Brian seemed to notice. "Sorry," he said frantically. "I make bad jokes when I'm nervous."

"It's fine," Mia said. "It's not like my ex is out to kill me or anything." Brian could sense the sarcasm and nodded with approval.

"I like you already," he said. "Rowan's said a lot about you."

She perked up at the sound of his name. "Do you know where he is?" She asked, hopeful.

"That I do," Brian confirmed as he reached back under the tree trunk. He pulled out another wrapped package. "He's going to need these when he wakes up."

"Is he okay?" Mia asked. Brian's face turned somber. "He looks a little rough," he said.

"Rough, how?" She asked.

"Rough as in...shot," Brian said. Mia's stomach churned, and so many questions suddenly flooded her mind.

"He's not dead," Brian assured her. "But he's not looking so good either. I got a camper nearby. We need to get him back there ASAP."

Mia rushed behind Brian as he strode through the woods. He seemed to know every nook and cranny out in the forest. He dodged over rocks and tree trunks as if he'd done it thousands of times before.

"So, how do you know Rowan?" She asked.

"Saved him from a bar fight," Brian said as he pulled away a tree branch for Mia to pass through. "He's got a temper from what I've learned about him. He really needs to get his shifting under control."

"He tried," Mia said. "But apparently the other shifters couldn't help him."

"No," Brian clarified, "Rowan wouldn't let them help him."

"What do you mean?"

"Rowan is pretty stubborn, I mean, you know that. Once they uncovered what Rowan's trigger was, he refused to cooperate with them."

"And what was that?"

Brian turned to face her, his expression confused, as if Mia should already know these things about Rowan.

"You, of course," Brian said nonchalantly. "But he said it could be from stress or when he's overwhelmed." "I mean, yeah, that's a common factor that brings on a shift. But usually, there's one thing. I don't know if he'd want you to know this or not...but Rowan feels really terrible that he didn't get to be with you. He thinks that he could have prevented a lot of horrible things from happening to you if only he had been there in your life."

Mia reflected on Brian's words and almost wanted to feel hurt. Rowan had been there for her in their childhood, and it pained her to think that he couldn't be with her. But there was something wrong with his logic, despite his best intentions.

"I had to make my own mistakes," she told Brian somberly. "Even if he was there, I don't know how well he would have been able to stop them from happening."

"It's all a lot easier to look back on what we should have done, isn't it?" Brian asked. "Even when it's too late."

They finally came to a clearing, where a large tree trunk had fallen on its side. Mia's eyes trailed to the sharp points of wood jutting out from where the tree had broken from its roots. They followed the trunk, all the way towards the branches, where a wolf was lying on its side, its breath heaving.

"Rowan!" Mia cried as she ran towards him.

Brian stayed behind, watching as Mia collapsed on her knees by Rowan's side. He had an entirely different demeanor from the menacing one she had witnessed in the cabin. He lay perfectly still, except for the rise and fall of his chest as he breathed.

Mia believed that Rowan was still in there. His eyes were closed, his breaths ragged as they left his muzzle. Mia looked at his sharp rows of teeth, less intimidating now that Rowan was out cold. She carefully placed her hand on the back of his neck, her fingers trailing through his rugged fur. She was almost afraid to be this close, but now Brian was here, and if Rowan awoke in a frenzy, his friend could certainly bring him back down to earth.

Bending down towards his ear, Mia gently stroked Rowan's back. "Rowan, it's me," she said calmly. "I'm here." The wolf's body took a deep ragged breath, and soon its eyes opened, a beautiful hazel looking back up at her. But his expression was pained. He whimpered softly, his ears tucked firmly on the back of his head. Mia shushed him gently as she felt the slightly cold touch of blood that had stuck onto Rowan's fur.

It was matted down, and Rowan whined in protest, small sharp cries of pain as Mia took her hand away from the wound on his shoulder. She could see where the bullet had hit, and most likely it was still in there.

"What can we do?" Mia asked, pulling her sleeves over her hands to keep out the cold. Brian shrugged as he knelt down on the other side of Rowan.

"We can try to carry him back to my camper," he said with determination. But judging by his face, Mia could tell Brian was skeptical.

Brian slid his hands under Rowan's limp body. "It's alright buddy," he whispered as he began to lift Rowan's head from the ground. Rowan whined louder, and the more Brian moved him, the more upset he sounded. "I know it hurts," he said. "But it's for your own good. Trust me." He tried again, but Rowan, still a wild animal at heart, let out a sharp yelp of pain as he snapped his jaws out at Brian.

"Are you serious?" Brian said, yanking his hand away. "Didn't think you'd be the one to bite a friend."

"Join the club," Mia said, holding up her bandaged hand.

Brian shook his head. "I don't think he's going to come with us like this," he said. "We're going to have to try to get him to shift."

Mia was puzzled. Rowan was always trying to keep himself from shifting. How would they be able to convince him to do the opposite, let alone while he's an animal?

"If I'm his trigger," Mia said. "What can I do to make him shift?"

"Maybe it just helps him to hear your voice," Brian suggested.

Mia bent closer towards Rowan, softly stroking the top of his head. She knew how strange this was, but she didn't know how much time he would have, and they needed to get him out of the forest before Grey and the others would find all of them.

"Hey," Mia said quietly to the wolf beside her. "I'm not sure if you can understand all of this or not, but I think Grey and the others might have found me in the cabin. They could be on the way right now."

Rowan didn't move. He stared straight up at the sky, his breath heavier than before. Mia gave an unsure look towards Brian.

"Rowan, you have to get up," she said with more determination. But Rowan wouldn't comply. Mia somberly lifted his head, being careful not to let her fingers get too close to his teeth, and lowered it onto her lap. Rowan was struggling to hold on, and Mia could feel herself getting more frustrated that she couldn't bring him back.

"Please, Rowan," she pleaded. Rowan's eyes began to flutter, and soon Mia realized that maybe they were already too late. "No!" She cried. "Rowan, wake up!" Her heart was breaking right in front of her as she clutched her best friends head towards her chest. She looked at Rowan's ribcage, just barely lifting. He was slowing down, inching his way closer to death. Mia shook him, frantic. "No, no! You have to stay!" She commanded, feeling her face burning despite being out in the freezing woods.

Mia looked up at Brian with tears welling up in her eyes. "It's not working," she said. Soon her body felt as limp as Rowan's. She rested her head against the wolf, her tears flowing onto his fur. He smelled like earth and the cold night air, and a familiar musk emanating from his skin. If only she knew how to bring him back. She had finally found him after all this time, only for him to be taken away from her once again. She felt a large hand clasp on her shoulder. But it wasn't trying to comfort her. It was trying to warn her.

"Mia," Brian said, very serious. "Looks like we're not alone here." Mia looked up from Rowan's body, her eyes blurred from crying.

"Damn it," Mia said under her breath, feeling the panic rising in her throat. From the trees surrounding them, they began to emerge, one by one.

A large black wolf, as dark as the night, stepped forward first. He raised his head to the sky and howled. Mia's blood ran cold, and she clutched Rowan closer to her. The others followed soon after, wolves of varying sizes, but all of them were dark and threatening. They joined the black wolf, harmonizing with his howls into the night.

"It's Grey," Mia said, her voice shaky. Her fingers felt numb, and not even Rowan's thick fur could warm them back to life.

"We should get out of here," Brian said quietly.

"I'm not going without Rowan," Mia said firmly.

"So what are we doing here?" Brian said as he walked closer to the center of the clearing. "We going to stay and fight?" He held out his arms, in a weak attempt to protect Mia and Rowan from the wolves.

"I don't think we have another choice," Mia said.

The wolves didn't make another sound as they inched closer towards the trio. They jumped from the trees on the hill down into the small clearing, circling menacingly around them, their bodies low to the ground. They were enormous, much larger up close than when they had first appeared.

Mia stood next to Brian, reaching down to grab a large stick from the ground. It was thick and sturdy, and she wasn't certain just how much damage it would do, but it would have to be enough. After all, she had the strength of a bear beside her. The wolves were even closer now, and Mia stared right into Grey's eyes. She would hit him first, she decided. He had been the source of enough violence in her life.

"Right when I put on clothes..." Brian started, but before he could finish he bent over at the waist, holding his arms out in front of him. In an instant, he contorted and twisted back into a bear. He roared up into the sky, and the wolves seemed to step back a few inches. Mia held tightly to the stick in her hands. She swung it from side to side at a wolf that was getting to close to her. She wondered which ones were Craig, Trent, and Rico, and wondered if they'd try to attack her first or let Grey make the first move. The wolf bent low, avoiding the stick, keeping its eyes locked onto hers. Mia's knees felt weak, and suddenly she wasn't so sure about their plan.

Brian roared, a staggered string of guttural cries ripping harshly from his throat. His breath made small clouds from his muzzle, and to Mia's surprise, he lifted himself up on his hind legs, swatting his massive paws in front of him in warning. The wolves began to growl now, one at a time as they watched Brian. The clearing became a standoff, with neither side willing to make the first move. It was agonizing for Mia.

She looked over at the fallen tree, where Rowan lay. Rage welled up inside of her. If she had to fight, she would fight for Rowan, whether he was still alive or not. She raised the stick high above her head and rushed straight for the black wolf, Grey.

Brian ran diligently beside her, his breaths laborious as his enormous body of muscle and fur carried him. With a piercing cry that tore at her throat, Mia swung the stick at the black wolf. The wolf was too quick, and grabbed for the stick, ripping it roughly out of Mia's hands. Mia stumbled back, losing her balance, but she kept her feet firmly on the ground. The other wolves watched them, waiting for their chance to attack. Mia wondered why they didn't just attack them at once.

The black wolf swiveled around and rushed for her, but Brian swung his paw at it. His claws were like long daggers, swishing quickly through the air. It made contact with the black wolf, knocking it onto its side. The other wolves growled in protest and charged for Brian and Mia.

One of them, a smaller wolf in the pack, lunged for Brian's shoulder, latching on with his jaws. Brian reared back in protest as he shook the creature from his back.

Mia was already losing hope. There was no way they could take down all of them, even if they tried. But before she had another chance to think of a new plan, the black wolf stood over her. The air around them grew cold, and the wolf shook back and forth until he revealed himself as a human.

Mia didn't want to look at him. She couldn't bear to see Grey's face again. But something about him seemed off.

"It looks like we've finally found you," a deep voice said. Mia opened her eyes. It wasn't Grey at all. Instead, a large man with dark skin stared down at her. A large scar stretched from his forehead to his left cheek. Unlike Brian and Rowan when they shifted back, the man was actually wearing clothes, a plain sweater over some jeans.

"Who are you?" Mia asked. The man nodded at the other wolves, and one by one they began to shift into men and women. They had an air about them, a mysterious aura as if they were part of an ancient tradition.

"We're old friends of Rowan," the man said.

Brian shifted back into a man, gathering his clothes from the forest floor in a huff. The wolf closest to Brian was a young boy, about the same age as Rowan, when he had first turned. His eyes were bright, shining in the moonlight, which revealed a soft set of freckles on his nose.

"Sorry about that," the boy said to Brian, pointing at Brian's shoulder. "Got a little carried away." Brian nodded at him while still in shock from the sight of all the shifters surrounding them.

"Now, let's see what we can do for our friend, shall we?" The man said as he headed for the fallen tree. "It looks like we have some catching up to do."

CHAPTER 16: THE PAST

The pack functioned as if it were a busy hive of bees. Each shifter had their particular task, all for the purpose of setting up a camp further into the woods. Mia and Brian had followed them to their meeting ground shortly after they had pried Rowan from under the tree. Rowan was still a wolf, and the man had looked down at him with sorrow as he carried him through the forest with ease.

Mia perched herself near the fire, which was being built by the young boy who had attacked Brian. She stared at the fresh flames that were struggling and smoking under a loose pile of sticks, trying to grow brighter and hotter. Tents had been set up, creating a circle of safety around the fire. Mia watched as the shifters worked. It was if they had done this routine many times.

The man emerged out of a tent, his face grim. He took a seat next to Mia.

"He's going to be okay," he said.

Mia sighed with relief. Finally, just for a moment, she could get her head straight now that she knew Rowan wasn't on the edge of life and death.

"What did you do?" Mia asked.

"What we always do with gunshot wounds," the man said. "Fortunately the bullet was easy to retrieve. We've had some bad scrapes in the past with hunters."

He looked down at his hands, still slightly caked with Rowan's blood. A woman handed him a washcloth and he gently wiped away at his fingers with it. When he was pleased with the cleanliness, he held out his hand for Mia to shake.

"I'm Josiah," he said. "Alpha of the Lost Shadow Pack."

Mia almost hesitated to shake his hand, but then she clutched it, regardless, feeling his warm hand still damp from the washcloth. She tried not to think about Rowan's blood. She realized that this was the wolf that

Rowan had seen at the waterfall the other day, the one that he didn't want to tell her too much about.

"I'm Mia," she said. "Sorry for trying to attack you. I thought you were someone else."

"You mean the wolves from the town nearby?" Josiah asked.

"Yeah," Mia said. "How did you know?"

"We smelled them out when we had first arrived. We thought it was strange that they weren't marking their territory, though."

"Do you know them?" Mia asked. "Is that why you're here? I'm still new to this whole wolf pack thing. I'm not sure if you keep in touch with other packs like you."

Josiah looked at the young boy, still poking at the fire. "Tex, I think that fire's looking good," he said in a fatherly tone. "Why don't you see what Raquel is up to?" The young boy nodded, his gaze floating between Josiah and Mia. He knew something serious was about to be discussed and he hurried away.

"We're not here for the other wolves," Josiah said, getting straight to business. Mia admired his no-nonsense attitude, although his serious tone made her feel unsettled.

"You're here for Rowan," she said with certainty.

Josiah nodded solemnly. "I didn't want Tex to hear," he said, looking over at the young boy. He still had a youthful glow around him, like he wasn't quite sure about the dangers of the world just yet. "Maturing as a shifter is a strenuous process," Josiah explained. "I should have been more careful when I was training Rowan."

"So you were the wolf he was talking about," Mia said. "I heard he didn't agree with some of your methods of teaching."

"That's true," Josiah said. "Rowan was such a strong boy, with plenty of potential. But there was something holding him back."

"Me," Mia guessed.

But Josiah shook his head. "That's partially correct," he said. "Rowan felt that he was responsible for you. He protected you once, long ago, but he felt that by being with us he was just wasting the time he could spend with you."

"What about his trigger?" Mia asked. "Brian said that once you revealed that it was me, Rowan left."

"Rowan left because of his guilt," Josiah corrected. "He had made some mistakes. I'm sure he's told you about that girl that was attacked. But he may have not told you about this." He pointed to the long, ragged scar that dragged down over his eye.

"Rowan gave you that?" Mia asked, feeling a lump in her throat. "That's just part of it, but yes," Josiah said. "We were trying to teach him to shift back. It's not always a grueling process, but it does take time. If he had stayed, he would have been able to control himself to the point where he wouldn't have to be in pain."

Mia stared down at the crackling fire. The smoke burned her nostrils, and she stared at it as it rose towards the treetops. "Rowan was having trouble," Josiah said. "Not every trigger comes from a direct cause as he thinks. Behind every trigger, there's an emotion attached, a much deeper meaning than what appears on the surface."

"What do you mean?" Mia asked.

"I could see why Rowan thought it was you," Josiah said. "But if he had just tried to understand, he would have realized that there's something hidden behind his fear. Unfortunately, he was still wild, and he lashed out. It scarred me physically, but I think it was his own guilt that scarred his mind. He ran from the Lost Shadows, and we've been trying to find him ever since."

"Seems like a lot of work for you to come all the way out here," Mia said.

Josiah shrugged. "Because of Rowan's mistake, we've been chased from our land for the time being," he explained. "Hunters spread through the area, picking off some of our kind. Shifters have to be especially careful. If one of us makes a mistake, the rest of us will suffer."

Mia pondered Josiah's words carefully. She gazed at the worn faces of the other shifters as they set up their tents for the night. Who knew how long they'd been living like this?

"I know we might seem destitute," Josiah said. "Some shifters can keep their secret, like Rowan. But before he ran away, he was just as broken as these people were. The Lost Shadows exist for those who don't have a pack to belong to. We're not a gang or a club that meets for fun on the weekends. We're a family, made up of outcasts."

"Then why doesn't Rowan want to go back?" Mia asked quietly. "Rowan is fighting something deep inside of himself," Josiah said. "There comes a point where our training can only go so far. When it comes to the ghosts that haunt us, one can only find an answer in oneself."

"So, you're not upset about what happened?" She asked. "Even when Rowan forced you guys out from your home?"

"No," Josiah said. "Rowan had made a mistake and a dangerous one at that. But like I said, we're a family. We will grow and learn to try again."

Mia stared down at her boots. She thought of what would have happened if these wolves had been Grey and his pack instead of the Lost Shadows. She had felt so helpless, and knew that if Rowan could have been there then maybe they would have had a better chance. But there was something else conflicting with that belief in her mind. It picked at her brain, and soon she could see a new possibility.

"Can I see him?" She asked.

Rowan was surrounded by several pack members, each of them cleaning up blood, bandaging the wound on his shoulder, or placing a cloth over his head. Brian was there, checking on Rowan's condition. He could barely fit inside the tent. The others worked carefully and efficiently. As soon as Mia entered the tent, they lowered their eyes, collected their materials and shuffled past her without words.

Brian reached over, patting Rowan's forehead. "Hang in there, buddy," he said as he headed towards the tent's opening. "He's all yours," he said to Mia jokingly.

Mia looked at the tired and battered Rowan resting on a cot, his skin on his chest gleaming with sweat. His eyes fluttered open, and he tried to sit up as soon as he saw Mia.

"You're here," Rowan whispered hoarsely. Mia sat on the edge of the cot, tucking her hair behind her ear.

"Of course I am," she said quietly as she ran her hand along his dirty cheek.

Listen," Rowan said. "About what happened...?"

"Don't worry," Mia said. "I know it was an accident. Josiah cleared up some things for me."

"I see you've met the Lost Shadows, then," Rowan said, a slight hint of bitterness in his voice. "I didn't think they cared for me enough to come all the way out here."

Mia reached for his hand, running her thumb softly against the top of it. "They're running, Rowan. Just like you."

"Because of me," Rowan said, defeated. "Just add it to the list, I guess."

"But they came back for you anyway," Mia countered. "They're just trying to help."

"Now you sound like one of them," Rowan said, inching himself lower towards the bed. He winced as the bandages crinkled against his shoulder. Mia could tell he was getting annoyed with her, but there was no way she was going to let him fight against what was good for him.

"I don't care if I sound like one of them," Mia said. "I've realized that the Lost Shadows and I have something in common."

"And what is that?"

"That we care about you, deeply enough to be fighting for you."

Rowan's jaw clenched. The shadows from a nearby lantern flickered over his face. It reminded Mia of the night she had embraced him, seeing him covered by that same shadow looming over him. "The first step to cleaning up your mistake is to realize you've made one," Mia said. "The least you could do is try to know that these people don't hate you."

"How could I?" Rowan asked. "And how could you not? I've hurt you already, Mia. Look." He gestured towards Mia's bandaged hand over his. "How many more times can I mess up before I lose you again?"

"It was an accident," Mia said. "I'm more upset that you're not willing to try to get over what should have been left in the past."

She had hoped that Rowan would somehow understand, maybe hear the strain in her voice desperately trying to call him back. She knew Rowan would feel alone if he finished training with the Lost Shadows.

"Please, Rowan," she said. "You can go back. Finish your training. Learn something from this."

"My whole life has been made up of mistakes," Rowan said, his voice tense. "I don't think there's anything they can do for me now."

"What about me?" Mia asked. She felt Rowan stiffen beside her. "Was I a mistake to you? What about when I gave myself to you? Was that a mistake too?" She could feel her voice getting louder, but she suppressed herself before she started raving again as she had done with Louise at the diner.

Rowan fiddled with the edge of the blanket around him.

"Josiah told me something," Mia said.

"Josiah doesn't know-"

"Quiet!" Mia commanded. She could feel Rowan's shock emanating from him. She had never talked this way to him, not even when they were young. But there was something Rowan had to hear. As far as Mia knew, it was what was best for Rowan.

"You can only be helped so much. There's something inside of you; something that only you have to deal with. Now whether you accept help is up to you. But if you're so afraid of losing me, just know that it's not going to be because you're scared of biting me again."

"What do you mean?" Rowan asked. The concern was rising in his voice. "Mia, what are you doing?" His voice was hard to hear. He sounded scared, childlike even. "You sound like you're saying goodbye," Rowan said.

Mia's heart hammered against her chest, blood pounding in her ears. She couldn't bear to say goodbye, and she knew that she wasn't. She did know something, though, that she had put so much into Rowan when really she knew what she had to do.

"I'm not saying goodbye," she said. "But I will if we both can't learn to get ourselves under control."

"Mia," Rowan said, so quietly that it made Mia's heart break even more.

"Josiah's words weren't just for you," she said. "In fact, I think I learned something from them myself."

"No," Rowan said. "You're not doing what I think you are." He tried to sit up, but he clutched at his wound, angry. "Mia, you'll be killed!"

"I know," she said. "I almost was when I ran from the cabin. But he's still out there, Rowan."

"Then just wait for me," he said. "I'll recover, and we can do this together."

"You've done enough for me," Mia said. "I know you feel upset that you couldn't be here to help me after you became a shifter. But that's all in the

past now. It was wrong of me to force my mistakes onto you. I've been trying to get you to fight this with me, only to realize that maybe I should fight
this myself."

"We can be there for each other!" Rowan argued, but Mia's mind was
racing down a one-way street.

"Yes, we can. But it can only get us so far," she said to him, her voice soft
and pained. Mia leaned over and closed her eyes, pressing her lips against
his forehead in a soft kiss.

"I love you, Rowan," she whispered. "I have always loved you."

She pulled her hand from his grip. She was suddenly plagued with determination. All this time, she had always believed that Rowan needed to
be there to save her. But this was her battle to take on. She looked back over
her shoulder as she pulled apart the flaps of the tent. Rowan stared blankly
at her, and she thought about the pain he must have been feeling. But she
knew as long as they had their shadows looming over them, they wouldn't
be able to be together.

"I love you," he said, a look of deep concern on his face. It was as if he
was looking at her for the last time, despite her promise that she would return. As Mia ducked back out into the cold forest, still buzzing with activity from the busy pack, she felt slightly afraid that perhaps she wasn't so sure.

Regardless, she pushed those feelings aside as she strode up to the fire,
where Josiah was sitting with Tex and several others trying to keep warm. "I
need some help," she said firmly.

"What do you need us to do?" He asked.

"I just need to know something," she said. Josiah looked to the others,
then up at Mia quizzically.

"Alright," he said. "We're listening."

Mia balled her fists at her sides. The question burned at the back of her
mind, and for a moment she felt like she couldn't actually believe that she
was going to ask it. The others looked at her, waiting with baited breath.
Finally, she took a breath as she remembered that she was doing this for
Rowan.

"I need to know how I can kill a shifter."

CHAPTER 17: PREPARATIONS

Mia trembled as her feet carried her on her new mission through the forest. Brian had severely tried to convince her to stay, but she knew that if she did, it would only be a matter of time before she put the rest of the Lost Shadows in danger, including Rowan. With Josiah's words still in her mind, she thought endlessly about Grey and his pack. Every shifter had a weakness, and she was mulling over what Grey's was. Somewhere in her mind, she had already figured out the answer.

Rowan was on her mind as well, his somber face still etched into a ghostly figure in her vision. She desperately wanted to stay, but not while she knew Grey was out on the hunt. Who knew what he might to Rowan if they found him? Rowan was better off with the rest of his pack. If he had been alone, there was no way he would have been able to protect Mia, even though he had tried to convince her of the opposite.

Just moments before, Mia had prepared herself. To her surprise, she really didn't need to pack anything at all. She knew that there was another weapon she would have to yield, one that had to be sharpened. She sat for a while with Josiah and told him everything. He helped explain the tools that she needed to bring. She would not find herself cornered again, not like the last time she had tried to run from Grey.

She put her hands into the pockets of her jacket, one of Rowan's old ones that she had grown to like. She felt the worn insides of the pockets, and the pilling fleece fabric brushing against her fist as she clutched something folded inside. It was growing warm from her body heat, her thumb rubbing against the casing nervously as she continued her walk. A silver knife. She'd never really carried a weapon before. She knew Grey was into guns, but he had never let her carry one in case she thought about using it on him. This knife felt ominous and dark in her pocket.

As she grabbed hold of a tangled root to pull herself over a steep hill, she worried just how far she would have to go for this plan to work. She could feel the branch pulling out from the side of the hill, her fingers slipping over the wood. As she fell back, she felt something pressing against her back. She turned to see the muzzle of a wolf, pushing her further up towards the ledge. Another was beside her, and Mia felt a twinge of gratitude that she had decided to include them into her plan.

The wolves worked together to help Mia until she was able to find solid footing on the upper ledge. She was surprised to see how well they could understand her and figured that since they had more training, these wolves were able to use their human intelligence.

Mia desperately hoped that they were still there. If they were at the police station, then her plan would be much more difficult to carry out. She knew the geography here. After all, she had grown so familiar with it just by staying with Rowan for a few days. She had learned the nooks and crannies and hoped that she could use them to her advantage.

The wolves trotted behind her as she moved through the trees, ready to follow her orders. Mia wasn't sold on letting the Lost Shadows help her at first, but she couldn't help but think about Trent as he clutched the bars of her prison cell, his mouth practically foaming over the scent of her blood. She realized that she didn't have another choice.

She had hoped it would be Rowan, but she knew he wasn't ready yet. Sure he had led her out from the police station safely, but how would he feel once he saw Mia's ex face to face? Grey hadn't been there at all, and Mia knew that if Rowan were to see him, his shifting would be out of control and unpredictable.

She ducked down with the two wolves behind a rock to stay in hiding. The wolves lowered their heads, their bodies twisting quickly back into more human shapes. Soon, there were two women beside her. They both had an athletic build with defined muscles through their black, long-sleeved shirts. They were perfect guardians to accompany her, recommended to her personally by Josiah. There was Kara, with short black hair, a nose ring, and sharp eyebrows always intensely knitted. The other was Shay, who had her thick black hair twisted into a long braid. Her skin was bronze, and her eyes a piercing yellow.

"We're in luck," Kara said with a wicked smirk. "I can smell your target now." She sniffed the air again and screwed up her face in disgust. "Yikes, is that bear pee? God...what a smell."

"Calm down, Kara," Shay whispered. "We don't need you going into a frenzy just yet." Mia peeked up from behind the rock. In the distance, she could see the back door of the cabin ripped from its hinges. Smoke rose high into the starry sky. The fire was still going, which means that Grey and the others might be inside. A soft yellow glow emanated from the windows of the cabin, partially obscured by the thick curtains Rowan had placed there.

"Are you guys ready?" Mia asked, wondering how she would even be able to get her feet to move forward any closer.

"Whenever you are," Shay said dutifully. As Mia stepped away from the rock, a hand reached out and clutched her wrist.

"Question," Kara said as she held tightly to Mia, pulling her back down to the ground. "How do we know that your ex is actually in there?"

Mia froze, and for the first time, she questioned the configuration of her plan. She knew she would have been attacked by those men if she had stayed in the cabin earlier.

"You said you could smell them," Mia said. "Isn't that enough?"

Kara looked uncertain. She made a strange awkward face.

Mia was annoyed she wasn't giving her answers. "Is there something you're not telling me?" She asked.

Kara shrugged. "I mean...you didn't actually see him, did you? This Grey guy?"

Mia had never felt so foolish. She knew the men were trying to break into the cabin. They had pounded on the door and everything. She had even heard their voices outside, low and growling.

But she hadn't seen them. How could she be so sure that it was Grey and the others? A dark realization crept over her as she lowered her head to the ground.

"I didn't even think I could be wrong," Mia said. Another hand reached for her, this time it was Shay.

"Hey," she said calmly. "It doesn't hurt to check. If they're there, we'll still be able to carry out our plan."

Mia sighed, once again nervous as she stepped out from the rock. Kara and Shay followed closely behind, their eyes darting around the woods surrounding the cabin. They emerged from the trees, passing by the tree stump used for chopping wood. Mia looked down at it, noticing the piles of wood neatly stacked nearby. Her eyes trailed to the empty slit marks pierced through the wood of the stump, and she stopped in her tracks. "What's wrong?" Shay whispered.

Mia's eyes burned into a long, thick slit deep in the wood. She could feel the cold night air consuming her.

"There's no ax," Mia said as the color drained from her face. "It's always right here."

Kara and Shay exchanged nervous glances. For a moment it seemed like they were regretting what they had gotten themselves into.

"Here, let me," Kara whispered as she navigated herself in front of Mia. Shay followed suit, spreading out her arms to her sides as if something was going to jump out at them at any time.

The door was still swung wide open, the hinges barely hanging onto the wood of the opening. They couldn't hear any sounds coming from the inside of the cabin, but a sharp glow from the fire flickered wild shadows on the walls of the sitting room. Mia's imagination would have gotten the best of her if she had come here alone. She stayed close behind Kara and Shay as they inched their way through the doorway.

"Maybe they're hiding elsewhere," Mia whispered. She felt Shay elbow her gently in the side and watched as Kara raised a finger to her pursed lips. As they stepped further inside, Mia's eyes widened at the chaos that lay before her.

The cabin had been torn to shreds, worse than when Rowan had taken off after he had shifted. The couches were ripped, their stuffing was strewn across the floor in large pieces that resembled snow. Thick claw marks covered the walls, etched forever into the logs of the cabin. A fire, one that Mia never lit, was dying now unkempt and glowing softly under the mantle.

A shadow flickered over the coffee table, now flipped over on its side. Mia had a startling realization, as she broke from the group and quietly bent down on the ground. She sorted through shredded papers and splintered wood until she found them. Her heart sank as she looked down at the remains of her and Rowan's ornament, both pieces smashed into raggedy chunks of clay. A white powder was clumsily covering the spot where they lay. Mia felt a void forming in her chest. How could they have done this?

She sifted through the pieces, the painted letters no longer recognizable. It took everything inside of her not to cry, not in front of Shay and Kara. But it was the last remaining thing that she and Rowan had shared, a small piece of their history now crumbled in front of her.

Carefully, she swept up what she could. Shay and Kara watched her, while also keeping an eye around the sitting room. Mia stared down at the pile, wanting desperately to pocket it and try to salvage it. But the damage was irreversible. A hand clasped on her shoulder, and she was whipped back into reality. She remembered she was still in Rowan's cabin and enemies could still be lurking about. With a stabbing pain of regret, Mia stepped away from the shattered ornament. She couldn't take it with her no matter how badly she wanted to.

The two shifters carefully made their way towards the kitchen. It looked worse than the sitting room, broken dishes covering the floor. Mia stepped on something that cracked under her boot. She stepped away, looking down at the sparkling shards of glass where the brick had landed after it had flown through the window. She knew then that it had to be Grey and his friends that did this to the cabin.

Kara looked at Shay, signaling in a made-up language to her. Shay nodded, understanding as Kara separated from them, creeping down the long hallway towards Rowan's room. Mia looked sadly at the destroyed kitchen. She remembered the small moments she had shared with Rowan here. How he had buried his face in her hair while she cooked. The smell of warm bread and stew the first night she had found him after years of subconsciously searching for him. She clutched her jacket closer to her. It felt colder in here now, all the warmth of the kitchen sucked out through the jagged hole in the window that Grey had made.

She stood quietly next to Shay until she heard Kara's voice from the bedroom.

"All clear," she said. Shay took a breath as if she had been holding it this entire time. Glass clinked as Kara emerged from the dark hallway back into the kitchen. "So, we were right," she said. "I can definitely smell this guy, and I'm picking up some others as well. He's certainly not alone."

"He should have three other friends with him," Mia said.

She expected Kara to agree but was shocked to see her shaking her head, her eyes suspicious. "There is more than that," she said. Mia took a step back, panic radiating throughout her body.

"I think you need to see something," Kara said, her voice deeply concerned.

They made their way down the hallway. Mia could feel the darkness swallowing her up as she stepped closer towards the bedroom. Not too long ago, she was excited to enter this place, fueled by her desire for Rowan and all that he wanted to give her. But now this place felt as if it were under a curse, hollow and horrifying, torn apart from the inside out.

They spread out in the room, and the moon shone out on the wall above the headboard of Rowan's bed. Kara pointed up to it. "Found the ax," she said. "He's certainly made his mark." Mia had to squint to get a better look, but as she stepped closer to it, the ax was lodged into an image painted on the wall. She kicked aside an empty spray paint can, and stared in horror at the image dripping down like blood on the walls.

The words 'Feral Blood' stretched along the wall, and underneath that was a crude drawing of a skull, opened wide as a wolf's head emerged from it.

"Your ex is a Feral Blood," Kara said. She stared down at the ground, kicking her feet against more broken glass near the window. The air was cold in the bedroom too, whistling through the cracks in the glass and seeping over Mia and the two shifters as they stared at the ominous message.

"You know them?" Mia asked.

"I know of them," Shay said.

"Me too," Kara said. "And not exactly good things either."

"But it should be just Grey and his friends," Mia suggested. "Maybe they're just trying to scare us."

To her surprise, Shay was also shaking her head. "Kara's right," she said," I'm picking up a lot more than just a few scents.

"No way," Mia said. "How could there be more?" Her breath was shallow, and the room seemed to spin around her.

"Grey's the alpha, right?" Shay asked. "He probably sent his two friends as scouts. Those police officers you mentioned. Now that he's found you here, it looks like he's brought his entire pack with him.

Mia suddenly felt like she couldn't stand anymore. Her knees gave out as she sat on the bed to keep herself from falling. "Where do you think he is now?" She asked. She looked up from her hands, to see Shay staring straight at the symbol painted on the wall.

"Shay..." Kara said in quiet horror. She stretched out her name as if time had suddenly slowed down.

Shay said nothing and turned quickly on her heels as she bolted through the doorway, down the hallway. Mia felt Kara's hand gripping her arm, urging her up from the bed.

"Come on, Mia. Quick!"

Mia looked back, taking one last look at the horrifying image as the red paint dripped from the wall and onto the knitted blanket that once belonged to Rowan's mother. She felt lost, only feeling the pull of Kara as they rushed through the dark hallways, through the rooms littered with broken furniture and splintered wood.

The air whooshed around them. Mia barely had time to react, only following after Kara, clutching her hand as they slid gut-wrenchingly fast down a hill covered in leaves. They hit the ground hard. Mia felt a harsh spike of pain jolt from her ankles to her knees upon impact, but they had to keep running, ducking under tree branches.

Up ahead, Mia could see Shay in her wolf form far ahead of them. She ran, her head low to the ground as her body bobbed up and down with each step. Kara cupped her hand against her lips.

"Hurry, Shay!" her screams seemed to tear from her lungs, and through the entire forest. Birds were shaken from their nests at the sound, their wings beating against the night.

"What's going on?" Mia asked, her head still dizzy as if she were in a trance.

"This was all a trap," Kara said, her eyes saucer-wide.

"Grey is headed for the Lost Shadows camp!"

CHAPTER 18: COMPROMISED

Rowan couldn't fall back to sleep no matter how hard he had tried. His entire body felt heavy, as his memories floated above his head like ever-changing shadows. He had already caught word of where Mia had gone and had been stopped by several Lost Shadows from leaving his tent. He knew Kara and Shay were strong shifters and would be good protectors for Mia in case anything happened. But Rowan couldn't bear the thought of having to stay behind once again, while Mia fought for herself.

He thought about the night that he and Mia had shared together. It all felt so far away now, and the image of his feral teeth biting into Mia's hand filled him with so much guilt. How could he have hurt her like that?

Josiah stepped into the tent, carrying a bowl of his special fall stew.

"You need to keep your energy up," he said as he took a seat next to the cot, placing the bowl onto Rowan's lap.

"I'm not hungry," Rowan said; his body tensing. Josiah had always made him uncomfortable whenever he tried to help him. Rowan thought it was just because he didn't like Josiah, but the more he thought about it, he realized what the true cause was.

He looked down at the steaming bowl in front of him. It smelled amazing, and his stomach growled violently as he stirred the contents. Pieces of pumpkin, fresh zucchini, and onion stared back up at him. All of them were most likely grown from the Lost Shadow's garden at their home base.

He almost didn't want to take a bite, not wanting to please Josiah in the slightest. But his hunger was overwhelming, and he reluctantly took a bite, hiding the pleasure in his face as the sweet and savory flavors rolled over his tongue, the warm stew instantly reviving him. It had a strange familiarity to it, and it reminded him of the stew he often made himself. He realized just how much he had taken away from him when he had left the Lost Shadows.

"She's stronger than you think," Josiah said as he watched him eat. Rowan kept eating. "I understand why you care for her so much."

"I can't tell how much of that is true," Rowan said. "I've hurt Mia plenty of times."

"How so? If you don't mind me asking?" Josiah said. He had a warm presence about him, which annoyed Rowan to no end. The Lost Shadows alpha always knew how to discuss a problem; how to make each pack member feel special. Trying to get closer to Rowan, bringing him food, and talking softly to him, were all just tactics to try to pry information from him.

Regardless of his tactics, Rowan felt as though he were at a loss. These thoughts would only haunt him more unless he could give himself up to Josiah. For once, he would have to give him what he wanted. Cooperation.

"When I first turned," Rowan began. "I left Mia behind. I didn't want to, but my parents thought it was best for me. They told me we could always come back. But I was angry, then, and out of control. The wolf was just finding its footing, trying to attach itself to me."

"A genuinely straining process, I know," Josiah said.

Rowan almost wanted to stop. He hated how fake Josiah sounded whenever he tried to talk calmly to him. It made him feel like a child again.

"Mia was hurt. All because I wasn't there," Rowan said. "She met Grey and he did terrible things to her. Now she's going out to fight him and once again I can't even help her." He could feel his jaw trembling, but he wouldn't allow himself to cry.

Josiah adjusted in his seat, avoiding Rowan's gaze. Rowan knew he could feel the tension between them growing. Josiah leaned forward, clasping his fingers together.

"Do you remember what I said to you while you were training with the Lost Shadows?" He asked.

Rowan looked down at his bowl, almost empty now. "You said this wouldn't be as easy as I thought," he said.

"That's true," Josiah said. "But I also told you something else."

Rowan searched his mind. Somewhere, there was a door that he had never opened. It waited there, urging him to open it. But Rowan was too afraid. He'd only let the small shadows slip out from underneath, the memories of his accident, how frustrated he had felt from the Lost Shadows' teachings, and how he had attacked that young girl a while ago.

But this time would be different. Rowan had never dared to question it, but he wondered at that moment what would happen if he were to open that door. He took a moment, racking his brain for the events that took place in that home.

A teenage Rowan stood outside of an enormous mountain home, tucked far away into the mountains of West Virginia. He had only a small bag of clothes and belongings, the things his parents would let him keep once they had told him to leave their home and pursue his new life as a shifter. He remembered how heavy his knock had sounded on the large front door, as he clutched the ancient and mysterious metal ring.

It swung open, and there stood Josiah, a tall and muscular man at the time. His short hair was graying at the ends, and he had an aura of power surrounding him. Josiah welcomed a reluctant Rowan with open arms. He introduced him to what would have become Rowan's new family if he had only tried a little harder to let them take him in.

There were plenty of other shifters, learning just as he was; adapting to their new environment. He ate with them and watched how close everyone was with one another. They truly were a band of misfits, from all the corners of the world and gathered under one roof. But Rowan felt cold. He felt like he could never be a part of them, and that he saw shifting for what it truly was, living with a chronic monster lurking inside of him every single day, always pestering him to come out.

His training began soon after. Day after day, he was singled out from the others as he was brought into the basement of the home. It had been converted into a training room, an empty wolf-proof space with hard floors and scratched up walls. Josiah pushed him, harder and harder each day, but Rowan just couldn't get the wolf under control. He would stay as a wolf for hours at a time, sometimes having to stay in the wolf-room until he could shift back. He believed he was a danger to the rest of the Lost Shadows.

Rowan followed his trail of thoughts as he wandered the path beyond the door in his mind. In a way, it was liberating to think through these memories, and he was startled to find that they weren't as painful as he had thought. But then he had arrived at a darker place. It had been years and Rowan wasn't making any progress. Josiah had sat with him. He had found him sitting on the roof, overlooking the mountains and the lights of the nearest mountain town glowing in the distance. Rowan longed to be back with them, to enjoy civilization once again as a regular human being.

Rowan remembered that night, crystal clear, unlike his other memories. He remembered the breeze on his face, Josiah's heavy presence near him as he had tried to comfort him. Rowan remembered how hard he had tried to block out Josiah's words. Little did that younger Rowan know that it would be just hours after that conversation that he would attack the girl, walking back from her friend's house through the woods.

Rowan forced himself back to reality. He had allowed himself to sift through the worst in his mind. All that was left behind was a small pearl of wisdom, one that he wouldn't allow himself to see before. He was angry and reckless then, and a strange tug in his chest suggested that for once, he put those thoughts aside. He looked at Josiah, allowing his heart to be fully open to him for the first time.

"You said it would always be a part of me," Rowan said, his face growing warm. "And that the true beauty of shifting is not that we can shift..."

"But because we can coexist as both human and animal," Josiah finished. "The wolf is not a monster. Yes, it's a predatory animal, but it is also amongst one of the most intelligent creatures on this Earth."

Rowan sat further back on his cot. Slowly, the pieces seemed to fall into place. He had been too angry to see them before, always pushing them from his mind. After he had made a mistake by attacking that girl, he had accepted that he would be a monster forever. But now, with Josiah here to remind him, there was so much more to shifting that he would have seen earlier if only he were more accepting.

"I'm sorry," Rowan said. "I think I owe you an apology for everything."

"Everyone makes mistakes in their past," Josiah said. "But only the bravest people will accept that they have a future."

"What do you mean?" Rowan asked.

Josiah smiled knowingly at him. "I mean, that there is something in your past that's keeping you from what you truly love the most. What that is, though, is up to you, and what you choose to believe is truly important."

His words felt thick in the air. Rowan could feel himself breathing them in. They settled on the back of his mind, creating a strangely calming effect. He felt as if something was unlocked inside of him.

"I'll leave you alone now," Josiah said in a joking tone. "I have lectured you long enough."

Strangely, Rowan was almost tempted to ask him to stay, to share more of his knowledge that was long overdue. But before he could say anything Josiah gave him a clever smile and left the tent, the large flaps closing behind him and leaving Rowan alone with his new thoughts.

Somewhere inside of him, the wolf was stirring. It seemed to stare at him through his mind's eye. At first, Rowan was made anxious by its presence. But he remembered what Josiah had said to him. Rowan was afraid of the wolf. He had tried too hard to keep it satisfied, only so it would leave him alone. But he could never escape that it was a part of him. The wolf seemed to be settled, perhaps because they were injured from the hunters before. He welcomed the wolf, and for the first time since he had lain bloody and battered on the forest floor fifteen years ago, he felt a strange peace washing over him.

The peace was disturbed, however, by a sudden chorus of howls from outside. He thought they sounded familiar. The Lost Shadows had plenty of signals while they were out, all communicated through howls. They could find each other faster, spread messages when they were separated, but most importantly let each other know when there was danger.

Rowan was able to recognize it in a flash. It was a rallying cry, a warning. Enemies and danger were close by. Rowan ripped his blanket from over him, his half-naked body quickly losing warmth as he stepped carefully towards the tent flaps.

The cries were louder, and soon he could make out the whimpering and yelps that others were getting hurt. Rowan felt an overwhelming duty to protect them. But when he tried to open the flaps, a figure hurried inside almost colliding with the cot.

It was Tex, the now youngest of the pack since Rowan had left. He was just a teen, much as Rowan had been when he joined the Lost Shadows. He was new to everything, and still thinking that he was a monster as Rowan had thought. Tex looked up at Rowan with terrified eyes, his forehead dripping with sweat.

"We're being attacked!" He cried as he trembled on the floor of the tent.

"Who's out there?" Rowan asked.

"I don't know," Tex said in a panic. "Another pack found us! I tried to find Josiah but—"he began to hyperventilate and Rowan felt sorry for him.

He pulled apart the tent flaps to peek outside. Sure enough, the camp was being ransacked by wolves. He watched as the other Lost Shadows shifted to fight back.

He needed to help his pack, but his first thought was Mia. She was still out there somewhere, and he had a feeling that this pack were here looking for her. That meant that amongst those wolves, sinking their teeth into the rest of his pack, Grey was sure to be lurking. Rowan felt overcome with rage. The wolf inside of him was prodding him to be violent, and for the second time other than wanting to mate, Rowan was glad to oblige it.

"Wait!" Tex cried out as Rowan was about to step into the camp. Rowan turned to see Tex rocking back and forth on the ground, his knees brought up to his chest.

"Please don't leave me here," he said quietly. Rowan felt a tug, an overpowering urge to leave Tex to find Mia. But he looked down at the young boy, frightened. It was a sight all too familiar.

Rowan bent down beside him, looking back at the tent. He knew the urgency of the matter, but it would be no good to the Lost Shadows if there was a casualty he knew he could have prevented.

"Hey, you okay?" Rowan said calmly. He reached a hand out, grasping onto Tex's arm. Tex shook his head. He was on the brink of tears.

As Rowan looked into his eyes, he felt as though he were talking to his younger self. He thought of all the words he wished he had listened to while he was training.

"Tell me what's going on," he said to Tex.

"I can't shift!" Tex cried in a panic. "I tried but I'm too scared. I can't! I just can't!"

Rowan shushed him, giving his arm another squeeze to help keep him grounded.

"Listen, I know it's pretty crazy out there," Rowan said firmly. "But I need you to focus on me for a second, okay?"

Tex nodded, his eyes flooding with tears.

"You can't shift because you're too freaked out," he explained. He took several deep breaths with Tex until he had managed to calm down.

Rowan was glad he could help him. He could feel his own energy improving just by assisting this new shifter in front of him. Slowly but surely, Tex was able to shake himself into his transformation, with Rowan talking him through the process carefully. He was pleased to see Tex calmly shift into his wolf form. Tex growled at Rowan in warning, but Rowan gently shushed him, knowing that Tex was still young and angry as a new wolf. He stepped aside, letting Tex take off running towards the camp, rushing for the nearest enemy by the fire.

Rowan scanned the clusters of fur and teeth, engaging in a fierce battle, out in the middle of the woods. He found what he was looking for. On the edge of the clearing surrounded by two other wolves was an enormous wolf with a menacing glare and dark brindled fur, red and peppered with inky black specks. His eyes seemed to stare straight into Rowan's.

Grey.

Rowan stepped out into the campsite, ignoring the crying and growling wolves colliding into one another. The only human in sight, he walked past the chaos, past the roaring fire and straight towards the wolf that had instantly become his enemy. He never let his gaze falter as he stepped over a fallen log. He could feel the wolf begging to be let out, and Rowan felt a sense of unity with it. He was a man, and an animal, and on this night he would finally let them meet.

With his muscles only slightly twitching, and his skin bubbling over his entire body, Rowan shifted perfectly for the first time. He bared his glossy white teeth at Grey as he rushed for him. Both he and the wolf longed for a taste of the enemy's flesh.

CHAPTER 19: PROTECTOR

"Oh my God..." Kara exclaimed as she looked down into the clearing. Mia stayed hidden behind a tree as she watched the chaos unfolding before her. She felt regret seeping into her, knowing that if only she had stayed there might have been something else she could have done. Then again, Grey and his pack would only find the Lost Shadows faster.

"I need to go down there," Mia said. "I know they're here for me."

Kara looked at her as if she were crazy. "You're not serious, are you?" She asked. "You'll be torn to shreds if you're not a shifter!"

"But maybe they'll leave the rest of the pack alone," Mia retorted. "It could be the only way to stop this."

A wolf bounded up the hill, its fur white and flecked with grey. It collapsed on the leaves next to Kara and Mia, exhausted as it shifted back into Shay.

"There's a lot of them," she said, her breath heavy. Kara leaned down beside her, tenderly brushing Shay's forehead.

"Oh shit! Look," she said, pulling her hand away. Blood was trickling from a gash above Shay's eyebrow.

Shay winced. "It's fine," she said, but Kara looked skeptical.

"Doesn't look fine to me," Kara said. Mia tried not to watch as Kara placed her hand gently on Shay's cheek.

"Let me take this next round. Okay?" Kara said in a more gentle tone. Shay was about to protest, but she clasped her hand around Kara's and nodded with determination. The scene tugged at Mia's chest, and she thought of where Rowan could be. She could see his tent still holding up on the edge of the camp, surrounded by fighting wolves.

"I can't see Rowan from here," Mia said. "I'm going with you." Before Kara could say anything, Mia has thrown herself from the hill and into the clearing, bracing herself against the leaves as she slid quickly towards another tree. She was getting closer now, her sights aiming for the tent.

With Kara following quietly behind, they kept sliding until they reached the bottom of the mound, and then they crept closer towards the

WOLF PACK CHRONICLES STANDALONE BOX SET

tent. Kara lifted up the back, allowing Mia to slide under the tarp-like fabric and into the tent. To her surprise, it was empty.

"Rowan's gone," she said to Kara.

Kara rolled her eyes. "Always running away, that one," she said, annoyed.

Mia thought the sounds were far more terrifying up close. Without even looking, she could see the teeth glaring and the claws shredding as wolves collapsed into violent heaps out in the clearing. She almost felt too scared to leave the tent, but she knew now that Rowan was out there somewhere, and that he could have shifted just moments before she arrived.

Without another thought, Mia ripped open the tent flaps and bounded outside.

Mia, wait!" Kara cried out, but Mia had a mission of her own. The cabin was just a distraction for her, just Grey trying to freak her out and assert his dominance over her, but Mia wasn't going to let him chain her down any further.

Reaching into her pocket, her hand clasped around the leathery covering on the object she had been carrying, given to her by Josiah. A silver knife. She scanned the campsite, looking for any hint of Rowan. Suddenly, she was knocked onto her side with incredible force. She reached out to catch herself, and the knife flew into the air and landed in a pile of leaves nearby. Mia panicked as she turned to see herself face to face with a large wolf.

"Grey?" She asked as she stared into its eyes. But she had a strange feeling that it wasn't him. She crawled clumsily backward, her eyes locked with the monster's in front of her. The wolf bared its teeth at her, its jaws slowly opening, to strike at her throat.

An earth-shattering roar cut through the forest as something large bounded for them. Brian, in his massive bear body, knocked himself straight into the wolf. The wolf rolled against the leaves with a terrified yelp. It lowered its ears as Brian crept towards it, sweeping a massive paw into the wolf's face. Mia looked away, not wanting to see the damage that the bear had done.

Another wolf approached them, who Mia recognized as Kara. Kara nudged at Mia to stand, helping her to her feet.

"Thanks," Mia said. "Both of you."

Brian shook his head from side to side as he sniffed at Kara next to him. Kara did the same, acknowledging that their alliance was safe.

"We need to find Rowan," Mia told them. "I'm not sure you can understand me or not." Kara nudged at Mia again, as if to assure her that she understood. She turned towards the fire and ran. Brian followed. Mia ran behind them, trying to catch up. She had to step aside as the wolves fought around her, almost finding herself getting snatched up in a wild pair of jaws with every other step.

It was if she were running down a hallway with knives slashing at her every which way, waiting to cut into her skin and make her bleed all throughout the forest. As the path seemed to clear before them, Brian roared again. They had found what they had been looking for.

"Rowan!" Mia cried as she saw a grey wolf being attacked by three wolves, while an enormous wolf looked on. It was Grey, and he was waiting for his chance to sink his teeth into Mia's best friend. Mia looked at Kara and Brian.

"We have to help him," she commanded. Brian and Kara understood and rushed for the pile of wolves entangled in a fierce battle.

Brian knocked a heavy-weighted wolf aside from Rowan, which Mia assumed was Trent. That just left Rico and Craig, whom she picked out almost immediately. Craig was a wolf with dark-speckled fur. Mia could see Kara struggling with the both of them, and couldn't let another Lost Shadow get hurt. Their numbers were dwindling, and she wasn't sure how long they could keep up the fight. She turned around and ran for the blazing fire pit, grabbing a sturdy stick poking from the flames. She lifted it carefully from the rocks, admiring the glowing fire spreading from the top like a torch.

She ran back for the wolves that were attacking her new friends and Rowan.

"Back off!" She warned; her voice harsh as she held tightly to her makeshift weapon. The wolves heard her cries, but most of them seemed to ignore her, not wanting to give up their fight so easily. But Mia wouldn't give up. Swiping the fire from side to side, she could see one of them shying away from the fight. Rico.

Something clicked with Mia as she stared into Rico's scared eyes, watching his ears and his tail tuck behind him. She swished the stick closer to him as he whimpered, until she cornered him near a tree, the glowing blaze blaring between them.

The wolf was scared of fire. It was his trigger.

Mia struck Rico without hesitation. He yelped as he fell to the ground, suddenly convulsing. His head shook, almost vibrating right off his shoulders. Within moments he was a human curled on the ground, naked and afraid. Mia took a step back from him as he crawled towards her, malice in his eyes. Before he could reach for her, a black wolf latched its teeth onto his bare arm. Josiah shook him with tremendous force, almost enough to rip Rico's arm from its socket. Rico's screams were drowned out by Brian's roar as he swiped Craig off of his back.

The fight was slowing down, as both packs lost stamina as well as soldiers for the battle. Mia scoured the clearing for Rowan. She caught just a glimpse of him as his body disappeared into the trees. He was going after Grey! Mia trembled, her gaze drifting from Brian and Kara to the woods where she was sure to lose Rowan again if she didn't do something fast.

She crept back into the forest surrounding the camp. Rowan was chasing Grey, their bodies small specks now almost out of her view. Mia tried to chase them, but her knees gave out. It was the first time she had realized how exhausted she was, especially after having run so much on this night. Her body just couldn't take her any further. Every muscle was aching and burning. Her hair clung to her sweaty forehead, stinging from the cold air. She braced herself against a tree, staring into the inky blackness.

The forest seemed much more menacing now, containing haunting secrets and terrible evils lurking and hiding around her. She scanned the forest, hoping that she wouldn't find herself face-to-face with any Feral Bloods. She had seen enough violence tonight and her body was letting her know it.

She forced her feet to take another step, even though they burned under her weight in protest. Her shivering fingers clung tightly to the trunk of a tree, as she could feel her ragged breaths struggling to take form in her lungs. How much longer would she be able to go on? Another step and she was tumbling into a cluster of sticks covered in ancient moss.

How many times had she been alone in this forest? Most of those times, there would be someone that would end up finding her, pulling her out from the darkness. It was Rowan, or Brian, or even the Lost Shadows that somehow found their way to her. But this time, she knew she was truly alone. Knowing this only made things more difficult for her.

She stared up at the moon as it glared from above, a beacon of warning, but its light wavered over her like a warm blanket. Sleep was pulling at Mia's eyelids, caressing her busy mind to a quiet hush. No, she thought, I can't. She struggled onto her hands and knees, fighting against the tugging urge to lie back down. She wandered through the trees. It seemed no matter what she did, she would always end up in the forest alone.

But she knew she didn't have to be. A cloud of exhaustion brought her strange images, and for a moment Mia questioned her sanity. The trees were all starting to look the same, and soon they seemed to twist and form until they were the cruel claws stretching at the sky, the same she had seen when Rowan tackled her in the forest.

These memories seemed to fuel her. She had played it over and over so many times in her mind of what she could have done differently. In most of her fantasies, she would pry the wolves from Rowan and fight back against them. She couldn't count how many times she had imagined that.

She had always regretted running away that day and leaving Rowan behind. She had run from her parents, from Grey, from the fact that maybe it should have been here out in the woods instead of Rowan. Rowan had been right, they could have made it if they were together. Together...then why was Rowan trying to fight Grey on his own?

The more Mia focused on these thoughts, the more they acted as coals, added to a train's engine. They were burning inside of her, growing bright and hot as they told her to keep running, but this time she was running for something else.

Somewhere, just a few more steps away, Rowan needed her. He was weak, after all, and who knows what kind of chance he would stand against a wolf such as Grey. Suddenly, Mia found herself inviting the nightmarish thoughts. They revived her, her own fears and regrets pushing her to keep moving until she was breaking out into a full sprint.

Rowan was always saving her, and she had gotten too comfortable that he'd always be there. But now it was her turn. Tonight, she would forget the past and shed her regrets of what could have been. As her boots thundered against the mulch and rotted earth, Mia was determined to grasp what she had long neglected...the present.

CHAPTER 20: PAST AND PRESENT

Sounds were confusing in the dark, the shadows playing tricks on Mia as she forced herself to keep moving. Little rustlings distracted her, sounding like much larger rustlings coming towards her. She didn't even stop to think of what could jump out and grab her. The forest was alive, especially in the night. As she continued, she could hear a new sound in the distance. Rushing water.

It grew louder now, like continuous thunder crashing. Mia pulled apart the tree branches to find the jagged and crooked rocks lodged in the dirt, spreading down as they met the mouth of the waterfall that Rowan had taken her to. Did Rowan bring Grey here on purpose? Mia wondered this as she navigated down the steep terrain, clutching onto the rocks the best that she could.

Her hand slipped, and she plummeted further down the ledge. Her heart caught in her throat as she stretched her arm out to grab a fallen tree branch. She kicked up the dirt around her as she looked down towards a cliff just below her. There, Mia could see one man standing over a wolf.

Mia looked up at her hand and closed her eyes. She couldn't see who it was down there, but she had a mission regardless of which man would be waiting for her at the bottom. With a final breath, she released her grip from the tree and crept from rock to rock until she was finally on the ledge.

As soon as her foot touched the rocks, she wished she had never let go of the branch. The man had heard her and turned around. Though only the moon was out, Mia could see the grim features of Grey as he smiled at her. He had a strange air about him, one that Mia had never even seen when she was with him.

Even as a human he was still an animal with a hint of lunacy in his wide eyes. Mia's heart stopped in her chest. She thought that she had finally escaped from Grey's clutches, but it turned out that there was far more power to him than she had once believed.

"Hello Mia," Grey said. His voice was eerily casual as if they were old friends catching up on the street. To him, he hadn't been abusing Mia for the few years they had been together. He was just here to win her back.

"Grey," Mia said, her voice firm and lacking emotion. She had wondered about this moment for a while, fearing what her first encounter would be with Grey if he had found her.

"It's good to see you," Grey said. "You look great, really." Mia's eyes fell onto a limp Rowan, bloody and battered, and just barely hanging on. He had been through so much already with his encounter with the hunters before, and Mia was worried if he even had any strength left in him.

"What did you do to him?" Mia asked. Grey looked at Rowan, nudging him slightly with a steel-toed boot. He still wore his clothes, which made Mia believe that he had far more control over his shifting than other shifters had.

"It's okay," Grey said, holding his hands out in front of him. "He's not going to be a threat to you anymore."

"Interesting to hear that from someone like you," Mia said. She wouldn't have dared say these words to him while they were together, but Grey had been one of the reasons why she and Rowan couldn't find their way back together.

"I can't believe you would say that to me," Grey said, his tone oddly friendly, although she heard a hint of the psychotic in his voice. "After all we had been through, even after what I told you the last time you ran away, you still managed to leave me."

"Why wouldn't I?" Mia said. "It's not like you gave me any reason to stay." Grey seemed to falter a bit at her words; his expression flickering in the shadows from the moonlight. He took a step closer to her, and Mia took one step back. She didn't want to be close to Grey, not until she was ready.

"I gave you everything," Grey said. "I was alongside you through everything. Or did you forget all of that once you saw your little friend here? Your best buddy."

The way he said it sent a shiver up Mia's spine. He had no business talking about Rowan.

"This is what you ran away for?" He chided with a scoff as he turned, lifting his boot to kick at Rowan's stomach. "I would have expected a lot more from you. A truly pathetic rebound if you ask me." Rowan gave a soft yelp, and it filled Mia with an incredible fury.

"Don't you dare touch him again," Mia warned.

"I'm really hurt, Mia," Grey said, holding his hand over his heart as if her words had actually pained him. "I thought you'd really be happy to see me. You didn't even say anything when I was in town." Mia's jaw trembled as a cruel shadow latched onto her. It had been Grey out in the streets that day.

"You knew," Mia said. "You knew that I was here the whole time."

"I know we've never talked about this," Grey said. "But being an alpha, I need eyes and ears everywhere. I knew you hadn't met the trio yet. Craig, Rico, and Trent already had the perfect job. Police officers sure are trusted in this town, and I thought they'd be perfect for bringing you back to me. It wasn't long before they caught onto your scent." He moved closer to her, his teeth pressed together in a terrifying smile. She could almost feel his breath on her skin as he said "Your sweet, sweet scent."

"Get away from me," Mia sneered as she brushed him off of her. Grey seemed almost impressed with her fire. She had never dared show this kind of feistiness towards him before.

"You've been spending a little too much time out here in the wild," Grey said. "It's starting to make you a little wild yourself."

Mia held her ground as she waited for a perfect opportunity. Her hands trailed towards her pockets. As far as she knew, she had something that Grey didn't, a weapon. As her fingers reached into her jacket, she was horrified to discover that there was nothing there but air and pilling fabric. The silver knife was gone. She tried to conceal her panic now that Grey was so close to her. If she lost face, he would know that he had an advantage over her.

"How did you find the cabin?" Mia asked, masking the tremble in her voice by speaking through her clenched teeth.

Grey scoffed again. "I must admit, those bear markings had us fooled for a moment," he said. He hovered closely around Mia, almost circling her now, despite the size of the rocky patch near the roaring waters. "The best part about living in a small town—and this is a rooky mistake, Mia—is that people talk. Everybody talks. I'm sure you thought you two were clever hiding out in the woods. But all it took were a couple visits from the police and pretty soon we start hearing stories about a man living alone out in a cabin."

Mia shivered; the panic setting in that she didn't have a weapon. How on earth was she supposed to deal with Grey if she was empty-handed? The way he looked at her had chilled her to the bone. He towered over her, his thick frame obscured by shadows. Before she could step away, his hand lashed out, locking around her arm. Mia knew it would leave a bruise. It had in the past. His grip had shocked her, brought her back to a place where she cowered in their apartment. She had once stared into Grey's drug-filled eyes as he threatened to take her life.

Mia stood her ground, her gaze never leaving Grey's no matter how much she wanted it to.

"Well, you've got me," Mia said. "Think you can keep me this time?" This seemed to anger Grey even more, and Mia found herself hurtling backward into a boulder lodged in the dirt. She tried to hide the pain as her body collided with the rough stone surface. "You're not exactly off to a good start," she said in a cruel tone. Grey bounded for her again, but Mia rushed for the nearest rock, pulling herself onto it. She only made it inches before she felt a hand grab at her ankle, ripping her from the safety of the boulder and throwing her back onto the ground.

She knew she couldn't run anymore. Grey was too fast and much stronger than she was, equipped with his incredible shifter strength. Before she could roll away from his grasp, Mia felt Grey's hand clutch around her throat.

Her eyes widened, regretting taking that extra step to talk back to him. She swallowed hard, despite the grip of Grey's fingers tightening against her windpipe.

You must think you're so clever," Grey said through his teeth. "Running away, finding another wolf pack to protect you. Well, look at you now. Back where you started, aren't you?"

Though her body struggled under Grey's grasp, Mia's mind had to stay busy. Without a knife, she would have to resort to another tactic to defeat Grey. It was hard to focus, though, as Grey continued to choke her. Mia lifted her legs, kicking wildly at Grey in a rough attempt to keep him from knocking her out.

His hands held firm, though, and Mia found herself staring up at the sky as her vision began to blur around her. It was getting harder to breathe as she felt herself fighting against Grey's malicious intent. Grey squeezed even harder, the look in his eye far more sinister than before. Mia choked and sputtered as Grey leaned his face closer to hers, the hairs of his thick beard brushing against her skin. It made her stomach churn. "Shouldn't I be enough for you?" He whispered harshly.

Mia was hanging on, just wavering on the edge of consciousness. As the oxygen around her grew thinner, she knew Grey was close enough for her to use the only weapon she had...words.

Whether it was physical like fire or psychological like past guilt, every shifter had a trigger. And Mia had just enough information on Grey, gathered up in her mental vault from their horrible relationship, to pinpoint what his trigger might be. With a strained breath, she managed to wheeze the words,

"Never enough..."

Grey's eyes darted back and forth across her face, and at first, Mia was unsure if he had heard her words. But she could feel his fingers just barely letting go from her neck. She seized the moment, waiting to say just what she needed to get Grey back into a wolf.

"You were never enough," Mia said to clarify.

"What the fuck did you say to me?" Grey said, more shocked than angry. Mia could already tell it was working; she just needed to wield her words carefully.

"You're tough," Mia said through chokes and sputters. "Think... you're so cool... with your wolf pack doing things for you. Just look now."

Grey eyed her with suspicion, but he appeared more surprised that Mia was the one telling him these words. His palm was sweating now, slipping against the skin on Mia's neck. Mia smirked at him.

"I know what you're scared of," she said. "You've always been scared of it because you know it's true. That's why you always threatened me whenever I tried to leave."

She braced herself as Grey yelled into the night, his breath a ghostly fog as he raised Mia into the air with one arm.

"Shut up!" He demanded. "You don't know anything!" Mia clutched onto Grey's arm with both hands. Out of the corner of her eye, she could see Rowan. He had stirred, just slightly but she didn't want to call out to him. She had captured Grey's attention and wanted to keep it that way.

Mia swung her feet until she could land a kick in Grey's face. It was enough to turn away, only for her to plant another one along his cheek. He groaned in pain as the soles of her boot made contact with his skin. Grey faltered back, lowering Mia back towards the ground and allowing her another chance to breathe.

"I know something, right now," Mia said, her hands trying to tear away Grey's fingers from her throat. "That I've got you to myself out here. Your pack isn't around to have your back."

"Right. And what chance do you even have against me?" Grey asked. He seemed more panicked than earlier, and Mia felt confident her words were starting to grab hold onto his mind.

"It's two to one now," she said.

"Two to one?" Grey asked as he shook his head. "You think your new boyfriend here is going to do anything to me?"

"He doesn't have to," Mia said. "I just know that I'm not the one alone."

She let the word hang there, and Grey seemed to take the bait. She had found his trigger. "Getting a little nervous, Grey?" She said, feeling Grey's hands trembling against her throat. "It's scary knowing you're alone, isn't it?"

As she said it, she imagined a grim sight. It was Rowan at thirteen, staring down an entire pack of wolves. For a second, she felt connected to him somehow. She was in just as frightening as a situation, though she wasn't as terrified as she thought she would have been. Though Rowan was unconscious, he was still right there beside her, fighting with her as he struggled quietly back onto his feet.

She kept her eyes locked on Grey, even when he was telling her to shut up.

"They're not your friends," she said. "They're all just scared of you, just like I was. Take them away and you have nobody left in your life."

"STOP IT!" Grey screamed.

His cries were lost in the roar of the waterfall. Mia could feel his hand trying to grab her again, though his knuckles were weak.

"You're trying to fight it," she egged on. "But you know for a fact that you're alone, and you always will be."

As soon as the words left her mouth, they almost felt like a magic spell, as if she knew the ancient sayings that would release her from Grey's grasp. Grey faltered backward, dropping Mia to her knees as he struggled. He held onto his head with both hands, screaming in a fit of rage as if he were being plagued by an irritating noise.

"Mia..." he said as he tumbled backward. He was teetering near the waterfall, and Mia knew she only had a precious few seconds.

She kept going, screaming over the waterfall as she proclaimed her love for Rowan, how Grey would amount to nothing but being a pathetic person that tormented others for his own benefit. The words fell from her mouth like stones, heavy ones that she had longed to say. They seemed to hit Grey right in the face, and within moments he was convulsing on the cliff's edge. His body eerily shifted, ghosting between human and animal as his jaws outstretched into a gruesome muzzle.

Just as he seemed halfway through, Mia took a step closer. She braced herself, ready to finish him off. But before she could, Grey had cried out in agony as a flash of white teeth snapped from the shadows, latching on to his ankle. Mia watched in horror as Grey got himself stuck in between shifts. He rolled helplessly on the ground, his arms vaguely resembling wolf paws as she seized against the rocks.

Rowan lifted himself over Grey now, his hackles raised as he crunched his jaws harder into Grey's ankle. Grey screamed a horrifying combination of man and wolf shrieks as he stumbled towards the edge of the cliff.

Mia watched Rowan shake Grey with such ferocity. She could see he was getting himself too close to the cliff's edge. With a cry she rushed for Grey, her body making contact with his deformed ribcage. He had felt light as a feather at her touch, and Mia watched as he tumbled into the misty falls without a sound.

It was silent, save for the rushing water beside them. It was as if Grey had simply disappeared in front of them. Just to be sure, Mia stood over the edge and stared down into the water. Grey's body was there, hanging limp and lifeless over a rock. She could see the dark smear of his blood bathing the side of one of the boulders.

Then, in a second, Grey's body was washed from the rocks and disappeared into the violent river.

Something grabbed tightly to Mia's leg, and she let out a startled cry thinking that it was Grey. But she looked to see that Rowan had shifted back into his human self, and was weakly smiling up at her. Mia ducked down beside him, taking off her jacket to drape around him. She tucked his wet hair behind his ear, and tenderly kissed him on his scratched forehead.

"Thank you," she said. Rowan nuzzled against her hand.

"Thank you," he said. "Glad we could finally work together for once." He smiled, his teeth still bloody from biting Grey. He noticed and wiped it with his arm in embarrassment.

"I think I figured out what you meant back in the tent," Rowan said, his voice exhausted. Mia shushed him, pulling him closer into her lap. His body curled up on her knee as she stroked his hair. She was just as exhausted as he was, and there was no need to discuss anything serious now.

"I used to hate myself every day for not being there for you," Rowan said. "But what I didn't realize, is that you're here, right now. And we don't have to live in all of that. That shadowy past that keeps us apart."

Mia looked down at him, wiping a red stain of blood from the corner of his lip.

"Stay with me then," she said. "Here, in the present."

Rowan gathered his strength, leaning up to kiss her. Mia turned and kissed him softly on the cheek.

"Um," Mia said. "Let me kiss you when you don't have the blood of my ex in your mouth."

"Right," Rowan said. "Sorry."

Mia lifted Rowan to his feet. They struggled up the hill, clutching onto the boulders together. Mia clutched tightly to him, glad that finally, they could exist in this new space together. Now that the evil was gone from Mia's life, their next battle would be navigating through the present and the unpredictable future.

"Need a hand there, buddy?" A voice said, reaching down to grab Rowan's arm. Rowan grunted as Brian stood on the ledge to pull him up, his body hurriedly covered up with a sweater and sweatpants. The rest of the Lost Shadow pack stood beside him.

"What happened to the others?" Rowan asked, appearing to take notice of the numbers.

From the group, Josiah stepped forward. "They're being tended to," he said calmly. "By the looks of it, you should probably get back to your tent too."

"And the Feral Bloods?" Mia asked. Shay emerged, being supported on the arm of Kara.

"Chased them out," Shay said proudly. "I don't think they'll be coming around here for a while."

"They won't need to," Josiah said. "We'll be heading back to our home shortly. After all, we got what we came for, haven't we?" He cast a knowing glance at Rowan. Rowan avoided his gaze, somewhat nervous. He glanced over at Mia, and suddenly she felt a pang of sadness as she realized that she didn't have Rowan for as long as she thought.

"You're going back with them," Mia said definitely.

"I have to," Rowan said. "I need to finish my training. Tonight was just another reason to get this under control." He brushed Mia's hair from her face. Mia shuddered at his touch, suddenly longing to be closer to him again, her body intertwining with his. All to herself.

"Okay," she said quietly. She couldn't bear the thought of being separated from him.

"I can't keep letting this get in the way of what I love," Rowan said as he held her close and kissed her forehead. "And that's you."

Mia trembled in his arms, dreading the goodbye. But Josiah had other plans for both of them.

"You know, Mia," he said. "That the Lost Shadows home base has an opening."

"An opening?" Mia asked. "For what?"

"We'll need someone to help oversee the pack, and possibly train the incoming shifters."

"But I'm not a shifter," Mia said. "I don't see how much use I could be to you all."

"I see you and Rowan have learned some things about triggers that I think may be a useful contribution to our pack," Josiah said.

Mia beamed as the rest of the pack agreed with Josiah, mumbling their approval. She looked right into Rowan's eyes. "Then I accept," she said with a grin from ear to ear. She had been lifted right out of her sorrow, and back into the arms of the man that she loved.

EPILOGUE

Mia carried her bag of groceries at her side as she followed the rugged path through the forest. Her feet hopped from stone to stone over a creek as she made her way back home. She knew she wasn't supposed to, but she still liked a bit of recklessness every now and then. The leaves were green again, to her relief. The past two winters had been insufferable for her, and she was looking forward to feeling the sun on her shoulders again soon.

She came to a tree, where a single rope trailed from the trunk to the ground. A zip line that she had helped to build not too long ago. A child stood on a platform made of plywood, her hands gripping onto the long bar as she took a leap of faith. Mia stopped to watch the girl, as she giggled all the way down the zip line and landed in a pile of leaves.

It was great to give the kids something to do in between training. As Mia continued on, she turned to see the child emerge from the leaves as a young wolf. She shook off the leaves that were clinging to her ears and ran in the direction of the main house.

It had been a couple blissful years for Mia. After Grey had been killed, she had felt lost for a while. Not because she needed Grey in her life, but because she had been so used to having him in her life, lurking around every corner and threatening to make his return that she didn't know what it was like to have a life that wasn't always in fear.

Luckily she had someone that could guide her through it, not to mention the help she had received from the Lost Shadows. Mia smiled to herself, grateful for the love that surrounded her. Her hand rested on her belly, large and round. Soon, there'd be an addition to the pack. On the back of Mia's mind there lingered the strange question of just what kind of child she was going to have once it emerged from her womb.

She was disturbed by a rustling nearby. At first, she thought it was just the child playing, but the young wolf had long since disappeared. Mia walked faster now, checking behind her. She knew the pack wasn't too far away, but she still couldn't shake the strange feeling she would sometimes get while walking through the forest alone.

Then, from behind a tree, a large figure leaped out in front of her. Mia gasped at the sight of the large grey wolf, lowering its head in front of her.

"Oh my!" Mia cried in an over-exaggerated tone. "There's a wolf out here! Somebody save me! He's absolutely rabid!"

The wolf shifted with ease, in fluid-like motions until it was Rowan standing in front of her. His messy hair was now cut short, clean and presentable, though he knew Mia still liked how he used to keep it. He was fully clothed, wearing a dark-green park ranger uniform. That's what the haircut was for, to keep Rowan presentable for his daily job.

Rowan lunged for Mia, carefully bringing her into his strong loving arms.

"Excuse me, ma'am," he said, very serious.

"Ma'am?" Mia said in shock. "I'm pregnant but I'm not an old woman, Rowan."

"Sorry...Miss," Rowan said with a wink. "I heard there was a predator out here, and I'm here to save you."

Mia smiled at him, wrapping her arms around his neck. "What's a park ranger like you going to do to fight off a wolf?" She asked softly.

Rowan shrugged. "Well, it just so happens to be that I am a wolf myself," he joked. "And I'm actually here to claim my territory." He reached up to grab her hand, holding it up to his lips to kiss it gently. His eyes regarded the bright shimmering ring on Mia's finger. "Seems as though it's a little late for that," he said.

Mia pulled away, still holding onto Rowan's hand as they continued to walk.

"What's happening in the wild these days?" Mia asked.

"Brian's been staying in the fire watch tower," Rowan said. "He says he's got his eye on one of the conservation program's interns."

"Uh-oh," Mia said. "Think she could be his mate?"

"Not sure," Rowan said. "We'll see if she can get over the bear-shifting hurdle first. You know, like you had to with me?"

"I didn't even have to," Mia said. "I already loved you then."

"You still got freaked out," Rowan said matter-of-factly.

"Well, yeah! You were a wolf!" Mia argued.

They chattered on like this until they came to the large cabin where the Lost Shadows stayed. The cabin branched off into separate smaller cabins, and Rowan and Mia had one to themselves.

The cabin was similar to the one Rowan used to have, though it was hard to get Rowan back to that cabin after what Grey and his pack had done to it. He was still able to salvage some of his books, along with his cooking pots and his clothes. What he didn't take was the box he had kept in his closet. He figured that the past should remain where it was and that there was no point in uncovering what needed to stay.

"The pack should be getting back soon," Mia said as she placed the groceries on the counter of their cozy kitchen.

"Shay and Kara have been on patrol today. Glad to see that the hunting has settled down for the season." Rowan sifted impatiently through the bag, pleased to find a chunk of beef wrapped in packaging. "You know," he said. "If you wanted meat, I could just get that for you. You know...for free."

"Yeah, but I prefer to have my meat in one piece, thank you," Mia smirked.

"Well then," Rowan said as he crept up behind her. "Do I have one piece of meat you might be interested in?" He nibbled on her ear and Mia shrieked with delight.

She smacked him on the shoulder, though his offer didn't sound too bad.

"Oh, wait here," Rowan said as he remembered something. He came back with a small red box, wrapped neatly with a bow. "Happy anniversary," he said with a smile as he handed Mia the box.

Mia took the gift, glancing at the over-excited Rowan. As she pulled off the covering, she could feel warm tears flooding her eyes. She pulled out Rowan's gift and laid it flat onto her palm. It was a clay ornament, half of a heart, with another shape inside. 'st, tes,' was painted on the front.

"It's incomplete," Rowan said. "But no worries. I just happen to have the other piece." He reached into his pocket, producing the other half of the ornament. "*be, ma*" was painted on his.

Mia excitedly put the two halves together. They made a single heart with a single message: *'Best mates'*

"Get it?" Rowan said. "'*Mates*' is like the word 'friend', but you know...you're also my mate." Mia laughed but noticed that the two pieces didn't exactly fit together; almost reminiscent of the old ornament they used to have.

"Rowan," Mia said. "What's this hole in the middle?"

"Check the box," Rowan said. Mia pushed the other paper away in the box, finding a small circle of clay. It was painted to look like the face of a baby. Mia laughed even harder as she completed the ornament, the baby's face perfectly joining the two halves.

"Do you like it?" Rowan asked, not sure if Mia's laughter was good or bad.

"I love it," Mia said. "But we definitely can't show anyone this. The baby makes it a little weird."

"Deal," Rowan said as he embraced her. Mia wiped her eyes as she leaned into his shoulder. He was warm and welcoming, like the home they could finally share together.

Mia leaned up, her lips pressing against his. Rowan was her best friend, her dearest love, her wolf.

The present had never looked so good.

END

Shadow of the Wolf

Central City Wolf Chronicles Series

Amelia Wilson

CONTENTS

PROLOGUE

No place for anybody.
   Certainly no place for a wolf.
   A scattered rhythm of paws thudded against the pavement outside of the abandoned warehouse. They were just far enough outside of the city for curious eyes not to find them.
   The pack was swift, made up of at least ten members that gathered in tight formation, their ragged panting making clouds in the frigid night air. They reached a chain-linked fence, where each of them took turns to scramble under it to reach the main yard.
   The building hadn't been touched for years, the windows were broken from rocks thrown by careless teenagers and wandering drunks. The wolves followed carefully behind the alpha as he led them through a hole in a brick wall, into the echoing emptiness of the warehouse. It was cold and damp, smelling of mildew and dying rats. Some of the wolves were nervous, although none of them would dare show it in front of the alpha while he was leading a mission. One false move and they could be exiled back onto the streets.
   Once safely inside, the alpha, who had serious olive-colored eyes and red brindled fur, turned to face the sea of grey and light-colored markings. With a faint whoosh and a jagged pattern of blurs, the alpha shifted effortlessly into his human form, and pressed his back against a crumbling brick wall. He was handsome. Rugged, with stubble along his sharp jawline. His human eyes were just as serious as his wolf eyes had been and his trimmed hair was a deep brown with subtle hints of dark red.
   The others took notice to shift alongside him, all of them forming tighter circles. The men and women waited patiently for their orders.
   The alpha regarded his pack with pride. All of them were dressed similarly in black athletic clothes. They had a very important mission to attend to this night. One of the members stepped forward, a grimacing young man with glasses and neatly combed hair. "My map says it's one of those doors,"

he said, pointing to either side of the main floor of the warehouse. Two hallways split off, curving ominously in different directions.

"Split up," the alpha said. "Beta, you'll lead the second group. Sound off a warning if you find anything."

"Don't you think we should stay together?"

"We don't know how much time we'll have to find this thing."

Without listening to another word, the alpha leapt over a railing, and landed firmly on the dirty tiled floor below. His polished boots scraped against the shattered glass as he led his half of the pack towards the right side of the room.

The hallway was dark, lit only by the glow of the small flashlights that each pack member carried. The alpha carried on ahead of them, his eyes darting wildly around the room, waiting for danger to spring on them at any moment. He knew something dangerous was here, although he wasn't sure what. All he knew was that there was a threat, not just to his pack but also to the four other shifter factions scattered around the city.

The group approached the end of the hall, where a dark corner waited for them. "Scouts," the alpha commanded. Two scouts, the youngest of the pack, stepped in front of him to peek carefully around the corner. The alpha waited as they assessed the situation. "I smell something odd," one of the scouts noted.

"Like a shifter?" The alpha asked.

"No, metallic," the other scout said.

"Blood, then."

"Perhaps."

"You should always assume the worst," the alpha said firmly, and then he waved for the others to follow him around the corner.

It was an eerie sight. Furniture and old machines seemed to have been ripped from their places. Papers from a much earlier time were scattered carelessly, like small ghosts. As the pack reached the middle of the hallway, they felt an earth-shaking rumble under their feet that vibrated under their soles. The alpha held out his arms, telling the group to halt.

Once the shaking had ceased, a low and deep groan rolled down the hall, echoing off of the walls and into the ears of the startled shifters. A strange wind seemed to pass over the group, almost like a phantom's breath. A monster? Or shifter? Whatever it was, it didn't sound human. The alpha felt a shudder pass through his entire body as if something invisible had passed through him. But he brushed it aside. They had come this far. He couldn't bring himself to back out now.

Another groan, and soon dust and dirt were crumbled down from the ceiling. The shifters hurried, trying not to stumble over as the floor shook again. "Should we signal the others?" A voice asked nervously from the back.

"Are you feeling unsafe?" The alpha asked, raising an eyebrow.

"Well...no, sir," the voice mumbled, trying to mask their discomfort.

"Then we should keep going? Don't you think?"

Nobody would dare challenge him, not even with the ominous rumbling and moaning that continued to sound all around them, shaking their bones and their souls inside them.

Finally, they saw a light. A faint almost candle-like glow was peeking out from a barely-open door. "The blood is stronger here, sir," one of the scouts mentioned.

"Whatever's been saying hello to us is probably on the other side," the alpha replied. "Should the attack team head in first?" another voice whispered.

"No, let me," said the alpha, his hand reaching out to touch the scratched and battered metal opening.

Just as he was about to open it, though, a new sound erupted in the hall. A warning howl, followed by the skittering of claws against tiles as the other half of the pack rejoined them. The beta, a black wolf with a streak of white, slid to a halt, gracefully shifting back into human form to face the disappointed alpha. His face was stained with worry and a hint of fear was mixed in.

"What happened?" Asked the alpha.

"We were jumped," answered the beta, sweating and out of breath. "They came out of nowhere, and...they took Henna."

"Who did?"

"We...we don't know."

The alpha contemplated the answer, but he didn't have time to pull his soldiers back. A loud and strange chanting came from the other side of the doorway, and a sharp clanking as if dozens of knives were being dropped on the floor.

"Stay close," the alpha warned his beta.

"But sir, we don't know what's here. It could be—"

"What? A monster? Spare me the fairy tales, please."

Without another thought, the alpha slammed his shoulder into the door. He could sense movement and smelt wolf on the other side. The room was wide and empty, the only light coming from a ceremonial circle of candles flickering against the walls.

The alpha could feel the warmth of his pack behind him, but he urged them to wait. As he stepped further into the room, he made out the dark outline of a hooded figure sitting cross-legged in front of an odd symbol etched in red, dripping down towards the floor.

Blood.

The marking was of a star, cut in half by a flying arrow. The figure in the center was whispering, his voice low and haunting as he spoke in a foreign tongue. While he did, the walls quivered again, and dust rained down on the alpha as he moved closer. The figure seemed to be lost in his own mind and he raised his arm towards the sky—something long and sharp was in his hands. It was a dagger, made of a clear, icy gemstone that glittered in the candlelight.

In one quick motion, he brought the weapon down, plunging it right into his own chest with an agonizing cry. "Hey, stop!" The alpha shouted. But of course, he was too late. The figure turned to face him, its red eyes glowing through the gaping void in his hood. "You should run," the figure warned, his voice a demonic growl. "He'll be coming soon. And you will die in his wake."

He began to convulse and to the alpha's surprise he saw several dark shadows shooting wildly about the room, before they disappeared into the dark corners. However, one ominous jet-black shadow wafted from the figure's dying body. It hovered threateningly, foreign whispers and gravely voices coming from it as it flew closer to the alpha.

Howls sounded from the distance. Warnings came from the concerned pack in the hallway. Something was coming—or was it already here?

The leader's eyes widened and he turned on his heels to sprint back towards his pack, but the shadow lashed out for him, gripping him by the throat with an inky black tendril.

The alpha's cheek was slammed against the cold tiles, and glass prickled into his cheek as the shadow wrapped itself around him tighter, like a ghostly snake. He watched in horror as the shadow moved over his chest, spreading like blood from a wound as it slithered up his neck. Then it slid right in between his lips, down his throat, and settled in his belly. The alpha sputtered and choked, hearing only the faint yelps of his pack members as they fought something he couldn't see.

"Fall back!" The beta cried over him as he tore into the room, and latched his arms around the choking alpha. As the alpha was dragged back into the hall, he could only just see a cluster of fur and gnashing teeth as another pack attacked his.

Then, there was a blinding light, burning bright in his mind's eye and then there was nothing.

Krista awoke with a gasp, drenched in a cold sweat. What was that light? Those flashes of gruesome images in her mind? Wolves running. An abandoned warehouse. Those piercing olive eyes. An ominous shadow. The very thought of that monstrous creature made her feel nauseous and she tumbled out of bed to vomit into the sink. As she ran the faucet, she clutched the edge of the bathroom counter, her breathing heavy and her chest tight.

Was that a dream? Or was it another vision?

1. FORTUNE

To Krista Sinclair, the office of a fortune teller was almost like a museum mixed with a hint of a grown-up's playground. Colorful chiffon curtains floated down from all corners of the room, with glittery sequins sewn into them. A gold fountain trickled on a nearby shelf, next to a porcelain statue of a hand, labeled with all the answers for palm readings. There were charts of star signs, of planets and their positions that brought the inquirer good fortune or bad luck. A purple neon sign in the shape of a crescent moon seemed somewhat out of place—it was a more modern touch that Krista had added against her mother's wishes, just to spice up the room a bit.

A hand, adorned with black nail polish and gold rings, was spreading out a handful of tarot cards, one by one, onto a sparkling tablecloth. The back of each card was decorated with a silver star, lying in wait. The hand reached up to light a stick of incense, wafting the musky vetiver-like smell around the dimly-lit room.

Krista closed her brown chocolate-colored eyes and gave a subtle hum as if summoning her power from the Earth. Some of her clients actually believed she was, even though most of Krista's act was for show. She did like how it made the experience just a little more "magical" for them.

"So, Mrs. Remy, what would you like to find out today?" Krista asked as she pulled her deep red hair up into a curly ponytail. A frail woman in a woolen coat sat nervously in front of her, her gloved hands clutching tightly to the purse in her lap. "Please, tell me if I should move on from Eustace or if I should still hold onto him," Mrs. Remy said with desperation. "I feel like I'm missing something."

"So...the usual?" Krista asked. The woman only blinked at her, and Krista dutifully starting turning over the three card spread. Past, present, future. Krista studied them carefully, giving a casual "I see..." for variety, even though Mrs. Remy always had the exact same spread.

"The Two of Cups in your past means you've shared a strong bond and a lifelong commitment. I assume this relates to your late husband?"

Mrs. Remy leaned in, hooked on every word Krista had to say. It honestly put Krista off a bit. She didn't mind putting on a show, but it sometimes rubbed her the wrong way if a client latched too tightly on to their fortunes, hungry for answers she wasn't even sure were true.

"What about right now?" The old woman asked. Krista rubbed her thumb along the corner of the Queen of Swords card in front of her. "It seems that you have a decision to make that's troubling you," she said.

"That's why I'm here, of course," the old woman scoffed. Krista smirked at her. "The Queen of swords is a strong woman, like yourself. However, she thinks with her mind, not with what's inside her heart. I know it seems tempting to follow your heart, but you've been clinging to your painful memories for a while now."

The old woman grimaced as if she'd known what she had to do all along.

"But it's not all bad," Krista reassured her as she pointed to the last card. A single man staring back at her. "Your future is occupied by the Emperor. I see a strong and sturdy man. Perhaps you'll meet him soon."

"Is it Eustace?" Mrs. Remy's eyes flickered.

"The future is always uncertain," Krista reminded her. "But because of the, erm, circumstances of your late husband, I should tell you that I can't bring him back."

It broke her heart to see the woman looking so upset. She reached across the table, cupping her fingers around Ms. Remy's fragile ones. As she did, she saw the flicker of an old man's face in her mind, smiling and holding hands with Mrs. Remy. Another vision—a real one this time. "It's not too late for you, you know," Krista said quietly. "There might be someone you already know who has an interest in you."

She didn't always let her visions affect her readings, but she felt that the old woman was a special case. After thinking for a moment, Ms. Remy raised her head. "I think you may be right," she said with finality. "I think I'm going to call that man from the assisted living home after all."

"That's a great start," Krista said with a soft smile. The woman snapped her purse open, and handed her usual payment over to Krista. "For your trouble," she said. Krista thanked her, packing up her cards and saying a quick ritual before closing her reading.

On her way out, Mrs. Remy turned to Krista. "My dear," she said. "Have you ever read your own fortune? With you being so connected to the spiritual world, you must be curious about your own love life. Aren't you?" Krista was startled to see the woman wink at her and she waved her hand dismissively.

"I'd like to try to keep my feet in the present if you know what I mean," Krista replied.

"Interesting," Mrs. Remy said. "I thought for sure you'd use your gift for fun once in a while."

"Well, I wouldn't exactly call it fun," Krista said with a slight laugh. "After all, a job is a job."

"Well, it sure is an exhilarating one, I'll tell you that." The old woman said her goodbyes and left Krista alone in the cold dim room.

Krista locked up for the night before ducking behind a secret curtain and heading up a flight of stairs. The fortune teller's shop she had inherited from her mother had an upstairs part that served as her private apartment. It was a stylish, yet simple studio, with a couch, a coffee table, a small kitchen area, and a corner with a bed just big enough for her. With a heavy sigh, Krista turned on some light techno music and lit some purple candles, before eventually making her way over to the fridge which was stuffed with six packs of beer and leftover Chinese takeout.

She cracked open a nightcap, sipping the foam from the top. She stripped off her sweater and scooted out of her tight jeans before throwing on an old baggy t-shirt and sitting cross-legged on her plush carpet. Mrs. Remy's words were still echoing in her mind. *"Use your gift for fun once in a while..."*

She looked over at the boxed-up pack of tarot cards—her mother's old practice deck. They seemed to be waiting for her on the edge of the coffee table. They were a gift for taking over the family business. Krista's mother was still alive, though to Krista she might as well have been a ghost. She hadn't spoken to her daughter for about a year, ever since she went to find herself on a "spiritual journey" to the Himalayas without even saying goodbye.

A phone buzzed next to her with a new text message. Krista eyed it nervously. "Dinner?" read the message from a man named Chris. Chris from the bar the other night. He was in business or IT or—whatever. Something boring that she couldn't remember. She hadn't had much luck with men lately. Any time she met one, they managed to make her feel like a freak by the second date...if she was fortunate enough to get to that stage. Whenever the conversation got around to careers, she always got funny looks. Whether people believed her or not, it still made her feel, well, freakish, and had done ever since she was small and just learning about her visions.

Her visions were often the reason she preferred to stay a recluse. It was hard to have a relationship, or even just a friendship when you constantly had flickers of a future about to go sour. They had been getting stronger in the past week, which only made her more anxious. All day, she had been distracted with that face she had seen the other night in her dreams. Handsome, stubbled, and with piercing olive eyes. He seemed to be looking right into her and it sent a quiver through her chest.

What did he say he was? A shifter? Krista thought. She waved her hand above her head. It sounded like bunk to her. It was a dream, not a vision. Although that shadow... there was something about it that made it all feel real.

Still, she wondered. *Never check your own fortune,* was her personal rule as a psychic. The thing about Krista's fortunes was that most of the time they were bound to come true, at least... that's what she thought.

She thought of the way Mrs. Remy's eyes had shone when she had said how exhilarating it was to have your fortune told. Her mind wandered and her hand hovered between picking up her phone to text Chris Whomever or picking up those damned tarot cards. Maybe if she did just a small reading, she could discover a hint about that stranger in her dream.

"What the hell?" she shrugged, chugging the last of her beer and slamming the can on the table. Anything was better on a Friday night than getting all gussied up and pretending to be interested in Mr. Whomever. She politely reached for her phone, and composed and sent a polite "No-thank-you" text before grabbing her cards.

They felt different in her hands this time, almost taboo. She even checked over her shoulder to see if anyone was watching her break her one and only rule. The cards fluttered softly as she shuffled them while thinking of a question to ask them. Only one floated to the top of her head.

"Is my dream just a dream? Or is it something else?" She spread out three cards: Past, Present, and Future. Why were her hands shaking? It definitely wasn't the first time she'd done this. However, it was one thing to tell other people's futures. When it came to her own, she found herself frightened and a little overwhelmed.

She took a deep breath and turned over her the first card, representing her past. Three of Swords—a single heart pierced by three blades—a past struggle or strained relationship. She rolled her eyes. *That's probably thanks to Mom*, she thought. Her present card was The Fool—a light-spirited looking man with a dog running at his side, which represented the possibility of a journey, or a new start. Strange... Krista thought. With some hesitation, she turned over the last card. Oddly enough, it felt the heaviest out of all the others. Her heart pounded in her chest as she brushed her thumb along the edge of the card. She flipped it as if she was ripping off a Band-Aid.

Her eyes widened. If she had been living in a horror movie, thunder and lightning would have ripped ominously through the room. But it was just her, in her tiny studio, alone with the horror of the future.

The scene depicted a castle-like structure, with lightning striking into the crumbling brick. Two figures were falling from the windows, screaming as they tumbled towards the unseen ground. The Tower—a notorious symbol of danger...and that something horrible was headed her way.

Krista stared blankly, trying to reinterpret the meanings. After all, the cards weren't always crystal clear. Her eyes kept gazing down at the couple falling to their doom, and suddenly a piercing sting vibrated in her skull. She saw the shadow again. It latched onto her chest before it lunged, mouth agape, right towards her face.

2. INTERRUPTED PEACE

Ryland was supposed to be recovering. But, he couldn't stand sitting around when he knew his incompetent beta, Tristan, was out running things in the Rogue's hideaway. For the past two days, Ryland had been giving orders to his pack from his bed, using Tristan as the unfortunate messenger.

He clutched at the ache in his bandaged side. When he winced, he could feel his skin prickle, the tightness of his healing wounds stretching over his skin. The infiltration of the warehouse didn't go quite as planned, with him running straight into that bone-chilling ritual and the rest of his pack being attacked by unfamiliar wolves.

They had taken Henna, one of his strategists. Who knows where she could be now, assuming she was even still alive. That was a dark thought for Ryland, but he had seen so much during his time as an alpha that he was sure nothing could surprise him.

Except for, of course, for this lingering pain that sometimes pulsed through his limbs and fingers. Ever since the encounter with that shifter, the one with the crystal knife, Ryland hadn't felt quite the same. There was some seriously evil dwelling in that place and the shadow that had engulfed him had only confirmed Ryland's hunch. He clutched at his wrist, clenching his fingers into a tight fist. As he looked at his veins, he swore he could still see the shadow inside of him, traveling through his bloodstream in dark syrupy waves.

"HARDER! Keep up that right hook, Trevor!" Ryland's voice boomed over the expansive training room of the Rogue's warehouse. His pack was currently one of the strongest in Center City and they were working their hardest to stay that way. The pack was split into pairs, men and women, and the wolves were taking turns sparring with one another. Some of them threw him cautious glances, and then carefully adjusted their fighting stances, to their alpha's amusement.

Ryland stood at his usual post, on a walkway that hovered above the matted floor. He leaned over the railings, studying the way each member delivered powerful kicks, punches, and bites. The sight of their diligence made him proud, although something about it felt slightly tainted. He still couldn't figure out how to shake that feeling, not even after being alpha for five years. No matter how hard he pushed the Rogues, they could have always been better.

Any other alpha from any other corner of Center City would have said their pack was the strongest. But, if the Rogues came up in conversation, they quickly changed the subject. Ryland had run a tight ship for as long as anyone could remember. Hardly anyone would have the guts to bring up the time the pack had almost split up.

Ryland massaged his temples in his calloused hands. He had a pounding headache—one that he thought would go away if he joined the rest of the pack on the training floor. They usually wrapped up though, whenever he had the time to get to the mat.

"Shouldn't you be sleeping?" A voice startled Ryland from the nearby stairs. He caught his breath, relieved it was just his beta approaching. Why was he feeling so jumpy lately? Tristan, a lanky figure with neatly combed black hair and stylish black-framed glasses, was always dressed nicely for any occasion except a mission. He was also notorious for getting in the way, according to Ryland.

"I can't sleep," Ryland grumbled. "Not until we can figure out whom those shifters belonged to." He pointed down to the pack below, which had now moved on to sprints across the lengthy floor. "Why weren't they out here, earlier?" He asked Tristan. "I practically had to drag them out of bed this morning."

"That's because I had told them to take the weekend off," Tristan said, casually adjusting his glasses.

"Excuse me? Who gave you permission to do that?"

" Ryland—"

The alpha raised a warning eyebrow at Tristan, who quickly corrected himself. "Sorry...*Sir*, but you were in bed for a few days. Besides, the pack was feeling a bit...battered from our altercation in that warehouse. I figured everyone could use some rest before we get our bearings on this...new situation."

Ryland could feel the hairs on his neck standing up. A strange rumbling took over his nerves, and for a second he wanted to lash his wolf jaws out at Tristan, sinking them right into his throat and tasting his blood.

"Sir?" Tristan's voice interrupted the disturbing image. Ryland snapped out of it. He realized his hands were shaking as they clutched the railing. "I've noticed that since the attack that you've been increasingly irritable. More so than usual I would say."

"I'm fine," Ryland said, trying to get his thoughts in order.

"You know, we sent the scouts back shortly afterwards," Tristan said. "They examined that room, the symbol on the wall, and the blood on the floor."

"Was it Henna's?"

"Another shifter's, sir. They found the body somewhere else in the warehouse. Looks like a Stalker to me. I've messaged their alpha to let them know."

"Did they see anything else?" Ryland asked. "The other things I mentioned."

"Ah. I've talked with both scouts and neither of them said anything about seeing any shadows, or a crystal dagger."

Ryland sighed. He didn't want to bring it up out of the fear of looking crazy, but the shadow had been haunting him ever since that night. He had tried looking into it himself, poring over some of the texts he'd picked up from other shifters in his family. He didn't think of himself as superstitious, but whatever he swallowed in the warehouse wasn't normal, and it was making him feel strange—violent even.

He watched his pack growing tired from their sprints, and wondered if any of them would be attacked next. They still needed to find Henna. He had a feeling that one of the other packs might know about her disappearance.

"Dinner's on for everyone as usual," he told Tristan. "After that, you and I need to meet. We need to start making some moves."

"Moves?"

"We need to stay at the top of our game. Call for a faction meeting. We don't know who this pack is. They could be trying to interfere with our peace treaty and the last thing I need is a war on my hands."

Tristan reached into the pocket of his blazer, and pulled out a pen and paper. "Should I call all four factions?" He asked.

"Wait, what is that?" Ryland pointed at Tristan's hands.

"A pen and paper. More reliable than my phone."

"Geez...you really are like him sometimes," Ryland shook his head.

"I thought that's why you chose me as your beta, sir."

Suddenly a slight groan caught Ryland's attention and he realized he was clutching the railing so hard now that it was taking a new shape. He pulled his hands away, and both he and Tristan noticed the small indents that his fingers had left behind, forever embedded in the metal.

Ryland stepped away, too embarrassed to meet Tristan's concerned gaze. He smoothed himself out, stopping at Tristan's shoulder on his way out. "I brought you into this place, Tristan, but I can also throw you back out," he threatened. "Don't forget that."

"Somehow you always manage to remind me," Tristan said calmly. But Ryland didn't quite hear him. His head was heavy with a dull pain, followed by strange hushed tones, almost like whispers. He couldn't understand what they were saying, but he was filled with the desire to hunt. To consume. *To take life...* was the one phrase that rung above the rest.

3. THE SIGN

Wednesdays were always the slowest, so Krista took it upon herself to close up for the day. She swept the rugged wooden floors of her shop, looking out at the rain dripping down her windows. Her place was in a quaint neighborhood just slightly out of the craziness of the city. She could see Central Towers in the distance though, which made for a lovely view at night.

Krista pulled down the pictures of her mother and her from a shelf and dusted them off. It was odd to see herself smiling in the photographs. She loved her mother, but still held some resentment towards her.

After all, her mother had pulled her out of high school and had made her finish out her teen years locked up in the shop poring over tarot cards and star maps. Krista had wanted to go to college, but her mother prioritized her training over everything else. Whenever Krista asked why, she'd only be met with the same answer: "You're meant for something else, just you wait."

Krista had waited...and waited... until she turned twenty-seven, with no 'something else' in sight. It was shortly after then, that her mother had decided to hand over the shop and disappear from Krista's life, without officially pronouncing her ready for the world. Krista thought she'd be more upset, but it was actually a relief to run the place her way, without someone breathing down her neck all of the time.

She shrieked as something crawled across her hand. A cellar spider, long and spindly. She cupped it in her hand and placed it in the nearest corner. "You might have better luck finding lunch up there," she told it quietly.

Out of the corner of her eye, she saw a figure outside, buried in a black hoodie as they tried to get out of the rain. She followed it until she heard the door jiggle, followed by a muffled groan of annoyance. *Who the hell?* Krista thought as she made her way to the peephole. The figure shifted their weight back and forth. Contemplating whether they should knock.

In any other circumstances, Krista would have pinned the guy as a burglar or something. But, as soon as he lifted his head, she could just see the hint of olive green under the figure's hood. She froze in her tracks. Certainly this was a coincidence. Anyone could have eyes like that. Still, she was curious and opened the door as far as the chain lock allowed her.

"Hello," she said, struggling to make eye contact. "We're actually closed—"

"I know, I saw the sign," the man said. "But I've been trying every psychic around Central City. Everyone's saying I should come to you."

His voice was smooth and deep. Krista hardly heard what he was saying to her and when he removed his hood, she could hardly stand. It was the exact same face, the one staring back at her from her dream.

She closed the door, unlocked the chain at once, and let the man inside. Her mother had warned her about handsome men and the trouble they brought, but her mother was very far away and this was Krista's shop after all. She couldn't pass up on such an opportunity.

"Uh, have a seat," she told him, and the man sat calmly at her round table, in her usual spot.

Krista shifted her weight and made a face before clearing her throat.

"What?" The man asked. "That's my seat," Krista said with polite firmness. "You said to take one."

"And now I'm asking you not to take *that* one."

Visibly confused and slightly annoyed, the man got up and took the other seat. It seemed as though he'd never been told 'no' before. Krista got comfortable.

"So, you are...?"

"Ryland. Ryland Iker," The man stretched out a heavy hand. Krista could feel his callouses when she shook it and immediately pictured him doing some sort of hard labor. She nearly blushed at the thought. Her mind was already getting carried away at the sight of the handsome face, but then she remembered her visions and the awful futures they often foretold. Just before she let go, she felt a slight tingle spreading across her fingertips. A vision was creeping up on her, but she tried to distract herself to keep it at bay.

"I'm Krista," she said. "What brings you here today?"

"I need to know...if you know anything about ancient curses?" Ryland said with all seriousness.

"Curses? This is a joke right?" Krista asked, her cherry lips curling into a smile. She watched the man close his eyes, frustrated and strung out.

"Forget it," he said, about to get up from his chair. "I knew this was a stupid idea..."

Krista wondered if he was just crazy, but if this was the same man from her dream, she didn't want to lose him so quickly. Not before finding out if he was somehow connected to the mysterious shadow and the terrifying future the cards had told her about. "Wait," she said. "Stay. The least I can do is to give you a palm reading before you head out."

"Will that help at all?" Ryland asked, skeptical.

"It might, if it's done by the best psychic in the city," Krista said matter-of-factly. Ryland inched back into the creaky chair, looking around and waiting for something to happen. "Uh, first I need your palm," Krista said trying not to laugh.

Ryland seemed so uptight, and his muscular figure almost made his chair look too small for him. It was comical in a way. "What? Like I need to hold it out for you?" Ryland asked, clearly not wanting to look like a fool.

"Obviously," Krista said. "It's a palm reading. Which hand is your dominant hand?"

"My right."

"Can you spread it out for me please?" She watched Ryland with a careful eye. He seemed to stiffen slightly. "Can I use my other one?" He asked. "I've uh, injured my right hand."

" I guess we can make it work," Krista tried to smile, but when she looked at Ryland she had the feeling that he wasn't the joking type. Still, he reached his left hand across the table, his palm open.

As she stared into the crevices and valleys of his hand, the first image that popped into Krista's head was the tower card, fire wavering from its windows. Two people falling to their doom. She took Ryland's hand in hers with caution, feeling a faint jump in her chest when she touched him.

"Now, let me just take a look—" Krista leaned forward to study him. Ryland leant back casually in his seat and looked out the window as if he were waiting for a doctor to remove a splinter and not for someone to determine his fate. Krista pressed her thumb against an empty space where Ryland's heart-line should have been. As soon as she did, she felt a sharp stinging in her forehead. With incredible force, she clasped Ryland's fingers in her own, holding tightly to him while her mind soared off into another place, past all time and space until she was staring into a black void. She couldn't hear Ryland trying to bring her back to reality, only a cacophony of roars and howls. Her entire body felt heavy as if she were a weight being hurled through the nothingness.

Then, in rapid flashes, she saw dozens of images pass through her mind, like cards being shuffled. There was Ryland, crouched on the floor in agony. He seemed to rip out of his skin as he transformed into a howling wolf. The wolf then stretched out as if made of liquid, twisting and curling into a horrific shape, until it resembled the same shadow Krista had seen in her dream. The shadow grew larger and larger, and a row of white teeth emerged from it. With a single breath, a massive wave of fire billowed from the shadow's mouth. Then, it began to laugh, a gravely disturbing sound that chilled Krista to the bone. It seemed to have noticed her, and in an instant, it spread open its grotesque jaws and swallowed her right up.

Krista didn't even know she was on the floor. The first thing she saw when she opened her eyes was Ryland, hovering above her. "Are you alright?" He asked, his eyebrows tightly knitted.

Krista sat up, clutching her head. It was the strongest vision she had ever experienced. She noticed Ryland's hand was clutching her arm. In a panic, she tore away from him. Who was this man? Judging by her vision, Krista wanted to assume he was a monster. So many thoughts buzzed in her mind. "Did you see something?" Ryland asked.

"I think you should go," Krista said firmly. Ryland had some kind of secret—one that she thought it was best never to know. Who cares if he was the same man from her dream? There was obviously some strange darkness connected to him that she absolutely did not want to be mixed up in. "Can you please just give me another chance?" Ryland tried to protest. Krista was already rushing him out the door. "I'm so sorry for the inconvenience," she said. "But I'm suddenly feeling...uh, very sick."

"Did you see something bad?" Ryland could barely finish his question before Krista shut and locked the door immediately behind her. She realized she was sweating, and her heart was still pounding like a hammer in her chest. She could hear him mumbling under his breath as he walked back up the street.

She couldn't sleep at all that night for fear that she would see something else. Her encounter with Ryland had only made her worry that she'd have another horrific vision. By the time she'd finished her third beer, she was starting to feel her psyche settle down. It was one of the more effective ways of keeping the visions at bay. As she drank, she perused her mother's library, hoping to find something on ancient curses.

She felt bad—regretful for kicking Ryland out of her shop. She was always so eager to use her abilities for others, but for some reason she just couldn't bring herself to help him. Maybe she was afraid, not just because of the vision, but because perhaps this vision had something to do with her own reading. Would this strange evil have something to do with her future? Perhaps it was that damned tower card she had seen?

Krista gave up on the books and looked out of the window of her studio. Whatever evil was out there, she didn't want any part of it.

4. NEGOTIATIONS

Ryland sat on the edge of his bed, unraveling a strand of gauze from around his wrist. His right hand had been killing him over the past few days, aching and burning. As he removed the bandage, he was horrified to see a dark ominous splotch under the skin of his wrist. There was a black lump that hurt to touch. It was spreading, whatever it was. Dark tendrils wove around his veins, pulsing in strange patterns up his arm. He had been wearing long sleeves to hide it from the rest of his pack, but couldn't do anything to mask the searing pain he felt each day.

What the hell was wrong with that fortune teller, kicking him out when he didn't have anyone else to turn to? Angry thoughts swirled in his head—something he noticed was becoming quite common. However, he also remembered how she had looked when she touched his hand. Her eyes had rolled into the back of her head and she had convulsed violently in front of him. Ryland had thought she was embarrassed or something, which is why she had kicked him out. She seemed different after she awoke. She looked at him so strangely, as if she was terrified of him.

Ryland wrapped a fresh bandage around the shadowy wound. Who wouldn't be scared of something like this? That Krista girl must have seen something unexplainable, which led Ryland to believe that maybe she could be what he was searching for, though her kind hadn't been sought out in centuries.

His door creaked open and Tristan stepped inside. "They're waiting for you," he said calmly and he opened the door wider for Ryland. Ryland finished wrapping his wrist just in time, pulling his sleeve down before Tristan could see. He still hadn't told anyone, even though he knew he should. He was worried about what they'd think. He had been having increasingly violent thoughts lately and didn't want anyone to think less of him, if they found out.

"Let's get this over with," he said as he followed Tristan towards the meeting room.

Shifter faction meetings were often held at the round table in the
Rogue's warehouse, in a special room reserved for such things. Since Ryland's pack was the largest, it occupied the top of Central City and served
as the 'head' of the five packs. The other four occupied each corner of the
city, all of them bound by a peace treaty, set up by Ryland and his former
beta a few years ago.

Ryland sat with Tristan at his side, and with three of his best pack members behind him: Geoff, a foot soldier; Kalyn, a strategist and Tory, a scout.

"I will call the roll," Tristan said above the noise of the meeting room.
One pack of shifters was rowdy enough. Having all five together in the same
room was asking for trouble. "Please make note if you are here. Furies."

"Present," said Sam, a broad-shouldered woman, and alpha of the all-fe-
male pack, The Furies. Her amazon-esque posse stood proudly behind her,
ready to settle any disputes.

"Nightcallers," continued Tristan.

"Here," raised the hand of Rizz, a spiky-haired punk whose pack occupied the top right corner of the city. His pack members were all clad in
leather and metal studs, eyeing the Furies with suspicion.

"We don't have time for formalities..." Ryland grumbled as he stood up.

"This is the standard procedure," Tristan corrected him. "You know,
like in every meeting?"

"We clearly know why we're all here," Ryland said. "Ben of the South
Stars is here, and so are the Stalkers. Now, with that out of the way, we can
get to more serious matters."

Tristan's eyes fluttered as he took a seat and opened up his notebook. "I
feel so left out, Ry," A grating voice called out from across the table. Ryland
clenched his fist at the very sound. "Didn't feel like introducing l'il old me?"
Declan Burr, a redhead with an unkempt goatee, kicked his boots on the
table and leaned back in his seat. Declan was Ryland's rival and alpha of the
Stalkers. He was also incredibly annoying.

"You're awfully cocky for someone who's just lost a pack member," Ryland said through his teeth. Declan, for once, decided to keep his mouth
shut.

"Onto the first matter of business," Tristan said. "The Furies have reported some strange activity recently?"

"We've been seeing this symbol spray painted everywhere," Sam said, sliding a piece of paper across the table. Each pack leaned in to get a better look. It was a star, split in half with an arrow. Ryland recognized it as the same one that had been crudely etched in the warehouse. "Any scents attached to them?" He asked.

"Ben and I have discussed this," Rizz said as he adjusted his nose ring. "Someone's definitely leaving scent markings around, but it's not from any of you guys."

"What's stranger is that there isn't a pattern to them," said Ben, a brooding man with long hair. "Our scouts have been recording the marking sites. They're too sporadic to determine anything."

Ryland pondered. A new pack in Central City? There hadn't been one since the peace treaty was arranged.

"Has anyone managed to find any information on Henna?" He asked the room. Everyone fell silent, curious eyes darting from one side of the table to the other.

"Nigel is missing as well," Ben said quietly.

"So is my beta..." Sam said with a hint of sadness.

Ryland tried to feel out the room. He didn't want to assume any of these alphas was behind this. Even though peace existed between them, Ryland still had doubts about where everyone's loyalty stood. Anyone could be recruiting shifters outside of the city to do their bidding, and this thought made Ryland suspicious of almost everyone in the room.

"You mentioned Declan lost a pack member," Rizz said. Declan shifted in his seat, avoiding eye contact with anyone. If anyone was behind this it would be him. He was a conniving man after all, and before he had become the alpha he had been a lone wolf with his own rules, and a cunning negotiator between all of the packs.

"The Rogues found the body. According to Ryland, he had been stabbed with a crystal dagger," Tristan said regarding his notes. "The killer took his own life with it, and apparently there was a strange shad—"

"A circle was drawn around the area," Ryland interrupted. If he couldn't tell his pack about the possibility of a curse, he certainly couldn't tell the rest of the shifter factions.

"You seem a little antsy, Ryland," Declan jeered. "Something you don't want to tell us?"

Ryland felt his anger simmering. "Shifters are missing, Declan. Someone is sacrificing them and we need to know who it is and why they're doing this. We're going to need each alpha to spread out their packs and gather as much information as we can."

"Shouldn't we all be working out a plan?" Declan countered. "I know you like to think you're the one and only leader of Central City, but with you making all the decisions for us, it really makes me wonder...are you trying to cover your tracks?"

"Oh, for heaven's sake..." Tristan sighed adjusting his glasses. The other alphas leaned away from the table, not wanting to get caught in the crossfire.

"You're quick to make accusations," Ryland said. "Perhaps you're making them before anyone else, so that they won't suspect you."

"Why would I kidnap my own shifter?"

"Well, why would I do the same?"

"Because I think you've turned into a power hungry bastard ever since your brother left the pack."

Ryland's temper was on a rolling boil now, about to spill out everywhere. Before he knew it, he was flying across the table, shifting into a dark-red wolf that lunged, jaws first, at Declan. The other alphas and their packs stepped away from the table, watching as Declan revealed his inner wolf. Ryland sunk his teeth right into his neck. Nobody would ever talk about his brother again. Not after they saw what he'd do to Declan.

It was chaos as Tristan tried to break up the pairs of gnashing teeth and threatening growls. Declan's hackles raised, his lip quivering as his jaws lashed out again and again at his rival. Ryland knocked him across the room, sending him crashing hard against the concrete wall with a weak yelp. Declan reverted back, his forehead bleeding along with his lip.

Ryland stood above him, placing his foot right on Declan's chest. "Your silver tongue won't help you here," he growled, sweat dripping from his brow. "I'll kick your ass a thousand more times if it'll help you learn your place."

Declan wiped his split lip, and grimaced at Ryland. "I think it's safe to end this meeting," Sam said, standing up with the other alphas. "Since our unofficial leader has decided to make a scene instead of leading the negotiations."

Ryland could hardly look at them as they filed out of the room. He didn't know what came over him, and even though it was satisfying to beat Declan, he worried that it cast him in a different light. *"Who needs them anyway?"* He thought. *"I know what I have to do, not them. I'm going to have to figure this one out on my own."*

"Or together…" Another voice seemed to say. It was faint, and not threatening like the other voice he had heard before. In fact, it almost sounded like the fortune teller he had met. Ryland shook it off. He really hadn't been resting as well as he should have been.

That night, Ryland stepped into the training room. The rest of his pack had probably already heard about the meeting and his outburst by now. As soon as his sneaker touched the mat, he noticed that everyone was more rigid and they all eyed him carefully. Not with their usual respect…this time they seemed different. Ryland took to a punching bag and told it about his day. One by one, the pack members began to leave, and he soon realized what that look in their eyes was.

Fear.

Ryland slammed his fists into the bag.

"Sir," Tristan called to him from the edge of the mat. His nicely-shined shoes didn't belong on it. Ryland stopped the bag, resting his forehead on it. "There's nothing to talk about. Declan ran his mouth and I did something about it."

"I'm not saying he didn't deserve it. But, you do have to keep in mind your responsibilities as alpha. You set an example, not for yourself but for the rest of the pack. I know you hate lecturing, but something has to be done or your behavior will drive the other packs towards breaking the treaty."

Ryland nodded. There was only one other person who had spoken to him this way, and it hadn't ended well for him. As Tristan left, Ryland clutched at his wounded arm, his veins contracting inside of him. This poisonous curse was making him this way and, if he wanted to remain the strongest alpha, he'd have to put a stop to it, fast.

But first, he needed to go for a walk.

5. PARTNERS

Krista awoke to the sound of rustling in the office downstairs. Sometimes the dryer would make more noise than usual. She just had to turn it off and restart it. Carefully, she slipped on a pair of sweatpants and a t-shirt, and walked towards the stairs in her bare feet.

She was barely awake, and the alcohol had hit her pretty hard from earlier. As she made her way to the main floor, she stopped dead in her tracks. It wasn't the dryer at all. Someone...or something was creeping about, rifling through her papers, and opening her cabinets. Krista suddenly felt more alert, pressing herself against the wall to listen.

There were voices, speaking in hushed tones. Was it that Ryland guy? Coming in to cause some trouble after she had kicked him out? As she reached the final step, she realized that the three men standing in the fortune-telling room were most likely complete strangers, and all of them were wearing dark clothes and plastic wolf masks.

They stared up at her, dropping her things to the floor. She stared back at them, and for a long moment, there was a deafening silence between them. "Ah, I told you she was home," one of them said, his deep voice muffled under the mask.

"W-who are you?" Krista asked, her voice cracking. "What the hell are you doing in my shop?"

"We're here for you of course," another masked man said in reverence. "We've come to bring you home, Oracle."

"Oracle? What the f—"

Before she could finish her sentence, one of them pulled out a long, silver blade. It glimmered in the dark and it was pointed right at Krista. "Thanks, but I'm staying home," Krista said, backing up the stairs. The men moved closer. "You can't run. We've been given specific orders to bring you back alive."

Krista didn't need to hear any more. She turned and bound up the steps. She could hear them hurrying after her, trying to squeeze themselves up the cramped stairwell. She rushed into her studio and slammed the door shut, promptly dragging a nearby table in front of it. Just as it was in place, a fist slammed through the wood. She screamed at the sound.

She ran for the kitchen area, grabbed the biggest knife she could find and stabbed it into the gloved hand. The man reared back with a pained cry while the others rammed their bodies into the wood, trying to break it down. Krista's stomach dropped, and she felt frozen in place. The only way out was the window next to her bed, and even that was a risk. But any risk was better than being dragged off by the creepy masked men.

She made a run for the coffee table, swooping up her mother's pack of tarot cards and ran towards the window. She struggled with the screen and checked behind her just as the door splintered open, flying off its hinges and landing with a heavy thud on the floor.

As a last resort, she cut through the screen with her knife. There was hardly a place to put her feet, but she managed to scramble out just before she heard the men say where she was going. They'd be coming down the stairs and outside to grab her. Krista hung from the windowsill, her feet swinging in the cold night air.

Closing her eyes, she let go, letting herself fall into a cluster of bushes under the window. The branches scraped under her t-shirt, scratching against her elbows, but she barely had time to react. Her feet moved on their own as she ran for a fence, jumping over it into someone's backyard.

She checked behind her, but there was no sign of the men following her. She kept running for another fence, and as she did she heard a low growl. A large black wolf was behind her! She'd never even seen one out here before. It looked hungry—its teeth were bared at her as if waiting to attack.

Another fence. Krista jumped over it, feeling the breath of the wolf as it snapped at her bare ankles. Its claws skittered at the fence as it tried to jump after her, but she had already made it to a neighborhood sidewalk.

And right into a man's chest. She collided with him, as if she had hit a brick wall, and her knife skittered to the concrete. Two arms latched around her shoulders, and she flailed and kicked wildly at them, trying to escape. "Let me go you piece of shit!" She screamed.

"And here I am, coming to apologize," a voice said. The arms released her, and Krista stepped back to see Ryland looking down at her. "It's you," she said, out of breath.

She heard another growl from nearby. Both of them swiveled and saw the dark wolf-shaped shadows at the end of the street. "They're after me," Krista turned to Ryland, desperate. He looked at the wolves with anger, but not fear. She pushed further into his chest, coaxing him to move. "Hello! I'm trying not to die here!" She cried. She felt his strong hand grip her arm and she was nearly pulled off her feet as Ryland took off with her into the night.

They came to a nightclub, beats pounding through the walls and onto the sidewalk. Ryland took her down a dark alley off to the side, and made his way towards the 'staff only' entrance. "We can't just walk in here," Krista said. Ryland looked at her coldly. "You can take the front entrance then," he said. "Good luck getting past the bouncer while you're wearing sweatpants."

"Can't we go anywhere else but here?" She suggested. As an answer, Ryland pushed open the door, and let a thundering beat out into the alley.

"They can't track us in here," he said over the music, pulling her inside.

Krista tried to shrug his hand away, but he led her down a red-lit hallway and into a supply closet. "Let go of me," she said. Ryland promptly removed his hand. "Whatever," he said. "Not like I saved your life or anything..."

"Thanks...I guess," Krista said quietly. "You just happened to show up at the right time."

"I was actually on my way to your shop," Ryland clarified, grabbing a handful of paper towels and searching the shelves. "You looked horrified the other day. I wanted to know what it was you saw."

"You knew I saw something?"

"I thought it was pretty obvious. Unless your convulsing was from a seizure or something," he shrugged, finally finding a bottle of something. He knelt down next to Krista, his face just inches from hers. She could feel his breath on her cheek, and she felt her skin flush as if he had left an imprint. "What are you doing?" she asked when he grabbed the edge of her t-shirt. His fingers brushed lightly against her side.

"You're hurt," he said, pouring rubbing alcohol onto a paper towel.

"I can do it," Krista insisted.

"Fair enough," Ryland pulled back, the warmth of his touch leaving her. Krista dabbed the paper towel, and winced as the alcohol came into contact with her scraped-up skin. "I didn't know there were wolves in Central City," she said.

"That's because there aren't any wolves here," Ryland said. Krista's confusion led him to explain. "They're shifters. People with the spirit of a wolf inside of them. They can transform themselves—they have superior abilities—that kind of stuff."

Krista couldn't help herself, and her laughter found its way out. "That's ridiculous," she said. "How do you know that?"

"Because I am one," Ryland said matter-of-factly. Krista nearly keeled over, almost in hysterics.

"You laugh about shifters and yet you're a psychic?" Ryland said sternly.

This made Krista stop. I guess it wasn't that hard to believe, especially after all the strange things that she'd been seeing lately. "There were men in my shop earlier," she said. "That's why I was running in the first place. And then the wolves came."

"Men? What did they look like?"

"I don't know. They were wearing masks. Wolf masks. They were going to kidnap me. They called me something weird...what was it? Oracle?"

She looked into Ryland's eyes, only to see that he was dead serious. "So I was right," he said quietly.

"What do you mean?" Krista asked. Again with the mystery and ominous comments.

"You need to come back to my place," Ryland said. "It's not safe for you to go back."

"Can't I just stay somewhere else?"

Something in Ryland's eyes looked desperate. He clearly didn't want her to stay somewhere else. "I hate telling you this, but you are very important right now," Ryland said.

"Excuse me?"

"Your gift is incredibly strong. I sought you out because of it. Now I've realized that other shifters are trying to get you too."

"But why? What's so special about me?"

"You can see into the future. That's one of the most important gifts of all. You might actually be...the oracle."

Krista didn't know what to make of it. She could barely control her visions as they were. How was she supposed to believe she was so important? But the way Ryland kept looking at her told her that something serious was going on. The strange visions, the shadow haunting her dreams, the wolves chasing after her. It was all starting to make some sort of sense. On top of that, she was thinking of her fortune. She was The Fool, about to go on a journey, but one that surely led to destruction and danger.

"Alright," she said. "I'll go. But the second things get too sketchy, I'm out."

Ryland seemed somewhat pleased with her answer. As she followed him out of the nightclub she could only hope that she wasn't being played for an actual fool.

6. IN THE CARDS

It was bizarre for Ryland to see an outsider, a non-shifter, inside the Rogue's base. As he lined his pack up in the training room, he briefly wondered what they were going to think of Krista. Then, for another moment, he wondered why he was even thinking about her. Why did it matter to him if his pack liked her or not?

"Krista, these are the Rogues," he said, once Tristan had brought her into the room. The Rogues straightened up at the sight of her, as if Krista were royalty coming for a visit. Ryland took pride in them.

"Wow, very...tight formations," Krista commented.

"They're just as good at displaying themselves as they are at fighting," Ryland said. "Probably from all the hard work I've put into making them that way. "

"Nice to meet you all," Krista seemed slightly apprehensive. Ryland wondered if it was because she had never seen shifters before, and here she was suddenly surrounded by them. He introduced each pack member to her before dismissing them for training. "Would you like to watch them fight?" Ryland asked, eager to show off the skills of the pack.

Krista shrugged. "Don't we have some important things to discuss?" She asked.

"Just watch, only for a second," Ryland insisted.

He knew she didn't seem all too interested, but he didn't want to pass up on demonstrating the Rogue's strength to an outsider. He led Krista up the nearby steps to reach the upper-level walkway, making sure not to take her near the railing he had crushed the other day. "They train every day, four hours max," he said.

"And that's not exhausting for them?" Krista asked.

"They need the exercise. Gotta keep them sharp and ready at all times."

"For what?"

"Well, I'm hoping you'll help me figure that out." He turned to look at her. She turned and gave a small smile, keeping her arms crossed as she leaned against the railing. He realized he had never really seen a woman so comfortable in his presence. The other women in his pack wouldn't even look at him or lounge in the warehouse on their days off. His eyes trailed from Krista's fiery-red hair down her arched back, noticing the way the fabric of her t-shirt clung to the curves of her supple breasts.

Even though she was wearing sweatpants, he could still make out the shape of her—curvy with a tight waist he pictured wrapping his arms around. He tore his eyes away, feeling a strange quiver in his stomach. Maybe it was just the curse, but this feeling wasn't as hostile.

He had a slight urge, an ache to release some of his tension. It was common for a shifter to feel this way, especially if they didn't have a mate. He quickly pushed it from his mind. She was gorgeous, sure, but he was already caught in a mess. Advancing things with Krista would definitely make things more complicated.

A yelp from below broke his chain of thought. Dozens of faces turned up to look at Ryland. A wolf lay on the ground, whimpering next to his sparring partner. Ryland's jaw tightened. Accidents were one thing, but weakness had to be dealt with. He left Krista on the runway to watch as he stepped onto the mat. "What's going on?" He asked the sparring partners. The wolf shifted back into a blonde man, holding his arm at his side.

"I dislocated it," he explained quietly, avoiding eye contact with his alpha.

"Let me see," Ryland said, taking the arm in his hands. Both shifters seemed nervous as they eyed him. In a flash, Ryland shoved the shifter's arm violently back into its socket. The cracking sound echoed, making everyone around them wince. They could feel the shifter's pain as he tried to stifle his cries.

"Get back to fighting," Ryland said firmly. "Pain is just another obstacle."

The rest of his pack had nothing else to say. "This isn't a break," Ryland clarified to them. "I didn't say you guys could stop." They followed his orders. They were used to this sort of thing.

"What do you think?" He asked Krista once he rejoined her.

"Could be better," Krista said, leaving the railing.

"I agree. They're a little slower today."

"Not them. You. You're way too hard on them," she said. Ryland was confused. He was the strongest alpha in Central City. Why wouldn't he be hard on his pack?

"You're telling me how to lead my pack?" He asked her, a hint of gruffness in his voice.

"I guess so," Krista said, and then with a devilish smirk she asked him, "What are you going to do? Kick me out?" Ryland was flustered.

"If they get too comfortable, they'll walk all over you," he said. He wanted to give her a bigger piece of his mind, but decided to hold his tongue instead. For once, he couldn't think of a better comeback and he admired Krista's hidden fire.

"This is your room," Ryland kicked open the door to reveal what was practically a small cell. No decorations, hardly any furniture, white walls. The standard model for a Rogue. Krista's first reaction was to test the bed. It squeaked slightly as she sat on it, bouncing up and down for a moment. Ryland turned his eyes away from her moving breasts and cleared his throat.

"Definitely a downgrade from my place, but I'll manage," Krista said.

"We'll see about getting you some clothes," Ryland said as he noticed that she was still barefoot. "And probably a shower too."

To Ryland's shock, Krista sniffed her armpit instinctively. Who was this woman he'd brought into his place? "You can tell I stink?" Krista said with wide eyes.

"Wolves can smell something from miles away," he said. "So, yes."

"Yikes," Krista said, and laughed a musical laugh. Ryland found himself latching onto it. He had dedicated so much time to being an alpha that he had never really had the opportunity to be around women that much. It was an interesting change, to say the least.

Tristan's head leaned in the open doorway. "You wanted us all to talk?" He asked. Ryland ushered him inside and shut the door. Krista's eyes darted from the door to him. "You're safe," Ryland assured her, which made her relax.

"Let me be the first to ask," she said. "What's all this about an oracle? And how I'm supposed to be one?"

"An oracle?" Tristan asked. "Like the ones mentioned in the old shifter texts? I thought they were a myth."

"Hear me out," Ryland said. "Krista had a vision when I saw her. Hopefully, she's willing to tell us about it." His eyes shifted over to her.

"Do you get visions often?" Tristan asked her.

"I didn't use to," Krista explained. "But one night, I had a really bad one. I thought it was a dream until I met Ryland and then I had almost the same vision."

"What did you see?" Tristan prodded.

"I saw you," she said to Ryland, then pointed to Tristan. "And I think you were there too. It wasn't entirely clear. But there were wolves and a giant shadow that I can't seem to get out of my head."

"Like the ones I mentioned," Ryland said. Hopefully having Krista would make him seem less crazy about this curse.

"Then I did a reading," Krista continued. "With tarot cards. It said there was something evil in my future. I can only assume it was about this, right?"

"Can you do a reading for us now?" Tristan asked. "Do you think you could tell us more about what's been going on with the shifters going missing?"

"I can try," Krista said, reaching into her sweatpants pocket. She pulled out a beat-up stack of cards and shuffled them, watching the two shifters nervously. She laid out several cards and studied them.

Ryland waited impatiently—he wanted answers. However, after a few long minutes Krista gathered the cards and shook her head, trying again, and then again. "What's wrong?" Tristan asked.

Krista seemed slightly distracted and a little embarrassed. "I'm, uh, I can't pick up anything," she said quietly.

"Well maybe try reading my palm again," Ryland suggested. He sat on the bed next to her, feeling the warmth radiating from her body to his. Krista took his hand, spread out his fingers and closed her eyes in concentration. But there was no convulsing or sputtering. She simply opened her eyes and let go. "Nothing..." she said somberly.

Ryland stood alone in the center of the training mat. He had told Krista to stay in her room until he could figure out a plan. After her visions had failed to come, Krista seemed distraught. Ryland worried that maybe he had made the wrong choice. Maybe she wasn't the oracle after all. Then, he remembered he had read something about a tool—an ancient family heir-loom—that Krista might find useful. If he could recover it, then maybe she'd have a better chance of seeing into the future.

His fist pummeled a punching bag, over and over. He shifted, snapping his jaws at the moving target. As he did, something caught his attention. A scent, one that he hadn't encountered in a very long time. A faint musk wafting from afar. He turned his head toward the source, but the smell disappeared as quickly as it had arrived. It was a ghost from the past, and although he tried to push it away it still managed to haunt him.

Christoph?

7. HISTORY

Krista couldn't stand the cramped feeling she got from the walls of her cell, as she began to call it. A couple of days had passed since she had been taken to the strange shifter base. Sometimes she'd get to walk around, and would witness men and women turning into wolves. They were fascinating—people caught between two worlds. Krista found herself relating to them somehow. Surely her clients would be wondering about her and why her shop hadn't been open for a while. Yet, Krista felt that she didn't have to worry about it. She was in a new world now, one that promised something better for her abilities.

But something was off. She was discouraged that she hadn't been able to summon her visions the other night, and she could sense that Ryland and his beta were feeling the same. How was she going to be an oracle when she couldn't even muster a brief hint of the future? She still wasn't even sure what she was supposed to do as an oracle.

No matter how hard she tried, she found herself staring at a blank slate. Maybe it was just nerves or the environment. A white prison-looking cell certainly wasn't doing any good for her psychic energy. She needed to get out and get some fresh air, which is precisely why she snuck out of her room to explore the rest of the Rogue's warehouse.

She actually loved the black sneakers Ryland had left for her. What he lacked in hospitality he made up for in style. The Rogues all wore hip athletic clothes, mainly in black. The jogger sweatpants and the tank top she had chosen were particularly comfortable.

Trying her best not to look out of place, she wandered down the maze of hallways, most of them containing supplies and dorm rooms like hers. The warehouse had been converted, from top to bottom, into a functional facility, almost like the inside of a nice gym you'd see in the city, though it definitely didn't look like it from the outside.

She found the kitchen, communal showers (which she only used late at night), and several reading rooms for the younger shifters to do schoolwork in. Finally, after perusing the hallways, she found one in particular that had nothing but a single room at the end. She felt her stomach flutter at the sight of a "Keep Out" sign, wondering with burning curiosity at what could be inside. Ryland was off with Tristan and there was no telling when he'd come back. She figured she'd have just enough time to peek in.

Double checking her surroundings, she snuck over to the door and just tested the doorknob lightly. Unlocked! But it was dark inside. She felt along the wall for a light switch. As it flipped on, she couldn't believe how this room could possibly be in the warehouse. It was a scholar's paradise that gave off the coziest vibes. Krista immediately felt herself sinking into the comfort of the room, admiring the strings of lights along the walls, the shelves stocked with books, and the old rugs and floor pillows nestled around an antique table.

It was all so out of place. *This has to be Tristan's room for sure*, she thought as she ran her fingers along an elegant chestnut wardrobe, tempted to peek inside. But there were other matters to attend to. Tristan had mentioned something about ancient shifter texts. Perhaps she'd find something about past oracles in one of his books. Her eyes drifted along the shelves until she found one that seemed promising. *"Ancient Tales of the Shift,"* was etched in gold on the ragged cover. She sat on the pillows in front of the table, poring over the pages. There were old illustrations, anatomies of shifters and the like.

One section caught her attention. It was a portrait of a woman, steeped in reverence. She was dressed in a flowing hooded gown, her arms outstretched and her eyes completely white. She was floating, wisps of energy surrounding her. Krista immediately felt like a stark contrast to this powerful woman, but still took the time to read the block of text next to the image.

"The Oracle's spirit inhabits but one woman, sometimes months, sometimes centuries apart. From the day she is born, the woman who houses the spirit devotes herself to the craft of clairvoyance. The Oracle's spirit often becomes more prominent in times of crisis, when she is most needed. Once the host has mastered summoning the Oracle's spirit, she will be granted unimaginable power."

It sounded pretty exciting to Krista, although she felt a flicker of anxiety taking her over. Suddenly she felt that she couldn't take in any more of the text. The more she read about it, the more inadequate she felt about her own abilities. She replaced the book on the shelf, and instead studied the trinkets and bottles that were laid out in the empty spaces. It reminded her of how her mom's shop used to look before she took most of the valuable things with her. Krista recognized some items as potions. She popped the cork out of one and took a whiff. It was ghastly, like soured milk.

She read the label: *Brittlesbane and Hogstooth*. Now, she wasn't a witch or a herbologist in any way, but she knew those ingredients were used to ward off evil spirits. Most of the contents had been consumed already, and she wondered why Tristan would need to take it.

Already she felt as if she had spent too much time in the room, but there was so much to see. There were sketchbooks, filled with images of wolves and one ripped image that Krista recognized as a shadow. As she made her way back to the table, she noticed an open book flipped over onto its pages. As she picked it up, a slip of paper floated to the floor. She grabbed it and saw that it was a picture of two little boys.

One of them had glasses, a toothless grin and dark hair with a hint of red. His arm was around the other boy who was dressed in a baseball uniform. Krista didn't think much of it, assuming the boy with glasses was Tristan. However, something caught her by surprise.

As they both stared up at her, she noticed that they both had the same pair of deep olive-green eyes. She dropped the picture immediately, then flipped over the book. Letters, addressed to 'brother', but which had obviously never been sent, sat waiting in the pages of what seemed to be a scrapbook. There were more pictures, and slowly the realization sunk in that this wasn't Tristan's room.

It was Ryland's.

"I thought your orders were to stay in your room," A voice startled Krista, making her flip the book back over in a panic. She stood up from the antique table, her hands at her sides, straight as an arrow. Ryland sauntered over to her from the doorway, picking up the book. He noticed the old picture tucked into the crack and grimaced as he closed it. "Snooping around, I see," he said. He sounded different, more aggressive than sarcastic.

"I'm really sorry. I thought this was Tristan's room or something. Either way, I shouldn't have been snooping."

Ryland ignored her. Krista hated how cold he was all the time. If only there was a way to lighten him up. "I learned about the oracles," she told him. "Since you never got around to telling me. You mentioned something about a tool, an artifact that I could use. Something that could maybe help us."

"I was just about to retrieve it, actually," Ryland said.

"Fantastic," Krista sighed. "I need to get out of this place."

"I didn't say you were coming with me."

Krista exchanged a stern glance with him. If she was supposed to be helping him, then why was he keeping her locked up?

"Why not?" She challenged. "Too *dangerous*?"

"Too *complicated*," Ryland corrected her. "I just need to run in and run out. I'd just be waiting for you to catch up."

"I'd watch your words if I were you," Krista said. "For all we know I'm carrying the spirit of a very powerful oracle."

Ryland thought for a moment. Her words were taking some form of shape into his mind. Finally he gave an annoyed growl. "Fine," he said. "But don't think I'm going to rescue you if something goes wrong."

"I jumped out of a window to escape evil shifters," Krista said with a smirk. "I think I can handle myself just fine." She brushed past him on her way out. "Come on," she said. "Let's go fetch."

8. BONES

"So, what are we looking for exactly?" Krista's voice emerged from behind a tombstone. Ryland scoped out the old cemetery, his eyes trailing over the towering headstones and cracking monuments that belonged to the dead. He tried to catch a scent hoping to avoid a run-in with those shifters, but the air was too cold and stung his nose. He was confident he could take some of them down in a fight. But it would be a whole other obstacle to keep Krista alive. He shouldn't have brought her along.

"My great grandfather's tomb is just around here," Ryland said from another row of graves. "We're looking for bones."

"Well, there are plenty of those around here." Krista joked. Ryland managed to crack a smile. It had been a while since he laughed at something so cheesy, but he would never let Krista see that. He stepped over the raised bricks in the warped stone pathway, scanning each of the names on the large mausoleums, made of dark stone. "Shifter blood runs strong in my family," he said. "I come from a long line of alphas. Most of them are buried here. I've been going through my family's records lately, and found that when he died, my great-grandfather was buried with a bag of ancient oracle bones."

"That's the tool we're looking for?" Krista asked.

"Precisely. Once we have them, you can use them to help you see into the future. Then we can finally figure out what's been going on around here."

"So...what exactly has been going on?" Krista stepped out of a row of headstones, nearly bumping into Ryland.

"Shifters are going missing. Most likely they're being sacrificed. My pack and I caught word of a powerful weapon being developed, though we're not sure what it is. When we investigated a potential lead, we were attacked and found a sacrificial room." He almost didn't want to tell her about the shadows. But if Krista really was the Oracle, any piece of information might help her figure out the mess they were in.

"Nobody in my pack saw this," he added. "But I attacked a shifter. Tried to stop him from killing himself with a crystal dagger. But I was too late, and I saw...a strange shadow come out of him."

He looked over at Krista, who stared straight ahead as they walked past more mausoleums. She was deep in thought about something and seemed slightly disturbed. Maybe she thought he was crazy. But he continued on. "I think the shadow might have something to do with a curse," he said. "I used to think that was all bunk. But...things have been different lately since we left that place. Ah, here we are."

They stopped in front of an elegant vault made of stone. The roof stretched into a pointed top. Two doors waited for them, elegantly decorated with golden patterns. The large plaque above the doors read "IKER" in sharp letters. "My family has expensive taste," he said as he reached into his pocket, producing a key. As he turned it and opened the door, however, he was startled to find nothing but a wall of brick on the other side.

"What the hell?" Ryland said.

"Does your family have a sense of humor too?" Krista scoffed. Ryland paced, wondering how they could get inside. Moments passed before he even realized Krista was gone. "Ah, here's something," she said from the other side of the vault. Ryland wandered towards her, wondering what she could possibly be up to. Krista proudly pointed to the back of the structure, where a small section of bricks had been removed towards the top. "Give me a lift?" She asked. Ryland was skeptical, but she was serious.

Begrudgingly, he ducked down, letting Krista straddle her thighs over the back of his neck. He lifted her, feeling her weight on his shoulders and the sides of her jeans brushing against his cheek. Her slender fingers wove into his hair while she tried to find her balance. With his arms wrapped around her thighs, Ryland felt a brief shudder that he tried to shrug off. He was getting warmer now, his mind wandering to more intimate thoughts of Krista. But once her body left him, so did those thoughts, and Ryland could only watch with silent admiration as Krista shimmied inside.

Taking a risk, he peeked at her tight, round bottom before it squeezed its way past the bricks and disappeared onto the other side.

"Are you coming?" Krista's muffled voice called out.

"Not quite," Ryland muttered under his breath. He shifted, his paws scraping against the stone as he leaped up, clumsily trying to get through the wall. He realized he was stuck, and panicked, but felt Krista's hands grabbing his paws and tugging at them. His wolf, for some reason was angry and frustrated, and told him to bite at her, but he resisted.

He shifted back as he hit the bottom. Krista stared at him in surprise, with a flashlight in her hand. "What? He asked. You've seen people shift already."

"Yeah," she said, impressed. "But not you. That was kind of awesome, actually."

This time, Ryland let her see his smile. He took the light from her, shining it over the rows of plaques. Eventually, it fell on a large stone coffin. Terrance S. Iker. "This is it," Ryland said as he and Krista struggled to push aside the lid.

"Hey Great-grandpa," he said to the dust-covered skeleton inside.

"Yikes. This is so disrespectful," Krista said with a wince.

"If we're saving the world, I'm sure he'd understand," Ryland said. He reached in, touching the old bones of his great-grandfather's arms and spreading them apart.

He stepped back in shock. They were gone. The velvet pouch with the oracle bones had already been taken, somehow. "Damn it!" He cursed as he turned to kick at a stone wall.

"Oh Ryland, look!" Krista took the flashlight and pointed it at a freshly laid brick wall, messily closing off the front doors. "Someone clearly didn't want us to come in here."

"Whoever they are, they've walked away with our prize," Ryland muttered. He clutched at his arm that was spreading a burn throughout his body. He coughed as he held his chest. Whispering flooded his ears, telling him violent and terrible things. He felt like exploding, to tear himself open just to be rid of them.

But then a hand touched his shoulder, and immediately silenced them. "You okay?" Krista asked. Ryland realized he was crouched on the floor, and recovered himself.

"Fine," he said, clinging onto the feeling of peace that she brought him.

As they made their way towards the main gate, Ryland caught a scent. "They're here," he said. "The shifters." He grabbed Krista's hand, and then he saw them, nearly a whole pack lined up under the yellow lights on the cemetery path. They growled in warning, all of them dark blurs blending in with the night. Then they ran. "Shit!" Ryland pulled at Krista's hand, turning around to run deeper into the cemetery. Their breath melded in the dark, clouds rising from their mouths. Ryland's legs burned and his chest ached from the cold. There had to be another exit. A flash of teeth lunged out at them from a nearby headstone. Ryland rammed his shoulder into a wolf, feeling a bite sink into his flesh. He threw the wolf to the ground, as he cried out in pain.

With his back against Krista's, he gazed over the headstones, wondering where the next enemy would appear. A threatening chorus of growls surrounded them. There was no way out. "I can hold them off while you run," Ryland said. "You want us both to die?" Krista asked. "Because that's definitely what's going to happen." Ryland then felt a tug at his elbow.

"Oh! This way," Krista said. The wolves were getting closer, panting as Krista pulled open what looked like a large cellar door just off the path. "This is a better idea?" Ryland shouted, but Krista pushed him through and slammed the doors shut behind them, just as a barrage of claws tried to grab for them.

They could still hear them, their irritated growls as they clawed at the metal. They settled, running off as they tried to find another route. Then, Ryland felt Krista's breath on the back of his neck. "Close one," she said in the darkness. The flashlight clicked on, flooding them with white light. "Whoa, check this out," Krista said, shining the beam down a dark tunnel.

"I don't think we should...," he started to say.

"Could be another way out of here," she suggested and started into the nothingness.

Ryland followed her, the tunnel narrowing around them. Water dripped along the walls, spilling into small rivers near their feet. He could feel his body pressing against Krista's in the close quarters. "Oh my God!" Krista shouted with fright. Out of instinct, Ryland grabbed her and pressed her against a wood-covered wall. "What is it?" He swung his head from one side of the tunnel to the other. Krista put her hand on her heart and laughed.

"Just a rat," she said with a sigh. "What a relief. Thanks for saving me though." She winked as she gently pushed Ryland away and continued on.

"Geez, don't scare me like that," Ryland scoffed. Out of the corner of his eye, he noticed strange shapes painted along the walls. "Point the light here," he told Krista. Krista turned, her shoulder awkwardly digging into his chest. "Sorry," she said with an awkward smile. Ryland could smell the flowery scent of her hair as it brushed against his chin. It was so easy to wrap his arms around her here, though he knew he absolutely couldn't.

He regained his focus, concentrating instead on the sprawling artwork along the walls. "It's some kind of story," Krista said, using the light to follow along with the tunnel.

There were rough images of men. As they walked they became more and more wolf-like until they were on all fours. Dark shadows floated in patterns along the wall, pouring out from the wolf-men. They reached the end and discovered a haunting image waiting for them there. There was a woman, made in blue, trapped in a box. Next to it, the shadows from the wolves blended into a massive wolf monster. Its jaws were agape, fire pouring from it.

"I've seen this before," Krista whispered. "When I first touched you..."

"This was your vision?" Ryland asked. He followed her gaze towards the wolf monster. Inside it was the light shadow of a man. Ryland stared at it, clutching at his arm again. Was that supposed to be him?

9. DISTRACTIONS

They were startled to find that the tunnel brought them out near a grimy river flowing under an overpass. The city was just a short climb up a nearby hill. Krista was relieved that they had made it out alive. Those shifters were terrifying to run into. But what stuck with her the most were the paintings on the wall. They looked as if someone had made them recently. Who else could know about these shadows? Who was that woman, drawn in the box? Krista felt her heart beating. Something was coming together, though she wasn't quite sure what it was.

> Meanwhile, Ryland was steaming with rage, throwing curses left and right. "We were so close!" He lamented. "Who the hell would have thought to break into that place anyway?" As he raged in his tantrum, Krista's eye caught something near the tunnel.

"What's this?" she asked, holding up a scrap of fabric. It was a patch, the kind you'd sew onto a jacket.

The pattern was a wolf's head, partly covered in shadow. Ryland raised it to his nose and grimaced. "Figures," Ryland said. "This patch belongs to a rival pack, the Stalkers. I should have known Declan had something to do with this."

"Declan? Is he your brother?"

Ryland turned quickly and eyed her with a wave of fierce anger that she'd never seen in him before. It was startling. "What do you know about my brother?" He growled. Krista could only think of the picture of the two boys. The boy in glasses with his arm around Ryland.

"Nothing at all! I just know that you have one," she said. "Geez, what's with you?"

Ryland took a breath. "Sorry," he said as he started following the river towards the overpass. "It's just...not my favorite thing to discuss."

"Why not?" Krista prodded. She learned Ryland had this way of shrugging everything off. But she had a feeling that underneath, there was something else about him that she wanted to crack into. After all, what would a hot-headed, combat-driven guy like him be doing in a beautiful room full of books and cozy pillows?

She sat down beside him on the riverbank. It was cold, and they were tired from their fruitless journey to get the oracle bones. Without them, Krista wondered if she could be any more help to Ryland and his pack. If she couldn't, at least she wanted to help Ryland at this moment.

"Well?" She nudged at his side. He was firm as a rock and didn't budge. "His name was Christoph," Ryland said curtly. "We grew up together, but very different. He was more scholarly. My parent's pushed me to go into sports and pretty much everything else in my life. Christoph, not so much. We spent our entire childhoods competing with each other, but we were still best friends at the end of each day."

"What happened to him?" Krista asked. Ryland's brow was furrowed. He rested his elbows on his knees. Krista eyed them, wanting to put her hand on one of them to comfort him.

"I got a baseball scholarship. He got his literature degree. We regrouped and formed the Rogues in Central City shortly after," Ryland said as he ran his fingers through his hair and looked up at the sky. "He said I should be alpha. He was my beta. That was already a mistake. I wanted to train the pack, to teach them to be the best they could be. He wanted to make it into more of a community. We couldn't compromise. I kicked him out."

"Seems a bit harsh."

"That's what I thought. But, I figured if you're trying to lead the strongest pack in the city, some sacrifices have to be made."

"You really care about your pack, don't you?"

"It's the only thing I have. And because of this curse, I fear it's driving them away." Krista watched as he stared down at his shoes.

"Are you even sure that it's a curse?" She asked him.

"The rest of the pack doesn't know it but...I'm positive that it is a curse of some kind," Ryland said. His hand clasped absentmindedly around his arm.

The more Krysta studied him, the way his jaw clenched and how he shifted his weight made her feel that there was something else behind Ryland's tough façade. "You have it, don't you?" She found herself asking. Ryland's eyes shifted sideways at her, and suddenly a tremor wavered through her body. "The curse. It's why you didn't let me see your right hand for the palm reading. It's why you have those potions in your room. You're trying to stop it."

Without fear, she reached over, grabbing his right arm and drawing it towards her. She pulled up the sleeve of his jacket, turning his hand palm up under hers. She felt him pull away.

"Don't," he said, but she held tightly.

"It's okay," she said. "I want to help you."

He relaxed under her touch. Krista carefully unraveled the gauze around his wound. There was a single black splotch, like a raised bruise, spreading out inky black tendrils along the rest of Ryland's arm. "Does it hurt?" She quietly asked. Ryland nodded. "It's been spreading," he said.

Krista could hear the pain in his voice, and her heart softened for him. Sure, he had been harsh towards her when they had met, but at this moment she felt like another Ryland was next to her. Maybe this one was gentler, kinder. She traced the dark markings with her fingertips.

"I need to find the cure," he said. "I can't lead my pack like this, and I don't know how much time I have until..."

"Until what?" It was like an ominous blanket of darkness was suddenly draped over them.

"I don't know," he said. "That's what I'm trying to find out. But I have a feeling it's not going to be good."

"Do you think it's the same thing we saw in the tunnel?"

"Maybe..."

They sat in silence for a while, listening to the rush of the nearby river and the whooshing of cars on the overpass. Neither of them knew what time it was, but it was getting late. It was a moment before Krista realized she was still holding Ryland's hand. Something inside of her told her not to let go. Despite her wishes, though, he slipped his hand from hers and wrapped up the black wound.

"I meant to tell you during your reading," Krista said, trying to conjure up something to say. She liked this softer side of Ryland and wanted him to stay as long as possible. "I noticed you don't have a heart-line."

"A what?" Ryland asked.

"Look," Krista turned her hand over to show him, tracing her fingers along her palm. "In palmistry, your heart-line gives you insight to your love life," she explained.

"But I don't have one. Does that mean I'm doomed to a loveless life, fortune teller?" Ryland smirked. It was charming and sweet.

Krista knew she was walking down a path she never wanted to go too far on. "Well, it means a lot of other things too," she said with a laugh. "Palmistry was never my strong suit, though. That was more of mom's specialty. She basically taught me everything I know. Of course, it was all against my will."

"Sounds like my parents," Ryland scoffed. "They pushed me every day, from school to baseball, to piano lessons, my life has been one booked schedule."

"That's rough. But at least you got to go to school. I spent all my time locked up in the shop learning tarot and everything else under the psychic sun."

"But you're very talented because of it."

"I don't know. Mom used to tell me this was all going to help me in the future. I guess if she's a powerful psychic I should trust her. But sometimes, I'm not even sure if I'm doing any of this the right way. I tell people their fortunes, help them shape their futures, but how can I even be sure that any of my work is good? I mean, these are other people's lives I'm dealing with."

"Well, if I've learned anything from being an alpha, it's that at the end of the day, you've given it your best. The best thing to do is be even better tomorrow."

"Hmm, I like that."

Ryland turned to her, and while he looked into her eyes, Krista felt her hand being turned over in his. "You're so keen on telling me about my love life," he said. "But what can we learn about yours?"

Krista felt a flutter in her chest. She felt embarrassed even mentioning her love life in front of him, if she could even call it that. "Funnily enough," she said. "I have a strong heart-line, but it hasn't quite, uh, shown itself these days."

"What do you mean?" Ryland asked.

"Well, I feel like psychics get a bad rep. People automatically think I'm a con artist or something, or that I'm going to trick people out of their money. There's also the whole clairvoyance thing. Sometimes when I'm, uh, on a date or anything, I can see a glimpse of the future with that person."

"I bet a lot of people wished they had that."

"It's almost like my own curse, all jokes aside. It kind of scares me to be with someone if I can peek at what's going to happen next."

"Isn't that the point? What's love without some risk?"

He was still holding onto her hand. Krista wondered where this was going...if it was going anywhere. Her mind was buzzing, and already she was wondering if she was going to have a vision right there. She only hoped it would be something good.

"Can I take a risk?" Krista said quietly. The world seemed to silence around them.

"Will it put your life in danger?" Ryland asked.

"Possibly," Krista said. She turned her hand over, holding onto his as she leaned in. She could feel Ryland's anticipation on his lips even before she pressed hers onto them. At first, it was soft, two people trying to figure out where the other stood. But then, Krista placed her hand on Ryland's warm cheek, her fingers brushing his stubble.

Ryland moved in closer, his warmth pressing against her as he pulled her waist closer towards him. He was going along for the ride, and soon their kiss was fiery. Hands entangled in each other's hair, lips exchanging deep, passionate kisses. Krista felt a shock traveling through her, spreading towards her loins. This wasn't a vision, it was all so real.

Ryland's nose brushed against hers. His eyes opened softly to look at her before kissing her again. Soon, his hands traveled somewhere else, his fingers brushing against her skin as he inched them under the fabric of her sweater. He pressed Krista onto her back, and she looked up at the towering skyline as he laid next to her, leaning on one arm and searching her with the other. His fingertips tickled her sides, gently gliding up her stomach as they kissed.

Krista could feel the bulge as soon as Ryland slid up against her. It grazed along her leg, pressing into her jeans, wanting so badly to explore her as well. Her mind was flooded with all kinds of thoughts. She was nervous, excited, and a bit terrified. But she held on, her hand wandering towards Ryland's crotch. He gave a slight moan at her touch, which fueled her to keep going. She clutched him tightly, noticing how large he was.

He was breathing heavily now, almost hungrily. His hand had just barely reached her breast, and he cupped it under his palm, kneading it, wanting to tear the delicate fabric between them. Krista sighed onto his lips as her hand trailed past his waistband, her fingers running along the band of his briefs. She went for it, sliding her hand over his elongated cock, and Ryland exhaled in response. She liked this other side of him too, a man that wanted to be putty in her hands. She could feel him pulsing in her grip and rubbed her thumb along his tip until she could feel the beads of warmth seeping from it.

Ryland let go of her breast, tightly clutching her waist. He bent down for another kiss, his lips pressing hard against her.

"Ow-" Krista gasped, feeling a sharp sting on her lip. Ryland quickly pulled away.

"I'm sorry," he said. "I'm so sorry...I just...I don't know what came over me." Krista touched her bottom lip, examining her finger to see a droplet of blood on her fingertip. "It's fine," she said, but the shock of Ryland's bite exhilarated her. She wanted to continue, but Ryland left her, standing up to brush himself off.

"I got carried away," he said.

"It's okay, really. I did too."

Ryland cleared his throat and steadied his breath. "I think we should, uh, be more careful," he said in a more constricted tone. "I mean, I don't want either of us to get hurt."

"Sure," Krista said, quiet and defeated, though she tried her best to hide it. "It's probably for the best."

"I'm glad you understand," Ryland reached down his hand, and Krista absentmindedly took it.

"So, should we call it a night?" She asked, a slight tug pulling at her chest. Ryland nodded curtly. "We found this Stalker patch. I think we should look into it tomorrow. You...can accompany me again if you want."

"Of course," Krista said, and watched as Ryland wandered up the hill, his hands thrust in his pockets. She could still feel the imprint of him, the touch of his hand on hers. As she followed behind him, she wondered if that was the first and last time he would ever touch her.

10. WRONG TURF

Ryland examined the patch in his hand. It reeked of Declan and his pack, with a slight touch of musk that reminded him of the wolves they had encountered in the cemetery. He sat on the cluster of pillows in front of his antique coffee table, resting his head on it as he mulled over the events of the night before. Without the oracle bones, he wasn't sure if he would be able to get a clear reading from Krista. He wondered about the bricked-up wall that covered the entrance to his grandfather's tomb. If someone had already taken the bones, why would they go to the trouble of bricking up the wall to keep others out?

Something had also deeply disturbed Ryland. The only person with access to his books was Tristan, and he could have known about the Oracle bones as well. The more Ryland thought about it, the more he began to question his beta. But he couldn't think of a reason why Tristan would betray him.

He found his thoughts drifting to other parts of the night. A flash in his memory came over him. His hands running along the smoothest skin he had ever felt. He could still hear the soft moan escaping her lips as he kissed her. Maybe it was because he had opened the door for her. He hadn't told a single soul about the curse, so what had made him so comfortable that he'd told her? She had barely spent any time around him, yet anytime she was near his instincts were dying to be unleashed. Maybe because he wasn't used to being spoken to the way Krista spoke to him. He wondered what would have happened if he hadn't stopped himself.

His thoughts ceased in their tracks as if they were on screeching brakes. He couldn't allow himself to go there, to indulge in thoughts of Krista when his life and the safety of his pack were on the line. If he pursued her any longer, it would just make trouble for him and everyone around them. Hadn't Christoph always warned him to stay away from girls?

Still, he lifted his head slightly, stretching out his fingers to look at his palm. His eyes traced along the empty space where his heart-line belonged. A knock on his door brought him back to reality, and Krista stepped inside with a steaming mug. He was wondering when he'd next be seeing her. They hadn't spoken at all about what had happened between them and probably wouldn't dare to.

Krista made herself comfortable beside him as if she had shared the space with him for years. She pushed the mug towards him. It had a calming floral scent. "Chamomile," she told him. Ryland looked into the cup. "I don't drink tea," he said, turning his attention to a bottle containing a makeshift potion. It was awful, but it helped with some of the pain the curse was dishing out on him. Before he could drink the potion, though, Krista's hand snatched the vial.

"Well, now's a perfect time to start," she told him, pushing the cup even closer. "Come on, it'll make you feel relaxed."

Ryland eyed her hand clasped around his potion. He sighed and took a sip of the warm beverage. His senses detected just a hint of honey had been added to sweeten it up. "So, without the bones what are we supposed to do?" She asked. "Are you going to tell the other packs about the curse?"

Ryland handed her the patch they had found near the tunnel. "Not yet," he said as she studied it. "We have to make a stop at one of Declan's old territories. For all we know, one of his shifters may have stolen the oracle bones."

"Why don't you ask the other shifter factions?"

"It'll get back around to Declan. We're all connected and I'm trying to keep this whole thing as contained as I can."

He looked over at her, watching her mind working. Yesterday had actually been somewhat enjoyable for him, having Krista come along, and he was willing to let her be his companion again.

It was an old fish market near Central City's bay area. Declan and the Stalkers often used to hold meetings in this place. That is until the peace treaty had been made and territorial lines were drawn to keep the factions in their place. It wasn't quite clear why Declan was a rival to Ryland. Perhaps it was because he didn't have to work hard to form a strong shifter pack. Either that or it was just the fact that he was an absolute asshole. Ryland figured it was the second option. Declan was smug, and always had something up his sleeve. It wouldn't be a surprise if he was really behind the shifters disappearing.

Ryland reared his head and covered his nose with the sleeve of his denim jacket. Though it was long abandoned, the old market still had a leftover fishy smell that clung to the walls. Krista made a disgusted sound as she ducked under the broken beams and followed him.

"Are you sure we'll even find someone in this place?" She asked.

"Surprisingly, the scent led me to this place, ," he replied. "But I'm not picking up Stalker scent anymore. In fact...it's more like...something familiar."

He wandered into an empty corridor, where a row of unused freezer rooms was lined up. The further he explored, the stronger the scent became. Then he realized he was smelling the same thing as he had smelled in the warehouse, just before he was attacked with his wretched curse: Blood.

"Krista?" he asked, worried that it was her blood being spilled without him even knowing. He would have sighed with relief if he hadn't seen her eyes rolling into the back of her head. He rushed over to her, catching her as he knees gave out. As soon as he did, she came to and clutched at her head. He caught a whiff of her vetiver-smelling hair. It reminded him of ancient magic and mystery.

"Fish smell really got to you, huh?" Ryland joked. Krista flashed a smile but was obviously distraught as she caught her breath. "A vision," she said. "It just...snuck up on me."

"What of?" Ryland felt his heart quicken. "Did you see where the bones are?" Krista shook her head. "No," she said. "I saw a wolf. It happened so fast, but I saw a yellow arrow, a concrete room and a patch of brown fur." She seemed deeply disturbed, to Ryland's horror.

"Come on, it might be here." He helped her to her feet, gently guiding her by the elbow towards the hallway. The smell of blood was growing stronger as they kept moving. "That's the arrow!" Krista suddenly exclaimed as she pointed ahead of them. A professionally-painted yellow arrow pointed down another dark hallway, barely lit by the sun that bled into the cracks in the concrete.

They followed it, Ryland worrying about what they would find on the other side. He hoped it wouldn't be Declan. He would never admit it, but he felt that Declan's strength nearly matched his own, even if he did kick his ass in the warehouse the other day.

"This concrete's looking awfully familiar," Krista whispered in the dark. Ryland could pick up a hint of trembling in her voice. He knew he wanted to go first, just to keep her from seeing anything too gruesome. They passed by more freezers, but as soon as they reached one at the end of the hall, Ryland picked up two more scents. He held his arm out to stop Krista, his eyes widening.

Shifters. Two. But neither of them was Declan, or of Stalker blood. He didn't want it to be true, not after hearing about what happened with the other packs. But as he inched closer to a cracked-open freezer room, he had his horror confirmed. As he pulled open the door, he felt a searing pain in his arm, and a fierce wriggling under his skin that he tried to stop but to no avail. The curse was attracted to this place and in seconds he'd find out why.

There, in the center of a large empty freezer, were dozens of candles lit in a circle. A dark figure hunched over something large on the ground, whispering strange words that Ryland picked up from time to time. He couldn't bear to let the same scene play out again. He kicked open the door with ferocity and shifted into his wolf form, bounding towards the figure.

The figure turned and cried out in shock, quickly shifting just as Ryland sank his teeth into his shoulder. Ryland shook him, a growl rattling in his throat as he threw the stranger against the wall. He reeked of that mysterious pack musty—almost like sewer water and rats.

He felt a bite in his neck, digging into his veins. Suddenly, Ryland felt overcome by a tremendous rage, unlike anything he had ever felt. It was a fire burning in his chest. He needed to shed blood, to taste his enemy and rip him to shreds. Ryland backed off from his enemy, taking a nip at his heel while dodging the gaping jaws headed right for his side.

They were a flurry of fur and gnashing teeth until the enemy shoved Ryland into the flames of the nearby candles. Ryland yelped and struggled to roll, cleansing his back of the flames. As he did, it gave the other shifter a chance to escape. He could only watch as the wolf shifted back into a hooded figure, frozen as he stared at Krista. Krista was trying to close the door to keep him from escaping. It was clear that the shifter had taken an interest in her.

"Don't touch me!" Krista's cries were amplified in Ryland's ears. The figure bent down and it one swift motion, it had carried Krista off into the hallway. Ryland growled as he tumbled to his feet, chasing after the man in the hood. His paws skittered along the concrete, while fish and blood mixed in his nose.

He was gaining on him, but the man turned a corner sharply and Ryland found himself skidding into a wall. Krista's cries echoed through the hall as she tried to break herself free from the man's shoulder. As Ryland caught up to them, he saw that she had somehow been successful. She fell to the ground, while the man held his eye in agony, blood spilling through his fingers.

Ryland's feet left the ground and he soared towards the man, his jaws open. He landed on his chest, growling in his face. The man tried to shift, but could only muster a slight change in his face.

"Who are you?" Krista shouted at the stranger. "Who are you working for?"

The man squirmed under Ryland's weight. He seemed calm—an older and more experienced shifter—but Ryland could see the real terror in his dark eyes.

"I thought you would know the answers to that, Oracle," he said.

"You know I'm the Oracle?" Krista prodded with disbelief.

"Of course. I was promised a higher rank if I brought you to the pack," the man said, his voice cracking under the pressure. "Along with the bones and the wolf soul."

"You have the bones," Krista stated. "What is your pack planning?"

"I am bound to my pack by blood. I will never betray them, even if it means sudden death."

Ryland couldn't bear to hear him talk anymore. The violent thoughts and urges were overwhelming him and the lack of information from the shifter only infuriated him more. He lashed out with his jaws, and as he did, he felt as though five long seconds were slipping away, right before his eyes, with no memory of how he lost them. He couldn't even hear Krista's terrified screams.

When he came to, there wasn't a man anymore, only a ragged pile of flesh and blood attached to the bones of a man. Ryland shifted back, quickly removing himself from his kill. For some reason, the pain had subsided inside of him, as if a thirst had been quenched. He could still taste the rusted iron on his tongue as he wiped his face.

Krista was staring at him, trembling. As he tried to move closer, she scooted herself away, her eyes locked on his.

"Are you okay?" He asked quietly.

"Do you always do that?" Krista's voice was barely a whisper. His heart sank. He didn't mean to, and he didn't want to. But the curse felt otherwise. He could only shake his head and held out his hand, hoping desperately that she would take it. She didn't.

"He has the bones," Krista said her eyes avoiding his. "He was going to take me to his pack."

Ryland bent down next to the fresh corpse, so she wouldn't have to. He searched every pocket until, finally, he found a dark satin pouch. He shook it, hearing the crackle inside as if stones were rubbing together. Opening it, he discovered it was the oracle bones, small and pearly, and etched with ancient runes.

"Is that them?" Krista asked from afar. Ryland nodded. He understood why she didn't want to be around him, but it still stung him.

"You said you saw a wolf," Ryland said. "Was it him?"

"No," Krista said.

That's what Ryland thought. He didn't want to believe the third element of Krista's vision, but it didn't stop him from trailing back to the freezer room. There had been two shifters after all. Some candles remained, casting a faint glow over the lifeless carcass of a wolf in the center of the room. He bent down in front of it, placing his hand on the cold body in reverence.

He had found her, just as the other alphas had found their missing pack members. Ryland felt a twist in his chest. "Who is it?" Krista asked.

"Henna. A great strategist," Ryland said. "She was an excellent contribution to my pack. If only her boundless knowledge of strategy could have helped her sooner."

He found an old tarp and covered the body. "Should we talk to Declan?" Krista suggested from the doorway. "This wasn't Declan," Ryland growled. "This was something much worse."

11. ALPHA

Krista stayed in her room until the pack meeting was about to take place. She felt it would be best to clear her mind of what she had witnessed. It occurred to her that there was something far more sinister going on inside of Ryland. She thought that their exchange on the hillside might have given her some more insight, revealing his more sensitive side. But, watching him attack his enemy was so shocking to her, that it made her question how much of it was Ryland and how much of it was the curse raging inside of him.

At that same moment, she had also felt something horrifyingly strange when Ryland tore that man apart. It was as if she had seen it through his eyes, and felt her teeth grazing against the flesh as if somehow *she* was Ryland doing the killing.

She mindlessly shuffled her tarot cards in her hands, wondering if she should do another reading for herself.

Ryland had taken the pouch of oracle bones with him, perhaps to study them. Krista didn't dare ask for them, even if they were supposed to be for her. She wondered if she could get Tristan to retrieve them for her but, before she could stand, he was already opening her door. "The alphas are waiting," Tristan tilted his nose down to look at her over his glasses.

Krista stared down at the deck in her hands, deciding that she'd pull one after all. Just one. As she did, she stared into the eyes of a red devil—The Devil—crouched above two humans, bound in chains. Her mother warned her many times about this card, a symbol of addiction and restriction. She placed it back in the deck, instantly regretting her decision as she followed Tristan to the meeting hall.

The alphas from all the Central City factions were gathered: Sam, Rizz, Ben. From what Ryland had told her about them, she was able to match their names to their faces as each of them sat in a circle. She noticed an empty chair, discovering that Declan was nowhere to be seen. There was of a seat reserved for her... next to Ryland. She cautiously sat, wanting to look at him, but also feeling afraid to. Was he the supposed to be the devil on her tarot card?

A heated discussion was already taking place, and nobody had even noticed Krista, an outsider, amongst them. "So you're saying we should gather our forces because you saw some drawings on a wall in a cemetery?" The tough Amazoness, Sam, asked.

"After everything—the kidnapping and murders of your pack members, you still won't believe us?" Ryland's voice rang over the chaotic rambling. "This is clearly a prophecy that will eventually be fulfilled in some way, and it's up to us to come together and stop it."

"But we don't even know what we're up against!" Ben growled. "It could be an all-powerful evil."

"It could just be bullshit," Rizz hissed through his teeth.

"We've explained this already," Tristan pushed up his glasses. "We believe we've found a 'prophecy' involving some kind of monster and an oracle. The latter is currently residing with us."

Krista felt hundreds of eyes on her as they turned their heads to get a look at this 'oracle.' She shifted in her seat but felt a warm touch on her thigh that made her shudder. Ryland was looking at her, his face leaning in towards hers and for a flash of a second, she thought of how he had kissed her. Suddenly, she felt a pull for that Ryland. Where was he now? Was he still there, right next to her? Or was she sitting next to the monster that was itching to eat her next?

"It's okay," Ryland's voice silenced her thoughts. "Relax. You're with us."

But Krista couldn't relax, especially when the entire room expected her to stand and address them. Ben seemed to do it for her. "Sounds like a myth to me," he scoffed. "You bring a human girl in here and expect us to believe she's carrying an ancient spirit of clairvoyance?"

"As a matter of fact, I am," Krista heard herself say. She didn't know how she did it. The words seemed to slip from her mouth, and she tried to gather them back up. "I mean, as far as I'm aware," she retracted.

"Tch. I thought we all outgrew those shifter fairy tales," Rizz scoffed. "If you know what's good for you, you'll smarten up and stay in your own world's politics."

Krista tensed beside Ryland. The words hit her like pinpricks. Weren't nightmarish visions enough to earn her place at the table? Did she have to carry shifter blood in order to have a seat?

"Krista isn't just some smoke and mirrors fortune teller," Ryland silenced the doubting voices of the other alphas. "Her power is incredible, and you should be grateful for it." Krista was taken aback at this. This was the Ryland she had discovered. He turned his head and gave her a gentle, knowing nod, which comforted her. There was someone on her side—just one person who was willing to believe in her.

She was also surprised to see Ryland rolling up his sleeve. "What are you doing?" She whispered harshly, grabbing his arm to stop him. "I thought you were-"

"No point in keeping secrets now," Ryland said. Krista just barely caught a sly smirk peeking at the corner of his lips. He was going to tell them.

"She's doing everything she can to help us stop whatever the hell this is," he held up his hand high above for everyone to see. The curse had spread all through his arm, the whole limb nearly covered in inky black stains. The room gasped as they watched Ryland's veins swelling under his skin.

"What the hell is that?" Sam reached for a knife in her jacket.

"It's a curse," Ryland admitted, flashing his wound for all to see. "The night my pack member went missing, and we infiltrated the new shifter's warehouse, I encountered a strange shadow, one that decided to latch onto me."

"What does it mean?" Rizz asked.

"That's where she comes in," Ryland placed his sturdy hands on Krista's shoulders. "We've recovered my great-grandfather's oracle bones from the enemy shifters. They stole them for themselves and, by the looks of it, they're searching for the oracle too. What they need Krista for is unknown, but we have the advantage now and we should take it while we can."

"But who would steal the bones?" Ben asked. "These shifters are obviously being led by someone well-versed in shifter lore. I know that just by that fact that it's not any of you alphas."

"Except for Ryland," a voice called out from the back of the room. The doors were pulled open as Declan stepped into the room, holding a weighty trash bag at his side.

"You're late," Ryland sneered. Declan kept a straight face. "So you thought I'd show up after our little scuffle at our last meeting? How generous of you," he said. He looked straight at Krista, and she could feel him studying her lack of shifter blood. Nevertheless, he raised the bag high above him. "Thought you'd all like to know where my pack member went," he announced and he opened the bag. He grimaced as he tilted it upside down, dumping the contents onto the table.

The other shifters flew from their seats, the stench overwhelming as a severed wolf's head tumbled onto the table. It rolled down, towards Ryland who held out his cursed hand to stop it. Krista was baffled as the wolf's glassy eyes stared into hers—it's disintegrating jaws fell open to reveal a mouth full of teeth.

"Why the hell would you bring something like this here?" He growled at Declan.

"Turn it over," Declan declared. "I'm sure you'll find something well worth your interest."

Krista sunk further into her seat, trying to avoid the stench surrounding her. She watched as Ryland, still holding the head, turned it over to where a serrated knife met with the flesh. There was a thick piece of paper, drenched in blood, but still decipherable.

"An Iker sheds blood without sorrow. An Iker seeks vengeance. An Iker will split this city again, from its roots to its skies." Krista wondered if anyone else noticed Ryland's hand shaking as he read the note aloud.

"Ryland...*Iker*," Declan enunciated for all to hear. "Just what is it you're planning?"

Nobody would even look at Ryland, except for Krista. She knew the alpha had acted unpredictably before. He had, in fact, shed blood without sorrow. At least, that's what she thought.

"Funny how you think this is still my idea," Ryland said firmly. "I found my strategist stabbed through the heart in some sick ritual. Someone is obviously setting me up."

"They seem to be setting you up as well, Declan," Krista added. Ryland had stood up for her in this meeting, now it was her turn to stand up for him. She threw a knowing glance at Ryland, and luckily he understood. He reached into his pocket and threw the Stalker's patch next to the wolf's head.

"Where did you get that?" Declan asked.

"The end of a tunnel, near the cemetery where my family's precious artifact was stolen," Ryland said. Krista heard the entire room turn their heads to Declan.

"There's no use pointing fingers while a curse is upon us and shifters are being murdered," Krista said.

"She's right," Tristan said. "We're not here to settle disputes. We're discussing how to use Krista's abilities to determine this potential threat."

"Then why not right now?" Declan challenged. The other alphas nodded in agreement. Krista's heart quickened. She looked up at Ryland, and even he seemed concerned for her. The others didn't know, but he and Tristan were aware that she couldn't do a reading under pressure. Maybe, with these oracle bones, she would have a better chance.

"Alright," she said as she straightened herself up. Tristan approached her, holding the silk bag. It wasn't that heavy in her hand, but once she felt the bones settling in her palm, she started to grow anxious. *Not here*, she told herself. *Not while everyone's expecting this from me.* Standing before the silenced room, she clasped her hands around the bag and closed her eyes. Her mother had only briefly covered ancient runes, and Krista hoped it would be enough.

She could still see them watching her as she took a breath and spilled the bones onto the table. They rattled into place, and Krista's heart pounded as she watched the odd shapes settle. Already she felt a wave of power rising from them and wondered if the other shifters could sense it.

Her eyes drifted along the runes staring back up at her, odd curved shapes and twisted squiggles that she couldn't quite recognize. "I see the word, power," she told the room. Their skepticism grew, which only made her more nervous. Placing her hands on the bones, she tried to feel the energy wavering from them. There was something clearly there, she just didn't know what. Her mind's eye only brought brief flashes, like soft crackles of static in a pitch black room.

She couldn't do it. No matter how long she spent poring over them, she couldn't get a clear reading. Her heart sank as Declan scoffed from the other end of the table. "What were you all expecting? That she'd float up into the air and spout out the prophecy?"

The other alphas and their pack members mumbled their concerns, flashing disappointed looks at Krista. "I think this meeting has reached a conclusion," Sam said with a grimace as she stood up. "We're joined by a peace treaty, but I and the other alphas should look into this on our own terms."

As she left, the others began to follow her. Declan was last. "Congratulations to the strongest alpha," he said, his eyes narrowed. "I thought you were supposed to be good at keeping everyone safe."

Ryland scowled and held his arm. Krista felt her face growing hot, and for some reason when Ryland placed his hand gently on her back it only made her feel worse. She scooped up the oracle bones and placed them back in the bag. "It's not your fault," Ryland told her. "It just wasn't a good place or a good time."

"Or maybe they're right," she felt herself say. "Maybe I'm not the oracle after all." She pulled away from him, even though it hurt her to do so. Tears welled in her eyes as she headed for her room without giving Ryland another glance. "I'm sorry to have disappointed you," she said over her shoulder before she turned a corner and felt herself choking up even more.

12. DISAPPOINTMENTS

Ryland's paws thudded against the hillside, his mind running just as wildly as if he were in the cluster of trees outside the city. There wasn't much nature around for shifters to release their wolf's tension in, but the small pockets of forests were sufficient for Ryland.

He couldn't stop thinking about that note, and Declan's suspicions that he was the monster taking and killing shifters. His only worry was that somehow those words were true. Krista was terrified of him after he had killed that shifter in the fish market. What would stop him from losing himself like that again? What if he already had been?

His teeth sunk into a rabbit's flesh and he shook it in his jaws. He needed to hunt, to clear his mind of everything that had gone wrong in that meeting. The bones of his kill shifted in his mouth as he carried it off towards the Rogue's warehouse. It was much simpler to be a wolf. Kill, hunt, survive, everything was so basic this way. In the other world, there were far more complicated things to worry about. Power, leadership...love. Suddenly Ryland wasn't hungry anymore.

The note was still soaked in blood, but Ryland held it in front of a lamp beside his bed. No matter how many times he had read the words, he had a feeling that they weren't about him. Despite Declan's accusations, there was something about this that Ryland couldn't connect to. *An Iker seeks vengeance...but for what?* He wondered. Maybe it had something to do with Henna. But just because he had lost a pack member didn't mean he'd initiate a killing spree against the other factions. He had worked hard with them to bring peace, and couldn't understand why or how he'd compromise that.

Something else about the wording bothered him—how the note had said '*An* Iker,' not '*The* Iker.' His eyes shifted towards a book on his nightstand about curses, marked in the center with a colorful bookmark. He opened the book to look at it, staring at the photograph of himself taken just a few years ago. His hair was longer and unkempt as he stood next to a young man that looked very similar to him.

The two were smiling proudly in front of a warehouse, one where that had spent so much time and money to convert into a base for the Rogues (or a state-of-the-art gym for curious non-shifters) Ryland stared at the young man in the glasses beside him, a clumsy smile on his face as he squinted into the sun. His hair was neatly combed, but he was still almost a spitting image of Tristan. The young Ryland was laughing about something, perhaps making fun of his brother.

Ryland turned the picture over, looking at the scribbled note in messy penmanship on the back: *"Little brother and me, 2016. Birth of the Rogues!"* there was a small doodle of a paw print next to it. Ryland couldn't help but smile, although the sight of it tugged at his chest.

He could still picture Christoph, throwing his black track jacket over his shoulder on his way out of the warehouse. "Good luck, Brother," his last words echoed in his memory. "You're going to need it." But Ryland knew what was best for his pack, and that's what had made him the best. Yet, Declan's words still clung to him. After that failure of a meeting, Ryland was left with a feeling of incompetence. He had been so proud to be the strongest alpha, and it nearly killed him to know everything he had built was crumbling in front of him.

He held tightly to the photo, and a strange eeriness crept over him. There was something familiar about the curl of the 'L' in 'Little brother,' the short, concise letters written with a light hand. He held up the note from the meeting, the one that was crudely stabbed into that wolf's head. He couldn't bear to hold them up side by side. Instead, he shook his head and placed both items on the bed, before rolling up his sleeve.

It was spreading to his chest now, frequently taking hold of his heart and squeezing it like tight fingers. He clutched at the dark lines branching out across his skin, clenching his teeth from the pain. He held on as a wave of it crashed over him. Breathing was difficult, stabbing him as he began to panic. There'd been waves like this before, but not as strong as this. He rolled over, crouching into a ball on the floor as he tried desperately to ride it out.

His thoughts could only drift to Krista, how she couldn't get a reading for him. Questions were still unanswered. What was this thing growing inside of him? Then, the whispering came. It was louder than normal, incoherent. He could only remember the jabbering of Henna's murderer that day. Shaking violently on the ground, Ryland tried to relax.

He closed his eyes, surrounding himself with thoughts of his pack, of his devotion to his purpose as their alpha. But for some reason, it just wasn't enough. It was then he realized there was only one other thing he could really think about what seemed to coax him back down.

Krista could make him smile, almost like in the picture of him and Christoph. He had been worried that she'd be afraid of him, especially after how she'd acted during the meeting. Still, she did stand up for him to Declan. She'd been with him on this journey from their shaky start in that nightclub. There was something comforting in that, comforting enough to help bring him back down to Earth.

As he settled, the whispering ceased. But the room still felt heavy, as if a dark presence was hovering like a cloud. The weight left his chest, and he was finally able to sit up, holding his knees against his chest. He needed somebody to talk to, other than Tristan, who was too much like his brother. There was a softer presence calling out to him now, as if a light was seeping into the room.

He was going to see Krista. She'd probably still be locked up in her room, afraid of him, afraid of her failure with the oracle bones. First, he searched his bookshelf for anything on oracle bones. Maybe he could take it to her and help her feel better about the whole thing. Once he found a book that suited, he took a deep breath. Why was he so nervous? Maybe because he was worried about how she'd look at him. Then again, she was so quick to touch him, to hold his hand and examine his curse when anyone else would have been afraid.

He gathered himself together before pulling open his door. A small gasp made him freeze in his tracks as he stared right into Krista's widened eyes. Her fist was raised to the door and she quickly held it back at her side.

"Hey," Ryland said.

"Hey," she bit her lip, and suddenly Ryland forgot about everything as the sinking feeling left the room. Krista was wearing pajamas, a tight pair of shorts and a long t-shirt covering them, the hem just barely brushing the tops of her smooth thighs. It was the same ratty band t-shirt she'd been wearing when he rescued her that first time, and Ryland remembered his fingers trailing under it to tend to her wounds.

"Did you need something?" He asked after both of them realized they had only been staring in shock at one another. Krista relaxed with a slight laugh. "Sorry," she said. "You might think this is weird, but I just had...a strange feeling that you were..."

"Not doing so well?" Ryland finished. Krista nodded. "Actually, yeah," she said, her eyes slightly narrowed with suspicion. Ryland pulled the door open further for her without another question. As she passed by, he caught the scent of her hair again, the citrusy, musky scent of vetiver. It aroused his senses.

Her hand trailed to the book in his hand, hanging at his side. "What's this?" Krista asked. "*Interpreting Oracle Bones and Runes?*" Ryland quickly pulled it from her. "I was just reading," he said curtly.

"Reading?"

"Yeah."

"Then why were you just about to leave?"

"What do you mean?"

"You tell me. You're the one who opened the door," Krista shrugged.

"I, um, was going to find Tristan."

"He always goes to bed at ten o'clock," Krista gave him a knowing smile.

Ryland couldn't come up with a better excuse and left it at that. The woman was a psychic, after all. She'd have to know his true intentions. Krista sat on the pillows around his coffee table. Ryland was surprised that she was being so open towards him now, after avoiding his gaze earlier in the day.

"So, what made you think I wasn't doing well?" He asked. Krista seemed distracted as she found a pen and scribbled on a piece of scrap paper.

"I was trying to sleep," she said. "I don't know if you'll believe this, but I felt a strange pain in my chest and I thought it might have something to do with you."

"Couldn't stand to be away from me?" Ryland took a risk. It worked. Krista laughed her musical laugh, tucking a strand of hair behind her ear. "It's more of a theory I have," she said. "I know I haven't really shown off my...abilities as an oracle yet. But, I still think that maybe...I don't know.

Maybe, we're connected somehow. That my powers are also attached to your curse."

"An interesting theory," Ryland said as he took a spot next to her. His knee just barely brushed against her bare thigh as he sat, and he couldn't help but look at how her legs were delicately folded to the side. He noticed her bare feet, her toes curling as she worked diligently on her sketch. "Listen," he said, remembering that they had left off on an odd note. "About the other day, with the shifter-"

"Honestly, I was shocked, and quite terrified," Krista said. "But, it's okay. Something told me that it wasn't really you in there." She turned, her bright eyes looking right into his. Ryland was taken aback and averted his gaze to the table.

"It's spreading more," he told her sadly. "It's getting harder for me to figure out what's me and what's...this *thing.* "

"Well, if it makes you feel better. I think it was really you that night on the hill," she said with a smirk. "If you remember as well as I do."

Ryland did remember, and he wanted to continue where they'd left off. He'd been told so many times how dangerous it would be to fall in love, but with Krista sitting next to him, and the lamp on the coffee table casting a soft glow on her red hair, he knew that tonight he wouldn't be able to restrain himself.

"You've thought about it?" Ryland asked.

"Here and there," Krista said with a smile. Suddenly, it faded as she finished her drawing.

"It's that symbol," Ryland recognized Krista's drawing of the star, cut in half with an arrow, the marking left around Central City.

"I saw it in a vision," Krista explained, her tone shifting. "I'm really sorry about the meeting. I really thought it would help to try-"

"You don't have to apologize. I knew there were a lot of people there."

"It's not just that. I haven't been able to really use my abilities to help much."

"You found Henna and the oracle bones. I'd say that's extremely helpful." He didn't want her to feel inferior.

"I just feel like everyone is counting on me right now," she said.

"Tell me about it. I'm leading a pack that's terrified of me. I can barely hold an alpha meeting without something going wrong."

"It looks like we're both disappointments."

"You're not a disappointment to me..."

The way she looked at him was driving him wild, a plan of some kind forming in her eyes. He hoped it was the same as his. There was something enticing about being alone in the dim light with her, while the rest of the world was asleep. There was a warning, something pulling him away from her, but he couldn't resist it anymore. He had regretted that night on the hill, his pride too strong to let him keep going.

He took another chance, reaching out, just to cup his hand around her soft cheek. She closed her eyes and leaned into it, giving a cautious glance before she tilted forward on her knees, wrapping her arms around him while their lips met. Ryland didn't know what to do, but the touch of her lips had softened him, and he melted into her arms, holding her body tightly against his.

She kissed him harder, hungry for him. Ryland was going to chase this as far as he could, and he pulled her onto his lap, letting her silky legs weave around his waist as she pressed her chest into his t-shirt. Ryland felt her unrestrained breasts and longed to touch them again as he had the other night.

As they kissed, he began to explore. She wove her fingers through his hair while his fingertips trailed from her thighs, caressing the skin on her stomach before reaching for her supple nipples. She sighed softly as he worked his thumbs in small, delicate circles, the buds underneath them growing more aroused. She worked her hips into a slow grind, gently at first,. Those shorts were so thin, sending Ryland's imagination into a flurry.

"I thought you said this would complicate things," Krista breathed.

"It's even more complicated to keep myself away from you," he replied.

The room was hotter as their bodies grew more familiar. Ryland felt the blood pumping to other places, the more Krista ground into him, her hips swaying in a beckoning rhythm. She pulled away and smirked as she reached down to grab his throbbing erection through his jeans. Ryland felt a moan escape his lips while she caressed him, her fingers spreading far apart to cover every inch of his thick cock. She kissed him again, her lips trailing to his neck in a string of soft kisses. Ryland leaned back but found himself caught off guard as something sharp grazed against his skin.

"Ouch!" He pulled away from Krista, who only gave him a devilish grin. "You're not the only one who bites," she said, a wild look in her eye. Ryland found- himself wanting her right then, his arousal peaking into a deeper hunger—yearning to be satisfied. He grabbed her thighs, holding her around him as he cleared off the coffee table in one swoop of his arm before placing her firmly onto it. A heavy breath rose from Krista, her eyes excited for what was to come.

Ryland pulled the thin fabric from her legs and tossed them aside. He pulled his t-shirt over his head, turning so she couldn't see the dark markings across his chest. "I'll get the lights," he said, not wanting to frighten her with the curse. He felt a pair of arms lash out, grabbing for his waist as they spun him back around. "I don't care," Krista said, pulling her knees apart to reveal her lacy black panties. "Let me look at you."

Her eyes sized him up, and she seemed pleased with him. She sat up on her knees on the table as she undid his pants, slowly pulling down the zipper and everything else with it. Ryland felt goosebumps prickling his skin as she caressed her fingers along his tightened shaft. Her lips grazed against the veins in his cock, teasing him until finally, she put him in her mouth.

Ryland hadn't felt anything like this in so long—it was hard enough not to finish just from her lips alone. As she sucked on him, her tongue rolling from shaft to tip, he couldn't control himself any longer. His wolf was dying to mate and had been for far too long. Just as her lips rounded his soft tip, he grabbed her by the shoulders, pinning her onto her back on the table.

He hovered over her, pulling the last scrap of fabric from her legs. His wolf was sensing her heat, and he was ready to give her anything she wanted. He bent over kissing her thigh, his lips trailing to her blossoming flower. She tasted sweet, and Ryland couldn't get enough as he licked at her clitoris. Krista moaned softly under her breath, crossing her arms over her to pull off the rest of her clothes.

Ryland was nearly floored at the sight of her glorious breasts, heaving as Krista's breath quickened. There was a soft glow about them, but he stayed focused on her lips, his tongue navigating around them as they swelled to the touch. He prodded her, tasting further inside. Krista's back arched as he continued to pleasure her, until she was soaking wet to the touch.

She grabbed for his cock, guiding it inside of her. She took him in with such ease, her warmth seeping around him as he pressed further. Krista was shocked at the size of him, but the look in her eyes told Ryland she loved every inch of him. With his hands firmly planted on either side of her, he worked himself into a gentle grind inside and out.

Krista wrapped her arms around him, wanting his body to be closer to hers. He lowered himself, letting her breasts fill the space between them. Krista held on tightly, as Ryland began to thrust harder, her walls sliding around his veiny erection. He was struggling to hang on, and Krista's breathy moans were driving him wild. There was so much more he wanted to do to her before he finished, and he picked her up under her thighs, his cock still inside of her while he rammed her into the bookshelf.

Books fell from their place onto the floor as he fucked her harder. She was dripping wet now, her back arched as she closed her eyes and moaned in ecstasy. Her legs wrapped tightly around his waist as she bounced up and down on his cock. Ryland pressed her harder into the shelf as he grabbed for her breasts, one after the other. They were full in his hands, and he bent down to suck on them.

"I'm getting close," Krista whimpered. Ryland was on fire. He lowered her, turning her to penetrate her from behind. Her luscious, firm ass slammed into him as he thrust deeper. He grabbed it with both hands, his thumbs digging into it as he pulled it closer to him. Then, he reached around, his fingers prodding and rolling around her clit. Krista's moaning soared higher the more he pleasured her, until she finally and breathlessly exclaimed she was going to come.

He could feel every second of it as she contracted around him while she climaxed. His cock was throbbing now as he rammed her harder and harder, Krista crying out in pure ecstasy as warmth poured from between her lips, coating him completely.

It was enough to send him spiraling into his own wave of pleasure. His teeth clenched as he finished. He throbbed inside of her until he could no longer breathe until he had nothing left.

Finally, he removed himself. Their naked, sweaty bodies heaved as they caught their breath, relishing the act they'd just completed. Krista turned, tired and dizzy with pleasure as she wrapped her arms around him. "Definitely didn't see that coming," she joked between breaths. Ryland smiled, and at that moment he was overcome by a great sense of peace and quiet.

13. ALPHA

Krista sprawled out on Ryland's bed, her naked body barely covered by the fur blanket. She closed her eyes and sighed, never expecting to have shared such a moment with someone, let alone a wolf shifter...let alone Ryland. Since they made love, her body had been overwhelmed with a buzzing sensation that numbed her toes and fingertips. Ryland's hand reached down to move a strand of hair from her face.

"What have we done?" he asked, though he didn't seem too concerned.

"Quite the dirty deed," Krista said with a smirk. "You're lucky. Most guys hardly get a second date with me."

"Color me surprised," he said.

"Well, I kind of brought it on myself. As you know, I tend to keep to myself. It makes things a lot easier in the long run."

"Well, you haven't had a horrible vision of us yet, have you?"

Krista thought it over. "If you don't count the visions of ominous shadows and wolves devouring people, I would say that our relationship was going rather well," she said.

She rested in the crook of his arm, gazing at the dark patterns of the curse working its way through his body. "Do you really think we're connected?" Ryland asked as her fingers trailed along the black strands of skin. "It would make sense if you're the oracle," he added. Krista noticed him looking at her longer than usual, his eyes more concerned. "You still don't think you're the oracle, don't you?" he asked.

"I don't really know what to think anymore," she told him. "I have these visions, but the second I'm in front of everyone trying to show them my potential, I just...crack. It's all static to me. Maybe I just didn't train hard enough." She wanted to roll over—to settle and sulk in her failure from the meeting, but Ryland's arms drew her closer, his warm body mingling with hers.

"You've been training your whole life," he said calmly. "And you'll always be training. That doesn't make you a failure. You're only a failure if you give up."

The words settled over her, calming her busy mind. "What if we can't find a way to lift the curse?" She asked. "What are you going to do?" She turned her head to look up at him. He was deep in thought.

"I'm going to lift it," he said with determination. "My pack needs me."

"Your pack doesn't show it," she told him. "They seem afraid of you. In fact, I haven't seen them do anything else other than train. Don't you ever let them get out once in a while?"

"They're not afraid. They're devoted to their pack and its cause."

"And what exactly is your cause?"

It concerned her that Ryland took so long to answer. "To be the best, of course," is what he came up with. "Central City needs a strong alpha to keep the other factions together. A few years ago it was chaos. Territories were fought over constantly. We were all on the brink of war until my brother suggested the Rogues intervene with the peace treaty."

He tensed up, bothered as he looked down at his blackened arm. "This curse is my burden to bear, and if it isn't lifted we may find ourselves facing another shifter war."

"But why is it your burden? Weren't you the one who sought me out for help?" Krista asked.

"You don't understand what it's like having this," Ryland said fiercely, to her surprise. It was the other Ryland talking to her now, not the one she knew.

"I'm trying to do my best here," she retorted sternly. Cursed or not, she wasn't going to let Ryland's unpredictable anger get between them.

"Sorry," Ryland relaxed as if something had passed over him. Krista forgave him. She thought of how hard it must be to be an alpha, to have everyone looking up to you constantly. Then again, she remembered everyone had been counting on her with the oracle bones. Now the shifters were going out on their own—possibly going to give up on the curse and the prophecy altogether.

She rested her head against Ryland, listening to his breathing as the soft glow of the city radiated through the warehouse windows. Tomorrow she would try again. Ryland had dozens of reference books she could use. I can't give up now, she thought as she drifted off to sleep.

Usually visions and dreams were indiscernible while Krista slept, but tonight, something was taking a firm hold of her mind. It was if she were a ghostly spirit, soaring through all of space and time—an inky void splashed with colors that would take shape into things she recognized. She saw flashes of Ryland and her, their naked bodies entangled in one another in passion. A wave of satisfaction engulfed her spirit, but the images fast-forwarded into something much more terrifying that ripped her from her pleasurable fantasy.

Ryland and she disappeared, leaving Krista's ghostlike presence in the dark. Then, a voice called out to her as she found herself traveling through a dark tunnel, lit by a flickering candle in front of her. As the light danced on the walls, she caught a glimpse of the woman in the cage, the same drawing she had found scrawled in the cemetery with Ryland.

The voice was crying out in agony now, calling out for help. It sounded familiar, but it was wavering, warping into something inhuman as Krista drew closer to it. The tunnel opened up into a more cavernous area, though she couldn't recognize where she was. There was low chanting, and she felt intense heat.

Her vision was starting to falter now, and she could only see the blurred shape of someone. Without thinking, she heard her own voice. *"Ryland!"* It echoed thousands of times off the walls, reverberating back to her and shaking her to the core. Then, the screams came. Terrible wails of agony as her vision flashed to an image of a crystal dagger. The blade plunged into the blurred figure's side and they fell, face first, onto the ground.

Krista ran towards the lone body she recognized. Twisted vague shadows shaped like monsters watched them, all standing in a circle. As Krista turned over the body, her heart stopped. She was looking right into Ryland's cold, lifeless eyes. His body began to tremble, but Krista held onto him, desperately trying to cling to him. Suddenly, his eyes opened wide, and a deafening roar emerged from him.

In a flash, large tongues of fire burst from his mouth and shot out from his eyes, nearly setting Krista ablaze. It consumed them. She could feel the flames licking at her clothes, at her skin. She panicked—trying to put them out, feeling the intense searing pain the fire brought her. She refused to let go of Ryland, not until they were completely engulfed in flame. The last thing she saw was a dark -hooded figure, holding tightly to the crystal dagger. A flash shone in the middle of the hood, but she couldn't see who it was.

A gasp tore at Krista's lungs as she ripped herself from her nightmarish vision. Ryland was going to be killed, and she needed to figure out when and where or it was bound to come true. She clutched at her chest, her breaths ragged and her skin dripping in a cold sweat. Where was she? It was light now. The morning had come to ease her fear, but it couldn't erase the vision she had.

The bed was cold beside her. Ryland was up by now, training. Of course, she had trouble believing that. What if she had a vision of something that had already happened and Ryland had been killed in the night? She pushed that thought from her mind. She could only see the future, not the present, and she needed to warn Ryland before he did something dangerous.

Harsh voices emanated from the training room. Krista tied up her still-wet hair from the showers and cautiously stepped inside. There was Ryland, standing on the mats with Tristan and two shifters standing around in a circle. It was a relief to see him alive, though a tense argument was taking place.

"We can't send anyone out, not after what happened with Henna." Krista recognized Tory, a scout who often stayed quiet around the warehouse like everyone else. It was surprising to see him standing up to Ryland.

"I didn't train all of you so that you can cower in the warehouse whenever something goes wrong," Ryland commanded. His voice was rough. Not in his typical teacher-like tone. "And if you don't like that, you can go back to the streets where I found you."

"Sir, you should consider the meeting that took place yesterday," Tristan said firmly. It was odd for Krista to hear him this worked up. "The rest of the Rogues are worried the same thing will happen to them. If you have any respect for your pack, you'll keep them here until this whole thing is figured out."

"How the hell do you think we're going to figure this out, then?!" Ryland was heating up now. "We're not like the other factions. I'm not going to sit around and wait for someone else to clean up the mess. This is up to me, and my pack!"

Krista's feet were touching the mat now. Tristan gave a slight sigh with relief. "Maybe you can do something about this," he told her.

"What's going on?" Krista asked.

"This doesn't concern her," Ryland's face was twisted in anger now. The curse had really taken a toll on him and was continuing to work its horrors.

"She's part of this just as much as you are," a strategist named Kalyn stepped forward.

Ryland seemed taken aback. Nobody in his pack had dared talk to him this way, and yet some of his best were defying his orders. "I have a lead on where the murderers are," Ryland said harshly. "I'm gathering a team, and we're going to infiltrate it, just as we did the abandoned factory. It'll be small, contained—just a scouting mission. Nobody will get hurt. I will make sure of that."

Nobody seemed to believe him, especially Krista. Ryland clearly wasn't himself, and his own pride would be the thing that would end up killing him and anyone else he took with him on his mission.

"The factory was a scouting mission as well, in case you forgot," A flare of light flashed across Tristan's glasses, vaguely reminding Krista of her dream—the hint of light shining in the figure's hood.

"Ryland, stay," Krista said. Anything to keep Ryland here before he did something drastic. "I had a vision last night, a powerful one. I saw that you were going to be killed!" She frantically tried to explain what she saw, about the dagger and the shadows around Ryland's body, how the fire had shot out from his face and engulfed him and Krista. His response was simple, direct.

"Let's hope that's not the outcome, then," Ryland said, barely casting a glance at her. Krista was hurt, especially because of what they had shared the night before. Couldn't he see through this curse to realize that? The other shifters stood their ground, their arms crossed and their feet planted firmly on the mat.

"Well, since I won't be organizing any strategists for you," Kalyn said. "I'll be seeing myself out."

"Same goes for me," added Tory. "I'm not going to let any scouts die out there."

The two of them walked towards the double doors, unzipping their black track jackets and leaving them behind them as they followed one another into the hall. Krista saw that something about this scene had unleashed another wave of fury in Ryland, as he watched them disappear down the hallway.

"How dare you do this to your alpha?" Ryland fumed, his face turning blood-red. "After all that I've done for this pack!"

"You are doing absolutely nothing if you're sending us all to be slaughtered out there!" A voice rung even louder than Ryland's. Krista had never seen Tristan so upset and had no idea he was capable of such anger.

A cry escaped from her as Ryland's hand shot out and grabbed Tristan by his white collar. Their noses were just touching as Ryland's chest heaved. Krista noticed the dark webs spreading from Ryland's t-shirt collar up against his neck, his veins pulsing violently. It was only a matter of time before he'd be completely consumed. Tristan kept a calm demeanor, his face furrowed with frustration at the behavior of his alpha. "I chose you for a reason," Ryland growled.

"I'm not your brother, Ryland. No matter how badly you want me to be."

It only took one second. One second Tristan was standing, and the next he was thrown onto his back on the mat, his glasses flying from his face. Ryland clutched at Tristan's shirt, staining it with a spritz of blood as he shot his fist into the beta's nose. He punched him again, and again, despite Krista's desperate screams for him to stop. The other shifters only watched in horror, fearing they could somehow be next.

Tristan choked and sputtered on his own blood, and Krista couldn't take the sight of it anymore. Ryland was going to kill him. He was going to get lost in himself, transforming into whatever that thing was that tore apart that shifter in the fish market. She had to stop it.

"Let him go, Ryland!" Krista forced herself in between them, pushing them apart, trying to gain control of the unrecognizable monster in front of her. The other Rogues rushed to her side, shifting into wolves that circled around Tristan, growling fiercely as they too stood up to their alpha. A pair of jaws lashed out at Ryland, and he seemed to snap from his trance.

Ryland looked at Krista as if she had somehow betrayed him too. Krista kept trying, inserting herself further between him and Tristan.

"Look at you," she said with disappointment. It wasn't hard to show it, not after she poured everything out to him. "Look what you've done while everyone here has given you everything!" Now her voice was rising, and there was something liberating about it.

A silence hovered between them, thick and ominous. She had no idea what Ryland would do next. Finally, he made a motion and stepped onto the concrete. Everyone's silent gaze followed him as he found a nearby table, lifted it high above his head, and launched it across the room with incredible force. It crashed to the floor, a cacophony of splintered wood and screeching metal forming as it slid to a halt. Krista jumped at the sound. The wolves whined nervously in response.

"FUCK YOU!" Ryland hollered. "All of you!" He even looked at Krista as he said it, which felt like he was stabbing her with a dagger of his own. He was just a wounded animal, angry and scared. Nothing could be done about it now, not when he was having a full-on tantrum in front of all of the Rogues.

They fell silent as papers fluttered to the ground around Ryland's feet. He stood there, his fists clenched and his chest rising and falling. "I'll go on my own," He growled with finality.

"What part of my vision did you not understand?" Krista shouted from the mat. "Apparently my abilities mean nothing to you if you're willing to dive headfirst into this without hearing me out!"

"I don't care if you're the oracle or not," he sneered. Now his voice was unrecognizable. There was something different about his eyes. Krista saw strange yellow pools forming in them, which suddenly turned into a deep-red. "You're just about as useful as them." Ryland pointed to Tristan, who glared at him with such hatred. Tristan licked the red from his teeth, wiping the blood from his lips. Ruby-red streaked across his white sleeve as he wiped his nose, but he didn't care.

"You don't mean that," Krista said, her throat tightening. Hot tears formed in her eyes. "This is the curse, Ryland, not you. Don't let it take you this way."

"Trust me, it won't."

He kept walking. Krista hoped that he'd look back, just once. He didn't. He slammed his fist against a button on a far wall. The sliding door to the warehouse creaked as it slid open. Krista and the Rogues watched—the tension heavy in the room as Ryland stepped out and disappeared into the cold morning.

14. LONER

Ryland ran until his four legs burned and couldn't carry him any further. Everything that had just happened at the Rogue's base was just a blur swirling in his mind. Now he was in the forest, lost and blinded by his own rage. *Who needs them?* He thought. *I'm the strongest alpha, after all.*

As a wolf, all he wanted to do was find something and kill it. Searching through the trees, his nose picked up a hint of deer, grazing on some nearby bushes. He could smell the blood running through its veins, hear its heartbeat. He crouched low to the ground, ready to spring out at his prey.

But, he couldn't do it. He shifted back, leaning against a tree as he watched the doe take off into the thicket. Suddenly, he was overcome with a blanket of guilt. He looked down at his fists, still covered in Tristan's blood, the skin broken on his knuckles. "What have I done..." the words escaped his lips, and they felt so foreign to him. Who was he now? He thought he had been a strong leader, an alpha who swore to do what was best for his pack, always. Until he had let that damned curse get a hold of him. It gripped him, tighter than it had the day it first took hold of his soul.

He buried his face in his hands and, to his own surprise, he wept. The image of Tristan's battered face was burned into his mind. He could still hear himself, a voice he didn't even recognize, telling Krista she was worthless. How could he have allowed himself to get this far? He couldn't bear the thought of Krista's face, tears forming in her eyes that he had helped to create.

The night before had been so perfect. He had never felt such a level of calmness washing over him. Now here he was, alone in the woods. He thought about going back. He could apologize, although he wasn't even sure who would forgive him after the stunts he had pulled earlier that day. It was already a bad sign that he had fought Declan several days ago, but now he had allowed himself to go over the edge completely.

While it was happening, it had felt almost like a dream. It was as if he had lost himself again, somewhere in a dark void. Awake and aware, he now realized that he would truly have to do this on his own. The curse had nearly demonstrated its full potential, and Ryland knew that if Krista and the others hadn't gotten between them, he could have beaten Tristan to a pulp.

He wiped the tears from his eyes. It had been a while since he'd cried—the last time probably being when his brother had left. It was hard to bear the burden of the pack on his shoulders, and now he was wondering if he had only brought that burden on himself. Thoughts of Krista started to take over. He hadn't felt so close to someone in such a long time and her warning still echoed in his ears.

Now that he had cast aside everyone that mattered to him, he had no choice but to continue. He stood up from the tree trunk, feeling dizzy and tired. It was as if he hadn't even slept last night. He needed to press on. He felt a pinch in his neck and touched the swelling veins where the darkness was now spreading. Maybe Krista was right. He was going to die. Or would he die trying to stop it? He had been so lost in his own thoughts, that he didn't give her vision a second thought.

Ryland sat in a diner with his lone cup of coffee as he tried to piece his hunch together. He hadn't done it before, out of fear. The truth scared him, and he couldn't bring himself to face it. He reached into his pocket, pulling out two papery items from it and laying them both on the table.

The photo of him and Christoph smiled up at him. He flipped it over, hiding his brother's face and revealing his handwriting on the back. He held it up to the blood-stained note, his eyes darting back and forth between it and the photo's caption. He knew the "L" had a familiar curve, but this time he studied all of the letters, comparing every swoop and line in front of him.

It suddenly became clear. Tristan was close to him, but not close enough. Declan was a rival with his own agenda, but he would have no reason to suddenly start another war between factions.

Then there was the brick wall in his great-grandfather's crypt. Only one other person could have known about the oracle bones beside him. He flipped the picture back over, staring into Christoph's young face, nearly obscured by the glare on his glasses. He stared at the scribbled note: *An Iker sheds blood without sorrow. An Iker seeks vengeance. An Iker will split this city again, from its roots to its skies.*

"*An* Iker," not, "*The* Iker." Ryland understood now, but he didn't want to believe it until he saw it for himself. Something tugged at him, and again he thought of Krista. She should be coming with him. It'd be too dangerous to go alone. Then again, it'd be even more dangerous delivering the oracle directly to this mysterious shifter clan. Who knows what they had planned for Krista if he hadn't been there to save her from that shifter? He paid for his coffee and left, pulling his hoodie over his head as he braced himself against the cold. He had an Iker to find.

As Ryland drew nearer to the hillside next to the overpass, he felt a rock sinking in his gut. Everything about this was a bad idea. As he had said to the Rogues, he would have to do this himself. He paused, briefly, once he reached the end of the large culvert tunnel. Water was flowing out of it now, dirty smelling water that reminded him of the shifter he had killed. He looked out at the grass surrounding it.

He had lain here with Krista the other night, wanting to understand her and to feel her against him. How he had wished for that again, even though he didn't know if she would bother seeing him again. For all he knew, she had already packed up and left, like Kalyn and Tory. Quietly, he vowed he would mend things with her and his pack once this was settled, assuming he made it out of here alive.

Kneeling down, he ran his hand along the soft grass. It was comforting, despite the noise of the city bleeding from the overpass and the smell of sewage spilling out into the nearby river. He savored the grass, because where he was going, he wasn't sure if he'd ever get the chance to touch the earth again. He stared into the darkness of the metal tunnel that blended into concrete. It was ominous, cold air emanating from it and touching his face.

It was like a crypt of its own, and Ryland was willingly stepping inside to accept his fate.

The flashlight clicked on, shining a bluish-white beam around the tunnel as Ryland made his way deeper inside. He could have started in the cemetery, but he didn't want to risk running into any more shifters, even if it was the middle of the day. His shoes were already soaked through with foul-smelling water. It splashed up around his ankles, seeping into his socks, but he didn't care. All he could think about was how he was getting closer to those paintings that he had seen when he was here with Krista.

He could see them now, the strange depictions of a woman in a cage, a monstrous beast swallowing a man, fire engulfing the room. It was all too similar to the vision Krista had warned him about. If he was going to break this curse for his pack, he would have to keep going.

The tunnel would bring him back out into the cemetery if he continued to follow it as he had followed it with Krista. His ears perked up, catching the sound of distant water flowing. Rain must have been collecting in here for a while, but something didn't sound quite right about where the water was going.

It had been pouring out of the culvert ditch, but as Ryland got closer, he heard it branching off. The flashlight pointed at what looked to be just another part of the concrete wall, except there was something that was vaguely familiar about it.

Instead of concrete, there was a small hole covered with planks of wood, swollen with foul-smelling water. He remembered shoving Krista against it when she had seen the rat. Ryland hooked his fingers around the topmost plank and pulled. It came out easily, along with the others. Finally, he revealed another tunnel branching out, stretching into never-ending darkness. Ryland stared down into the dark water.

There was no way he could squeeze himself through the hole. Unless...He reached his hand through, shining the light until he found a place to hold the flashlight. Then, he shifted into a wolf, just barely able to wiggle himself into the hidden tunnel. He lifted his head, unsure if there was room for him to stand as a man again.

He took a risk and shifted back, grabbing the flashlight. The tunnel was just about the same height, and he was curious as to how it got here in the first place and why it had been boarded up. He noticed the tunnel had a distinct scent, compared to the other one. He could pick apart the different notes, sewer water, fur, wolf urine. Each one was a red flag for Ryland to turn back, but he refused to go back empty-handed.

Continuing on, he discovered there were more paintings along the walls. Men were shifting into wolves. There was a city, being overtaken by a large shadow made of darkness and fire. Ryland recognized two pointed ears sticking from the shadow's head. It made him shudder to think that very shadow was forming something evil inside of him. He shook it off. The curse was strong, but he'd never let it reach its fullest potential.

He followed the paintings, staring nervously as the story progressed. There was an image of a dark hole as if the earth was cracked open. Tiny people were falling into it, their limbs flailing as they were consumed by more fire. Whatever this shifter clan's purpose was, they seemed to be obsessed with the end of the world. Finally, the paintings stopped, ending with just one enormous beast. His jaws were opened wide as he pulled people into his mouth. A circle of wolves was around him, bowing their heads in reverence to him. Ryland figured the monster was some sort of wolf god. Did that mean he was the same? Again, his thoughts were running rampant, and he tried to distract himself by thinking of what he'd say to Krista once this was all over.

Then, the tunnel ended in a room and, to Ryland's, dismay it branched off into two directions, again. He closed his eyes, trying to gather his senses and to pick up any sign of the wolves. It was almost impossible to read the room with the overwhelming stench of the water rushing over his feet.

He shone the light to the left, then the right as he contemplated. If only Krista were here. Maybe she'd give him one of her visions to help give him some kind of clue. Taking a heavy breath, he chose the tunnel on the left. There were markings there, the same symbol of the star cut in half with an arrow. He figured that would at least be the best place to start.

The symbols, which were smeared across the wall in different shades of spray paint, glared at him. Ryland furrowed his brow. It was all starting to get too real for him now. Noises coming towards him told him he wouldn't be alone for long. They were almost like whispers, the familiar ones that Ryland had heard. His arm started to burn again the closer he got to them.

Luckily he was prepared. He reached into his pocket, producing a silver pocketknife that once belonged to his father. It was almost a joke, using silver on a shifter, but it was a useful metal to weaken a wolf's skin—to make them revert into their human forms. He opened the blade, brandishing it in front of him as the voices drew nearer.

They were human, but as the light shone on them, the group of figures panicked. "Intruder!" One shouted as he turned into a wolf. The others followed suit, and soon the entire tunnel reeked of mildew-coated fur and oily, musky skin. Hundreds of teeth flashed in the dark as they ran for Ryland. Ryland held his position, his knife at the ready. He would have shifted, but there were too many of them. Roughly eight wolves were crammed into the tunnel and he wouldn't be able to fight them on his own. Strongest alpha or no, any pack was still better than a lone wolf.

Ryland turned to the side as the first wolf approached, and plunged his knife into its ribcage, just as the wolf was about to take a bite of his arm. It whimpered as it fell into the dirty water. It shifted back into a man, covered in a hooded robe. The others growled fiercely at him, their hackles raised and their lips curled in wicked sneers.

They attacked all at once. Ryland felt the bodies piling on top of him, their weight slamming into him like a rogue wave. He nearly toppled back, but he held on, grabbing any handful of fur that he could and slashing his knife at it. If only he could weaken the pack to just a few, then he could shift and take the rest down on his own. The blade made contact with fur and skin. Ryland jumped back, trying to avoid the jaws of the wolves.

Teeth sank into his shoulder, and he cried out in agony as a wolf caught him in an iron grip. He caught the jaws of one, holding them open as a tongue lolled out at him, still trying to get a taste of his flesh. Flinging it off of him, the wolf slid to a stop against the wet concrete. He swung his knife into the wolf grabbing his shoulder, the blade catching it in the eye. It was overwhelming, trying to determine which one would bite him next. Suddenly, he realized in horror that his hand was empty. He shone his flashlight frantically in the water as the wolves circled him, only to find the blade shimmering in the water. Just as he was about to roll and grab it, a pair of hands reached around and covered his head with a black bag.

It was getting harder to breathe. Ryland could feel the fabric pulling into his mouth as he gulped for air, but the hands held tightly to him, suffocating him further. He was going to die before he had even found any answers, but he still threw his arms wildly at his attackers. He was taken down in moments, more hands grabbing at his shirt, pulling his jacket as they forced him to the ground.

"You idiots haven't eaten, have you?" A gruff voice asked. "Trying to sink your teeth in the first living thing you see?"

"Sorry," A more shrill voice said. "It's not often we get an intruder."

"Don't you know who this is?" A low gravelly voice asked. "We've been trying to get this bastard for a while now."

Ryland gasped for air. "Careful, we don't want to kill him." Someone said.

"You're right. The master's going to need him alive...for now."

There was devilish snickering, the last thing Ryland heard before a final struggled breath escaped his lips, and he fell, cold, to the ground.

Ryland awoke, only to find himself still shrouded in darkness. However, he could just see the soft golden glow of thousands of candles and torches through the fabric. The ground beneath him was dry, but cold, like the concrete floor of the Rogue's warehouse. Boots scuffled towards him—they sounded like thick rubber. He sensed a presence hovering above him.

"You did well, Eric," Ryland almost recognized the voice. It was cool and quite calm.

"Now, let's just see who the lucky final wolf soul is," the voice said. A hand pinched at the fabric, nearly pulling Ryland's hair as it was quickly ripped from his head.

Time is a funny thing. It slows down, it speeds up, and sometimes it screeches to a complete stop. Ryland felt all of those in the few seconds he looked into Christoph's eyes. Time had certainly changed him, and yet he was almost the exact same person who had left Ryland all those years ago. His brother's dark hair had a hint of red like Ryland's, and was neatly swept back.

Ryland's heart hammered in his chest. He had never thought he'd see his brother again, and certainly not like this. By the look on Christoph's face, he was thinking the exact same thing. "Ryland..." the name sounded so foreign coming from Christoph's lips. He too was surprised and looked at Ryland as if he were a ghost.

"You...you're the one," Ryland couldn't even find the words. Christoph stepped away from him, afraid to be close to him or else it would be real.

To Ryland's horror, his brother was shaking his head at him in disbelief. "How did you...No. Not you. I can't believe this..." he said with a shudder in his voice. He turned to face a heavyset shifter with thick facial hair. "Lock him up," he commanded. "This was not the plan at all."

"Wait! Christoph!" He never thought he'd call out to his brother again. Christoph wouldn't look at him, only turning away as another bag was placed over Ryland's head.

15. PARTING GIFT

It had been days since Ryland had left. Krista's eyes were closed, deep in concentration as she steadied her breathing. She had been trying to conjure up a vision, since her nightmarish one the other night, hoping to catch a glimpse of where Ryland could be. It felt as though she was drifting off into a deep sleep before she found herself feeling cold. The vision was clumsily chopped together, wavering like a flickering candle. The air was suddenly musty around her, and she could just about recognize a small cluster of yellow lights glowing in a dark room.

The rest was too hard to see. She could hear breathing, muffled and labored breathing from under a piece of fabric. Perhaps someone was suffocating Ryland. The thought of this made her chest sink. She couldn't bear to lose him, not after she had finally found someone to understand her.

At least she could hear the breathing. Maybe he was still alive—frightened and alone. Then, she could feel something more as she tried to feel out the vision more in her mind's eye.

Water. Rushing water. She felt how cold it was, and she could hear it running, even though she couldn't see it. Ironically, for having "visions," so many of her experiences focused on other senses. Then, over the water, and blending with it, was a voice. *"Ryland?"* It was nearly gasping, startled somehow.

Krista couldn't hold on any longer. The vision was fading now, and her eyes shot open as she gasped for air. She found herself back in Ryland's room, staring up at the ceiling over his bed.

Naked, Krista wrapped herself up in the fur blanket she had come to love since their night of passion. It was strangely comforting and reminded her vaguely of her wolf if she was even allowed to call him that. Rain pattered against the window to greet her as she woke up.

She hadn't been wallowing in her sorrow the entire time. For the past few days, she had been channeling her energy using every technique her mother had taught her. She'd alternated between studying and trying to trigger her visions. It wasn't her kind of thing to mope over a guy. It certainly wasn't new for her to be ghosted by one. However, Ryland was different, and she found herself missing him. Despite this, she was also bitter about how he had left the state of things. A conflict brewed in her heart. She wanted Ryland, to be closer to him and be his companion. On the other hand, she didn't know if she would ever see that version of Ryland ever again.

She had tried to leave the warehouse many times, only to be told of how unsafe it was. Even just going out for takeout required a pair of shifters at her side. Rush out, and then rush right back to the Rogue's hideout— the routine of the days she spent waiting for Ryland to come back.

Stacks of books covered the room. She had read so many of them. Useless facts and countless details of runes and magic swum in her head, yet she still couldn't bring herself to ask Tristan for the oracle bones. She had asked him many times if Ryland was going to come back. Tristan tried to reassure her, to help her understand that this was just part of Ryland's typical behavior to run off when things weren't going his way.

Something felt off about Ryland's disappearance this time. He certainly hadn't left on a good note with the Rogues or Krista. His words still hurt her, even though she wanted to give him the benefit of the doubt and believe that he didn't mean them. Before he left, he had declared he would follow his own lead and lift the curse on his own.

How could he have been so stubborn? Krista thought as she rolled her eyes at the thought of Ryland's pride, and how it had a habit of getting the best of him. She desperately hoped it wouldn't lead to his death as her vision had portrayed. What still haunted her, however, was the look in Ryland's eyes—how they had seemed to change color right before he told everyone off.

Maybe he knew he couldn't stop it, she thought. Maybe he was really an animal, aware that its death was imminent and thought the best thing to do was go off and get it over with quietly. If she believed that, then what was she still doing here? She had her own purpose to fulfill and without Ryland, how much of this was still up to her?

She dragged herself out of the bed, wrapping the blanket around her bare shoulders as she looked at the rain spilling down the window. With the sky so grey, it was hard to tell what time it was. Krista looked out at the heaps of metal scrap and factories that plagued Central City's downtown. She wondered if any one of these abandoned places was a potential hub for the enemy shifters.

I'm not going to sit here another day, she thought. *Not while Ryland's out there on his own.* Just as she had decided she was going to talk to Tristan, she heard a heavy creaking, as if an elephant-sized chair were being dragged across concrete.

The warehouse doors were opening. It had to be Ryland. He was the only one who used those doors on a regular basis. The other shifters had stayed put while he was missing except for the small side trips to accompany Krista.

She fumbled for some clothes, slipping into her typical garb of leggings and a sweatshirt. While she pulled on the sneakers Ryland had given to her, her chest leapt at his possible return.

She hoped he'd be ready to reconcile, and to apologize for his behavior before he had left. Krista ran for the door and into one of the halls, headed straight for the training room where the warehouse doors and Ryland would be waiting for her.

Her sneakers squeaked as she ran down the metal steps, her heart racing now. She tried desperately to push the thoughts of her vision from her mind, dismissing it as only a worry that didn't need to be pursued further. As she sprinted down the last hallway and pushed open the double doors to the training room, her eyes widened.

The loud creaking filled the room once more as the giant metal door began to close. Tristan was standing next to it by the button on the wall, his back turned to Krista. As she moved in closer, she discovered to her disappointment that Ryland was nowhere to be seen.

A shifter passed by her, a woman who gave a sad nod to Krista. Krista watched with confusion as the woman gave a polite wave to Tristan and ducked under the closing door. There were dozens like her, shifters walking off into the large alley leading to the downtown streets. It was a mass exodus of some kind, and as the doors closed with a hiss and a final clang, Krista realized that she was alone with Tristan.

"What's going on?" Krista asked. Tristan, surprisingly, was dressed differently than usual. It was strange for Krista to see him sporting a casual t-shirt and jeans. When he turned to face her, she noticed the healing bruises on his face where Ryland had punched him. He seemed tired. The sleepless nights had taken their toll on him too.

Krista waited for an answer, and Tristan tried to grasp for the words. Finally, he put it the best way he could. "The Rogues have...disbanded," he said curtly.

"What? Why would they do that?" Krista would have thought the shifters would wait for their alpha's return. Even if he had messed up, it was a huge change for the Rogues to pack up and leave all of a sudden.

"Because I told them to," Tristan said. Krista could tell this was a decision he had had to think long and hard about. Perhaps that's why he hadn't been sleeping as much. "There have been ...doubts circulating in the pack since the last pack meeting took place," he explained further. "Once Declan brought it to everyone's attention that Ryland couldn't keep them safe, the Rogues started to question if they wanted to be a part of the pack or not."

"But what about Ryland?" She asked. "He could be still out there. They didn't wait for him to come back first?"

"Why would they? You saw how he treated all of us before he made his grand exit." Tristan was still bitter about the incident, and it was apparent in his voice.

"That wasn't the real Ryland back there," Krista said defensively. "I saw something dark in his eyes. It had to be the curse talking, not him."

Tristan couldn't look at her and only shook his head. "I warned him," he said. "I tried to tell him his temper was getting out of hand. Look where that's gotten him. It's time he knows that he can't treat us this way, and come back as though nothing happened."

"So, you think he's just out moping somewhere?"

"I believe so. Declan's words really got to him during that last shifter meeting. I know he wasn't confident in his leadership abilities after that. I'm not surprised that he would take off for a few days."

"But he could be in danger. I heard him. Someone called out to him in one of my visions."

Tristan pushed up his glasses, this time wincing as his finger brushed against his bruised nose. "Are you still having those?"

"I've had one, yes," she said. "I have an idea of where Ryland might be. If we hurry, we can help him."

He was thinking it over, and Krista desperately hoped that somehow he still had some concern for his alpha. He walked away, disappearing for a moment into a small office. Krista's heart sank until Tristan reappeared with two black umbrellas, and a jacket draped over his shoulder. He handed one to her. "You lead the way," he said.

Rain pelted against the umbrellas. Krista was careful not to let the water drip onto her as she carefully navigated herself down the hill next to the overpass. As she drew closer to the culvert drain, she felt a tugging in her chest. She hoped that, if her vision was correct, Ryland could be somewhere in here. The rushing water immediately made her think that this was a good place to start.

"What's the significance of this place?" Tristan hollered from a safer location. Despite his casual garb, he was still iffy about the rain-soaked grass in front of him and stood like a plank at the top of the hill.

"When Ryland and I were looking for the oracle bones, we were chased by those shifters," Krista explained. "We found a passageway that brought us out here. In this drain pipe, there's a wall where we found those drawings—the prophecy."

"And you think Ryland's in there somewhere?"

"That's what I'm hoping, yes."

Krista's foot nearly slipped in the muddy earth as she crept closer to the tunnel. Her mind drifted back to that night she had spent with him, lying in the grass, his warm hand holding onto hers. She closed her eyes, just holding onto the moment for a second before letting it go.

She whispered a wish to herself that Ryland would still be alive once they got to him. Something was off about the culvert drain. Where water should have been pouring out, there was only a small trickle, as if it were a faucet running without water pressure.

Looking up, she discovered that the hole in the drain had been boarded up. A heavy metal sign was nailed to the boards: 'Danger! No Trespassing! "

"I don't understand," Krista said. "This wasn't here before."

"Perhaps they've just added it," Tristan suggested.

"No, something is strange about it." Krista moved closer, studying the letters. "This isn't an average city-issued sign," she told him. It was black paint, crusted over and running clumsily down the sheet of scrap metal, homemade and recently crafted.

"I think someone else made this," she added.

"How do you think we should proceed?" He asked. "We don't have the tools with us to get this open."

Krista pondered, her mind reeling with thoughts of Ryland trapped inside the tunnel. She mentally retraced her steps, quickly remembering the cellar-type doors next to a headstone. "The cemetery," she said. "There's another way into the tunnel. If we can head over there quickly-"

Tristan was already turning his back, his hand in his pocket as he wandered back up the hillside. "Where are you going?" Krista asked, impatient.

"I'm not picking up any signs of Ryland here," Tristan said.

"Of course you're not. It's raining," Krista insisted. She could tell there was something Tristan wasn't telling her, hence the poor excuse. "You don't want to find him, do you?" Krista asked as she followed him. Tristan stopped in his tracks.

"I don't need to," he said coldly. "I've been his beta for the past few years, ever since Christoph left. Ryland believes he's the strongest alpha in the city. Even if we do find him, it will take an extreme effort just to coax him back to reality."

"But what if he's in danger, or if the curse is finishing him up? Does that mean nothing to you at all?"

Tristan wiped the droplets of rain from his glasses. "Ryland clearly doesn't need me anymore, or any of us for that matter, or he wouldn't have left the way he did. For all we know, he's already taken care of it." His face was sad as he held out his hand for Krista to take. Krista ignored it, walking up the hill on her own. Tristan reached into his coat pocket. "It was an interesting ride, to say the least. I'm sorry if this was a fruitless journey for you. For a moment, I really did believe you were the oracle."

He opened his hand, holding out the silk bag of oracle bones. "I think Ryland would have wanted to give these to you," he said. Krista took them, the weight of the bones shifting over her fingers as they landed in her palm.

"What about the warehouse?" She asked. "What are you going to do with it?"

"I'll give it a few more days," he said. "I'll have to clear out Ryland's room, but the rest of the equipment, along with the warehouse will be put up for sale."

So, that was it, the end of the Rogues. Krista really couldn't believe it. "Can I stay there until he comes back?" She asked.

"I don't have high hopes," Tristan said. "Get back to your shop and your clients. The Rogue's are gone, but I'll contact a few shifters to keep an eye on your place just in case."

He held out his hand again, this time for a handshake. Krista, her mind plainly elsewhere, shook it. She could barely feel his hand in hers. All she could think about was Ryland.

She knew she couldn't go to the cemetery alone, and though she felt a tugging in her chest, she wondered if Tristan had been right about everything. Maybe she had been fooling herself this whole time.

A cab came to pick her up next to the overpass. Tristan paid the fare and gave a slight, sad wave as the car drove away. Krista watched him disappear through the rain-soaked window, and then she stared down at the pouch of oracle bones in her lap.

Tristan was right—it had been quite the ride.

Krista just couldn't come to terms that it was all over now.

16. BROTHERS

The cell was cold, like everywhere else in the tunnel system. Ryland stared hopelessly at the flickering candle beside the metal bars, just barely granting him enough light. He refused to eat, and his head was beginning to feel heavy like the rest of his body. For the past few days, he had wondered where Christoph was. Maybe their first encounter, since their estrangement, was too overwhelming for him. He never liked confrontation, always keeping to himself with his books when an issue arose.

His stay in the makeshift dungeon had been miserable. The cage was made of old bars welded together from old pieces of iron gates, presumably taken from the cemetery. Ryland could no longer tell when the days became nights. The only sounds he heard were the yelps and howls of the mysterious that his brother led.

Some was unlocking a large door near him, which meant that it must be a mealtime. It was the same thing of old scraps, which made it even more difficult to determine what part of the day it was. Ryland sat up. He had not shown any signs of weakness, once, in the presence of these shifters. He was battered and tired, but he held his head as high as he could.

It wasn't the usual shifter bringing him his meal. Instead, there was a woman carrying a battery-powered lantern. She held the door open for Christoph to walk into the room. It was still so strange for Ryland to see his own brother this way. His face had aged slightly, but he still looked like the little kid with glasses that Ryland used to play catch with.

Although he barely had the strength, Ryland stood to meet his brother's gaze. "I was wondering when you'd show up," he said to Christoph. Christoph seemed disturbed. "I needed some time to...prepare," he said. "They told me it was you, but I needed to see it for myself."

"What do you mean?"

"Hold out your arm."

Ryland didn't have to ask again. He rolled up his sleeve, revealing his now completely blackened arm underneath. It was painful to the touch, almost like horrible sunburn that never went away. Christoph examined it, his jaw tightening in the glow of the lantern's light. "Damn you, Ryland," he said through his teeth. "Why did this happen to you?"

"You think I planned for this...thing?" Ryland asked. "A shifter killed himself in front of me and this...curse...latched onto me."

"You interrupted my sacrifice's ritual," Christoph said shaking his head. "We recovered the body and the crystal dagger after your pack cleared out."

"Ritual? What have you been up to all this time?" Ryland asked. Christoph paced back and forth along the bars of the cage. "You remember what great-grandfather used to talk about? About the ancient shifters and how they received their powers from the wolf gods?"

"That was just a fairy tale he'd tell us at family gatherings."

"See, that's what I thought —until I had some time to myself to think it over. After you and I had...parted ways, I spent some time brushing up on my history. The ancient shifters knew they could awaken something incredibly powerful if they could use a ceremonial knife to harvest wolf souls."

"You're losing me here," Ryland said. Christoph placed his fingers on his temples. "I forgot I have to put things simply for you," he said. "I've been building my own pack since I left the Rogues. There are shifters here without a faction. They wander aimlessly around here, seeking guidance and direction. I've been taking them under my wing, and we've built our base here under the cemetery in Central City."

"What does that have to do with you killing other shifters?"

"We've only been taking the ones that intrude on our rituals. The shifter texts revealed that if one could gather enough wolf souls, they could be joined together in a living vessel to summon an incredible power."

"And I'm the vessel, then?"

Christoph turned from Ryland, and Ryland could sense his brother softening somehow.

"You weren't supposed to be, " he said, his voice somber. "We sent a shifter to a private space to practice the final ritual. He was our host until you appeared. I was told an enemy pack had arrived and sabotaged the ceremony, but I didn't know that it had been the Rogues. "

"That's what this is, then?" Ryland held up his arm. "The wolf souls are inside of me, now?"

Christoph shook his head. He reached into the pocket of his ragged coat and pulled out the dagger Ryland had seen before. It glistened in the lamplight—a long, polished crystallized blade emerging from the decorative handle. Soft pulses of blue energy spread through it, forming patterns in the gemstone.

Christoph admired the shape of it, his gaze following along the sharpened blade. "Great-grandfather wasn't just buried with the oracle bones," he explained.

"The wolf souls are contained in the crystal dagger, our ceremonial weapon. However, the final soul comes from the host, who must lose his own life to the blade. What's taking place inside of you isn't a curse, it's the weakened spirit of what we'd been trying to summon. It's been feeding off of you, searching for a way out."

"Why haven't I heard of this? I've read every shifter text and not one mentions anything about this ritual."

"You should remember where your private library came from," Christoph said, pushing up his glasses. "I knew every title on those shelves by heart, and I knew there was one that couldn't be brought to anyone else's eyes, including yours. So I took it. After all, I was building a pack of my own. That day I left was the day you became my enemy."

He stared straight ahead, deep in his own mind somewhere. It seemed as though there was more he wanted to say, but not with foreign ears around.

"Leave me," he said finally to his shifter companion. The woman beside him left the lantern next to Christoph on her way out, closing the door behind her. The silence between Ryland and his brother was overwhelming, a game of who would be the first to crack.

"This isn't a pack at all, Christoph," Ryland said. "This is a cult."

"I don't like to use that phrase, but yes. If you must call it something, you could consider us a cult that worships the ancient spirit."

"I wouldn't have thought a scholar like you would get caught up in brainwashing practices."

"I'm not brainwashing anyone! Not like what you've done with the Rogues! Turning them all into combat automatons for your disposal!" Christoph's voice echoed around the chamber.

"I'm their alpha," Ryland said firmly. "I was doing what's best for them."

"You still don't understand. We were all afraid of you! Do you think the Rogues stayed out of respect? I tried to help you see that, to tell you it should be a community."

"So you left and formed a cult? Is that the community you've been seeking?"

"Nothing's changed, Ryland. I've found a way to move on, to prove myself stronger than the others without making a display of myself."

"What about all those symbols you've been leaving? Or the wolf corpses you've carelessly left behind in your wake? Your cult killed my strategist. That sounds like quite the display to me!"

"Henna?" Christoph's voice was softer now.

"You didn't know?"

"I told them to just take anyone they saw falling behind."

Ryland couldn't believe these words were coming from his brother's mouth. Christoph had been such a kind spirit when they were younger. Now he had turned into a thoughtless killer, a cult leader hungry for power.

"I should have never kicked you out," Ryland said. "So many lives would have been spared if not for you. I might have been amongst them."

"Don't," Christoph warned. "Don't...remind me."

"About what? How you're going to kill your own brother for power? I may be tough on my pack, but I'd never take life to prove myself worthy of leading it."

"Are you so sure about that? It was reported to me that someone tore one of my members to shreds when they tried to obtain the oracle."

Ryland felt the sting throughout his body. He knew he hadn't been himself when he had killed that shifter, but it was still painful to think about his lack of control over the ancient spirit inside of him, or how Krista had looked at him afterwards. An image of Tristan's face trembling against his fist tugged at his heart. He had done violent and terrible things, and he wondered how much of that was the 'curse' and how much of it was him.

"I found a picture of us when we started the Rogues," he said trying to shift his brother's thoughts to other places. "If you knew we'd be here today, what would you have said?"

"I'd say we were making a huge mistake," Christoph said. To Ryland's surprise, a small smile cracked on his brother's lips. Christoph sat down, leaning his back against the cage.

"I'm sorry," he finally said, keeping his gaze forward. "I'm sorry this has happened to you. If I had known it was you..."

Ryland sensed the conflict forming with his brother. He crouched down beside him, daring to reach his hand out of the cage and placing it on Christoph's shoulder.

"Then why don't you help me stop this?" He said quietly. "Help me purge this spirit, and maybe...maybe we could try this whole thing again."

Christoph didn't turn around. His shoulder felt cold under Ryland's touch. "It's not that simple," Christoph said.

"We can both be alpha. Help me rebuild the pack. We'd be unstoppable together."

"I have my own pack to think about now. I've come so far for this—years of research. So much blood spilled-"

"So what? Let me out of here. We can drop all of this. You can even take your pack with you." He reached again between the bars, handing Christoph the very photograph he spoke of. Christoph held it, unable to tear his gaze away from the two young men staring back at him.

"My pack doesn't serve me alone. Their diligence lies with the Ancient One," Christoph flipped a switch, standing and pulling away from Ryland's touch. "And so does mine."

He picked the lantern off the ground, casting crooked shadows around the chamber. "He'll be here soon," he said. "And we'll prepare you for the final sacrifice."

"Are you listening to yourself right now?" Ryland cried out. "Please tell me you're aware of how crazy all of this sounds!"

Christoph froze in place. "I always wanted to be the best," he said. "You've had your chance, Ryland, throughout our entire lives. Now it's my turn."

"Christoph!" Ryland clutched at the bars, shaking them furiously. His body and heart ached, and he silently wished this evil spirit would help him rip the cage apart. But his brother kept walking without giving him another glance.

Then, Christoph turned, keeping his gaze on his feet. "We still need the oracle, you know," he said. "Word has spread that you're somehow connected to her. I'll have you know you'll be reunited soon."

"Don't you touch her," Ryland growled as he rattled the cage bars.

"I can't have her power interfering with our final ceremony," Christoph said.

Ryland remembered the image painted on the wall. The blue woman locked in a cage. Christoph was lost, and though he was furious, Ryland wondered if there was any way to get his brother back. Ryland had lost him once before, but perhaps there was a chance, a chance that Ryland had wished for so long ago.

Once the door slammed and Christoph had left him alone, Ryland sank back down to the ground, holding his head in his hands. *"Krista, you have to run"*, he thought. He hoped that if only he could think of her long enough, he could somehow manifest his thoughts into hers. If they were as connected as he thought, maybe he could reach out to her. Two spirits calling to each other in the unseen realm.

"Please, Krista. Please, be somewhere safe..."

17. ORACLE

"Alright, Krista, just close your eyes and concentrate on the light." Her mother, Helene, always had a stern voice with never a hint of charm to it.

"Mom, for the last time, I don't even see a light!" The sixteen-year-old Krista ran her tongue along her braces, her eyes partially opening to look at the wild-haired woman standing in front of her, dressed in long curtains of eccentric fabric. She vaguely resembled Krista, the same light-colored eyes, full of wisdom, and elfin features.

"That's why you have to concentrate. The spiritual realm is hard to reach. It requires all of our practice and attention to access it."

Krista sat cross-legged on a pile of pillows, trying to steady her breathing as she meditated. Her mind kept wandering. What did she eat for lunch today? How many times would she have to study her tarot deck before she finally understood it? When would she finally be able to go back to school and to her friends. She'd probably be in math class if it had been an ordinary day. So many thoughts mingled in her mind, creating a wall of static. Finally, she opened her eyes with a tired sigh. "I can't do it. I've got nothing."

"Can't is just an excuse."

"No, really mom, I can't. I don't know why you keep pushing this on me after I've told you. I don't have the 'gift' or whatever you call it." She tried to stand up from the pillows, but her mother placed her hands firmly on her shoulders and pressed her back down.

"I know you're too young to understand," she said firmly. "But my power is fading, and it'll only be a matter of time before I have to leave you here."

"Is that what happened to Dad?"

Helene's eyes flitted away from Krista's gaze. "There are some people that don't understand this gift," she said quietly. "Your father was one of them. If you stay away from men, you won't have to deal with such things. Now, let's try again..."

"Please, Krista. Please, be somewhere safe..."

Krista's eyes opened, and for a second she was startled to find herself back in her loft above the psychic's shop. She could have sworn she had heard Ryland's voice calling out to her in her sleep. A cluster of beer cans clattered onto the floor as she sat up on the couch. Last night had been rough. She had forgotten the state the shop was in before she had run away from it. It had taken hours for her to clean it up to a state where her clients would even be willing to return, if they were after she had disappeared without warning.

She cooked herself a quick breakfast with the only ingredients that weren't spoiled in her fridge. As she ate, she took a quick peek outside the window by her bed. There were two shifters circulating around the shop, their eyes and ears open for any suspicious activity. Not only did they make Krista feel safer, but they also brought her a strange sense of comfort that she didn't have to leave the world of shifters entirely behind her.

As she put her bowl in the sink, her attention was drawn to the silk bag of oracle bones on the counter. She reached out for them but hesitated. Ryland's words echoed in her mind, about how she should never give up. She still hadn't heard anything about his whereabouts. She wondered just how long she should wait until she gave up.

The sign on the door flipped from closed to open as Krista unlocked the door to her shop. She glanced at the shelves, now neatly tidied up and filled with her mother's belongings. Before she could reach out and grab one of the books, the bell on the entryway gave a slight ring.

"Oh, Mrs. Remy! It's nice to see you come in so early," she said.

Mrs. Remy's purse dangled over her arm as she shuffled her old body into the store. "Do you know how happy I was to see that you were open?" she said with a warm grandmotherly-like smile. "I tried to call the shop many times, only to find you were closed."

"We had to make some...repairs," Krista said. "I needed the vacation anyway."

"Don't we all? I hope you had time to relax."

"Oh, I could still use a few more days of rest." Krista nearly laughed at the irony. If only Mrs. Remy knew everything she had been through and the things she had experienced in the shifter's world. The thought of it had only made her sad now. Once again, she found herself back in her shop, carrying on business as usual. Even the devoted Mrs. Remy had shown up. Life was normal. *As it should be*, Krista shrugged.

"Are you here for a reading?" She asked the old woman and she went to pull out a chair for her at her reading table. To her surprise, Mrs. Remy shook her head. "Not at all, dear. In fact, I'm here to give you a thank you gift." She dug through her purse, and handed Krista a packet wrapped in tissue paper. Krista unfolded it and revealed a lovely delicate headscarf.

She nearly gasped as she unraveled it, staring in awe at the glittering moon and star patterns embedded in the black chiffon. "Oh, this is far too generous, Mrs. Remy-" she began.

"Go on," Mrs. Remy prodded. "Try it on!"

Krista smiled at the fabric as she wrapped it carefully around her head, letting it drape over her shoulders. She turned to look at herself in the mirror. "My God," she said. "I'm nearly the spit and image of my mother!" As soon as she realized it, she felt a heavy weight on her—a feeling of power surrounding her.

"Now you look like a real fortune teller," Mrs. Remy said, admiring the contrast of the fabric against the red shock of Krista's hair. "I'm paying it forward if you will. After all, you've done a lot for me to help me find happiness."

"So you asked out that man in the assisted living home after all?" Krista asked with a knowing smirk. Mrs. Remy surprised her again as she shook her head once more.

"Oh, heavens, no. He turned out to be a real snore fest," she said. "Quite literally. He fell asleep during our lunch date. But, luckily I was at the grocery store the other day when I bumped into an old friend of mine from my college days. We picked up right where we left off. He has just lost his wife too, and we've been seeing each other ever since."

Krista was taken aback. Her visions were bound to come true at some time or another, and it completely floored her to hear Mrs. Remy's outcome had been different. "I thought for sure you would have hit it off with that other man," Krista said, almost to herself. Mrs. Remy was still all smiles. "Life has a funny way of surprising us, doesn't it?" She asked. "I better get going. I hope you like your gift. I'll be back next week for our scheduled reading."

"Of course, Mrs. Remy," Krista said with a warm smile, though her mind was stormy now. "Same time, same place."

"By the way, who are those handsome men standing outside your shop?" The old woman prodded. "Is there a 'someone' in your future now?"

"Not quite," Krista said, a flutter of sadness in her chest. "They're just inspecting the place."

The little bell rang against the door as Mrs. Remy smiled at each of the shifter men standing by the entrance.

"Anything wrong?" Krista asked them.

"Nothing out of the ordinary," one of them said.

"And no sign of Ryland?"

They only shook their heads at her. She gave a sad shrug as she turned her attention back to reorganizing the remaining upset behind her counter. Those evil shifters had made quite the mess during their search for her, and she still had a few things to put back in order.

As she swept away the remains of a broken clock face and a pile of junk mail, she noticed a hint of black ink looking up at her. 'Krista' was written on it. Her stomach did a flip. Was it a note from Ryland about his whereabouts? She could only hope as she sifted the trash to the side and pulled it from the rubble.

It was sealed with wax, certainly not Ryland's style, but he was full of surprises. She slid her finger under it the seal, breaking the envelope open and pulling out the letter inside. As soon as she opened it, she realized it wasn't Ryland who had written to her.

Her mother's handwriting was concise. She was surprised she had even found the note in the shop. It seemed as though her mother had left her a goodbye message after all, despite Krista's belief that she wouldn't. Krista sat in her usual chair by her reading table, focusing deeply on the note:

Krista,

By the time you read this, I'll be very far off on my spiritual journey in the Himalayas. There are monks there that claim they can strengthen a psychic's abilities and I must train with them to learn their ways. Funny, we are always learning, aren't we? Even though I've left you everything, including my shop, there is still plenty for you to learn.

Before I go, I will leave you with my advice. Our gift is incredible—how we can see into the future. However, you should always remember one thing: the future is an unknown shape, which we must grab hold of and mold into something new. Whatever shape you make of your future, I hope that you'll eventually understand the power that you hold deep inside yourself. No vision or spell or tarot card spread can tell you otherwise.

I love you and hope you'll understand my leaving. Take care of the shop, but more importantly, take care of yourself, always. You hold a very important spirit inside of you—one that will reveal itself in due time and one that you should never doubt. Goodbye, my daughter. May blessings follow you everywhere you go.

Much love, and plenty of magic,
Mother

Krista's hand shook and she read her mother's words over, and over again. Here she had thought she was forgotten about and that her mother left her without even muttering a goodbye—that all of her training had been for nothing. But, as she sat, mulling over the goodbye note, she began to realize there was something important that she had missed.

She left the note on the table and grabbed Mrs. Remy's gift, before bounding up the steps. Although she felt shaky in her abilities, she knew that her mother had believed in her all along and that she might have another chance to use her power for something great.

Slamming the door behind her, Krista grabbed the silk bag on her counter and headed straight for her coffee table. She sat cross-legged on the ground, looking at the old pack of tarot cards. It felt like so long ago that she had done the reading for herself. Now she had a whole new understanding of what being a psychic meant. It wasn't in the cards, or in the lines on her palm.

She shook the contents of the bag into her hand. For the past few days she had been studying her runes, but none of it would mean anything if Krista didn't believe in the one final element she needed to read the prophecy.

Her breath felt heavy in her chest as the bones rattled back and forth, their message yearning to be determined. If her vision for Mrs. Remy hadn't come true, then who's to say that her vision of Ryland would come true as well? She could only hope she had enough time.

She stopped shaking the bag, and took a deep breath. Finally, it became clear to her why she couldn't read her cards in front of Tristan and Ryland, or why she couldn't understand the oracle bones during the shifter meeting. Krista believed the future was always certain, and that only brought her a fear that stunted her abilities. It's why she was too afraid to pursue a relationship with anyone, or too scared even to leave her shop, or indeed why she had gone home instead of looking for the one man who understood her.

The oracle was inside of her. It always had been. Now she was trying to speak, loud and clear. *The future is uncertain*, she told herself, *and there's no reason to fear something you can't see clearly.*

She picked up Mrs. Remy's present, wrapping the delicate chiffon scarf over her head. It was her own ritual, and for once she felt as though she was in perfect control of this moment. Now, she was more than a psychic. Her thoughts already felt like magic flowing through her brain. She felt a rush of energy—her veins pulsing as she finally untied the bag. "Give me sight," she whispered to the bones, to the oracle guiding her hand as she flipped the silk upside down.

Time slowed, as the bones fell. Krista felt as if they were her own bones. They spread out, each of the tiny pieces falling into a perfect shape of a crescent moon on the table, as if they had their own consciousness. Krista felt a rush of excitement as she pored over them. There were twisted symbols, squiggles and ancient scrawling in an unrecognizable language. Yet Krista could understand all of them with ease. It was as if someone had lifted a curtain from her eyes.

The words flowed from her mouth like honey as she clearly spoke the language of the bones. At first, she had been frightened, but then she thought of Ryland and the Rogues, of Tristan and the shifters that she refused to let die in vain. She would hold onto this strange magic that began to surround her and never let go until she learned the truth.

As she spoke, she noticed a faint glow emanating from the bones. She was reading the prophecy! Every word of it. An intense heat spread from her toes, all the way up to the top of her scalp, and she couldn't stop herself from shaking as pure energy began to flow through her.

She could hardly breathe. Her lungs were filled with cold, arctic air. The bones began to rattle on the table, shaking violently before they slowly levitated up into the air in front of her face.

Then, she heard a voice. It was a woman's voice, as stern as her mother's. It was almost like an ancient song to her ears. *"Hail, Krista..."*

"W-who are you?" It was hard even for Krista to speak, especially since there was nobody around to hear her.

"Do not be afraid, for you have awakened my spirit with the ancient words. The oracle hears you. I will grant you with sight." The words echoed, bouncing off every part of Krista's skull. She suddenly felt a rush of power flowing through her entire body as the oracle's spirit revealed itself to her.

Krista turned her head to the sky, the power suddenly overwhelming. She was surrounded by a distant roaring and felt as though she were flying through all of space and time. Her eyes widened, filling with a swirling blue light as she experienced her vision.

It was the clearest she had ever seen and it was as if she were standing right there. She heard the ancient words, and again she understood all of them.

"The power of old returns to the new. The Wolf God will rise once more. He will bring the Earth to its knees."

Krista felt the non-existent ground shaking beneath her. She saw flashes of Ryland, from the moment he had stepped into her shop, to the moment they had first made love. Then, she saw the dark shadow from her nightmares. It was tightening itself around Ryland, choking him and entering his mouth. Krista flew forward, further in time until she found herself in a pitch-black space. A fire began to erupt from the ground, as an enormous wolf monster, the size of a skyscraper, rose up. He was half-man, half wolf, his jaws agape as he laughed maniacally.

The fire began to spread, and Krista suddenly found herself standing on a busy street. The roads were cracked as if an earthquake had taken place. Bodies rushed past her, screaming in terror. She watched in horror as the massive wolf monster laid an entire city-scape to waste with its paw.

Buildings crumbled, and a massive wave of dust flew over Krista. She braced herself, but it passed right through her as if she were a ghost. The wolf monster grabbed a fistful of screaming people and threw them into his mouth.

Then, Krista heard the voices again, whispers in ancient tones. *"But the oracle will emerge, once again. Only she can dispel the darkness."*

The dust and debris flew around Krista like a massive whirlwind. A blinding blue light was cast on the streets as a cloud-like orb began to pick up everything around it. Pieces of buildings and cars were crushed under the gravity of the orb before they were sucked up into its gravitational pull.

Krista's eyes widened once she saw what was in the center. A woman, just like the picture she had seen in Ryland's old books. She held out her arms as if she could control every part of the Earth with her fingertips. Her ancient robes flew wildly about her. She floated in the center of her sphere of energy, as it moved up to the wolf's face. It growled and roared at her, but she was not afraid.

Instead, she simply held out her hand, placing it on directly on the wolf's nose. Then, as if an atomic bomb had hit the ground, a blinding flash of energy burst from in between the two forces, spreading out wide and covering the entire world.

Krista was knocked back, off of the street, back into space and time as she was being yanked out of her vision. White light still blinded her, as she heard the deafening roar of the wolf monster as it was defeated.

She woke up on the floor in a cold sweat, her heart throbbing violently in her ears. A gasp tore at her lungs as she sat up. The oracle bones fell to the table, scattering every which way, as their power was exhausted. She had done it. Finally, she had seen the curse, and everything it would bring.

Of course, she had witnessed and experienced the power of the oracle. She gazed at her fingertips, which still had swirls of blue energy racing around them. As she made a fist, the swirls conjoined into a handful of what looked like blue smoke.

Her breath still felt cold in her chest, and she quickly changed into her leggings and sneakers, the familiar outfit she wore with the Rogues. As she raced back down the stairs, she threw open the door and startled the two shifters standing guard.

"We have to gather the factions, now!" She said. "Something wicked is about to be awakened. It's time for us to stop it!"

18. AWAKENING

Ryland winced as the rope was tightened around his wrists. Even if he had tried to shift, he'd still be caught in the ropes. Two cultists were holding his sides as his feet were tied to a metal loop on the floor. His entire body was stretched out, preventing any sort of escape from his oncoming death.

"We have to cleanse him first," Christoph stood in the center of the cult's main room, where Ryland had first been reunited with his brother. They had spray-painted the symbol of their pack on the floor in black. Candles filled the room with an ominous light, casting terrifying shadows onto the wall.

A woman approached him, her face and body obscured with a long hooded robe. Ryland couldn't believe such archaic garb was being worn in a place like this. It only added to the cult's mystery. The woman held out a stick of sage, tied neatly together with a leather cord. She lit it ablaze, casting the smoke over Ryland as she incanted a chant.

The embers stung at his skin. At this point, the spirit had consumed nearly all of his body. "We have to do this soon," Christoph said without looking at his brother. "There'll be nothing left to give, if the spirit consumes him completely."

"Christoph...you can stop this right now," Ryland tried desperately to get his brother to understand. But Christoph was wrapped up in his own scheme. He was remorseful about sacrificing his own brother, but the wild look in his eye told Ryland that he wasn't going to change his mind.

"How much longer until the dagger is ready?" He asked the heavyset shifter by his side.

"The dagger is still being purified and blessed," the shifter replied.

"Are the exits sealed?"

"Since this morning, My Liege."

"Of course they'd call you their liege," Ryland scowled.

"This coming from the only alpha I've met whose pack calls him, 'Sir'" Christoph retorted.

Just in that exchange, Ryland thought there was a glimmer of his brother still inside of him. There just had to be a better way to coax it out.

The burning sage stung his nose and engulfed his senses. For some odd reason, it was making him feel dizzy and strange. He wondered if it was even sage that was being burnt. The room grew fuzzy around him—his brother's face slightly blurry as he moved about the room.

Again, he tried desperately to contact Krista, although he couldn't hear her from the other side. *"Please be safe"*, he kept saying to her, as he feared the shifters would be coming for her soon and locking her up. Christoph didn't want any flaw in his plan and was taking specific measures to prevent it from failing.

"Krista, I didn't run, He's going to kill me". Suddenly it became more real to him. *"He's going to kill me."* His heart ached at the thought. How he wished now that he could see where his pride had led him. If only he had been a more understanding alpha. If he hadn't pushed them so hard, he wouldn't be tied up and about to be sacrificed—spending his final moments in a cold and lonely dungeon.

"He's going to kill me..."

Krista heard Ryland's voice ringing loud and clear in her mind. She tilted her head down and her eyes cleared as she gazed out at the five shifter factions. They watched her with shock and awe.

"Ryland is going to be sacrificed by his brother," she warned. Her voice boomed, full of power in the Rogue's warehouse. Even though she hadn't been away from it for long, it was comforting to be back in its meeting hall.

"How do you know?" Rizz called from his seat.

"I have just heard his voice," she said.

As the blue clouds of energy faded around her, she placed her hands on the table. Nobody believed she was the oracle. Now, here they were, witnessing the true power that they had doubted. It was a slight shock to Krista, to say the least.

"I'm sure you can guess why you've been gathered here today," she said. "There is a spirit, an all-powerful being mentioned in shifter texts. He's the Wolf God, a symbol of fear and power in the ancient world."

"How do you know?" Sam asked.

"Because I've seen him myself," Krista's confidence was growing now. "He's bigger than any of us can imagine. I watched as he swallowed buildings and people whole."

"So, what about the curse?" Ben asked. "Is it part of this prophecy?"

"There is no curse," Krista said. "Ryland has been carrying the spirit of the Wolf God inside of him. Once he is killed and the spirit is finally unleashed, the Wolf God will wreak havoc on the city."

"From its roots to its skies..." Declan said quietly, remembering the note he had brought into the last meeting in his attempt to slander Ryland's name. "I had it all wrong," he added.

"You've learned your lesson, but now we can come together and right all wrongs," Tristan said from behind Krista. It was so odd for her to sit in Ryland's seat. She relished every moment of it. Fear was foreign to her now. At any other time she would have hidden inside of herself. But, now she had the power, and she knew the truth. Now, she just had to use it for its true purpose.

"We don't have much time," she said. "Each faction can round up a team, and we'll infiltrate the place where this dark presence is hidden."

"What's in it for us?" Sam said, nodding to her strongest shifters.

"Is it not enough of a reward to be able to stay alive another day on this Earth?" Krista's voice was rising. It was as if the oracle was speaking for her, giving her the right words to say.

The alphas looked to one another, each of them waiting to give a reply. Krista wondered if it would just be her taking on this mission. Even with her new abilities, she knew she couldn't take on an entire pack of wolves on her own, let alone the Wolf God if he were awakened. Surprisingly, Declan was the first to stand from his seat. The entire room fell silent as they waited for his answer. "The Stalkers will send a team with the Rogues."

"So will the Nightcallers," Rizz chimed in. "All she had to say was 'staying alive' and I was in."

"The Furies will provide aid," declared Sam

"And I give you some of my South Stars," said Ben.

Krista had to catch her breath. The support had been overwhelming and unexpected. She held her hands up, the static of electricity crackling through her fingertips. "Very well," she said, "let's assemble immediately!"

The shifters scattered from their seats, calling out orders to the shifters they had brought with them. The plan was beginning to form now, and as she turned she noticed Tristan deep in thought.

"Not what you were expecting?" Krista asked. Tristan shook his head. "I feel so foolish," he said. "It was wrong of me to doubt you. If you'll have me...I'd like to accompany you as well." He nervously shifted his gaze. "I owe it to Ryland," he added. "Despite how he'd left us and the Rogues."

Krista placed her hand on his shoulder. Suddenly, she could feel Tristan's emotions, as if they were traveling directly through her palm, up her arm to her mind. She felt his pity, his pain, and his desire to be better than he had been. It must have been another gift of the oracle, to be able to see and experience emotions this way. "None of us wanted him to leave that way," she told him. "What he did to you was wrong, but he is our alpha. The least we can do for him is save him and let him be accountable for his own actions."

How the hell did she get so wise? Krista couldn't help but smirk. Even though the oracle had been with her for her entire life, it was exciting to see her spirit come to life inside her. Even Tristan seemed surprised at her words, and Krista owned every second of it as she sounded the call to gather the wolf clans.

"*Hold on, Ryland...*" She thought, projecting herself into his mind. Already, she felt his fear and his pain, through the connection they shared between their spirits.

"*Help is on the way...*"

The words were just faint enough, but Ryland could hear Krista's voice, which filled him with hope. Never before had he heard her this way, and he could only assume that she finally knew how to awaken her power. That is unless he was just hearing things out of delusion. He hadn't eaten or slept well in days, and could very well be the victim of his own thoughts.

He struggled against the bindings around his limbs, like a fly in a spider's web. His body felt heavy hanging from the ropes that pulled at his muscles, threatening to tear his arms right from their sockets. His brother hadn't come back yet. Earlier, he had watched as Christoph debated heavily with one of his shifters, the large man with the beard before finally, Christoph left the room in a huff.

One by one, the circular chamber in the sewers was filling up with members of Christoph's shifter cult. Old waterlogged boards were placed on top of the system of rushing water, to create a makeshift platform for the ceremony to take place. Candles surrounded every corner, some of them held by cult members wearing long tattered robes. They had painted the symbol of their pack on their chests, and all of them wore plastic wolf masks. It reminded Ryland of something out of a fantasy movie, even though it was all very, very real.

The cult members formed a circle, some of them sitting along the strips of concrete on either side of the water. Ryland was in the center, staring in awe at the sheer size of his brother's pack. Ryland had no idea how he had managed to gather so many members. Christoph had impeccable management skills, which would have come in handy for forming a cult of this size. That and the promise of the power the Wolf's spirit would give them if this sacrifice was successful.

Finally, once the room was full, it fell completely silent. Ryland could only hear the ringing in his hears, and the thunder of his heartbeat pounding against his eardrums. Then, it began as soft as the first raindrops of an impending storm. One voice sang a note, low and ominous. The others added to the melody, one after the other, until a bizarre chorus was bouncing from every wall of the chamber.

The song continued in the language Ryland could only remember from the chaotic whisperings the wolf's spirit often spoke to him. Finally, out of the corner of his eye, he saw Christoph in the back of what appeared to be a strange parade of sorts. A female shifter held a long hooked rod with a lantern at the end, leading the rest of the party. Behind her was a man, a pillow held in both of his upturned palms. There was another man with a violin that only added another level of eeriness to the singing.

Christoph had a hood over his head. Whatever reservations he may have had seemed far behind him now. Ryland could feel his stomach churning, and a cold sweat formed on his brow. He clenched his teeth at the growing pain. They had stripped him down nearly to nakedness, and his muscles contorted as the wolf's spirit continued to eat at him. It seemed more aroused by the chanting, begging to be finally unleashed. Ryland wasn't sure what he should expect, other than he wouldn't stay alive long enough to see it.

The parade disbanded, spreading out into a row in front of Ryland. The music and the singing died down until once again there was a deafening silence. Christoph raised his arms in welcome. "The day is finally here," he announced, his voice echoing to every member of his cult. "You have all done very well, doing everything in your power to gather the wolf souls. Now, tonight, we offer them up to Sulous, the ancient Wolf God."

Ryland could feel his brother's gaze, despite the fabric obscuring Christoph's eyes. "Sulous has slept for many centuries. Now, he is stirring, alive and well in this gracious host you see before you. He longs to be released, to finally bring justice to this chaotic world."

He turned to face the cult members behind him. All of them were latching on to every word, grateful to witness such a monumental moment. Ryland, on the other hand, kept himself from rolling his eyes. Christoph was certainly the most theatrical out of the two of them. If he wasn't about to die by his brother's hand, he would have laughed in his face.

"Long ago, the shifters were headed for war and disaster. Today, they're only bound by a treaty that has only divided them further. When Sulous walks this earth, he will bring us all together once more. Shifters will join shifters, and we will live under the one true alpha. There will be a place for us in this world riddled with humans, and we shall reign over them until the end of time!"

The room ignited with cheers and raucous applause for Christoph to absorb. He laid his head back, taking all of it in as if he were fueled by their praises. "Aren't you glad I brought you all here today? Aren't you glad that all of you are under the Star of Sulous, and you will be the first to receive his blessing?"

More cheers as the cult members grew wilder now. To Ryland's dismay, they longed to see the Wolf God. He could only hope that somewhere Krista was making a plan. *"Where are you?"* He asked her.

"You have to hurry. Please, hurry."

Krista and the others ripped the metal sign from the front of the large culvert drain, chucking the heap of metal to the side. A wave of water rushed from the tunnel and down the hill. Luckily it was night, and the streetlights couldn't reach the secret entrance to the tunnel system.

Shifters were lined up, itching to get inside and all of them ready for whatever was on the other side. Krista stood on one end of the culvert drain, looking out at the army before her. Each shifter faction had gathered a team of what must be one hundred wolves. Each alpha stood proudly with their chosen pack members. Krista wondered if it would be enough. They certainly couldn't back up and do a recount. It would have to be enough.

Tristan was at her side. "Whenever you're ready," he told her. "We have to go now," she said. "I can hear Ryland..."

She turned to face the shifters. "I know that I am only new to your world, and there is much for me to learn. But, I've been around long enough to have seen the differences you all have. Each pack has their own strengths, their own weaknesses."

The alphas nodded as they hung onto her words. "You've been separated by those differences," she continued, her voice loud and clear in the dark cold night. "The shifter factions achieved peace, once before. But those lines separated you. Please, settle your differences with me, and tonight we will come together as one pack, and save this world that we all share!"

Cheers filled her ears, and she stood to the side as she let the shifters free. One by one, they transformed. The wolves rushed into the black tunnel, howling with reckless abandon as the five shifter factions blended together with wild excitement. Krista watched as Tristan turned into a dark wolf with a thin light stripe, in a flash. He led Krista behind the army as they began Ryland's rescue.

"We're in the tunnels..." Ryland lifted his head, his eyes widening. Krista's voice was becoming clearer now. Help was on the way as she had promised. But, would she stop Christoph in time?

Ryland could only helplessly watch as his brother lifted the crystal dagger from the shifter's silk pillow. The blade glimmered in the candlelight as Christoph brandished it. As he stepped closer to Ryland, he lifted his hand over his hood, pulling the fabric from his eyes.

"Now, brother, we will see who the strongest alpha is," he said. Ryland could hear the catch in Christoph's voice. "Christoph..." he could only whisper, his voice weak. "I can never come back from this. I hope you know that."

Christoph hesitated, his jaw clenched. He tilted his gaze away from Ryland's as he contemplated. "You think I didn't consider that, at all?" He said, pointing the knife in Ryland's side. Ryland winced as the blade pricked at his skin, already drawing a bead of blood, growing a fresh ruby red from the air.

Christoph stared with wide eyes at the blood, as if under some kind of trance. "I'm sorry, Ryland," he said. "Surely you understand wanting to bring the shifters together under one rule."

"Not like this..." Ryland mustered. "Wandering in the dark will only make things harder for you to see."

"Enough!" Christoph hollered, startling Ryland. The dagger was still digging into his side, but not nearly hard enough to pierce him completely. "I've had enough of this. Do you think I haven't suffered enough with this decision? For my own brother to host Sulous's spirit?"

He pointed at the cult members surrounding him. "They are all here because of me. How could I promise them something only to take it away? Surely you understand."

Ryland shook his head, tired and without the words to say that could make his brother stop. "If Sulous happens to grant you a long life, I hope you spend every day of it thinking about the day that you killed me."

He was pleased with those final words, but he needed to talk to Krista before it was all over. "*I'm sorry, Krista,*" he thought. "*Please forgive me, and know that I never quite understood love before that first time you touched me.*"

Cheers filled the chamber as the bloodthirsty shifters watched Christoph draw his arm back, ready to deliver the final blow that would awaken the mighty Sulous. Ryland stared hard into his brother's matching olive-green eyes. He wanted him to remember, to forever burn the image into his mind.

"*Oh, please, Ryland. Spare me with the theatrics,*" Krista's voice rang out, loud and clear, in his mind. Before Christoph could stab the crystal dagger into Ryland, the cheering slowed, mingling into a chorus of wolf howls and wild growling. "What is that?" Christoph turned to his posse behind him. They shrugged but readied themselves just as the tunnels were flooded with packs of furious and frenzied wolves.

At the end of them, Ryland could see a figure with glowing blue eyes approaching. He recognized her figure, even in the flickering candlelight. Krista had finally come for him. Despite everything, she had arrived and had brought reinforcements at her side.

The cultists scattered, each of them frantically shifting into their wolf forms and attacking the enormous pack of intruders. Howls filled the dark chamber, overwhelming Ryland's ears as an underground war raged around him. He watched as Tristan fought beside Krista, his teeth lashing out at anyone that got too close to her. Krista's mouth fell open with relief once she saw Ryland, and his heart was filled just to see her so close to him again.

A blue glow surrounded her, and Ryland could only smile knowing that the power of the oracle now flowed through her veins and that she had gathered the strength to awaken it herself.

And then, as quickly as it had come, it was all torn from him in an instant. He saw Krista's smile slowly morph into a terrified wail from across the chamber. At first, he felt cold as the blade slid through his skin. There was a pinprick of shock, like static that spread throughout his body. It wasn't until the blade was ripped from his side that he felt a fire washing over him.

He cried out in agony, and a loud roar was ripped from his lungs, rising above the howls of the fighting wolves. His eyes flitted to the ground, where he could see Christoph holding the crystal dagger in shock. It clattered out of his hand, the blood splattering onto the star symbol on the floor.

"My God, what have I done..." he mouthed as he crumbled to the floor and watched Ryland squirm in terror.

Ryland convulsed as he felt something pulling at his skin, tearing apart his muscles from their bones. His veins pulsed with pitch black blood, spreading through every inch of his being.

"It is time," a deep growling voice told him.

19. POWER

"RYLAND!!!" Krista's screams tore at her throat. She had been too late. After doing everything she could her vision still came true. With Tristan at her side, she rushed towards the center of the chamber, hoping to untie Ryland when suddenly the ground began to quake under their feet.

She tried to keep her balance, but the rumbling was so violent she stumbled to her knees. The other shifters ceased their fighting, turning to see what was happening in the tunnels.

A fire began to spread from Ryland's body. It started at his feet, licking at his heels before it shot up like a pillar that consumed his entire body. Krista felt a terrified scream radiate from her, and could only watch in horror as Ryland's shadowy figure was lost in the blaze.

She looked over and saw the boy she had recognized from the photos in Ryland's room, now all grown up. He stared up at the blaze in complete awe and fear. Christoph had brought the evil to life. She ran and grabbed him by the shoulders. "Don't you realize what you've done?!" She screamed into his face. Christoph's chest heaved as if he couldn't tear his gaze from Ryland's body.

The ground continued to shake, the shifters now scattering in terror as the fire grew into an enormous blaze. But, Krista couldn't feel any heat emanating from it. Through the blinding flames, she could see Ryland's figure...shifting—though it was nothing that she had seen before in the shifter's world.

Ryland's body ripped at the bindings holding him. The fire began to subside as a dark shadow grew larger and larger inside of it. Then, from the blaring red and orange waves, the shadow emerged. First, a single enormous paw stepped out, crushing the wooden planks in an instant. They fell into the rushing rainwater and were carried away.

Krista took a step back together with Tristan. Chaos broke out among the shifters as they scrambled from the water onto the concrete pathways. They stared with wide eyes as another large paw emerged, then another, and another, until finally a massive wolf the size of an elephant was revealed.

It was covered in black shadows that wafted from its fur like clouds of steam. Its eyes were glowing red, like the flames from which it had been born. It stood with pride and power, nearly filling up the entire chamber. The wolves scattered around its feet, some of them shifting back into humans.

The wolf raised its head and released a howl so loud that it made the Earth quake again. It reverberated from the walls, filling the tunnels, and bounced around Krista's skull. She held on to the concrete until her knuckles were white. Tears stained at her cheeks. It had been done. The ancient Wolf God was here.

Sulous gazed down, twin fires radiating from his eyes. His jaws just barely opened, revealing his enormous teeth stained with blood from the thousands of lives he had torn apart.

The room fell completely silent, frozen by the Wolf God's display of power. Krista watched as Christoph approached the panting beast. With every breath, smoke emerged from between Sulous's jaws. Christoph straightened himself before giving a low bow to the beast.

Even from afar, Krista could see him shaking like a leaf. "All powerful Sulous," he began, trying to maintain a hint of reverence through his shaky voice. "We have summoned you from your long slumber," he turned to his cult members, scattered amongst the other wolf factions. They all fell to their knees, humbled, their hands held out at the ready.

"We give you the shards of this earth to unite under your rule," Christoph continued. "Go as you wish, but first we ask that you bestow your blessing onto us, so that we may carry your strength as your devoted servants."

The echo of his words died down. As soon as it was quiet again, the mighty beast began to shudder. A low growl rumbled through his chest, emerging from his enormous jaws as a maniacal laugh. Christoph shrunk back in surprise.

Krista grabbed hold of Tristan's fur. He shifted beside her, not taking his eyes from Sulous. "Something terrible is about to happen," she whispered to him. "We have to get the other shifters out of here."

But Tristan was frozen in place, struck with fear as a booming voice carried over every living body in the room.

"Fools!" Sulous's voice was an earthquake in itself. Dust sifted from the ceiling into the water below. "You expect me to share my power with you? Your words of worship fall on deaf ears. I am a god of chaos and destruction, of bloodshed and mayhem. I thrive on the blood of anyone that stands in my way, including yours!"

In a flash, his jaws opened wide as he gnashed his teeth at Christoph. Christoph ducked out of the way, nearly toppling into Krista and Tristan. The Wolf God gave another hearty laugh as he swept his tail at the surrounding shifters. Cries and yelps filled the chamber as everyone tried to scatter or face the tragic fate of being eaten by Sulous.

"We're in way over our heads now," Tristan cried out over the roar of flames and growls of the massive wolf. But, Krista watched Sulous carefully. She felt Tristan grab her by the waist, pulling her just as a giant paw swiped at a cluster of shifters. Krista watched in horror as Sulous grabbed a handful of bodies, humanoids, and wolves, and shoved them into his gaping jaws. Their bones crunched against his teeth before he swallowed them all in one gulp.

He lifted his enormous shadowy body, his fur as black as night. With a powerful slam, he rammed himself against the ceiling of the tunnel, again and again. Krista felt someone slam into her shoulder, Sam. "We need to pull back," Sam warned.

"Sulous is trying to get out!" Krista shouted. "If he leaves these tunnels, he'll expose the shifter world to the humans."

Sam gave her an understanding nod, then shifted back into a large white wolf, rejoining the remains of her pack. Their army had tried to get to the Wolf God, nipping at its heels to no avail. Sulous took notice of them and swept his jaws down to try to scoop them up into his mouth.

At once, Krista was brought back to her vision. The Oracle had revealed to her a solution if only she could find the chance to apply it. There was an image of a woman, the pure spirit of the oracle, as she approached the wolf monster.

"I need to get closer," she told Tristan. "I can stop him, but I can't get there alone."

"What about Ryland?" Tristan asked. "He's not gone, is he?"

"I don't know," Krista said. "He could still be in there somewhere."

Her eyes darted about the room. She had yet to summon the oracle fully, since she had left her apartment. Fear was already beginning to set in once more, and there was not a single quiet place for her to gather her power.

Screw it, she thought. *I'll do it here if I have to, and it looks like I have to.*

"I need some cover," she said. "Just for a moment."

Tristan stepped forward, trying to keep his gaze on what the Wolf God would do next. The other alpha's caught sight of him, each of them hopping over destroyed concrete to get in position.

"What's the deal?" Declan asked.

"Surround Krista," Tristan said.

"The hell is that going to do?" Rizz's eyes widened in terror.

"Just trust me," Krista said. Then, to each of the alpha's surprise, she sat cross-legged on what was left of the ground. Water was rising around her, but she forced herself to concentrate.

Rizz, Sam, Ben, Declan, and Tristan. Together, they locked arms in a circle to protect Krista the best that they could. It wasn't much, but Krista was thankful for them. *Come on*, she thought, *focus...* the roaring of the Wolf God, and the cracking of the concrete as the ceiling was on the brink of collapse was all too much for her to hear, and she struggled to reach for her power.

She heard her mother's voice. *Look for the light, Krista...concentrate on the light.* And this time, she saw it. It shone bright and clear in her mind's eye, a white glow. She saw flashes of Ryland and felt the touch of his hand against her skin. She saw the alphas and their heart's intentions focusing on her. She even caught a glimpse of Mrs. Remy, and the beautiful scarf she had gifted her. Finally, she saw her smiling mother standing in front of her in a white void. *"You're doing great,"* she told her as if she were whispering the words right into her ear.

Krista felt the wind rushing through her hair, surrounding her in a wild vortex—the power coursing through her veins. *I am the oracle*, she told herself, *and I have all the strength that I need.*

In a rush of electricity, a ball of energy began to form from Krista's forehead. She kept her eyes closed, ignoring the chaos surrounding her. The energy grew larger, brighter and blue until it surrounded her completely in the form of an enormous orb. She felt her body being lifted from the ground weightless as her hair swept wildly at her face.

She spread out her arms, feeling the oracle working her magic. As she opened her eyes, blue fire emerged from them, illuminating the chamber and nearly blinding everyone around her.

The orb carried her off her feet until her body stood dead center. She refused to let go, her sights locked onto the monster turning to face her. Krista found herself just mere inches from Sulous's jaws that were filled with blood-stained teeth. To her surprise, the Wolf God shrunk back as her orb drew closer, not wanting to be touched by its magic.

"I should have known your arrival was imminent, Oracle," Sulous's voice boomed.

"Then you know full well what happens next," Krista's voice was just as loud, as powerful as a raging ocean. The Wolf God was unmoved, but the fire in his eyes flickered with uncertainty. "I will lay this world to waste," he roared. "And only you will live to walk amongst the ashes."

"Oh, please," Krista said. "That's honestly supposed to scare me?" She would not let on that deep down she was trembling, but the excitement inside of her was somewhat comforting. She was prepared for whatever was going to happen. Just as in her vision, she propelled herself forward, her arm outstretched towards the wolf's open mouth.

Sulous crushed another cultist under his paw as he ran for Krista, panting furiously. Fire shot out from between his teeth, ready to consume her entire being. But Krista wasn't afraid. She had to get Ryland back by any means necessary.

As they met in the middle, their two spirits collided. Krista, expected to be swallowed whole, but stayed put in her force field. It began to expand as she planted her hand firmly on the chilling wetness of the Wolf God's nose. Then, time stopped.

Sulous and Krista were frozen, the wolf in a permanent leap in midair, his teeth yearning for a bite he would never obtain, and Krista with her hand held against him as she was bathed in blue light.

Krista hadn't been prepared for this part. Nothing about her vision had included her body careening through a rainbow tunnel. She could hear millions of voices flying past her. It was cold, freezing, but Krista didn't shiver as she plummeted, down, down into an unknown realm.

The colors around her began to fade, dissolving into a murky blackness until she finally slowed to a soft hover at the bottom. She continued to float, searching, though she wasn't quite sure for what. There was only darkness in every direction, and not a single light to guide her except for her own.

She flew through the void as if flying through never-ending space. Finally, she spotted a soft white light approaching. A cold, wisplike presence revealed itself to her. It was a bearded man, but he was a ghost, his body completely translucent. He stopped when he saw her, squinting to get a better look.

"Are you an angel?" He asked, his voice hollow.

"No," Krista asked. "I'm looking for someone. His name is Ryland Iker."

"I'm not quite sure what that is...a name...I think I've forgotten mine. Forgotten...." He kept repeating to himself as he floated away, disappearing into the dark. A few others approached her. Some of them were lost but didn't know what they were looking for. Others just gave her an unblinking glance as they disappeared.

Krista found herself alone, until a woman's voice cried out in fear. "Hello? Is someone there? Can somebody please help me?" Krista headed straight for the source. Maybe they could help her find Ryland in this place.

Eventually, she found a woman lying on the non-existent floor. She was struggling to get up. Krista tried to take her hand, but the woman passed right through her, ghostlike.

"You...your spirit is still alive," the woman said in shock as she stared up at Krista. "How did you get here?"

"I'm looking for someone," Krista said. "Ryland Iker. Do you know him?"

"Ryland's here too?" The woman's face contorted into deep sadness. "Oh my God...those shifters...they must have..."

"Wait," Krista realized. "You're Henna. Ryland's strategist."

"Yes..." the woman's eyes widened. "That was my name! I had almost forgotten it."

With ease, she was able to stand up from the ground. It was then that Krista began to realize. She had somehow entered the spirit world, a realm where the dead roamed aimlessly. The oracle's power must have unlocked it when she had touched the Wolf God.

"Ryland's spirit is trapped here too, and it is not his time yet. I need to retrieve him. Does this place ever end?" Krista asked.

"There's a place where not even the dead will roam," Henna said, pointing into the dark. "Keep going, and eventually you will feel it. But, don't get too close. Whatever it consumes is doomed to stay here."

"I wish there was some other way to help you," Krista's heart sank at the sight of Henna forever trapped in the dark.

"You helped me remember," Henna said. "If I can hold onto my name, I can find my way back to where the others dwell, in the bright space." A smile crossed her lips. Krista still couldn't quite understand what Henna meant. Even though she was the oracle, there were still things that simply could not be explained, not even the mysteries of the spiritual realm.

All she knew was that there was still hope for Ryland, and the thought alone carried her forward in the dark.

"Ryland!" She called out to him. Despite the vastness of the realm, her words didn't carry far, as if a wall was constantly in front of her. It became suffocating after several moments, and Krista began to panic. She didn't know how much time she had in this place.

After what felt like hours of searching, she saw something other than darkness. There were white wisps, like clouds of smoke, aimlessly floating in a contained space. She felt a sharp pain in her chest, and she realized that she was in the place the dead had feared to tread.

Right in the center of the smoke, with his body being tossed around by the smoky tendrils, was Ryland. His eyes were closed, his spirit being attacked by a harbinger of death.

"Ryland!!" He couldn't hear her. Krista moved closer, still remembering Henna's warning. If the tendrils grabbed her, she'd find herself pulled in as well.

But she couldn't leave Ryland behind. She moved forward anyway until he was at an arm's length. She reached out, relieved that she could still feel the softness of his hair. He was still solid, but he was barely hanging on. His weakened head rose to look at what was touching him.

"Krista," he said, his eyebrows furrowed. "How did you get here?"

"Ryland, I can't explain right now," Krista's gaze kept drifting up to the white tendrils. They hadn't taken an interest in her yet, and she wanted to hurry and get Ryland out before they did.

"You have to hang on—you have to come with me!"

"I can't...I'm so tired..." Ryland rolled over in the white tendrils as if they were carrying him off to a deep sleep. Krista's eyes widened in horror.

"Ryland, the Wolf God has been awakened," her voice was more panicked now, as a tendril spiraled like a snake, turning from side to side waiting to attack her any second. "You have to get out of here so we can stop him!"

"Wolf God?" Ryland was struggling to remember. Death was approaching, coming to slowly pick apart his memory for good.

"Sulous is here. Give me your hand and I'll pull you out!"

"I can't...so...tired...It's warm on the other side."

"No! Ryland, stay with me! That's a lie, okay? Just listen to me! If you give in, you'll be dead forever." She was losing hope, but she remembered the words he had spoken to her before, as they lay on his bed and he stroked her hair. It seemed like a century ago.

"You've only failed if you give up," she reminded him. "You can't give up now, Ryland. Think about what's waiting for you on the other side."

"I don't have a pack anymore," Ryland said. "They've all left."

"No, just you wait and see. Your pack is still strong. They're waiting for you to come out and lead them." Krista couldn't bear to stand around and watch any longer. She threw out her hands, grabbing hold of Ryland's shoulders.

"You have to remember," Krista said. She felt like she was underwater now, her cries only lost in a wall of bubbles. Ryland swayed helplessly in her grip, but she refused to let go.

"Remember when you and I were on the hill?" She asked. "I told you that you didn't have a heart-line? Remember, playing baseball with your little brother? Or Tristan and his silly schedules and notes? You can't have forgotten about that!"

A white tendril lashed out around her arm. Krista cried out in pain. She couldn't hear the oracle's voice in here, to guide her. It was all up to her now. The tendril tightened its grip around her, pulsing as it seemed to drain the energy right out of her. She understood now why Ryland had a hard time leaving.

"Please, Ryland!" Her voice was desperate now as another tendril wrapped itself around her waist. It would only be a matter of time before it pulled her in as well. "We're not going to die here," she said. "I have a shop to run, and you have a pack to lead. Look at me!"

Ryland weakly lifted his head with all the strength he could muster. "Every shifter faction has joined together, because of you," she said. "Hell, even Declan is out there fighting to save your stubborn ass!"

She saw a glimmer in Ryland's eyes, as the olive green returned to them. It was working. He was slowly remembering. Krista felt herself being pulled further into the white smoky void. Her grip was loosening on Ryland.

"You are the strongest because you never give up, and you said that no matter what, you'd be even better tomorrow," she said, her head heavy and tired. "We have to make it to tomorrow, Ryland. I just want you to be there with me..."

Suddenly she felt herself giving in, despite her deep struggle the overwhelming comfort was washing over her. But then, she felt a pair of strong arms pulling her away from the smoking tendrils. Krista was drifting in and out as the darkness swept past her.

Her eyes fluttered open as soft warm lips pressed against hers. Electricity pulsed between her and Ryland and her heart pounded in her chest as they exchanged a powerful, passionate kiss. She felt his strength engulfing her now, and when he pulled away, she saw that Ryland was glowing with life.

"Let's get to tomorrow," he said with a firm nod. He placed Krista down, and they wrapped their arms around each other, their foreheads pressed together. Krista concentrated, calling on her power.

As soon as she did, she felt her and Ryland being pulled back again as if someone had pressed a rewind button. The spirit realm whipped past them, pitch-black fading into a tunnel full of color once again. Ryland buried his face in Krista's hair, his body heavy against hers as they approached a blinding white light hurtling towards them.

20. PEACE

Krista awoke, breathing in life. She was still in her orb, her hand on Sulous. Time had stood still between them, but the blinding light had followed her here, emanating from her touch on the Wolf God's muzzle. It expanded, filling the entire room until a massive explosion of magic launched her backward. A deep blue ring of light stretched out as her sphere shattered like glass, flying through every inch of the chamber and the tunnels surrounding it.

Krista flew back and hit a concrete wall, the wind knocked from her lungs as she fell to her knees. The alphas gathered around her, helping her to her tired feet. The world felt heavier here, the gravity pressing on her entire body.

She stared ahead at the Wolf God, now shaky on his feet. The remaining shifters watched in horror as Sulous swayed back and forth, the bright light on his muzzle engulfing his entire body. "No!" He shouted a final booming note that resonated in Krista's chest. The light quenched the shadows that made up his body, and he lifted his head in agony, giving one last roar before he fell.

His body crushed the concrete pathways, sending waves of dirty water through the tunnels. The Wolf God shrunk down as the shadows around him were eaten away. He opened his jaws a final time, but only smoke emanated from them, trailing out like a ghostly fog.

Then, he was silenced. Everyone stood back as faint blue shadows, spirits, flew up and disappeared into the air with long exasperated sighs. The light faltered, expanding and contracting until it finally began to fade, a low musical hum vibrating throughout the room.

The shifters crept out from their hiding places, the cultists mixed in with the five factions. Each alpha followed after Krista as she walked towards the light.

There, where Sulous's mighty body had once stood proudly, was a tired and battered Ryland. He was lying face-up, the light hovering above him. It was barely the size of a marble and drifted down into Ryland's open mouth. As it disappeared, a glow radiated throughout his body.

The dark strands of Sulous's spirit dissolved from under his skin as if they had never taken hold of him in the first place. He was healing, turning back into the Ryland that Krista had grown so attached to.

Once the light disappeared, Ryland's eyes fluttered open. Krista leaned over him, caressing his face with her fingers. She bent down to place a tender kiss on his forehead. Ryland's arms shot out around her, pulling her closer so he could give her a proper kiss to express his gratitude.

A wild chorus of cheers surrounded them from the shifters. Even Tristan had clapped once he saw his alpha alive and well.

Krista melted into his arms. It was such a relief to have him back. She pulled away, looking into those soft green eyes of his.

"Hey," she said, feeling her heart beating against his bare chest.

"Hey," Ryland gave a weak and tired smile. "I just had a strange dream about you..."

"Yeah, that wasn't a dream," Krista said. "It was very real."

"Look! You're blue!" Even though it wasn't really a curse attached to Ryland, it seemed that a huge entity had been lifted from him. His entire personality had flipped on its head, and he was filled with new, brighter energy.

Krista looked down at her skin—a soft blue glow was slowly fading.

"Oh, about that..." She began.

"You don't have to tell me," he said. "I can clearly see from here that you're an incredibly sexy oracle."

Krista's face grew hot. She gave a nervous glance around the room, reminding Ryland that there were hundreds of eyes watching them. Ryland winked at her, and she moved aside to help him to his feet.

He was shaky at first, but with some help from the other alphas and Tristan, he gained some balance. The crowd began to separate, leaving one other person who had seemed to disappear during the chaos.

Christoph clutched at his arm, which hung limp and broken at his side. He limped through the shifters and was instantly grabbed by Sam and Ben. Krista felt a shudder down her spine. He was a whole other monster they had to deal with, but instead of being hostile, Christoph was broken and drained.

From where she stood, her intuition revealed that he was afraid, and with good reason. His selfishness had almost cost her Ryland and the entire world.

"Brother," Christoph began, but Ryland held up his hand.

"You and I have a lot to discuss," he said. "But for now, rest, and reflect. Your cult, on the other hand, will have to disband, or they'll suffer under the rest of the shifter factions."

He nodded to Ben and Sam to take his brother away. Christoph struggled to walk, not even daring to look at the cult members that he had disappointed. The Wolf God and the Stars of Sulous would no longer be a threat to the world.

Krista took Ryland's hand, holding it tight.

"We also have a lot to discuss," she told him as she raised an eyebrow.

"Like what?"

"Like the massive temper tantrum that got you into this mess in the first place?"

"Can't I just bask in this attention for a little longer? I did just happen to come back to life after being possessed by a Wolf God."

"Of course you can," Tristan's voice cut in. "But first, let me just give you this." A fist flew towards Ryland's face. Krista gasped as Ryland's head flew back. He clutched at his nose, checking to see if it was broken. It wasn't.

Tristan shook out his sore knuckles, his face dead serious. "Consider that our talk...for now," he said.

To Krista's surprise, Ryland had actually cracked a smile.

"I think I rightfully deserved that," Ryland said. "You look good in a t-shirt, Tristan."

Declan stood by Krista's side. "Wherever you went, did you bring back a different Ryland?" He asked with heavy sarcasm.

Krista looked into Ryland's eyes and placed her hand on his chest. She stood on her tiptoes to kiss his cheek. "I think I brought back the right one," she said with a smile.

"Rise and shine," Ryland awoke to Krista's nose nuzzling his ear. She kissed his cheek until he finally stirred. He gathered her in the crook of his arm, but she pulled away. "Wait! Wait!" She said, and then she held up a steaming mug in her hand. "Hot tea," she explained and passed him the cup.

Ryland breathed in the floral scent. "Chamomile?" He asked as he took a sip.

"You remembered," Krista smiled as she got comfortable next to him.

"What day is it?" He asked.

"Tuesday."

"But wait...I feel asleep"

"Saturday, yes. You've been sleeping for days."

He couldn't believe he had slept for so long. But his body was feeling incredible for it. Maybe it was finally shedding Sulous's spirit that brought him his energy. "Have you missed me?"

"Since the day you first left," Krista said, her voice soft as she looked up at him. Her lips barely touched the outline of his jaw. There was a brief silence that hovered between them. Ryland wove his fingers through Krista's hair, knowing what still needed to be said.

"I'm sorry for the things that I had said to you," he explained. "I wasn't myself, especially on that day. Still, that's no excuse for my behavior."

"I understand. But now you have me to keep you in check," Krista joked.

"I'm just thankful that you were able to find me in time. I still don't know how you managed to gather the shifter factions so easily."

"Well, once I had the whole oracle thing figured out, it didn't take much convincing them."

"Have they said anything lately? The alphas?"

"They've been regrouping for now. The factions ...lost a few shifters during your rescue."

She noticed the concern on his face as he held onto his mug. "Ryland, there was nothing you could do," she had read his mind completely. "Even if you were able to fight alongside us, we still wouldn't have been able to defeat Sulous."

"You're right," he said. "I just know I have to go in front of the alphas again and explain myself. And...I think I need to resign as the Rogue's alpha."

"What do you mean?"

Ryland thought it would be best for everyone if he had stepped down from gathering the shifter factions. "These alphas came together when I couldn't," he explained. "If I try to lead them now, I'll only be a fool."

"Well, Tristan and I have an idea that you might like if you're interested," Krista smirked.

"Tell me."

"Tristan can tell you himself. I just came up here to have a little alone time before you get back into alpha mode."

"What makes you think I'm not in alpha mode already?" Ryland gave a sly grin and rotated himself on top of her, careful to place his mug of tea on his nightstand. Krista put her hands on his waist, caressing the deep V near his sweatpants. "Oh, I think I'm having a vision," Krista said.

"Does it somehow involve me inside of you?"

"Why, yes, I think that's what I'm seeing. There's something big and hard in my future."

"Hey, I'm seeing it too—maybe we're still *connected* somehow."

"Give me a few moments and I guarantee you'll feel a connection."

Ryland buried his face in her neck, his teeth grazing against her skin as he playfully roughed her up on the bed. Krista laughed into his shoulder, pressing her palms into his chest. It wasn't long until their clothes were thrown on the floor, and the alpha lost himself in the pleasures his oracle had to offer him.

"What was the body count?" Ryland asked Tristan as they wandered in the tunnels.

"About twenty," Tristan said, shining a small flashlight on a clipboard in his hands. "Three of those were Rogues. We've identified the others and have passed them along to their proper pack for burial."

"Thank you for keeping track of the data," Ryland planted his hand on Tristan's shoulder. Tristan jolted, not expecting the gesture. He stopped in his tracks while Ryland carried on.

"You're welcome, Sir," he said.

"Please, you can just call me Ryland."

He turned and saw Tristan hiding a smile as he carried on behind him.

"Krista's been helping keep watch during the cleanup," Tristan explained as they turned into the next tunnel. "All she has to do is flash them a glimpse of those fiery blue eyes, and they snap back into action." Ryland couldn't quite concentrate on Tristan's words.

It was the place where Ryland had squeezed through by himself. He was already anxious to encounter what was waiting for him on the other side. There was a phantom pain in his arm, and he shook his head to rid himself of the thoughts of the whispers that once haunted him.

"Are you alright?" Tristan finally caught on that he wasn't listening.

"This place really gives me the creeps," he admitted.

"I can understand why," Tristan said. "We've been extra careful trying to keep this clean-up under wraps. We wouldn't want curious eyes from the city poking around here and exposing us. Thankfully the television stations have been too preoccupied with the earthquakes to look into stories on an ancient Wolf God."

A cold shiver passed through Ryland.

"Tristan, do you think I should give up being an alpha?"

"Why would you ask something like that?"

"Well, because...I was thinking...that maybe you'd want to take over for the Rogues. You have excellent management skills, and the pack has always respected your decisions."

"While I'm humbled and honored at your offer, Ryland, I've been working something out with Krista that would hopefully bring all the shifters closer together. Believe it or not, I've gained some influence from your brother's practices."

Ryland shot him a nervous glance, but Tristan laughed it off. "We're not starting a cult," he explained. "We're just adopting his ideas of uniting the shifter factions. Oh, we're here. I'll have to explain later."

The room was as cold as the day he had left it. The smell still wafted around Ryland, dirty water and musty concrete. Members of the Rogues were scattered in groups around the chamber as shifters cleaned up pieces of concrete from the ground.

"We didn't want to kill anyone," Tristan said. "But we also didn't want to let your brother's cult get off so easily without proper punishment for their deeds."

Ryland looked across the floor of the chamber, noticing a soft blue glow on the other side. Krista sensed his arrival and turned to give him a wave.

"She's lucky to have you," Tristan said.

"Quite the opposite," Ryland said. "I owe that woman my life."

"There's a way to prove that, you know."

"I'm dating a psychic, an ancient oracle no less. Do you really think I could get away with a surprise engagement?"

A voice perked up somewhere in his mind.

"There'll be no talk of engagement until you take me on a proper date first!"

"Get out of my head!" Ryland called out to Krista. She gave him a playful smile and went back to supervising the pack of shifters hoisting concrete from the sewer water.

Scanning the crowd, Ryland noticed someone was missing. "Where's Christoph?" He asked Tristan. "He didn't-"

"He's still very alive," Tristan said. "But we've kept him separate from the others. We couldn't have him stirring them up again."

It was déjà vu, only the tables were turned as Ryland stepped into the smaller chamber nearby, where his brother was sitting against the bars of a cage.

"Hello Christoph," Ryland crouched to make eye contact. His brother was tired, his broken arm bandaged up in a splint. "Are they taking care of you in here?"

"Would be nice to have some reading material," Christoph said, his voice weak. Ryland turned to Tristan.

"Can you leave us alone for a second, please?" He asked.

The door closed behind Ryland, and there was a heavy cloud of awkwardness between him and Christoph. He figured the only way to dispel it was to keep talking— he hoped his words would tear down the walls that separated them.

"I suppose you're going to give me my sentence, then? Beheading perhaps? A stab through the heart?" He was surprised that Christoph was the first to speak.

"I'm not going to meet violence with more violence," Ryland said.

"Well, that's a first."

"A first in many firsts. I believe I've grown into a better person because of this."

"What about a better alpha?"

Ryland shook his head. "After you killed me...it really opened my eyes. I thought I could be the best on my own. But now I realize that it takes not only me but everyone else around me to be great."

"How sweet," Christoph rolled his eyes under the lens of his glasses.

"That includes you," Ryland said. Christoph looked up from his feet with curious eyes. "I can't let you out on your own, just yet. Everyone still thinks you're a psychotic cult leader. Hell, they're probably right. But...I want you to come back to the Rogues and get the help that you need."

"I can't do that," Christoph said. "After everything I've done to you..."

"I know what it's like to get lost in the dark. We don't have to stay there forever. I've learned that there are people who are always willing to pull you out."

He held out his hand through the bars. Christoph thought it over, his eyes were suspicious of Ryland. Ryland didn't pull away. He looked at his brother with sincerity and hope.

A smile spread across his face as Christoph took his hand and shook it with his remaining strength. "Okay," Christoph said. "I'll do it." It was almost as if they were kids again, making up for a minor argument, before they'd go outside and play ball in the backyard.

"Great," Ryland said, standing up from the cage. He knew it would take a lot more than a handshake to get his brother back on the right track, but it was a good start. "Oh, by the way, I actually did bring you some reading material."

He reached into his jacket, pulled out a square photo album, and passed it to Christoph through the bars. "What's this?" Christoph asked as he opened it up. "Oh, wow," he said as he realized. Ryland watched while his brother silently flipped through the pages, his mind deep in nostalgia.

"I'll see you soon," he said to Christoph.

"Yeah...you will."

They exchanged a final smile before Ryland passed Christoph a flashlight to look at the book some more. Then, he closed the door behind him to rejoin Tristan and Krista. He felt a wave of satisfaction, that finally, some things were falling into place for him, and that someday he would really have his brother back.

EPILOGUE

A gavel fell onto a podium, its hammering sounds filling the room and silencing the hundreds of voices in the Rogue's warehouse. Tristan adjusted his necktie and placed his hands firmly on either side of the podium. "Welcome, all of you," he announced. "To the first-ever gathering of the Shifters Union!"

The shifters from all five factions cheered from their seats. Behind Tristan was a long table, where each alpha had their own seat. Attached to the table was a new emblem, a gold star with a wolf's head in the middle.

Tristan shuffled his notes in front of him as he spoke into a microphone. "These past few months have been full of darkness and danger. As an ancient shifter oracle pointed out, we were once separated by our own differences. We drew lines claiming there was peace between us, only to drive ourselves further apart from one another," he cast a knowing glance at Ryland, who straightened up in his seat.

"But I have seen how the five shifter factions have come together in times of darkness and turmoil," he continued. "They have fought a mighty evil, and we are all stronger because of it. Now, as the head ambassador for the alphas, I am pleased to announce that we are erasing the lines that divide Central City. Today, and from now on, the five factions will unite as one union. Please give a round of applause for your Shifter Council."

More applause filled the warehouse as Ryland, Declan, Ben, Sam, and Rizz stood from their seats. They exchanged handshakes, hugs, and wrapped their arms around each other's shoulders. Never before had Ryland felt so accepted by the other shifters. From now on, he wouldn't be just an alpha—he was one of many powerful leaders. He would stand with his pack instead of behind it.

The Rogues, most of them returned after their exodus from the warehouse, clapped and celebrated Ryland for the first time instead of being afraid of him. Ryland straightened himself up for them, and as he did, he caught someone else clapping for him out of the corner of his eye.

Christoph, wearing a black Rogues jacket, stood in the doorway to the meeting hall. He smiled proudly at his brother and raised his fist in solidarity. Ryland returned the gesture before his brother put his hands in his pockets and returned to his room.

"Not too bad of a plan, huh?" Tristan placed his hand on Ryland's shoulder, pulling him from his trance.

"I'll admit, you had me worried when you said you were adopting some of the wolf cult's beliefs," Ryland said.

"He's doing better, isn't he, Christoph?"

"He still has a way to go, but I'm finally starting to recognize him again. Now, don't we have this meeting to continue?"

"You're absolutely right."

"You do the honors, *Ambassador.*"

Krista held her concentration, her mind focusing heavily on an object in a distant place. She could see a cave, tucked away in a misty mountain. Moss hung from the ceiling, and old burnt out torches lined the walls. Just up ahead, there was a skeleton in an opened stone coffin, its bony hands clutched tight around a folded square of fabric. *"A king,"* the oracle's spirit told her. *"Powerful and of shifter-born. He rests with the artifact, yet to be disturbed."*

Until we can find him, Krista thought. She admired the power that continued to flow through her even after she had used the oracle's spirit to defeat Sulous. Her power was even more enjoyable now that she could use it whenever she wanted. She hoped there would no longer be terrifying, nightmarish visions whenever she slept.

She adjusted her vision, now focusing on the ancient symbols scrawled in what appeared to be blood on the square of fabric. Squinting in her mind, she roughly translated it: *"Blood and bone are sealed for now, until the king is awakened to unleash his wrath."*

Before she could read any more, a door slam echoed in her mind and made her vision become unclear. Then, she heard footsteps rushing up the stairs in her loft. *"Krista! Did you find anything?"* Ryland's voice pierced through her thoughts, ripping her straight from her vision and back to reality.

As her eyes opened, Krista panicked and she fell towards the floor of her loft. She landed right in Ryland's arms and clutched her head. She felt groggy as if waking up suddenly from a nap. "Well, I did find something," she said. "Until I was interrupted..."

Ryland looked up at the place where Krista had been hovering. "Is there any way you can control the whole...levitation thing?" He asked. "I would think that before you go on a vision quest that you would sit somewhere safer. like the couch...or maybe your bed?" He gave a devilish grin, and Krista playfully pushed him away.

"How did the first meeting go?" She asked.

"Fantastic," Ryland filled her in excitedly on the shifter's pledge, that the alpha's would now gather and make decisions as a group rather than representing separate factions. After he had been rambling on for some time, he stopped when he noticed Krista's smile creeping across her face.

"What?" He asked. "Something wrong?"

"Not at all," Krista said, wrapping her arms around him. "I've just really loved seeing this side of you all the time. When we first met you were so broody," she contorted her face into an angry one. "Grrr, get away from me. Grrr, I'm cursed and nobody understands." Ryland picked her up and carried her over to her bed.

"Alright, Ms. Oracle. Let's not forget that you couldn't even read your tarot cards in front of me without freezing," he said as they sprawled out on the covers. Krista relished these moments the most, the quiet ones in her loft while she meditated in between clients coming into her shop.

"I found another artifact," Krista said proudly.

"What is it? A sword? Another dagger? We finally displayed that cursed ring that you found the other day."

"Actually, I think it may be some kind of shroud. It belongs to another one of those dead kings that are seeking their revenge, blah, blah, blah. The usual spooky stuff. But, we should probably pick it up soon. The oracle said it's been undisturbed, but you know how it is once someone gets their hands on an ancient artifact before we do."

"Well, where is it, then?"

"Scandinavia."

"Great, where the vampires live?"

"That's Transylvania."

"No, I'm pretty sure there are vampires all over that side of Europe..."

"Then we're going to need some more backup this time."

A bell rang as someone entered the shop. "Duty calls," Krista said as she sprang from the bed. "Have Tristan get our passports sorted out, won't you? I've always wanted to go to Europe!"

She leaned over and kissed him, relishing the peace and comfort that Ryland's lips brought her. As she sauntered away, Ryland pinched at her butt. "Anything in the cards about us going out to dinner, sometime soon?" He asked. Krista looked over her shoulder at him. "Hmm, is that sushi I'm starting to see? And maybe, if my vision comes true, I'll do a special spread just for you. You know, a private reading."

Ryland bit his lip and sighed heavily, as Krista walked down the stairs to meet her client. When she reached the bottom step, she grabbed her black scarf that was hanging on a nearby hook and wrapped it around her head.

She had come a long way and became an oracle. She had traversed the shifter world and brought back her very own alpha as a mate. As she took her seat and shuffled her tarot cards, she smiled at the power flowing through her, her own intuition.

"Now," she told her customer. "What would you like to ask the cards to-day?"

END

Secrets of the Alpha

The Reign of the Alpha Series

Amelia Wilson

CONTENTS

Prologue

A soft breeze filtered through the trees, moving the leaves together in the canopy high above Danielle's head. She giggled and remained still, letting the wind play with the loose strands of her hair. It was only here in the depths of the forest that she allowed herself to be free. The sounds of nature filled her ears like a gentle lullaby putting her at ease.

She glanced up to stare at the golden rays of light dancing about the boughs. The branches swayed and rocked, causing the light to bend and shift. She sighed at the sight, with a smile on her face. Her eyes remained fixed on the golden-yellow rays shining through the emerald-green leaves.

With the smile still playing at the corner of her lips, she moved through the forest as if it were her home. Every step she took was delicate and soft. She moved smoothly over the roots and rocks. The deeper she went into the forest, the more the stress of the city faded away.

"I have missed this place," she sighed stopping to study the wild yellow flowers springing up at base of a tree.

Ever since she was a child, Danielle was more at home in the forest, surrounded by nature, than she ever was in the concrete city. She moved over the roots, ducking under the branches hanging close to the ground. Squirrels jumped from branch to branch following her. Danielle reached into her backpack and pulled out a paper bag. She kept her eyes locked on the little creatures as she shoved her hand into the bag and pulled out a handful of nuts. She tossed the nuts in their direction and smiled as the furry animals scrambled to get them, before returning the bag of food to her backpack.

This forest had become a second home to Danielle and she spent more time here than she did in her apartment back in Seattle. Of course her roommate didn't mind her absence, despite her objections about coming here. Danielle pushed the thoughts of her city life out of her mind and focused on the rough bark that scraped against her fingertips.

As the trees opened up into a clearing, Danielle reached for the camera hanging around her neck. Through the tiny lens she scanned the meadow, ready to snap the perfect image. The sun's rays danced through the long golden grass, swaying in the breeze, and kissing each flower as it moved. She snapped the shudder of the camera capturing the scene. She pulled the camera away from her face and flipped through the images ensuring she had captured the right picture, before moving on.

She whipped her head up when a flock of birds took to the sky. A flash of cold air stole the warmth from her blood. Her eyes scanned the shadows before turning to the birds that were leaving the safety of the canopy in a wave of panic. Danielle's heart beat faster, and her eyes scanned the meadow frantically as well as the shadows, searching for a predator coming her way. Her mind raced through several scenarios as her heart drummed frantically in her chest. All she could envision is the park rangers hovering over her dead body. She pulled in sharp frantic breaths trying to steady her nerves as her eyes widened with awe.

Seven -large gray wolves emerged from the shadows of the trees. With a shaking hand, Danielle raised her camera to her eye and began snapping pictures. Her heart thundered in her ears as she moved carefully around the trees trying to capture the best picture she possibly could.

On her fifth snap, Danielle's eyes widened and her mouth dropped open. The gray wolves shuddered as if a cold breeze had chilled them to their bones. But as each wolf shivered, Danielle's eyes widened ever more, as their gray coats dropped to the ground. Slowly, each rose as man from the golden grass stark naked and unconcerned at their nudity.

"I knew it," Danielle whispered as her finger continued to press down on the shutter release to capture the images. A chill stole the warmth of her blood as one of the men paused to stare in her direction.

Danielle's heart sank, and she was thrown back to memories of grade school and of blushing at the pitcher of her high school baseball team. His eyes were as dark as he wisps of his hair that floated around his face. To Danielle he was the most stunning man she had ever seen in her whole life. From the way his thick shoulders rested to his branch-like arms, Danielle found herself daydreaming of all the things he could do to her.

She shook her head and rubbed her eyes panting with excitement.

"No way." Danielle blinked trying to focus. Her heart sputtered as she stared at the man in the clearing. He was gorgeous, and she was certain she was lost in a dream.

"Don't wake up" she mumbled squeezing her eyes shut. She sucked in a deep breath and she paused to peak through her eyelids. Sure enough, the dark-skinned man with the chiseled chest and hanging assets was still there in the meadow, his eyes locked on her.

She wanted to reach out to him, she wanted him to know she was there, but as she started to move, her inner voice screamed at her.

"Don't move. Don't say a word," it whispered and Danielle dropped the camera. For the first time in the forest, Danielle felt the sting of fear. The man stood with his eyes locked on her and she wondered if the shadows were enough to mask her from his view. For a single heartbeat, Danielle remained frozen to the side of the tree. Deep down she wanted to be caught, but the inner voice screamed louder than before. *Run! Now!*

Danielle ripped her pack off her back and took off into the woods. Out of the corner of her eye she saw the shadows shifting. The men took off in her direction moving faster than humanly possible. Danielle sprinted through the trees trying to outrun them. She twisted her head to look over her shoulder. They were moving like the wind racing through the forest. Danielle pushed on forcing her body to move faster. Despair filled her as the thought of being captured entered her mind.

"You can't escape us," they yelled closing the gap.

The forest may have been her second home, but she didn't have the skills these men possessed. Fear stabbed her as she tried to find an escape. Danielle's eyes darted about as the men grew closer. She paused trying to regain her breath. With nowhere else to run, her eyes shifted to the trees and the branches high above her head. Her only hope was a thick branch hanging above her head. Immediately she jumped and pulled herself up. Her knees scrapped the bark as she continued to climbed higher and higher into the tree.

"Come down from there, now" one of the men ordered. Danielle pulled herself up to a higher branch, hugging the tree refusing to move.

"We won't hurt you. We just want to talk."

Danielle glanced down before turning her head towards the sky. The branches of the other trees moaned and scrapped against the one she clung to. For a moment she wondered if she would be able to jump to the next tree. With a trembling hand she stretched out, trying to reach the adjacent branch. The crunching of the limb under her weight caused her to pause.

Fear stabbed her. She wrapped her arms around the trunk and hugged it, holding her position.

"Get her."

Without hesitation, three men took to the tree and scrambled up to where Danielle had planted herself. She squeezed the tree holding on to it tighter than ever. The men unwound her arms with ease and pried her from it. A gush of wind blew up through her hair and for a moment Danielle was flying. But when the thud of feet hit the ground she opened her eyes.

The tall tanned figure stood before her glaring at her. Danielle tried to resist glancing at his crotch, but her desire and curiosity won out over her fear. Her eyes flickered down for a moment before they dropped to the earth at her feet.

"What are you doing here?" The dark-skinned man asked towering over her.

"Pictures," Danielle stuttered as she kept her eyes averted from his gaze. "For work." Danielle tried to keep her eyes down, but she couldn't resist stealing another glance at the man before her. Suddenly, several hands were on her ripping the camera from her neck.

"Hey, that's mine." Danielle protested reaching for her camera.

"Not anymore," he said as he fiddled with the camera before finally smashing it on the ground. Danielle's heart broke as she watched the lens of the camera shatter into pieces at her feet.

"You didn't need to break my camera."

"Yes, I did. Now who else is with you?"

"No one." Danielle stared up at the man and straightened her back. Despite his size and his beauty, she stared at him defiantly.

"Is that so?"

Danielle didn't budge. She stood straight trying to keep her nerves under control. He nodded once. From the corner of her eye she noticed the men scattering like ants.

"What is your name?" he demanded.

Danielle crossed her arms and pressed her lips into a tight defiant line.

"Tell me yours first," she demanded in the same commanding tone. The man's eyes sparkled with interest as he gazed down at her.

"Derek. Now, yours." Danielle paused wondering why he was being so straightforward with her. For a moment she debated about whether to give him her real name. Something about the way his eyes pierced her soul caused her to shiver.

"Alice," she lied. "Alice Bane."

Derek's eyes drew in tightly as he leaned in closer to her. Danielle paused, trying not to let him intimidate her as he sniffed around her.

"You are not Alice." His eyes narrowed forcing Danielle to step back. "How do you know that name?"

Danielle's mind raced about trying to concoct a lie. But words failed her as her heart pounded in her chest. She exhaled and straightened her shoulders.

"Why?" Danielle challenged. She held her ground as Derek circled her.

"Tell me how *you* know Alice and I might let you live."

"Tell me how you know her and I might let you live." Danielle huffed crossing her arms. Although Derek was three times her size, she refused to give him the satisfaction of killing her without a fight.

"Tell me your name first, and I might tell you how I know Alice," Derek argued realizing his only option was to cooperate. He glared at Danielle mimicking her body language.

Danielle forced the fear down her ragged throat as she tried to speak, "My name is Danielle, and Alice happens to be my roommate. Now, how do you know Alice?"

Derek's eyes widened. His lips twitched at the corners fighting a smile. "Is she now?"

"Yes, and? So, how do you know her?"

"Alice and I go back a long time."

"That is hard to believe, Alice is an orphan."

"Is that what she told you?"

"Maybe."

"Well, Danielle, I am afraid Alice has been lying to you."

"Maybe you have the wrong Alice."

Derek leaned in closer and took a long whiff of Danielle before pulling away. He shook his head as a gleam of victory settled in his eyes.

"I don't think so," he said while the others quickly returned. Danielle didn't flinch as they closed in around her.

"Well?" Derek asked glancing at the younger man standing behind Danielle.

"She's alone."

"Well, it looks like you'll be coming with us, after all."

"Derek! You know the laws." The men protested. Derek raised his hand silencing them.

"What laws?" Danielle asked glancing around the group. Her heart sank into her stomach. She was outnumbered and in the middle of nowhere. No one would hear her if she screamed. No one knew where she was, except for Alice.

Hope filled Danielle as she thought of her roommate. If Danielle didn't come home, Alice would come looking for her. Maybe find her before... Danielle pushed the idea of dying out of her mind as she glanced at Derek.

"You took something that didn't belong to you," Derek started to say as he stole a closer step. She tried to step back but the heat from the man behind her held her in place.

"You have two choices, now," Derek leaned in closer. Danielle could feel the warmth of his breath on her face as he spoke.

"I can kill you now and put you out of your misery, or you can get on the phone with Alice and bring her here."

"Alice won't come here, she hates the forest," Danielle said trying not to let her urge to kiss him overpower her common sense.

"Does she now?"

Danielle nodded trying to hold herself together as Derek's musky scent of pine washed away her fear. She breathed in deep allowing herself to hold on to his scent and filing into her memory.

"She does," Danielle whispered trying to keep her voice from cracking.

"Why don't you call her and find out if she would come here to help you?"

"She said she would never come here. That if something happens to me here, she won't come."

"You leave me no other option then, but to kill you." Derek raised his hand up. Danielle sucked in a deep breath and closed her eyes waiting for the blow. If she was going to die, she couldn't think of a better way. She waited for the strike that would end her life.

The chirping of Danielle's phone caused Derek to pause. He lowered his arm and slipped his hand into Danielle's pocket. Danielle exhaled and opened her eyes praying Alice wasn't on the other end of the line. As the phone continued to ring, Danielle could feel Derek's gaze on her.

"Hello," Derek's voice was tender and soft, easing Danielle's fears a little. She sucked in a deep breath and strained her ears to hear to who was on the phone.

"Why yes, Danielle is right here. Would you like to speak to her?"

The pause in the conversation told Danielle all she needed. Danielle didn't have to call Alice, she was calling for her daily checkup. All Danielle's lies went up in smoke as Derek glared at her. Derek put the phone up to Danielle's ears. She paused before she answered.

"Hey," Danielle cringed, waiting for the sound of Alice's voice.

"So, who answered your phone? You didn't tell me you were dating anyone." Danielle exhaled letting relief wash over her.

"Carrie, now isn't a good time."

"Well, you haven't called me in a while, so I thought I'd call you."

"Carrie, seriously. I will have to talk to you later." Danielle nodded at Derek, who snapped the phone closed before Danielle's friend could say another word.

"It would be a pity if you didn't follow through with that promise."

"I don't understand," Danielle said, her heart sinking to her stomach. Thoughts of never seeing her friends again filled her mind.

"Call Alice, get her here, and you can see your friend again."

"Why do you want Alice here?" Danielle asked as her decision shifted.

"Let's say she and I have some unfinished business," Derek's words lingered on the air. Danielle chewed on her lower lip and held out her hand for the phone. With a wicked smile of victory plastered on his face, Derek dropped the phone into her hand.

"I doubt she will answer," Danielle said as she dialed the number.

"Let's hope for your sake, she does." Derek's eyes darted to his companions who snickered triumphantly. Danielle's eyes flickered about the group wondering which one would be the one to take her out.

The phone rang and rang and Danielle waited. She knew Alice would never answer on the first call. She snapped the phone closed and stared at Derek.

"Pity." Derek raised his hand once again and Danielle lifted hers.

"Alice never answers the first call. She will answer if you let me call her again. It's kinda our thing. Sort of a code we use. One means I'm fine, but the second call, she will answer." Danielle's eyes widened with hope. Derek nodded giving her a second chance.

"Make the call. And for your sake," Derek leaned in closer, "She better answer." Danielle nodded and dialed the number again.

Chapter 1

Yellow rays from the afternoon sun filtered through the thin curtains. Alice Bane dug her head further under the pillow trying to avoid the light as her eyes fluttered open. A soft moan beside her caught her attention, and she popped her head up. She rubbed the sleep from her eyes and focused on the stranger beside her. His chiseled bare chest and peaceful breathing rocked her to her core.

Carefully, she pulled the sheets away from her body and slipped out of the bed without making a sound. Her heart drummed in her chest as she tried to remember the events of last night. Pieces filtered through her blurred memory as she slipped into her skirt. A smile played at the corner of her lips as she got dressed.

"Leaving so soon?" a low husky voice broke her concentration. Alice whipped her head around. The fit young man rested on the bed —propped up on one elbow. A warm smile stretched across his face and he winked at her.

"I, um," Alice tried to place his name, but no matter how hard she tried to remember, it eluded her. "Hi," she sputtered while pushing her foot into her high heel.

"Hi," he said watching her with a spark in his eyes. "You don't remember anything about last night do you?" Alice's face burned from embarrassment as she shook her head.

"James," he said throwing the sheets off him. Alice's eyes widened as he moved from one side of the room to the other. She couldn't help but glance at his firm butt and his smooth muscular back. She sighed when he yanked his jeans up, covering the lower half of his body.

"Well, James," Alice cleared her throat and turned searching for her blouse among the clutter thrown about the room. The disarray in the room gave her an idea of the kind of night she had with him. The sex must have been amazing as her joints felt unhinged and her body was relaxed.

"Looking for this?" James asked lifting up her black blouse with one finger and dangling it before him. Alice looked at him and smiled. The spark of lust in his eyes ignited the passion in her. He flashed a crooked little smile waving her garment before him.

"Maybe."

"Well, if you don't need it," Alice's eyes followed the material as James tossed the blouse over his shoulder. The fabric drifted gently to the ground and landed in a pile of clothes in the corner. Before the garment landed, James stood beside her, wrapping his arms around her tiny waist and he pulled her off her feet.

The heat of his chest sent a flame through her. With a single kiss the passion sparked from the embers of lust. It didn't matter that Alice had forgotten his name, or even how she had gotten to his place. All she cared about was helping him out of his jeans again.

"Perhaps you can jog my memory about the events of last night? I seem to have forgotten some important stuff."

"Really?" James pulled her to him once again and pressed his lips to hers. Alice curled her body around his as they embraced. He tasted like honey and smelled like Axe body spray. She wondered for just a moment if he had by chance gotten up before her to shower, or if he always had that remnant of musk on his skin. The thought drifted from her mind as James' hand glided over her lower back before cupping his fingers around her ass.

Alice lifted her leg and curled it around his waist to hold herself to him. Their tongues drifted around each other as the lust burned hotter. Everything melted away except for James who held her attention.

"Are you hungry?" James asked pulling away as a low rumble interrupted them. The pang of hunger snapped at Alice's stomach. She couldn't ignore her rumbling growing from inside her. She giggled as she pulled away from James.

"I could eat," she said with a smile. "Or I should I just eat you?" Her eyebrow rose as she glanced at him. James lifted her up and brought her back to the bed. She dropped from his arms, landing softly on the crumpled up comforter and pillows.

James dropped to his knees as his fingers played with the hem of her skirt, pushing the fabric up her thighs. Once he had her where he wanted her, James moved in to the space between her thighs. His hot breath teased her as she arched her back waiting for his tongue to dive into her.

A low chirping from a phone pulled her out of her serenity. The tiny bells from the phone pierced her happy place and grew into an irritation as James nibbled on her inner thigh. She wondered if he could hear it, or if he was ignoring it. But when the chirping didn't stop, Alice lifted her head off the pillows and tapped James' shoulder.

"Are you going to answer that?" she asked hoping he would at least put an end to rude interruption. James lifted his head up and stared at her. He cocked his head to strain his ears and shrugged. The chirping stopped and Alice plopped back down into the pillows. Alice settled back down pushing James' down on her again when the rumbling of the phone vibrating against the wooden table started once more.

"I believe that is yours."

Alice scrunched her eyebrows together trying to remember the day. She didn't have work, so there was no other reason for anyone to be calling her. Her roommate Danielle flashed into her mind. She sighed with frustration rocking her head back and forth ignoring the sound. James waited to see what Alice would do. Alice shook her head and closed her eyes.

"It's my roommate checking in." Alice's eyes shifted to James who held his gaze on her face. His eyebrow rose with confusion and cocked his head.

"Is she your mom or something?"

Alice chuckled darkly and shook her head throwing her arm over her head. "She went to Yellowstone. I told her to ring me every day. She is letting me know she's still alive." Alice said reaching for James.

"One ring tells me she's fine, two and I better answer. It's a code we have," she explained. He smiled and nodded letting his shoulder slump down. Alice sucked in a deep breath trying to succumb to her desires.

"A code huh?" James nibbled on Alice's inner thigh again, inching his way closer to her secret flower. Alice exhaled as he drew closer, his hot breath tickling her as he moved. With his tongue stretched out, she felt a tiny wet flick of his tongue over her slit. Her leg muscles twitched in anticipation when the tiny bells of the phone interrupted once more.

"Oh for fuck's sake," she grunted. James pulled away giving Alice space. She twisted her body around and grabbed the phone from the side table. She glanced at the number and immediately pressed the green button.

"This better be good, you are interrupting something important," Alice blurted keeping her gaze on James. James rose from his knees and played with the hem of his jeans tempting her. He shook his waist and spun around teasing her while unfastened the button of his pants and inched them down over his hips. Alice tried to smile, but her attention was elsewhere. The silence from the other end of the phone held her hostage.

"Danielle? What's wrong?"

"Alice!?"

Alice shot up at the frantic tone in her roommate's voice. She was no longer concerned with James' attempt at seduction and shook her head. She pulled the sheets over her body to cover herself up, closing herself off. James' shoulders dropped with despair and walked out into the living room of the one-bedroom apartment.

"Talk to me—what's going on? Are you hurt? What's wrong?" Alice asked once James was out of the room.

"I don't know how to say this," Danielle panted. The fear in her voice had Alice's hair standing on edge. Her mind raced to calculate how long it would take her to find Danielle if she was lost in the backwoods of the national park.

"Do you have any broken bones? Are you bleeding? Lost? What?"

"I know what you are." The words Alice never wanted to her roommate to utter stopped her heart. Suddenly everything was clear. Alice pressed her lips together into a tight line while her eyes widened with fear.

"What you are talking about, Danielle? Tell me where you are and I will come and get you."

"Listen to me," Danielle panted. "I know everything."

"I doubt that," Alice said trying to keep the tone light and playful.

"Stop deflecting." Danielle's voice rose, taking Alice by surprise. In all the eleven years she had known Danielle, her friend had only lost her temper once. Alice paused as Danielle took a deep breath. "Look, I'm in serious trouble. I need you to come to Yellowstone. Now."

Alice froze. Every inch of her body tingled as the idea of setting foot in Yellowstone stole the air from her lungs. A lump of fear settled in her throat. She swallowed hard forcing the fear down as the ghosts of her past came back to taunt her.

"Danielle, if you are in trouble, you need to call the park ranger. He will find you faster than I can."

"No. It has to be you. These people specifically asked for you."

"People? What people?" Alice rose from the bed and raced to the corner where she plucked her blouse from the pile of clothes.

Her heart thundered in her ears making it nearly impossible to hear Danielle. Through her heavy breathing, Alice heard the phone crackle as it was switched between hands. She moved at lightning speed pulling her blouse over her body and slipping into her skirt before the silence on the other line broke.

"Hello Alice." She gasped.

"Derek?" Alice dropped her voice making it no louder than a whisper. She tried to hold back her anger as she glanced through the open door to James.

"Well, I'm impressed. I thought you may have forgotten all about me."

"What are you doing?"

"Enforcing the law."

"So help me, if you hurt Danielle I will kill you."

"That's funny. I thought I heard you threatening me."

"I don't threaten people, Derek." Alice hissed.

"Well, you see, dear Alice, your friend was in the wrong place at the wrong time and saw things she shouldn't have."

Alice didn't need any further information. Her heart sank as her mind reeled at the potential outcome for her friend. All Alice could see was Derek twisting Danielle's thin elegant neck, causing the light in her friend's eyes to go out.

"Are you certain?"

"I take it you didn't get the text," Derek's voice dropped causing Alice to flinch. Alice pulled the phone from her ear and glanced at the screen as a message popped up. Quickly, Alice clicked on the link. Her eyes widened as a video played.

There in the deepest part of Yellowstone National Park, a pack of wolves shifted to humans. Alice held her breath with her eyes focused on the screen in her hands. The camera jerked about as Danielle raced up the tree to safety.

"Oh Danielle," Alice sighed exhaling the air trapped in her lungs.

"Alice?" Derek's voice drifted over her pounding heartbeat.

"So, now you understand the situation," Derek continued as Alice brought the phone back to her ear.

"What do you want?" Alice hissed with hate.

"Justice, but I'll settle for a trade."

"What kind of trade?"

"You return home, or I will kill her."

"What kind of trade is that? You aren't offering a trade. You're giving me an ultimatum."

"Alice, I'm willing to let your friend go if you come back."

"I don't belong there."

"You're one of us." Derek yelled causing Alice to flinch. She flexed her jaw muscle as she thought of Danielle. There was no way Derek would simply let Danielle go, after she'd witnessed their secret first hand. There was only one solution for Alice, and that was to eliminate the problem.

"I may be, but I don't belong to you. You can't order me to come back."

"I may not be able to order you to come here, but if you don't your friend will be dead by the time I drop this phone."

In the background Danielle's cry stabbed Alice. Alice cringed with the realization that she had no other option but to go back. She had to take a life so she could save another. Alice sighed and dropped to the bed sitting in silence.

"You're going to kill her no matter what I do."

"Not true. I'll spare her if you take her place."

"Oh, so you want to kill me? Sorry, but I like my life."

"Then it's settled. You know, I thought that you cared for this human."

"Alice!" Danielle's screams pierced Alice's heart.

"FINE!" Alice shouted. "I'll come back."

"I knew you would come around eventually," Derek laughed. "I promise that your friend will be cared for until your arrival. Once you arrive it'll be up to you to decide her fate."

"But you said you would let her go!" Alice could feel the fire coursing through her veins. The animal in her was rattling its cage begging to be released.

"The terms of Danielle's fate will be decided when you get here. Oh and Alice, I do hope you get here soon. Her presence is making the others twitchy."

"So help me, if one hair is plucked from her head, I'll kill you myself."

"Well, that would be a fight worth waiting for." Derek's laughter pricked Alice causing her to anger burn.

"See you soon?" Derek said sharply.

Alice sat on the bed with the phone to her ear listening to the silence from the other line. Every breath she took was to calm her nerves. She glanced at the human in the other room. James flashed her a warm smile. Alice rose from the bed and balled her hands into fists. She knew she would be attacked the moment she stepped foot in the park. Hope seeped out of her as James walked into the room.

"You okay?" he asked his eyes filled with concern. Alice pressed her lips into a tight line letting the air escape from her nose. She didn't say a word. She glanced at James to speak. Hurt and rejection flashed across his face. She tried to smile but only shook her head and closed her mouth.

"Thanks for last night, I had fun," Alice's voice was harsh. She stole one last glimpse at James, hoping she could remain in the fantasy. But she knew that her existence would always put others in danger.

"Wait, don't you want some food? I ordered pizza." Alice paused at the door and turned to look at James. He was tall and handsome. Strong and endearing, but her heart froze as she stared at him.

"No, but I did have fun."

"So that's it? You're just going to leave?"

"This isn't the start of a beautiful relationship," Alice said flatly crushing all her hopes of starting something with James. The spark in his eyes faded as she tried to smile. "But thanks."

Alice reached for the door knob and pulled the door open. She slipped into the hallway and shut that part of her heart off forever. She raced towards the parking lot, letting her thoughts consume her. After all this time, she finally understood that she could never hold on to a relationship with anyone in the human world. The lesson was hard to swallow as she realized she had put her best friend in danger because of who she was.

"Hold on Danielle," Alice sighed. "I'm coming for you."

Chapter 2

Alice's heart skipped the moment she crossed the state line into Montana. Her eyes bolted from one side of the road to other before darting to the rear-view mirror. With each glance, she expected to find a pack of angry wolves waiting for her. But as she drove on, all she could see was the wide open country, lost to time.

The high-rise buildings of the city were long gone. Only lush green trees towering towards the sky and wide open spaces surrounded her. She sucked in the crisp clean air and exhaled allowing the pollution of the city to be expelled from her lungs. Her nose filled with the sweet aroma of honeysuckle and wheat. For a split second she wondered about pulling over but she didn't have time to lollygag—Danielle was in trouble.

Alice's mind shifted from the open space and serenity of the wild to the confrontation she was about to drive into. She clenched her teeth and gripped the steering wheel harder.

"What do you have up your sleeve?" she mumbled to herself while keeping a keen eye on the road. It was nearly twelve years since she had last seen him and their parting had been anything but mutually agreed. Her heart sputtered with worry.

Danielle was more than a best friend and roommate—she was a sister. There was no telling if Derek would keep his promise. He wasn't her alpha which made the situation worse. She wasn't bound to him in any shape or form, which meant that Derek could do anything he wanted to Danielle and there wasn't anything Alice could do about it.

She pressed down on the gas pedal, propelling her car down the road faster. She no longer cared about the speed limits or any other human restrictions. Her only thought was to find Danielle and run away as fast as possible. Her thumb drummed against the steering wheel as the trees whizzed by her in a blur. The animal within her growled, and she wondered if ditching the car wouldn't be a better way to travel.

She glanced down to the speedometer and shook her head. With the needle hitting over one hundred, she knew there was no way she would be able to run that fast. But, even 100 miles per hour wasn't fast enough. Her eyes narrowed and her body twitched as she remained behind the wheel, pushing her little Honda as fast as it could go.

It wasn't until she reached the large wooden sign that she finally slowed down. Her heart skipped and sputtered, as the needle dropped below the speed limit. She sucked in a deep breath hoping beyond hope she wouldn't have to confront anyone right here. She rolled past the welcome sign to Yellowstone National Park and smiled.

"Yes!"

Her fears dissipated as she came to a stop behind a long line of cars waiting to enter the park. Alice's head turned from side to side while her eyes peered into the forest. She tried to calm herself but her nerves were shot. Every inch she moved forward was like a notch on a noose around her neck. The air in her lungs burned the closer she got to the small welcome hut of the park.

"Get a grip, Alice." She mumbled searching the shadows of the trees. "They wouldn't be stupid enough to attack you here. Too many people."

She continued to follow the line of cars until she came up to a stop at the entrance. A stout young woman, wearing a brown shirt and khaki shorts, stepped out of the shack. She smiled and leaned down to Alice's window. Alice's eyes lingered on the poor girl and pulled in a deep breath. The scent around the park ranger was complex. Alice caught a hint of lavender soap mingled with coffee and chocolate but no traces of the musky animal scent.

"Good afternoon," the young ranger said extending a map of the park to Alice.

"I won't need that," Alice said shaking her head.

"Okay, well, when was the last time you came to this park?" the human asked. Alice's eyebrows rose in curiosity.

"Why does that matter?"

"It's a standard question to ensure people don't try to come more than once a year. Some new law in place to regulate the national parks." The girl appeared dumbfounded at Alice's question, but kept the smile on her face.

"It's been longer than a year."

"Well then, welcome. The park fee is $15 per vehicle. We would ask that you refrain from feeding the wildlife and if you intend on camping in the park, you will need to go the ranger's station for a permit."

"Even in the back country?" Alice asked pulling money from her wallet and handing it over to the girl.

"Oh, especially in the back country. Here at Yellowstone we want to make sure that everyone is safe. That's why we try to keep track of where our visitors are going. Then if there are any emergencies we will be able to locate you faster."

Alice's eyes widened. Hope filled her heart as she stared at the young girl. "Everyone has to check in with the ranger, then if they are camping in the woods?"

"Oh yes, everyone."

"Has anyone got lost in the last couple of days? I have a friend who came through here and called me for help. She said she is in trouble and needs help."

The girl pressed her lips into a tight line and glanced over her shoulder to her computer screen. Alice's eyes shifted from the girl to the little desk inside the hut and waited. The girl turned her attention back to Alice and shook her head.

"Sorry, no one has put up any alerts on missing persons, within the park. But they don't always send notices here to the welcome station. It would be best for you to go to the park ranger's office."

"Of course it wouldn't be that easy," Alice mumbled. The girl glanced at her and cocked her head. She had hoped it would be an easy rescue, in and out with no issues. But if the ranger's didn't know where Danielle was at, then it would take longer than she expected. All hopes of bypassing Derek's pack flew out the window.

"Excuse me?"

Alice smiled and cleared her throat.

"Where is that exactly?" Alice asked reaching for the map.

"Oh, well, here," the girl handed Alice the map again and leaned into Alice's open window to point out the ranger's station within the park. Behind her, she could hear the grumbling of the people behind her as they grew impatient. The girl pointed to the map moving her focus from Alice to the line piling up behind the Honda. Alice nodded and smiled.

"Thanks," Alice said as she threw her car into drive. The girl stepped back into her box and waved as Alice drove on.

"Nothing is ever simple anymore," Alice said trying to read the small squiggles representing the road from trails.

"But it would be wise to stop off at the ranger's station to let them know I am here," Alice argued with herself as she followed the signs on the side of the road until she pulled up into the small parking lot.

Alice put her car into park and stared at the log cabin with the words "Ranger's Station" painted on the awning. She killed the engine and got out. With one wary foot in front of the other, she walked towards the double doors and pushed through them. Her senses sparked as she sniffed the air. The hair on the back of her neck rose at the familiar scent of another wolf nearby.

"Great, just what I need," Alice grumbled, stalling at the entrance. "Well, you knew you were going to have to run into his crew, eventually. Might as well get it over with."

Alice twisted her head to take in fresh air before stepping further inside the station. The cool air-conditioned breeze swept around her hitting her with lavender and pine. The sickly sweet aroma knocked her back as if she had been hit with a brick to the head. She wobbled a few steps to the counter and clung to it for dear life. Through blurry burning eyes, she tried to find someone to help her. In the corner of the room, behind a faux desk, a strong young man sat with the paper in front of him and his feet propped up.

"Excuse me," Alice cleared her throat trying to shift through the different smells locked in the small room.

"Yeah?" the man huffed flipping through the pages of the newspaper. "What can I do for you?"

"I was told you could help me. I am looking for a missing person here in the park. Is this the right place?"

"Yep," he mumbled undisturbed by Alice's questions.

"Well can you tell me if anyone has been reported missing?"

"Nope." He said bluntly without dropping the paper.

"No, you can't tell me? Or no one has been reported missing?" Alice's face grew hotter with frustration. It was bad enough she could barely see through the fragrances assaulting her sinuses. But to have the ranger deliberately being stubborn was downright irritating her.

"No one is missing, and no one has been reported missing," he answered.

"Okay. Well, can I file a report on a missing person?"

"Go to the police."

Alice's face burned at the quick dismissal. Clearly she wouldn't be getting any help from the ranger. Her eyes narrowed before it hit her. The overwhelming scents in the office, the burning eyes all signs pointed to one thing; he was a wolf, and was probably ordered by the alpha to be a pain to anyone looking anyone else. Alice's balled her hands into tiny little fists as she tried not to let him irritate her.

"Look, my friend came out here four days ago. She registered here with you or someone in your office. I got a call from her yesterday saying she is in trouble."

"What kind of trouble?" the ranger asked with his face still buried behind the paper.

Alice's eyes narrowed on the paper trying to burn holes into it. She sucked in a deep breath and slammed her fists on the counter. "Wolves," she spit.

The ranger laughed keeping the paper steadily in his hands. "Wolves don't hunt people."

"You know damned well what kind of wolves I am talking about." Alice snapped. She stormed around the desk and ripped the paper from the park ranger's hands forcing him to pay attention to her.

"Hey," he grumbled as Alice crumbled the paper into a tiny little ball and tossed it into the waste bin.

"I understand you have orders to be a dick to me. So you might as well call Derek and tell him I'm here."

"Derek?" The ranger sat up straight and stared at Alice. His gaze was filled with awe and wonder. Alice stepped back taking in his confusion and understanding. She noticed his nose twitching as her scent drifted around him. His eyes grew wider as he rose from his chair.

"How do you know Derek?"

"Don't be coy. You have your orders. Now either tell me where I can find him, or tell me if a girl named Danielle Johnstone came in here and got a permit to camp in the back country." Alice demanded.

The man shook his head while keeping his eyes locked on Alice. She stepped back keeping a few inches of space between them in case he attacked. She watched every muscle in his body expecting it to twitch or shimmer giving her the sign he was about to shift and rip into her.

"I think we may have gotten off on the wrong foot here," the ranger said putting his hands up into the air and moving slowly towards the main desk. Alice moved back around the counter refusing to take her eyes off him.

"My name is Bash Allen, and I am a park ranger here at Yellowstone," he extended his hand towards Alice who simply glared at it and shook her head. He dropped his hand and adjusted his attention to the small laptop on the counter.

"So, if your friend got a permit, I can find it in our data base. But, you have to understand that not everyone stays within their permit ranges. A lot of hikers say they will be one place and then they wander into other parts of the park."

"All I need is a starting point. I can track her from there."

"With all due respect, Miss, this park is huge. I could help you."

"No thanks. I am sure you will notify Derek as soon as I leave this building."

"To be honest, I don't know this Derek person. I have heard his name thrown around a bit, but never met the guy."

"Sure," Alice huffed as she trained her eyes on the computer, as the names of everyone with permits for camping scrolled down the screen.

"I'm serious."

"I'm sure you are, but *with all due respect* Ranger, I don't trust any wolves in this area. Either you work for him and your job is to throw me off the trail, or you don't and you'll end up slowing me down. Either way—point me in the direction of my friend and I will find her myself."

Bash stared at Alice and opened his mouth, but the glare in her eyes changed his mind and he turned his attention back to the computer screen.

"Here," Bash said pointing to Danielle's name in the list. "You can start in the northeast territory of the park."

Alice stared at the map for a moment and nodded as she burned the image into her memory.

"Thanks," Alice said glancing at Bash. He smiled and stepped back from the computer. Alice moved towards the door and hesitated. She glanced over her shoulder and stared at Bash for a moment.

"I don't know if what you said about Derek is true or not. But if you do happen to call him to warn him I am here, give him a message for me."

Bash opened his mouth and shook his head, but Alice cut him off before he could say another word. "Tell him, I won't go down without a fight."

"Who should I say you are?" Bash asked keeping his eyes on Alice. She turned and glared at him.

"Alice Bane," she answered, yanking the door open and stepped out into the fresh air. The overpowering aroma of lavender, basil and pine drifted away from her as the door closed behind her. She sucked in a deep breath clearing her senses.

"Hold on Danielle," Alice whispered looking into the trees. Alice walked to her car, pulled open the door and climbed in. As she started the engine, she glanced towards the ranger's building.

In the window, she spied Bash standing with the curtain pulled back staring at her. The look in his eyes was soft and tender—reminding her of the look James had given her when she had left him. Alice turned her head and glanced over her shoulder as she pulled out of the parking stall and drove off.

The trees towered over her car and sunlight danced through the canopy. The soft gentle hues of the green and gold leaves stabbed at her heart. For a brief moment she actually missed this place. Yellowstone was the only place she had ever known that allowed her the freedom to shift and run wild. But the further she drove into the park; the more other more haunting memories flooded her mind.

There was a reason she had left, despite the beauty around her. The only reason she had returned was for Danielle. Alice sucked in a deep breath and her eyes drifted to the small parking lot on the right-hand side of the road. She slammed on her brakes and turned the wheel. Danielle's car stood there, in the last parking bay. Alice pulled into the space next to it and cut her engine.

She climbed out and scanned the area. A long trail wound up a slope and disappeared into the woods. Alice closed her eyes and pulled in a long deep breath allowing Danielle's scent to overwhelm her. A gentle breeze flowed around her and tickled the loose strands of her hair. Her eyes snapped open and she turned towards the trail.

"Please be okay," Alice whispered as she stared at the trail before her.

Chapter 3

Alice trekked over the rocky path stealing a few moments to appreciate the surrounding scenery. She couldn't help but let her mind wander to the past, letting childhood memories drift past her eyes. A faint smile crept over her lips when she thought of the times she had raced through these trees and fields with her family. Her heart swelled with each passing mile she crossed. The birds chirped and sang while she hiked along the beaten path. The warm summer breeze played with her hair while memories of a peaceful time played in her mind.

When she reached the clearing she paused. In the center of the open field, majestic elk took pause to study at her. She couldn't help but smile at the three heavy set creatures nibbling on the tall grass. At one point in her life, she would have stalked them and killed them, together with her father. But now, Alice just stared at them with wonder and awe.

"Hello," Alice said walking towards them with her hand stretched out as the thoughts of her father raced through her mind.

The moment the wind shifted, the elk took notice and jolted up from their grazing. They stared at her with caution, ready to sprint. Alice stretched her fingers out to them, but the instant they caught the whiff of the animal in her, they took off. Alice remained still, studying them as they bolted into the safety of the forest.

"They know what we are."

She turned her head with her mouth open. Beside her stood her father in his old hunting jeans and tee-shirt. Alice gasped at the sight of him. Tears rose in her eyes. She closed her eyes and rubbed them but when she opened them again, she didn't just see her father standing in the field, but also a younger version of herself. Side by side the two walked through the field. Alice reached out for the ghostly images, but no matter how hard she tried to touch them, they were always out of reach.

"Like all creatures, they know what we are," her father said to her younger self. "It is in their nature to run from us. We are predators to them," her father explained with a smile. Alice kept her eyes locked on her younger self as the girl shimmered, ready to shift into her wolf form. Her father stretched out his hand and clasped the young girl's shoulder.

"Leave them child, they are not what we are hunting today."

"But Daddy," the girl said and stared up at the man. He shook his head and nodded to the furthest edge of the clearing.

"I am pleased you want to shift and hunt. But when you let the wolf out, the human fades into the back of your mind and we are not yet far enough away from prying eyes. Be patient. I promised you a chance to play, but not so close to humans. They might see and you know what happens if they do. We can't risk exposing ourselves to them. Do you know what would happen if we were to shift in front of humans?" Alice's father dropped his head to glance at the child with love and understanding. The girl dropped her head and nodded.

"We would have to kill them," Alice answered. Her father lifted his hand up and placed it on the young girl.

"We must be careful and cautious."

"I understand, Father." The younger Alice glanced up at her father. Alice reached out her hand towards them but her father and younger self disappeared like fog.

Alice shook her head trying to force the memory out of her mind. A single tear ran down her cheek.

"I miss you Daddy," Alice sighed holding on to the memory as long as she could. The wind drifted around her kissing her skin as she stood hoping the memory would return. She closed her eyes letting her heart break for a moment more before she continued her journey through the field.

At the edge of the field, Alice paused and sucked in a deep breath. The scent of pine, honeysuckle, and jasmine filled her nose. She remained still letting the wind shift and sway about her. When she was absolute certain no other scents were lingering on the wind, she opened her eyes.

"This looks like a good spot," she told herself kicking out of her shoes and tucking them into the roots of the old tree beside the path.

Her wolf nose would be able to pick up Danielle's scent better than what she could in human form. With her eyes darting to and fro, Alice began stripping off her clothes. First, her socks, and then her shirt. As panic and fear bubbled in her stomach, she yanked off her pants and stood bare letting the warm summer sun kiss every inch of her body.

She walked over to a fallen tree with her belongings and tucked her clothes into the gap between the forest floor and the tree trunk. She took in a deep breath hoping to settle her nerves and she let herself relax. Her toes tingled as she dug them into the cool moist dirt and she concentrated.

"Come Alice, you have done this before," she told herself. She took in a deep breath and concentrated. Tiny prickings in her toes pushed up into her ankles before reaching her legs. She shook her arms and wiggled her body. Each moment that ticked by caused her more aggravation.

"Come on!"

She panted forcing herself to concentrate harder. Although three years had passed since the last time she let the wolf out, she couldn't let that stop her. She had never expected or anticipated shifting would be so difficult now. After all, her wolf had been clawing and begging to be released, when she was on the phone with Derek, so why was shifting taking so long now?

Alice gritted her teeth. Her body trembled while the tingling grew into jolts of electricity. Each heart beat felt like lightening zapping her insides. She closed her eyes and forced herself to take every bit of energy. But still, her body remained in human form. Alice opened her eyes and heaved in and out.

Every muscle in her body ached. She dropped down to catch her breath. Her head pounded while her lungs pulled in the fresh air around her. She stood straight and tried again. Every fiber in her body sparked and jolted her causing her extremities to twitch.

"What the hell?" she grumbled looking up to the sky. "I don't have time for this."

She shook her body trying to release the jitters before standing still again. "Don't think about it," she told herself. "Shift. You've done it before. It's like riding a bike."

Alice pulled in air from her nose and closed her eyes. In the back of her mind she heard Derek's voice mocking her.

"What's a matter? Big bad wolf can't come out to play?"

The very thought of Derek sparked the fire Alice needed. Before she could stop herself, her body split, releasing the wolf trapped within her.

Alice's front legs dropped to the soft moist dirt of the forest. She glanced down to find her massive gray paws under her. A deep rough laugh pulled up from her chest as she realized what she had done.

"Like riding a bike," she thought. Alice paused and lifted her head up towards the trees. New scents filled her nose. The subtle hint of roses filtered through the pine and aspen trees. Alice cocked her head to the left and paused trying to pinpoint the exact direction of the scent.

"There," she thought with her big blue eyes popping open. Without thinking, she pushed herself forward and left the trail behind her.

Alice raced through the trees with ease. She had forgotten the last time she had felt so free and alive. While she kept the scent in the front of her mind, she couldn't help but think of all the times she had raced through this forest with her family in wolf form.

The soft dirt sprayed behind her as she pumped her mighty legs. Each stride increased her speed and soon the forest was nothing but a blur. With the wind in her face, Alice followed the scent.

It blew her mind—all the things she could sense and feel in this form. As she raced further into the back country, she smelled every animal she passed. The musky stench of the grizzly bear, the dainty hint of rabbits, even the moldy aroma of the skunk filled her nose as she ran. But only one scent kept her going, the strong scent of roses that Danielle grew on their fire escape back home. No other person in the park would have that fragrance. It was the one thing she was certain of as the afternoon sun slipped through the trees.

Finally, Alice skidded to a stop letting the dirt pile up under her long nails. The sudden overwhelming stench of musky pine filled her nose. She shook her head trying to clear the air, but the scent burned her nose and overpowered the subtle fragrance of roses.

"Derek." The name sounded like a curse word in her mind. She ducked into the shadows and scanned the area. No doubt the scent was his. It was one of the reasons she couldn't stand to be around him. But as she stepped slowly away from the trail, she realized she would have to follow it sooner or later. After all, Danielle was in Derek's company and she would have to suffer to find Danielle.

Alice moved far enough away to let the robust scent drift away with the wind. Carefully, she moved five long steps to the south and paused. The stench wasn't as strong coming from the south as it was from the north. Alice turned her head towards the long steep slope that rose up into the mountains.

"So that's where you are," Alice huffed glaring up to the peaks. A smile played in her mind. Although she had been away from the area for a while, she still knew it like the back of her hand. She sucked in a deep breath and pushed through the scented trail. She counted her steps as she moved west. After all, a wolf's scent only lingered for the width of their body and Derek would never let a human ride on him in wolf form.

Alice exhaled sharply and took tiny whiffs expecting the scent of musk to intrude into her nose. When the air came up fairly clean, Alice sucked in more deeply. She glanced up to the sky to find dark clouds drifting her way. She knew if she didn't get to Danielle soon, she would be stuck in a storm that would wash away her scent, leaving Alice with no way of finding her.

Without risking another moment, Alice raced alongside the musk and rose scented trail that led up the mountain pass. From the time she was a child, she always loved this pass. It led to a secret lake that no human would ever find. That is where she knew Derek would have taken Danielle. Far enough away from humans, and secret even from the sky because of the large trees covering the water.

Alice raced up the embankment until she reached the top. She paused to gaze down at the lake below her. There was no way Derek would bring Danielle here alone. Alice's eyes scanned the trees for his pack. Sure enough, in the shadows, a wolf lingered under the shrubs.

"Well, there is more than one way into to this place," Alice thought as she turned and raced back down the slope. With time running out, she pushed her legs as fast as they would go. Each stride she claimed, she promised Danielle she would make it before the sunset.

With her lungs burning, Alice reached the second trail to the lake. She hurtled over the fallen branches and trees as she made her way to the water's edge. The moment her paws touched the moist sandy bank she paused and lapped up the cool spring water. Alice glanced up to the sky as the last light of day drifted behind the mountain top.

"Hold on Danielle, I'm almost there."

The soft blue light of night filtered through the orange and reds of the sun. Alice moved in the shadows keeping her eyes alert for any signs of Derek's men. It was the flicker of a fire, like a lighthouse beacon in the dark, that caught her attention. Alice paused and dropped to the ground. With her eyes trained on the fire across the way, she sniffed the air. The hint of roses lingered around her and all of Alice's doubts faded. Danielle was there, no question about it. Only problem was, how to snatch her without Derek finding out.

"Alright Alice, think. You have to be smart about this," she said to herself as she moved closer to the little campsite. "Derek is with her. He wouldn't just leave her out on her own like this. Think, what would he expect you to do?"

As her mind whirled with different strategies, only one scenario continuously came back in her mind. Alice sighed, there was no way she was going to be able to get Danielle out of Yellowstone without taking Derek out first. She sucked in a deep breath weighing her options as she drew closer.

A rustle of leaves not far from where she hid startled her. With her heart racing she ducked down. The lone wolf she spotted earlier trotted down the slope towards the small camp. Alice watched as the wolf shifted to its human form before getting close. Through the rustle of the leaves and the other animals around her, Alice honed her ears to listen.

"Well?" Derek asked.

"Nothing. Although I did catch a scent earlier, but it didn't have the fragrance you described earlier."

"What do you mean?" Derek asked in hushed tones making it nearly impossible for human ears to hear.

"It was roses mixed with coconuts. Maybe she isn't coming after all."

"Oh, she will come. Mark my words, she'll be here. Maybe not as soon as I had hoped."

Alice tried to keep still as she listened to the distant conversation, but every fiber in her body screamed for her to attack. Resisting the urge, she remained as still as possible. Although both men were in human form, she realized they would be able to shift faster than it would take her to charge them.

"Tell the others to come back tomorrow. I doubt she will be coming tonight." Alice heard Derek order and twitched at the underlying command in his alpha voice. Although Alice was not under his control, it was still clear that he held the rank and the others obeyed without question.

"Perfect," Alice thought. "Send them all away and open yourself up to me."

Alice kept her eyes on the shadows as they withdrew from the area. Her mouth dropped as she noticed the number of people moving quickly away from the area.

"So, you have added to your little pack have you?" Alice hissed. The dark shades of night drifted over the lake as the silver light of the moon faded from the clouds rolling in.

"Better make your timing perfect," Alice thought. "You will probably only get one shot at this."

She moved swiftly like the predator she was through the shadows disturbing nothing as she inched her way closer towards them in. Her heart raced as lightening cracked against the blackened sky. The rumble of the thunder caused her to pause and look up to the sky.

"It's now or never."

Chapter 4

Alice kept low to the ground as she inched her way closer to the campsite. With each step she took, she ensured her paws didn't touch a branch or twig. The last thing she wanted was to give her position away. Slow and steadily she moved, until the stench of basil washed over her. She held her position waiting until she saw Danielle with her own eyes. As she listened, she heard the soft drumming of a human heart beneath the low double thrum of Derek's beating heart. Alice sighed with relief to know her friend was still alive.

As Alice positioned herself to strike, Danielle's voice carried through the trees causing her to pause. Her eyes scanned the dark horizon searching for her friend. On the shore of the lake, she spotted Danielle sitting on a log beside the fire. A movement in the shadows caught her attention and soon Derek emerged and took a seat beside Danielle.

"How does it happen?" Danielle asked. Alice's ears perked at the calmness in her friend's voice. Alice popped her head over the boulder which she used as a cover to hide her from the fire. She rose slightly stealing a peak of Danielle. There, huddled with her arms around her, Danielle sat calmly while Derek stroked the fire. Alice studied Derek as he turned to face Danielle.

"What?" Derek asked as he moved further from the fire and took a seat beside Danielle.

"Shifting, how does it work? Do you have to concentrate or does it just happen?"

"If you are worried if I will spontaneously combust into wolf form, you don't have to worry. It doesn't work that way for me."

"For you? Does it happen like that for other wolves?" Danielle glanced over to Derek with wide eyes, filled with wonder and awe. Derek pulled back his head and laughed. The sound bounced off the surrounding trees startling the birds from their slumber.

"Those born this way can control themselves better than those bitten."

"So one can choose to be a wolf?" Danielle couldn't hide her curiosity. Every bit of her being leaned closer towards Derek as if he was a mighty sage.

"There are those that seek us out hoping to join the pack."

"What's that like?"

"You sure are filled with questions." Derek glared at Danielle and crossed his arms.

"I would apologize, but seeing as how I'm not sorry, I won't. Besides, you're planning on killing me so I thought..." Danielle let her words drift away.

Once again Derek threw his head back laughing at Danielle's innocence. He shook his head before rising to his feet. Danielle's eyes lingered on him as he moved with grace and majesty. Her stomach twisted from the butterflies flapping within her. She shook her head with her mouth open in awe of him. Everything from the way he moved to the sound of his voice drew her in.

"Are you going to answer the question? Or is deflecting a wolf thing because Alice does that all the time." The very mention of Alice's name caused Derek to twitch. A smile played at the corner of Alice's lips. The very thought of his discomfort sent chills of pleasure throughout her body.

"For those bitten, transformation only happens during a full or new moon. For those born this way it is a choice. They can walk around like humans and completely cut off the wolf. Or they can embrace it and change at will."

"So," Danielle paused gauging Derek's body language. "You were born this way."

"What makes you think that?"

"You said that you won't burst into a wolf, so you must have been born this way." Derek nodded as his eyes lingered on Danielle. The corner of his lips pulled up before he turned his back on her to tend to the fire once more.

"Or I could be the alpha."

Danielle's eyes widened as she stared at him. The more information Derek revealed the more Danielle's courage grew. She scooted closer to the fire. The flames licked the wood casting Derek's shadow around them. She realized she would never be satisfied until she knew it everything.

"Is that the leader?" Danielle asked hoping she wasn't crossing some forbidden line. Derek smirked while his eyes remained locked on the fire.

"Aren't you a clever girl? How did you figure that out?"

"The others. You ordered them to track me down and they did. Just now, one of them came up to the camp." Derek's shoulders stiffened. Danielle paused wondering how much of what Derek was saying was the truth or if the one who came directed him not to shift and so, he couldn't. She waited a moment before continuing.

"You told him to let the others go home. But why don't you think Alice will come tonight?"

"You heard all that? With those human ears of yours?" Derek turned and faced Danielle. The lightening crashed against the dark sky causing Danielle to jump. She sucked in a deep breath as Derek's features shifted from man to monster and back again.

"I did," she gulped. The hair on the back of Danielle's neck rose. Her eyes flashed around the camp as long howls tore through the trees. She jumped letting the fear control her. It was fight-or-flight time, and she was ready to run.

"What's the matter? Scared of the big bad wolf?" Derek teased watching Danielle's reaction to the sound.

"Please," Danielle huffed. "Wolves do not scare me. They are the most majestic creatures on the planet. And loyal to their pack."

"What startled you? Your heart is racing as if you are running, but here you are standing still beside me."

"Lightening is going to hit soon. We should seek shelter."

"You don't need to worry about the lightening. It never strikes this area. Some say it is protected by the trees."

"Nonetheless, I would like to move." Danielle didn't wait for Derek's approval. She quickly gathered her belongs and headed deeper into the forest. Derek was on her heels ready to reach out and grab her if she took off. Alice waited and observed the area and the situation, itching to take action. The sooner she was able to make her move, the sooner she could leave this place.

Thunder grumbled through the sky crashing against the surrounding mountains causing the sound to amplify. Even Alice wondered about where the lightening would strike as she remained hidden behind the boulder. Her eyes darted to the dark clouds blocking out all forms of light. Even with her enhanced eyesight, the shadows of night impaired her sight.

"Here is good," Danielle said stopping at a fallen tree. Derek laughed as Danielle sat down and crossed her legs.

"So how does one turn into what you are? You mentioned being bitten, but what happens after?"

"Why wondering if I will turn you?"

Danielle paused to give Derek's words weight and nodded. "It seems logical. Either you are going to kill me, or change me."

"What makes you think I am going to change you?" Derek leaned in closer parting his lips to flash his teeth. Danielle didn't flinch—she remained still with her eyes locked on him.

"Because I know you feel something for me."

"Do I now?" Derek laughed keeping his face inches from Danielle's.

"I believe you do. Why else would you keep me for so long? You could have killed me in the forest when you first found me videotaping. Instead you took me with you. Of course I could be a pawn in some fucked up game you have with Alice, but, why wait to take my life? Unless of course, you think turning me would hurt Alice more than my death." Danielle stared at Derek. His eye twitched as she spoke giving away his plan.

"Thought so. You want Alice to see you doing it and that is why I am still here," Danielle mumbled. Her mind raced to put the pieces together as Derek pressed his lips into a tight line.

Before Danielle could utter another word, Derek's hand cupped around her head and pulled her to him. His lips brushed against hers causing her body to burn with a desire she hadn't felt in years. Danielle didn't wait for Derek to pull away, she wrapped her arm around his neck and drew him closer to her. Keeping his lips locked to hers.

"I knew it," she finally panted when Derek pulled away. "You do like me."

"I have found myself growing fond of you," Derek confessed, flashing a crooked little smile at Danielle.

"I have that effect on people. So what happens now?" she asked letting Derek slip away from her.

Before Derek could answer a bolt of white light crashed down through the trees, hitting the edge of the water where Danielle and Derek had stood before. Derek's eyes jerked to Danielle and for the first time he stared at her with the same wonder as she had been staring at him with.

"How did you know that was going to happen?" Derek asked bewildered. Danielle shrugged.

"It was just a feeling. Sometimes lightening is attracted to me. Kinda like how tornadoes were attracted to Dorothy in the Wizard of Oz. I think it has it out for me to be honest. Luckily though, I learned to read the signs."

"Signs?" Derek's eyebrow rose as he stared at her.

"Oh you know, the hair on the back of the neck standing up. The tingling of the skin like when you stick your finger in a light socket." Danielle looked down to her fingers as she spoke.

"You never answered me." Danielle glanced up to Derek. "What's going to happen now?" Danielle paused and dropped her eyes again to her fingers. "With me?"

"That is up to Alice." Derek said flatly as his eyes drifted to the darkness that swallowed them.

"What's your problem with her anyway?" Danielle asked rising to her feet. She took a few steps closer to the camp as the small fire glowed in the dark.

"You wouldn't understand."

"Try me," she said walking back to the camp as the rain began falling from the clouds.

"Alice was my mate." Danielle paused letting the words sink in. She turned on her heels and looked at Derek.

"What?"

"It isn't what you think."

"Explain it to me. After that kiss, I certainly think I have a right to know if she is competition." Derek moved over to Danielle and glared at her with an intense expression that sent chills racing through Danielle's body.

"Alice belongs to me. Her father gave her away, so that she would join our packs together into one. But she ran away leaving both vulnerable."

"Alice is not one to run from anything. There must have been a reason for her departure."

"There was not. Everything was set. The moon was full and everyone had been planning the ceremony for weeks. However, word soon spread through the area that she was gone. In his grief, her father took his own life and her mother was forced from the pack to live alone. She took everything from her family."

"That doesn't sound like Alice." Danielle crossed her arms defending her friend and roommate.

"Maybe not now, but the real reason I didn't kill you right where you stood, was because of her scent. You smell like her."

"Seriously?" Danielle shook her head and turned away, striding back to the fire to get warm.

"Danielle, please." Derek reached out for her and with his fingers around her forearm, yanked her back to him. "I told you, you wouldn't understand. A wolf is bound to their family. Alice was a wild card and still is. She needs to pay for what she did to her parents."

"Why didn't you go after her when you first found out that she had left, if she was to be your mate," Danielle hissed the word 'mate' as if it were a cursed word. Her eyes shot daggers at Derek as she waited for him to explain.

"I tried, but I was not the alpha then. So I was ordered to stay put. But if it weren't for that order, I would have. I would have gone to the ends of the earth to find her." Derek dropped his hands from Danielle and stepped back.

"So, I'm the bait and you want revenge."

Derek nodded. "What happens if Alice doesn't show?"

"She will come for you—you said so yourself."

"But you paint her like a villain— maybe she won't show."

"Then I offer you the choice now." Danielle's eyebrow rose as her heart thumped in her chest.

"What choice?"

"To become a wolf and join my pack."

"Or?" Danielle's eyebrow rose with suspicion.

"Or, I can kill you now."

"I don't think you have it in you to kill me," Danielle challenged, squaring off her shoulders to glare at him defiantly.

In the darkness, Alice watched with her mouth wide open. Everything Derek said pricked and stung her like a thousand knives slicing her open. Each and every word spilled from his lips only threw more fuel to her fire. Alice crouched to her hind legs and let the strength of them spring her forward. There was no way she was going to let Derek continue to stamp her family's name deeper into the mud.

She bolted through the shadows of the night as Derek's body trembled. Danielle gasped and stepped back cautiously to avoid the snapping of bones as Derek shifted. Before Danielle could turn and run, Alice's howl ripped through the silence scattering every living creature for a three-mile radius.

Danielle stumbled back and crashed hard onto the ground. The scream she had built up in her lungs refused to come out as the gray wolf lunged out of the darkness with its mouth open.

Alice sank her teeth into Derek's hind. His cry rumbled and echoed over the lake. Alice knew that if he had others still around, they would be here soon. She had to act fast if she was going to save Danielle from his wrath.

"Oh my God," Danielle whimpered with wide eyes locked on the gray wolves. Her heart crashed against her chest, and every breath of air was a struggle between the screams. "This isn't happening," Danielle huffed trying to get her footing so that she could run.

But the fight kept her frozen in place. She had seen wolves battle before, but none were so brutal. Of course, Danielle was always a safe distance away. Yet, here she was in the middle of the fight locked between two creatures each playing for keeps.

"Please, stop!" Danielle cried out. The smaller of the two wolves charged the larger one. Danielle's hands flew up to her mouth trying to hold back her scream.

Then, rain poured down, soaking the wolves and Danielle until it became a sheet of water separating the human world from the supernatural world.

Chapter 5

Danielle trembled in the darkness of the forest. Her heart raced as she searched for Alice and Derek in the depths of the shadows that shrouded her vision. The snapping of branches and twigs rattled her nerves, causing her to jump at each and every sound that crashed through the night.

Though her sight was blurred by the limitations of her human eyes, she strained to see further. She took one weary and cautious step, pausing to listen. The clap of thunder in the distance shattered her resolve to find them. The rolling thunder made it impossible to locate the precise location of the wolves.

"Alice!" Danielle cried out with her hands cupped around her mouth. Her voice boomed through the darkness. Danielle paused and stood like a statue waiting for something to return to her. But the sounds that came back to her were jumbled and confusing. The howls and snarls from the wolves as they battled in the void, echoed against the tall mountains that surrounded her.

Danielle spun around trying to get her bearings, but no matter which way she turned, all the trees around her rose to the sky in the same shape. With no way to decipher which way she was going, she would only get lost. For a split second she wondered if anyone would be able to find her. In all the time she had spent in the back country and in different forests around North America, she had never once felt the prick of fear. Now it stabbed her with murderous intent.

"Derek!" her voice bounced off the side of the mountains that surrounded the hidden lake once again. Danielle dropped to her knees. Her lip quivered as the tears mixed with the rain washed down her face.

"Please," she begged. "Stop."

Deep in the woods the wolves paid no heed to the human's plea. The creatures snipped and growled protecting their own as the battle raged on. Alice snapped her jaw down around Derek's heel as his head whipped around to grab the back of her neck. Before Alice could wriggle out of his grip, she found herself flying through the air.

Her body snapped a young sapling as she crashed against it, with such force that the very air in her lungs burned. Alice tried to shake off the dizziness but she couldn't figure out which of the three Derek's she saw was the right one to attack. She tried to steady herself for the next attack, but as her muscles tensed to spring forward Derek shifted back into his human form.

"You can't beat me Alice," he gloated while watching the thin gray wolf stumbling about.

"You were never strong enough to beat me, so what makes you think you can do it now?" Derek circled around Alice and bent down. Alice growled with the hair on the back of her neck raised and her body poised to attack. Derek glared at her with a large branch in his hand ready to use it as a bat.

Alice snipped at Derek. He dodged her razor-sharp teeth and drew the branch back. Alice sidestepped and ducked as the branch whizzed over her head causing her hair to sway like the tall grass from the gust of wind rolling over her.

"I have to admit, I didn't think you'd return. I thought you would run like you always do. Apparently, this Danielle girl means a lot to you."

A low rumbled ripped through Alice's throat letting out a sharp growl. Without hesitating she lunged again, missing Derek by inches. He laughed, circling around Alice and then he shifted the branch from one hand to the other and back again.

"So here is what I am going to do," Derek smirked. His eyes remained locked on Alice as she circled around him. "I am going to turn her into one of us." Alice lunged at Derek and ducked down to sink her teeth into his calf. His scream filled the night air.

Before Alice unclasped her jaw, the branch crashed against her side forcing her off of him. She didn't know how much longer she would be able to keep fighting. Derek was stronger and she was losing. Another blow to ribs and they would shatter. Alice whimpered while reeling away from Derek. She glared at him knowing that she would rather he killed her than curse her friend with this life.

"All you had to do was turn her into one of us earlier, and we wouldn't be in this mess. But you never could stomach your responsibilities. Now, here we are. Just look at you. Broken, beaten, and unable to stop me from taking what I want, yet again."

Alice stumbled back trying to keep enough space between herself and Derek. Pain ripped through her body and she wondered how much more she could take. The gleam in Derek's eyes made it clear he wasn't going to stop until she was dead.

"But what would happen to Danielle?" she thought to herself missing Derek's swing once again. The pain was winning and her body was too weak to keep fighting him.

"Don't worry about Danielle, I have grown quiet fond of the human. And when she turns, she will be mine, and you..." Derek paused to laugh. "You will be dead."

"Derek!" Danielle's voice split through the trees and he turned to find Danielle standing like a dark angel in the shadows. The distraction was all Alice needed for one last hoo-rah. With all the strength she could muster, she bolted towards Derek and sent him crashing to the ground.

"NO!" Danielle shrieked helplessly. Derek's arm wrapped around Alice's neck and squeezed. Alice tried to wiggle her way out of Derek's strangle hold, but it was no use. He had her right where he wanted her.

"I'm so sorry, Danielle," Alice thought as the vision of her friend faded into nothingness.

Derek pushed Alice's body off him and rose like a victorious champion. He looked down at the crumpled body of Alice and kicked her in the ribs for one last gesture.

"Alice!" Danielle cried out through the rain. Although she couldn't see all that had happened, she knew her friend was in trouble. Derek emerged through the dark shadows with his hands opened to her.

"What happened? Where's Alice?" Danielle asked sucking in a deep breath and fearing the news. Her eyes drifted to the space between the trees hoping to find her friend coming through the veil of night as well. But when she saw only Derek, she knew.

"She is gone and we need to leave."

"No." Danielle screamed charging into the forest. Derek wrapped one hand around her waist, holding her back. Danielle pushed and slapped his arm trying to escape his grasp. Derek tossed the branch to the ground and curled both arms around her holding her to him.

"We need to find Alice. If you beat her to a pulp she needs help."

"What about me?" Derek asked twisting his leg to reveal the stream of blood running down his leg from where Alice nipped him.

"My God, what did you two do to each other?"

"What we had to do."

"I am not going to leave my friend out there. She could be dying."

"If she knows what's best for her, she *will* die."

Shock froze Danielle's heart. Derek's callousness was too much. She shook her head refusing to hear the truth. Her eyes focused on the trees and the shadows. Everything around her suddenly became very small. All she wanted to do was scream, but nothing escaped her lips.

"I don't believe it. Alice can't be dead."

"She may not be, but Danielle—" Derek switched on his charm and released Danielle. "You are not a wolf. You don't understand our ways. Alice was a threat to my rule as alpha. She challenged me. Those who challenge the alpha must die. It is the way of the wolf."

"She wasn't challenging your status and you know it." Danielle shoved her hands into Derek's thick chest, barely causing him to rock on his heels. He shook his head and grabbed her by the wrists stopping her from shoving him again.

"She attacked me. She knew what she was doing and she knew the consequences of her actions. Now you can either come with me now, or you can join her in the afterlife."

"You made it all sound so romantic—the idea of being a wolf. But after what you did to Alice, I would rather die than be one of you."

"That's the anger talking. You don't mean that."

"No?" Danielle glared at him. Her heart broke as she stared at him. Despite the fact she had only known him a few days, there was a spark between them. She had felt it when he had touched her the first time, and even now she felt it. Danielle dropped her head allowing the pieces of her shattered heart to prick her.

"Please, I know you care for me. We have something special. Don't make me choose between her and you. Please, don't make threats you can't honor."

"You think I won't kill you right here and now?" Derek growled, his eyes narrowed. Danielle stared back at him unafraid and shook her head.

"I know you won't."

"You know too much about me and my kind. You have proof that could cause our world to end with that stupid video. I gave you the choice to join us, but you refused. You leave me no other choice but to kill you." Derek stepped back and Danielle closed her eyes. The sharp sound of air whizzing through her teeth echoed in her ears and she closed her eyes waiting for the blow that would end her.

Derek stood with his hand raised and fingers like claws ready to strike, but the longer he stared at Danielle, the less resolve he had. He knew that in killing her, he would kill a piece of himself as well.

"I have to," he whimpered sucking in a shallow breath. "I have to kill you. It is the law."

Danielle remained still with her eyes closed and shoulders back. "Then do it."

Derek dropped his hand and stepped back conflicted. "I can't."

Danielle opened her red eyes and tears streamed down her face. "Please, if you are the alpha you can show mercy to Alice. She is more than a friend to me, she is a sister. I can't just leave her out there to die."

"Danielle, you don't understand."

"So, show me everything about you and your world. But please spare her."

Derek shook his head and he dropped to his knees. Never in all his life had he been dismayed by a plea. He was a strong wolf and ruled with an iron fist. Yet here, this mere human had him wrapped around her little finger. The idea of being vulnerable was a new concept for him and it frightened him.

Danielle stepped forward and cupped her hands around his face, as she dropped to her knees to face him. The anguish in his eyes broke her heart. She knew the only way she would ever understand was to turn. Danielle leaned forward and pressed her lips to his.

"Derek, I'll pledge myself to you and your pack. I'll let you bite me and join you."

"If," Derek added curling his fingers around her arms and pulling her hands away from his face.

Danielle nodded and continued. "If you help Alice."

"I would give you the world, if I could. But I can't. Alice has broken the laws."

"No one knows that but you." Derek shook his head.

"If I let her live, the pack will rise up against me and challenge me. It would be a blood bath."

"We can say she never showed up. She doesn't have to come back with us. I just need to make sure she will be safe. If she is hurt, I need to help her."

"You don't know what you are asking."

"I am asking that you put aside your differences and your laws to help my sister."

"Fine," Danielle yanked her hands away from Derek and stood. She shook her head as she glared at him. "If you won't help me, then I will go out there alone and help her myself."

Danielle didn't get more than three steps away before Derek was by her side. "I can't let you wander these woods alone."

"Please, I have been in forests all over the United States. I think I can handle myself."

"No. Not here you can't."

"You're just trying to stop me from helping her."

Derek shook his head. "No. I am going with you. There is nothing in our law that says that a human can't help. You aren't strong enough to lift her up so I am coming with you. Besides, there are more dangerous things in these woods besides wolves."

"I can handle myself."

"I'm not saying you can't. I am simply saying I won't let you go alone."

Danielle pushed the tears from her face and gave Derek a weak smile. She reached out her hand and took his. Derek glanced down at Danielle's hand wrapped so tenderly into his and smiled.

"Come on, I left her over here," Derek said grudgingly as he led the way back to the battle grounds.

Danielle's heart skipped and sputtered as she tried to find Alice in the darkness. One thing was certain—Danielle was pleased Derek had agreed to help. Trying to find Alice in the dark without a flash light would have been next to impossible. Danielle squeezed Derek's hand as she looked up at him.

"Thank you."

"I am doing this so that you honor your agreement."

"I will let you bite me so that no laws are broken, I promise." Danielle stared at Derek as he led the way through the broken trees and shrubs.

The rain fell around them. Every step felt as if Danielle was marching to her doom. She didn't know what condition she would find Alice in, but she knew she would help her no matter what. As they continued to walk into the night, Danielle grew more and more impatient. She twisted her head about wondering if Derek was leading her back to his town, or if he really was this far into the forest when he took Alice down.

"You okay?" Derek asked listening to the frantic beating of Danielle's heart. She nodded as she chewed on her lower lip.

"It's not much further, I can smell her," he said glancing at Danielle as she squeezed his hand.

"Can you hear her too?" Danielle stared at Derek with a pain that was too much for him to bear. He turned his head away from her and paused.

"Please don't get your hopes up. She might not have survived. I knocked her around pretty good. If she shifted to her human form, she will be battered and bruised."

"As long as she is still alive, and I can help her."

"That's what I am trying to tell you, you may not be able to help her."

"I'm not going to think like that. Alice is stronger than you give her credit for. She may be hurt, but I don't think you killed her."

"And if I did? Would you still want to be by my side?" Derek dropped his gaze and stared at the ground.

Danielle shook her head pushing all negative thoughts from her mind. "We will cross that bridge when we get to it."

Chapter 6

Soft silver hues filtered through the dark storm clouds and the moon peaked out from behind the clouds. Alice panted with pain trying to pull her knees up to her chest. Every inch of her body ached. Her head spun as bright sparks of light shot through her eyes each time she blinked. She tried to cry, but the salty tears leaking from her swollen eyes burned and denied her the release she wanted.

A rustle of leaves and heavy footsteps sent chills racing through her damaged body. She froze, holding in the small shallow breathe she was able to trap in her lungs. The rustling of the leaves grew closer. She tried to hold in the air, but her lungs and ribs wouldn't allow it. She exhaled sharply closing her eyes and succumbing to the inevitability of defeat. Derek was on his way to finish her off, and it sent her heart into panic mode. She swallowed down the lump in her throat and relaxed her body. She always knew she would die in this forest, she didn't think it would happen today. Alice kept her eyes closed and let the pain consume her. If she was going to die, she was going to do it on her terms.

"I'm sorry Danielle," Alice whispered realizing her friend would never hear her. She exhaled and let the darkness consume her.

Bash moved through the trees poking his head around each branch and trunk before moving on. The air had a hint of rust and salt that tickled his nose as he moved. He stopped by a large tree fallen from the storm. His ears perked up as took in the surrounding sounds. In the distance a husky voice rose and fell as the winds crashed against the leaves in the trees. He tried to focus on what was being said, but the words were not clear enough to understand.

"Where are you?" he whispered into the night. He let his eyes roam through the shadows and adjust to the silver light of the moon. "You are here somewhere, I can smell the blood."

Bash continued down the slope of the mountain and stopped. He saw the placid lake spanned out before him and gasped to see the open still water reflecting the moon. For a moment he believed he had entered into a new world. The lake reflected everything from the moon to the trees and even the side of the mountains that protected it.

"Wow," was all he could say, but he didn't have time to appreciate the scenery, a life was on the line and he had no time to waste.

Ever so carefully, he wove in and out of the trees making certain to remain masked in the shadows. He knew Derek's hearing was just as keen as his, but if he could move like other animals lurking in these parts, he had a chance to continue unseen.

A low gleam of red and orange caught his attention. Bash paused by the large aspen tree poking his head around the trunk. There he spotted the alpha. His heart sputtered, and he held his breath.

"Please," the girl begged. Bash glanced over to see a young girl standing beside the alpha. Bash could tell by the way her shoulders slumped down, she was upset. Bash glanced around the trees and made a break for the next trunk hoping for a closer view.

"Danielle, you don't know our ways. Alice knew what she was getting herself into when she came here." The alpha's voice was laced with his commands, but from Bash's view he knew they had no hold on the girl.

"So you're Danielle," Bash thought watching the girl with the alpha. "Then Alice must be around here somewhere too. Oh God, what if I am too late?"

Bash's mind wheeled about as he sniffed the air. The heavy stench of rust was overwhelming. He closed his eyes and allowed the surrounding sounds to fill his ears. Normally he hated all the things he could listen to, but tonight he prayed he would be able to pick up everything.

He stood in the shadows with his lungs full of trapped air and listened. Every sound exploded in his ears, from the drumming of the rain water falling from leaf to leaf, to the sound of the couple down by the lake. Then, came the faintest hint of a heartbeat.

Bash's eyes popped opened and his sight adjusted. A body rested, there in the nook of an old tree. Bash sprinted to it and pulled the leaves from around it. He leaned in close and pressed his head down. Alice's heart was still drumming but growing fainter by the moment.

"What did you get yourself into?" Bash whispered in her ear. Alice moaned ever so lightly. His ears perked up—in the distance he heard the woman's voice rising up from the lake.

"Please," Danielle begged. "I will let you change me if you don't let Alice die."

"Oh crap," Bash said scooping Alice up into his arms. "Hold on. I am going to get you out of here."

In her stupor, Alice's eyes rolled back into her head. A weak moan escaped her lips giving Bash the reassurance he needed. Without missing a beat, he pushed the loose strands of hair out of Alice's face and focused on the wounds. A salty rust scent caused his nose to wrinkle.

"You are losing a lot of blood," he whispered into Alice's ear. "Hold on," Bash cooed, hoisting the girl up into his arms. Without hesitation, he sprinted into the woods. Behind him hushed tones filtered into his ears. He glanced down at Alice. "I'll get you outta here."

Bash paused by a tree and set Alice down for a moment. He poked his head around the trunk and listened. In the space between the trees, he noticed dark shadows shifting and poking around the area they were hiding.

"I left her right here," Derek said scanning the area and pushing aside the fallen twigs and shrubs.

"Well where is she? Please tell me you didn't kill her?" Danielle's face was flushed with anger. The thought of her best friend dying alone broke her spirits. Danielle dropped to her knees throwing her hands up to her face. Instantly, Derek rushed to her side.

"I can track her, but you will have to keep up. And Danielle," Derek paused looking down at the distraught girl at his feet. "You'll have to prepare yourself for the worse."

"I wouldn't have had to if you hadn't done this," Danielle snapped. Derek stepped back and glared at her.

"Alice attacked me first, remember? She brought this on herself."

"You didn't have to fight back. You could have let her thrash you and then I could have explained the situation."

"It's not in my nature to let a weaker dog take me out. What would my pack say?"

"Your pack isn't here! It was just you and me and now Alice is gone."

"Danielle," Derek's voice dropped, and he fell to his knees, looking at Danielle. He cupped his hand around the girl's face and forced her to look at him. "Look, Alice may be fine. If she was able to run away from here, then maybe she isn't dying."

"But you don't know that." Danielle huffed, wiping the tears from her eyes.

"I don't know that. But what I do know, is that Alice is gone. We can pick up the search tomorrow. Right now, I want to bring you back to town so you can get some sleep."

"I can't sleep knowing my friend is hurting."

"I am not about to let you stay here alone. There are things in these woods that would kill you just for having my scent on you."

"Such as?" Danielle's eyes widened in fear as she scanned the area.

"I'd rather not say. Just know that you can't find Alice in the dark. We'll search for her tomorrow."

"But..."

"No." Derek leaned in and pressed his lips to Danielle's forehead. He pulled back and sighed. "If you want to be like me, you are going to have to learn to take orders. Right now, I am ordering you to come with me."

Danielle shook her head and rose to her feet. Tears streamed down her burning face and her eyes searched through the shadows. For a moment Bash thought the human had spotted him and he ducked around the tree taking cover.

"Come on," Derek said. The sound of heavy footsteps falling away from him allowed Bash to breathe more easily. He glanced down at the injured woman at his feet.

"Oh man," Bash said wiping the sweat from his brow. "I don't know what you did to piss him off, but you barked up the wrong tree, Lady."

He leaned down and picked Alice up. Her body slumped towards his. With one arm over his shoulder and the other dangling down towards the ground, Alice dreamed. The hushed voices and scent of pine mixed with basil filled her nose. She grunted and a hearty laugh rumbled.

"Sleep. We will talk in the morning."

Bash sprinted through the trees holding Alice close to him. With each mile he ran, questions filled his mind. He glanced at the girl in his arms.

Her hair drifted like flowers swayed by the wind. Even the blood splattered across her pale face reminded him of some Van Gogh painting he had seen as a boy.

"Almost there," he said coming up to a small cottage on the edge of Yellowstone National Park. Smoke rose towards the sky from the stone chimney.

Bash pushed through the door and rushed Alice to the couch. Ever so gently he placed her on the cushions and rushed back to the kitchen. He grabbed the needed supplies and quickly went to work on her trying to keep her from slipping into the next world.

"You are safe," he whispered. "Rest."

Bash splashed the warm water on Alice's face, cleaning up the dried blood. With every sweep of the wash cloth, he stared more intently at the girl lying helpless on his couch. His heart splintered as he clung to hope.

Chapter 7

"Where am I?" Alice lifted her throbbing head trying to focus. Every bit of her body ached as she rose up. The warm sunlight blasted through the open window and the pounding of footsteps echoed in her ears.

"My place," a familiar voice said. Alice flinched at the male voice. Pain ripped through her as thoughts of Derek filled her mind. There was no way she was going to be able to fight him now, not while she was so badly injured.

Alice tried to rise from the couch, but the world spun around forcing her lie back down. She lifted up her arm to protect her face in anticipation of another blow. But when the shadow blocked out the sunlight, she opened her eyes wider. There, standing with a bowl in his hands and a smile on his face, was the park ranger.

"What are you doing here?"

"I live here," Bash said moving slowly towards her. She leaned back as he sat down at her side and offered her a bowl of stew. The aroma of meat filled her nose and stifled the harsh basil fragrance that caused her head to ache even more.

"Why does your place smell so bad?" Alice asked taking the bowl. The heat from it soothed her in an unexpected way. She stared down at the steam rising from the contents and smiled weakly.

Bash laughed and remained by her side. "It's the only thing that masks the scent."

"What scent?" Alice asked, before turning to Bash to study the three images of him. She squinted her eyes focusing on the one in front as the other two images shifted into the middle person. She blinked trying to keep her focus, but the images waved and shimmered back into three distinct people.

"Of me," Bash whispered realizing he might be speaking too loudly. "You took quite a beating last night."

"You don't have to remind me."

"You should have let me help you."

"What could you do?" Alice grunted with distrust as she sniffed the bowl wondering if he had poisoned it. Bash cocked his head and stared at her.

"Well, you may not have been beaten to a pulp for one thing. What in God's name made you think you could take out the alpha?"

"You mean Derek." Alice corrected picking up the spoon and bringing a good spoonful up to her mouth. Her lips parted with some effort and she forced herself to eat.

"You knew he was the alpha of these parts. So why did you do it? You're lucky he didn't kill you."

"Why do you care? Aren't you one of his henchmen?"

Bash shuddered at Alice's words and shook his head. "No. I would never be a part of his tribe. I doubt he even knows what I am."

"But you're a wolf aren't you?" Alice asked through a mouthful of stew. The corners of Bash's lips pulled up. The half-smile was weak and he dropped his gaze.

"So why are you keeping me alive?"

"Look, you have no reason to believe me, and I could be killed for helping you, but Derek has no right to take another life. I don't care if he is the alpha in these parts."

"So you're a lone wolf?" Alice's eyebrows rose as she stared at him. Bash nodded. "Why? Don't you want to be a part of the pack? Who made you? By all rights you should at least have a bonded mate."

Bash shook his head. "But what about you? Why did you attack Derek?"

"He has my friend."

"Danielle?" Alice's head jerked up. She stared at Bash with suspicion.

"How do you know Danielle? Have you seen her?"

Bash glanced down at his hands before rising to his feet. He turned around and took a seat in the large rocking chair. Sucking in a deep breath he stared at Alice.

"After you came in yesterday looking for your friend, I decided to follow you. You were after all very concerned about her. Once I caught your scent, I understood what you were. I had to help. But I lost you by the trail." Bash glanced over to the counter. Alice let her eyes wander to the pile of clothes resting in a neatly folded pile.

"It took me nearly all night to find you. But when I did it was almost too late. Derek had whipped you good."

"He won't next time."

"Are you on some kind of suicide mission?"

"I can't let Derek take Danielle from me. I won't. She is my only friend."

"So you challenged the alpha and lost. Now she will be his. I heard her say so. She wants to be like us and the alpha will honor her request."

"Why do you keep saying he is the alpha? He is nothing more than a bully. He stole that title and everyone seems to just follow him because he says so."

"I don't." Bash said throwing back his shoulders with pride in his tone.

"How is that even possible? Unless," Alice paused and stared into Bash's eyes. The flecks of gold mingled with brown were nearly a caramel color. There in the depths of his eyes she found no signs of his being bonded to anyone.

"How is it you don't belong to anyone?" Alice asked pushing another bite of stew into her bruised mouth.

"It's a long story."

"What else do I have to do?" Alice said swallowing the food down before resting the bowl on her lap. "I can't go anywhere now and I can't challenge him anytime soon."

"If I tell you my story, will you promise to let things go?"

"No. Of course not," Alice jerked back as pain shot through her ribs. "Why would you ask that? A life is at stake. I can't let Danielle become one of his tribe members. It wouldn't be fair to her. She doesn't know what she is asking." Alice puffed trying to get the words out through the pain. Bash rose from his seat with his arms out. Concern flashed across his face.

"I appreciate everything you have done for me I do, but I can't sit here and let this happen. I have to stop it." Alice tried to stand. Her knees wobbled under her weight as she tried to make it to the door.

"Please, don't go. Stay here and get some rest. Derek won't change her today. He has to wait for the new moon."

Alice paused and whipped her head around to glare at Bash. "How do you know that?"

"Sit down and I will tell you." Alice glared at him but didn't move.

"I won't force you to stay. I promise. But maybe you will understand that we have a little time on our side to rescue your friend."

Alice moved back to the couch carefully and sat down. She crossed her arms around her chest trying to hold herself together as Bash rocked back in his chair.

"I understand how these things work," Alice said. "I know more about my kind than you could possibly comprehend. Every wolf that is created is bonded to someone. That's what makes the pack so strong. So why aren't you bonded? Were you born this way, like me?"

"You can be born into this life?" Bash's eyes opened wider and Alice snapped her mouth closed. She shook her head and sucked in a deep painful breath.

"Yes. You can be born into this life. Those that are, are typically the alphas. Which is why Derek can't be the leader of this tribe. He was bitten a long time ago by my father."

"I was bitten too," Bash confessed. "Bitten and left for dead."

Alice shook her head as the pieces began falling into place. "That is why you are not bonded to anyone. When you shifted for the first time, no one was there to show you. But if Danielle is bitten, and Derek is there she will be bonded to him for life. Her freewill and choices will be stripped from her. Derek will take away her love for me."

"How does that work?" Bash asked leaning in closer.

"First, tell me how you were changed."

Bash pinched the bridge of his nose and leaned back. Alice studied him as he struggled to remember the remaining images of his human life.

"I was scouting the new terrain here at the park. I was told to tag the wolf population to see if any were migrating back to Canada. After all, it has only been a few years since we reintroduced the wolves here."

"One day, I was out tagging the wolves when I saw one in the distance. I tracked it until night. I made my camp and was cooking dinner when it attacked me. It bit me over and over again. Each bite was like a million needles pricking me at once. I thought it was strange the way it worked on me.

Normally wolves bite and clamp down, but this one released its grip on me and attacked again."

"Somehow I managed to get into my tent and to call for help. I was evacuated from the campsite and spent several days in the hospital recovering. I can remember the doctors saying it would take weeks for me to heal, but it only took days. Everyone was amazed. However, when the first new moon came four days later, a change happened."

"You turned into a wolf."

Bash nodded his head with a sober express. "Yes. I was alone when it happened. The pain was immeasurable."

"Were there any other wolves around you when it happened?" Alice asked not realizing she was leaning in closer toward Bash as he told his story.

"No. I was in my apartment. When I came to, the next day, I found an eviction notice for disturbance and a note saying the apartment doesn't allow animals. I left that place and came here. I don't think the park even knew it had this place, so I claimed it."

Alice turned her head about the small cabin. Through her blurred vision she focused on the fireplace. In the nook between the hearth and the pit she noticed a small paw print and gasped.

"You can stay here," Alice said with a faint smile. "I doubt my father would mind."

"What?" Bash glared at her trying to make sense of her words. Alice rose to her feet and walked over to the fire place. She pressed on a small stone and wiggled it out. Carefully she reached in and wrapped her fingers around the box left inside the nook.

"What is that?" Bash asked as Alice pulled out the box and handed it to Bash.

"Something that will help you during the new moons. This place once belonged to my family. My father crafted everything you see. Except the furniture—that's new."

"But this place has been abandoned for years."

"Twenty to be exact. The contents of that box will help you as it helped my mother."

Bash's eyes widened as he opened it up. Inside lay a handful of herbs. He glanced up to Alice with wonder.

"It is wolfs bane. It helps those like you to manage the pain of shifting. Trust me, it works."

"But how?" Bash wondered picking at the dried herbs in the box.

"My father roamed these parts well before wolves were reintroduced. He came across a female hiker one day. She was gravely injured, and he knew the only way to save her was to bite her in the hope that the wolf gene would mend her. She mended, they fell in love, then had me." Alice smiled as she pointed to the small paw print by the fire place.

"Wow." Bash's jaw dropped as Alice moved back to the couch and sat down.

"You're telling me."

Bash scrunched his brows together studying the herbs. "How does Derek fit into all this? And why did you go after him?"

"Danielle came out here to study the wolves. She was just in the wrong place at the wrong time. I won't let Derek change her. I know what it did to my mother. She was forced to love my father even though she may not have, otherwise. I can't let that choice be taken away from her. I can't."

Tears flowed down Alice's cheeks and Bash bolted to her side. He sat down beside her, wrapping his arm around her shoulders.

"Let me help. We can find her and save her together."

"Why would you help me? I am no one. I'm just a lone wolf with no pack of my own and Danielle is the closest thing I have to family."

"Because, I don't want to find you dead somewhere in the forest. There is something about you that makes me..." Bash didn't finish his sentence. Alice leaned closer to him and pressed her lips to his, silencing him.

***

"Are you sure this is okay?" Danielle asked as she clasped her arm tighter around Derek's arm. The sinister glances from the townsfolk had startled Danielle. Every voice in her head screamed for her to run, but Derek only smiled and leaned in to whisper in her ear.

"It's okay, no one will harm you as long as you are with me."

"But they don't like me," Danielle said wondering how many people could hear her hushed voice.

"You're human. They don't like the idea of an outsider coming around, but they won't dare touch you."

Danielle kept her eyes trained on the three women standing like statues outside a small shop. Their eyes bore into Danielle as she and Derek walked past them. Danielle tried to remain calm, but her nerves were shot and all she could think of was Alice somewhere in the woods.

"Here," Derek said coming to a stop in front of a single storied brick building. He reached into his pockets and pulled out a set of keys. Danielle listened to them jiggle as he unlocked the door and held it open for her.

The moment she was inside, relief washed over her. The daggers and spikes thrown at her vanished as she stepped inside. Her eyes widened to find a typical hotel room, fully furnished.

"You're surprised," Derek laughed. "What did you expect to find?"

"I don't know," Danielle answered walking further into the room. She brushed her fingers over the dresser wondering if everything she was experiencing was nothing more than a dream.

"This is all too surreal. Everything is very human here."

"We are human," Derek said with a bite of pain in his voice.

"But not just human."

"No. We are not just human, but it doesn't mean we have to live like savages."

"What else is more than human?" Danielle asked turning her attention to Derek. Her eyes flashed to his pants as her eyebrows rose. A smile played at the corner of Derek's lips.

"Are you sure you want to find out?"

Danielle couldn't help herself. With everything that just happened, she needed something to take her mind off reality. She stepped forward with her fingers at the hem of her shirt and pulled it off. Derek's smile grew as he watched the human strip bare for him.

"Danielle, you don't have to do this."

"I want to," she said pressing her bare breasts against Derek's body. Her lips brushed the base of his neck while her fingers traced his spine.

"Please," she begged. "Bring me back to reality."

Derek didn't need to be told twice. He wrapped his arms around her back grabbing Danielle by her wrists. Moving with care, he lifted her hands up and clasped both her wrists with one of his hands. With a hunger consuming him, Derek crushed his mouth to Danielle's and parted her lips with his tongue.

Between Danielle's legs, she felt Derek's fingers graze over her thighs until he found her wet spot and he pushed his fingers into her. She sucked in a shallow breath as he entered her. The pressure of his fingers eased the moment he began pumping them in and out of her.

"Is this what you wanted?"

"More," she whimpered with her hands over her head. Derek's hot breath caressed her bare flesh as he released her hands. In one swoop, Derek lifted Danielle off her feet and moved her to the bed, but then he dropped to his knees. With her legs draped over his shoulders, Derek leaned closer.

Danielle shivered with pleasure to feel Derek's hot breath on her thighs. She closed her eyes and her mind to everything but him. For the time being she wanted nothing more than to melt into him. He was strong and sincere but more importantly, he filled the hole in her heart she hadn't known was there.

Derek moved with care ensuring his tongue lapped every inch of her thighs. Her tender flower of flesh opened up for him and he dove in with his tongue. Danielle sucked in quick shallow breaths as Derek's tongue lapped over her clit. She reached down and pushed Derek's head closer to her. With two fingers, he peeled back the layers of her flower and pushed them into her.

"Yes," she hissed with her legs squeezing around his head. "More."

Chapter 8

Alice's eyes fluttered open. With an outstretched hand, she felt the cool fabric of the empty sheets next to her. She rose abruptly scanning the room for Bash. Everything was in disarray. Clothes were flung about the floor and the cold sheets were a distinct reminder that she was alone. Her heart sank as thoughts of her previous suitors filled her mind. She thought of James and wondered if he had experienced a similar feeling of rejection when she had left him.

"So, this is how they felt," she mumbled realizing she was alone in the room—in just a small cabin tucked away in the woods which was filled with silence also. A stab of regret shot through her. She tugged the sheets closer to her, wrapping herself in them and then she slipped her legs over the side of the bed. Although the pain Derek had unleashed on her still jabbed at her ribs, she rose to her feet.

Her legs wobbled under her weight for just a moment before settling. She scanned the room again with a clear head. A smile pulled up at the corners of her lips when her eyes drifted over to the mirror on the back of the door. A small white sheet of paper was stuck there as a note:

"Be back soon."

Alice smiled and with the sheets still wrapped around her body, she made her way through the door and out into the living room. The odor of basil lingered in the house and caused her nose to wrinkle.

"I need to ask him about that," Alice mumbled walking into the kitchen area. She pulled open the refrigerator and leaned down peaking inside. The shelves were bare, with only a few boxes of take-out and a quart of milk left in a half-gallon container.

Her stomach grumbled as she closed the door and stood. "What did you expect?" she asked herself moving to the cabinets. As she pulled open the doors, she found even less food on the shelves. "Total bachelor pad," she said glancing around the living room.

Her clothes were still sitting in a neat folded pile, from earlier. Although Alice had no issues walking around in the nude all day, at some point she was going to need them. She moved carefully, trying not to cause her body to spasm as she snatched her clothes and made her way to the bathroom.

A smile lifted her spirits when she noticed the same pink tile-lined bathtub, from when she was a child. She sat her clothes down on the sink and dropped the sheet. Reaching down, she twisted the knob that released the water. As steam filled the room, she turned to stare at herself in the mirror.

Bruises speckled her body from her shoulders to her waist. If she had gone to a hospital, the doctors would have assumed she'd been hit by a bus. But with her keen eyesight, she could still see the remnants of Derek's bite marks on her arm and she grunted.

"You've looked worse," she said dropping her eyes to inspect her legs. Although there was an angry red blotch where Derek had torn her skin, it was nearly healed. All that was left was for the color to come back.

Alice stepped away from the sink and climbed over the edge of the tub. Leaning down, she flicked up the spout allowing the shower to switch on. The warm water flowed over her body washing away her pain. As she let the heat rise, her mind drifted to Danielle.

"I don't know how it was before, but hot water doesn't last," Bash's voice startled her. Alice jumped in the shower and pulled the curtain against her.

"I didn't even hear you."

"Sorry," he said and his cheeks turned a darker shade of red. " I knew there was nothing in the fridge, so I got us some dinner."

Alice glanced down to find he was holding two large white plastic bags. "I hope you like Chinese."

"Thanks," Alice smiled relaxing. "I'll be out in a bit."

"You can use up the hot water, I don't mind."

"Or you can join me," Alice hinted winking at Bash. His cheeks flushed and he shook his head.

"I would love to really, but you kinda wore me out earlier. Hence the food."

"Food is overrated," Alice teased, throwing back the shower curtain. Bash turned his head away and clenched his jaw.

"What?"

"I... I'm sorry about last night."

"I'm not." Alice smiled wickedly. She moved about the small bathtub trying to tempt him further. But with each advance she made, he kept his back to her.

"We shouldn't have done that in your condition."

"If there is one thing I love about being a wolf, it's how quickly I heal." Alice glanced down at her battered body. "These will be gone by tonight. Then maybe you can rough me up yourself."

Bash flinched at the thought of hurting Alice. To him, she was an angel sent from heaven and it was his duty to protect her at all costs. He shook his head and stepped out of the bathroom.

"You finish your shower. The food is here when you want it."

Alice stood stunned, as Bash disappeared behind the closed door. She turned to glance at herself once more before shame washed over her. She nodded once and turned her attention to the warm water flowing over her body.

"That's a first," she mumbled soaking her head and clearing out the dirt from her romp in the woods.

After the last bit of brown water had flowed down the drain and the water had turned cold, Alice twisted the knob and got out. She reached for a towel and dried herself. Her clothes were a bit damp from the moisture in the air, but she didn't mind. Once she was fully dressed and her wet hair was in a bun on top of her head, she stepped out into the living room.

Bash gave her a weak smile and gestured to the meal he had set up for her.

"Where did you go?" Alice asked moving to an open chair at the table. She sat down as the aroma of food drifted around her, blocking out the stench of basil, for the mean time.

"To town."

"How far away is the town?"

"A few miles. I didn't expect you to be up when I got back, but I figured you'd be hungry so I left."

"Thank you. This all smells wonderful." Alice sucked in a deep breath letting the food fill her nose. But as she breathed in the pungent stench of basil slaughtered her once again.

"What is up with the basil? I smelled it in the office and it's all over this house."

"Basil keeps the others away."

"What others?" Alice asked digging into one of the small containers of food. Bash cocked his eyebrow up staring at Alice as if she should already know the answer. When Alice didn't respond he shrugged and smiled.

"The other wolves. Derek's pack. It masks my scent from them."

"How did you figure that out?"

"Well, I've been here for a while, and none of them have found me yet, to force me to be a part of their little tribe."

"Doesn't mean that it repels them."

"Well you don't seem to like the smell of it."

"I don't," Alice confessed through a mouthful of food. She dropped her eyes.

"Well then, I don't think they like it either. I've got used to it. It used to burn."

"Did you see Danielle in town?" Alice asked hoping against hope that maybe her friend had gotten help. When Bash didn't answer she glanced up at him. His face was white, and he quickly shoveled food into his mouth.

"Bash, did you see Danielle?"

He dropped his eyes concentrating on the food in front of him. Alice waited with her eyes locked on him.

He pushed the food down his throat before he answered, "Yes."

"I have to go to her," Alice dropped the container and stood up. Bash was up in a flash also and he reached for her. His fingers curled around her arm restraining her from moving.

"Let me go," Alice hissed glaring at his hand before casting her eyes up to meet his gaze.

"Alice, please, listen. Danielle is surrounded by Derek's people. If you go charging into town, they will rip you to shreds."

"I have to get my friend out of there."

"I don't think she wants to leave."

"What do you mean?" Alice pulled her arm out of Bash's grip and stood back.

"She was with Derek. Her arm around Derek's waist. They seemed like a happy normal couple walking down the street. I don't think he is keeping her against her will. I think she wants to be turned."

"You can't be serious." Alice plopped down to the chair, defeat crushing her heart. "She doesn't know what she is getting herself into."

"Maybe she does," Bash said grabbing the container of food. "What if Derek told her everything? And she still wants this life?"

"She can't have it. I won't let her."

"You can't make that decision for her."

"You know what will happen to her! She'll have no free will. Her life will change. Think about it. If you had a choice about becoming this way, would you have made that decision? You had no clue you would change during the new moon. But if you had, would you have done it knowing that each month you would turn into a wolf?"

Bash paused and stared at his food. He poked at the chicken with his chop stick before looking at Alice.

"Yes, I would make that choice. It would be better than dying."

"But she isn't in a life and death situation, so she is choosing wrongly."

"Actually," Bash chewed on his lower lip trying to find the right words to say.

"What?" Alice snapped.

"I heard that Danielle taped him shifting. Her life is in danger. Either she turns into one of us, or she will be killed. Maybe, she knows what she is getting herself into and she wants this life."

"No. She doesn't. I doubt Derek has told her everything, which is why I need to find her. If she wants to change so badly, then I will bite her myself. But I can't let him do it and I won't let her face this alone."

"I still have free will and I was bitten," Bash reminded Alice. Alice shook her head.

"Derek won't leave anything to chance. He will be there when she turns to ensure her loyalty to him."

"Maybe she has fallen for the guy. I mean from what I saw, they looked like a new couple. She was all over him and he was all over her."

Alice shook her head and tears began pooling in her eyes. "She can't be with him."

"Why? What is it about him that you can't stand?"

Alice whipped her head up, wiping away her tears. "He killed my family. I won't let my best friend be with a murderer."

Bash leaned back and stared at Alice. His lips pressed into a tight line as her words sank in. "That definitely changes things."

"I don't care that she wants to be a wolf. It would make my life so much easier not having to hide that side of me when I am around her. But to have him change her—no. I won't allow it."

"Alice," Bash leaned in and stretched his hand to touch hers. Deep within his eyes, Alice saw nothing but love pouring out of him. "I will help you. But you have to promise me, that if your friend chooses this life, you will give it to her. You can't turn into Derek and take away her free will."

Alice stared at Bash and nodded. "I promise I will do what she wants, but we have to find her first and get her away from him."

"I'll help you. But you are going to have to trust me."

Before Alice could say another word, Bash was by her side. He cupped his hands around her face and pressed his lips to hers. The kiss was soft and sweet and it filled the void in Alice. With the kiss, all of Alice's fears and worries faded. She knew she could be complete with Bash—that he held the keys to her future. However, a dark voice rose up with in her.

"You can't trust him," it snickered. "He will betray you just like Derek did. Wolves cannot be trusted."

Alice pulled away from Bash and with a weak smile she nodded.

"I do," she whispered.

"We still have time before we have to do anything. Tomorrow we will go into town and find out where she is."

"Then what?" Alice asked and her mind raced with different plans of rescuing Danielle.

"We will talk to her. Find out what she wants and go from there."

"Or," Alice's had a darker thought. "We kidnap her and take her away from this place."

She nodded again and puckered her lips to Bash's. The bitter scent of basil filled her nose, and she smiled weakly at him.

"Tomorrow," she agreed.

Chapter 9

"So, what else do I need to know before I become like you?"

Danielle smiled at Derek. She wrapped her lips around the plastic straw and sucked. Her eyes remained locked on him, pulling him into them greedily. Derek chuckled darkly allowing his eyes to wander about the small restaurant.

Several eyes glared at them and Derek shifted his head. The bystanders turned their heads and made no further eye contact, once his eyes landed on them. He shifted in his seat and lifted up one hand over the lip of the table and took Danielle's. The heat resonating off him sparked a fire within her. She batted her eyes letting them undress him. A crooked little smile played at the corner of his lip.

"Tons."

She wiggled herself closer to him, her eyes wide with wonder. Derek's body shifted to meet her. She was like a magnet pulling him in closer. He shook his head fighting the pull and sighed. She traced her fingers over his knuckles sending chills coursing through him.

"Like?" Danielle's voice broke into his daydream. He blinked out the fantasy of ripping her clothes off and taking her right there.

"Well, for starters," he cleared his throat, pushing the thought out of his mind. "You'll be stronger than you are now. Your ears will pick up things miles away, but sounds will be so much clearer, that it'll be like they are happening right beside you." Derek chuckled as Danielle cocked her head.

"What?" she asked sticking her tongue out to play with the plastic straw sticking out of her drink.

"You may experience headaches from the noise at first. But over time you will get used to it and be able to tune everything out."

Danielle nodded her head, pulling another mouthful from her cup. Her mind raced with all the possibilities that stretched out before her. Never in her wildest fantasies had she ever consider the notion of werewolves to be real. Now that she knew they were, she wanted to be one more than ever.

"Anything else?"

"Well," Derek dropped his gaze and played with Danielle's fingernails. "You will see things differently."

"How?"

"The colors will be brighter, more vivid. You will be able to see further than you ever thought possible."

"This all sounds amazing." Danielle giggled trying to contain her excitement. The more Derek told her the more she felt compelled by this new life change. Her heart raced as she glanced around the small room.

"Tell me something," Danielle said staring at the girls in the corner. The three women with long brown shoulder length hair and piercing eyes glared at her. "Will I look different?"

"What do you mean?"

"Like them?" Danielle nodded to the woman. Derek shifted in his seat and sighed.

"No. But if you will bring with you a beauty that is uniquely your own. Everyone is different." Derek paused and turned his attention back to Danielle. He rubbed her hands with his, trying to hold her gaze.

"If you are wondering if you'll be stunning, you will be. No doubt about that. You will also be almost invincible."

"Really?" Danielle perked up. Her fears and insecurities vanishing at the thought.

"Only one thing that can kill us," Derek sighed. Danielle flinched and her mind quickly raced to Alice. Her heart beat frantically in her chest as she hung on Derek's words like a lifeline.

"What?" Danielle nearly shouted. Derek shook his head before dropping it again. He didn't say a word but simply lifted his fingers to his neck and scrapped his nails over his Adam's apple. Danielle's mouth dropped.

"So that's how you know Alice is alive," Danielle said keeping her eyes on Derek. He nodded with his lips pressed into a tight line.

"Did she have a choice?" Danielle asked slipping her hands out of Derek's. His eyebrows pressed together studying her.

"What do you mean?"

"Did you create Alice?" Derek's laughter filled the room, causing the others around them to take notice. He shook his head.

"No. Some of us are born this way. That's why she was able to..." Derek stopped speaking and straightened his shoulders.

"What?" Danielle moved in closer seeing the distress in his eyes. "Or are you not allowed to say?"

"There is a lot I am not allowed to tell you."

"Because I am human." Derek's eyes narrowed sending chills racing down Danielle's back.

"Can I ask how you know Alice? She must be someone important to you, to go through all this trouble to keep me hostage."

"Do you still think you are my prisoner?" Derek gasped.

"I know I am. That would be the only reason for you to keep me close to you. I mean, you haven't let me out of your sight since you brought me here."

Derek moved closer to Danielle. His hot breath caressed her face as he spoke in hushed tones, "It's not safe for you to be here unaccompanied. The others..." Derek's eyes shifted to the group in the corner. Danielle flashed a quick glance and ice ran through her veins before she pulled away. "...would kill you, but I'm not going to let them."

"Why would they want to kill me?" Danielle whispered as her eyes jolted to the trio of girls still in the corner booth who were glaring daggers at her.

"Because of what you know about us. Humans are not allowed to know such things. Yet, here you are in full knowledge of what we are and, even more, you have proof. Your very existence is putting a lot of people on edge. Humans have been in the dark about our kind for eons. If your footage of us went live, what do you think would happen?" Derek paused with his eyebrow raised.

"They would hunt us to extinction," he finished not allowing Danielle to answer.

Danielle nodded. "That explains the looks."

"Don't worry. As soon as you are turned, they won't be so hostile. In fact, they will treat you like family."

"So everyone is kinda related to everyone else here, huh?"

Derek nodded, "By birth or by bite, yes. We are essentially a large family and would do anything to keep our secret."

Danielle pulled back and smiled. "So, when will you change me? If that is all there is to it, change me right here."

"It doesn't quiet work that way."

"Well why don't you tell me how it works? Then we can let everyone know our plans so the staring will stop."

"Maybe if you got rid of any proof that could leak our secret, they might stop."

Danielle lifted her hand up. Derek stared at it briefly wondering what Danielle was doing.

"Give me my phone. All my videos, and footage are linked up with my cell phone. All I need to do is delete the last forty-eight hours of footage. We can go to the cameras and smash them for extra insurance." Derek leaned back.

"What?"

"We already smashed the cameras around our hunting area."

Danielle's face turned white. "Oh."

"But here," Derek pulled out her cell phone and placed it into her open hand.

"Thank you." Danielle quickly keyed in her password and began fiddling with the phone bringing up the link to the footage. With a small smile playing at the corner of her lips, she deleted her files and then the app.

"There, all gone," Danielle said handing over her phone once more to Derek. Derek examined the phone and the apps she had uninstalled before nodding once. He kept his eyes locked on her. With a sudden swoosh, Danielle watched as he smashed her phone into several pieces on the concrete floor.

"You didn't have to do that," Danielle gasped. "I said I deleted everything."

"It's not that I don't trust you. It's just an added security." Derek shifted in his chair and Danielle's eyes followed his gaze. The girls in the corner booth flashed enchanting smiles before rising. They each nodded once and made their way out of the restaurant.

"What is with those three?" Danielle asked leaning back in her chair, watching the girls disappear into the crowd.

"You could say they are enforcers."

"What is their job? To be total bitches?"

"Be careful Danielle, they can still hear us," Derek warned.

"I don't care. It's not like I haven't done everything you have asked me to do. I deleted the evidence, I am planning on joining this tribe of people. What more do they want?"

"Actually, they don't want you to join."

Danielle's eyes popped open at the news. She tried to wrap her head around what she could have done to piss them off, but came up empty. "What did I ever do to them?"

"You are with me," Derek said flatly. "They are kinda territorial and feel like you are over-stepping your boundaries."

"I don't get it."

"That's because you are not one of us yet. You are still human and don't understand the hierarchy of the situation."

"Well maybe if you explained it to me I would."

Derek sighed and with a weak smile he nodded. "Fine, but not here. We have to go someplace quiet were the walls don't have ears."

Danielle rose with Derek. He stretched his hand out and led her out of the small diner. As they walked down the street, Danielle noticed the glares had ceased. The fear and intimation she had once felt was gone. She breathed in deeply, following Derek to his car.

"Get in, we have to go to the woods."

"Okay," Danielle's voice quaked. Although she didn't know what Derek was planning, deep in her heart she knew he wouldn't hurt her. She got into the truck and waited for Derek. He climbed in and slipped his key into the ignition. The truck rumbled to life and before Danielle could say another word, they were driving down the street heading out of town.

"So, are you going to tell me how you know Alice?"

"I've known her for several years."

"How many to be exact?"

"Sixty-five." Derek answered reluctantly. Danielle's eyes widened and she searched for signs of aging on his face.

"That's not possible."

"It is when you are a wolf. We don't age the same way as humans. Time doesn't have such a strong hold on us because of our ability to shift."

"So, will I stop aging?"

"Not exactly. You will age when you can learn how to stop shifting during the new moon."

"So how old is Alice then?"

"In human years, 75."

"How do you know her?" Danielle pressed again, trying to keep her voice under control. Her nerves rattled as the trees swooshed past the window in a blur. She didn't dare turn her attention to the speedometer for fear of knowing how fast they were traveling.

Derek licked his dry lips and kept his eyes on the road. His fingers tightened around the steering wheel and he sucked in a deep breath.

"You see this forest around you?" Derek asked. Danielle tried to look through the window but everything was such a blur all she could do was nod.

"This place was once ruled by two tribes of wolves. One tribe came from northern Canada. They were gray wolves, powerful and cunning. Humans introduced them to this area hoping to restore the ecosystem that had been destroyed by the eradication of the red wolves that had once lived here. But the red wolves weren't completely gone. There were a few of us that remained."

"When the gray wolves came, the two tribes fought over territory for hunting grounds. In order to broker a deal, the gray alpha offered his daughter to the alpha of the red wolves. The idea was to bring the two tribes together to live in peace. But the daughter ran away from her responsibilities and was never seen again."

"So Alice was the gray wolf's daughter, and you were the red wolf." Danielle whispered putting the tale together in her mind. Derek nodded.

"Alice was to be mine, but she ran away leaving me and her family."

"What happened to her family? I mean if wolves live so long, surely they are still around."

Derek shook his head and stole a glance at Danielle. "They left these parts in search of her and they never came back."

"If the gray wolves are gone, then why the hostility? I mean wouldn't they be welcomed back to their lands?"

"This is not their land," Derek hissed stomping on the brake and causing the truck to come to a skidding stop. "They are not allowed to return after all that they did to my people—my tribe. It was only after they left, that my tribe grew."

"I'm sorry," Danielle gasped staring into Derek's murderous eyes. He sucked in deep breaths as his hands trembled.

"No," Derek huffed regaining his senses. "I'm sorry. I told you, you wouldn't understand. But after you change, everything will be made clear to you."

"Are you planning on killing Alice, if you see her again?"

"I should have killed her in the forest, but I didn't. If she shows her face again, I will have no choice."

"You can't do that! She is like a sister to me. Please."

"You have no say. You are still a human."

"And when I am like you? Will I have a say in her fate?"

Derek glared at her, refusing to answer.

"You can't kill her. You can't. After all, it is your fault she is here. She came for me and you told her to come. Surely there has to be some diplomatic solution, if you invited her."

"You don't understand," Derek snapped. "You have no say in her fate when yours is still up in the air."

"What do you mean up in the air? I told you I would become like you. If that means that I will have a say in Alice's future, then I want it more now than ever. I won't just stand by and let you kill my friend."

"Why are you defending Alice so much? She lied to you. Family doesn't do that. Family sticks by you no matter what."

"Families lie all the time to protect the ones they love. And I love Alice. She was there for me when no one else was. She found me on the streets and took me in. We are sisters and I won't just sit here listening to all the things you are going to do to her because of what you did."

"What I did?" Derek seethed. His eyes grew narrow as he bared his teeth.

"You kidnapped me, you challenged her, you made her come back, and she did come back—to save me. Now, if I can save her—bite me now so that I can make my claim for her life."

Derek's face dropped. The tension and fierceness vanished from his features as he stared at the human sitting beside him.

"You would do that for her? You would go to those lengths to save her?"

"Yes." Danielle squared her shoulders and glared at Derek with complete resolve in her eyes. Derek nodded, plopping back into his seat. He released the steering wheel and stared out the window.

"Are you willing to take her place by my side?"

"Yes," Danielle answered quickly. "If you spare her life."

A small smile played at the corner of Derek's lips. He twisted in his seat to face Danielle. The innocent girl kept her composure, wondering what was happening in this wolf's mind.

"You will make good on your promise."

Chapter 10

The light of the day faded into the soft hues of night. Alice stood on the porch of her family's old home allowing memories to flow through her like water. She brushed away the single tear that had slipped down her cheek the moment the screen door had slammed shut.

"You okay?" Bash asked. The old wooden boards moaned under his weight as he walked closer towards her. Alice shrugged, turning her attention from the distant trees to him.

"Been better." She tugged her jacket up over her shoulder and shifted her focus back to the trees before her. Somewhere in the distance the echo of an owl's cry faded.

"You're thinking of Danielle aren't you?"

"I just don't understand how all this happened. Last week she was with me in Seattle, arguing over chores, and now here we are. The one place I never wanted to come back to. Out of all the places in this park she had to visit, why did she have to come into his territory?"

"She'll be fine." Bash wrapped his arms around Alice's waist and settled his chin on her shoulder. She snuggled into his arms letting him hold the pieces of her together.

"I have to go for a little while," he whispered in her ear. "I won't be gone long."

"Where are you going?" Alice turned her body around to face him. She stared up at him, her eyes filled with worry. Bash lifted his hand up to brush the back of it against her cheek.

"To the ranger's station. Apparently some other hikers have gotten lost and they need my help to find them. It won't take me long. I will be back soon."

Alice nodded trying not to let her emotions get the better of her.

"Don't worry. Derek won't find you are here and he won't come looking for you."

"It's not Derek I'm worried about right now."

"Alice, Danielle will be fine. You have to trust me on this." Alice stared up through the canopy of the trees, keeping her eyes locked on a sliver of moon drifting through the sky.

"It will be gone tomorrow night."

"I know. That is why I will help you find her tomorrow. But..." Bash's words trailed off. Alice twisted her head to look at him. His eyes were on the wooden planks at their feet.

"You will be turning too," Alice finished. "I know. It's the reason I am worried. What if I can't do this without you? What if something happens to me and Danielle is trapped with Derek forever?"

"Nothing is going to happen to you. You are too stubborn to let anything happen to you." Bash flashed Alice a tender smile trying to fill her with hope. "Besides," he added, "You'll find Danielle and you'll be able to make the right decision."

Alice nodded as he slipped away from her. "Don't worry."

Alice kept her eyes on Bash as he moved towards his jeep parked in the dirt driveway. He lifted his hand to wave goodbye, before opening the door and getting in. The low rumble of the jeep filled the forest causing the birds to take flight. Alice watched the feathered creatures soar into the sky as the headlights washed the trees with light.

"I'm sorry, Bash." Alice's voice dropped. She kept her eyes on the clouds drifting past the moon. "I can't wait until tomorrow."

As soon as he was out of sight, Alice glanced around her. The only way she could find Danielle would be to face her fear and go into town. Before her inner voice could stop her, Alice stripped her clothes off and shimmered. The instant her wolf split through her human self, she took off running through the forest.

The cool moist dirt sprayed up behind her as she raced through the forest. Darkness fell around her, but she didn't mind. She enjoyed getting lost in the shadows. In her wolf form nothing could stop her. Alice let out a sharp howl of enjoyment letting her animal nature free. With Bash on his way to the ranger's station and the town in front of her, she knew she would have to be fast.

She pushed her muscles to dig deeper. Her legs moved in harmony as the wolf bobbed and wove through the trees. Each scent came alive in her nose, from the sweet-scented rabbits hiding in their holes to the crisp clean fragrance of water pouring down the stream of the mountain. Everything crashed against her as she moved making her more alive than she had ever felt before.

A snap of metal and the hint of a rust smell caught her off guard. Before she could come to a full stop, she had let out a howl of pain. Her face crashed into the dirty ground and pain ripped through her hind leg. Alice's heart drummed in her big ears. Her eyes darted to her hind leg and she saw a bear trap was clamped around her leg.

Before she could transform into her human form to release the lever, a net sprang up around her pulling her high into the trees. She thrashed about trying to get out of the ropes that snared her, but the pain in her leg was too sharp for her to concentrate on much else.

She let out a low howl pushing it from her chest to her throat and out of her mouth. Her cry echoed through the trees. Alice closed her mouth realizing that her howl wouldn't just be heard by Bash, but by every other wolf in the area.

"Idiot," Alice scolded. "You may have just brought the whole town down on you."

Through her pain, Alice tried to focus. She pushed the sharp burning sensation to the back of her mind and then, slowly she let her human-self shed her wolf's coat until she was fully human once more. She glanced down at her leg and grimaced at the sight of the metal piercing her flesh. Blood gushed from the wound and she pried open the metal trap releasing her leg.

The bear trap dropped to the forest floor and clanged against the rocks below her. Alice turned her attention to the knot above her head. Searing pain rolled through her in waves. She reached up to the knot trying to free herself, but with each movement a new pain ripped through her body.

"How the hell did you get up there?" Bash was staring up at her. His eyes were full of concern and pain.

"Don't ask," Alice gasped through the pain. "Please, just get me down."

"I should have told you about the traps," Bash apologized walking over to the large tree that had the rope wrapped around it. He pulled out his pocket knife and started cutting the rope. One strand at a time, the rope became looser.

"You knew about these things?" Alice huffed watching Bash work on the rope.

"They've put them all around the border of the town."

"What? Why? When?" Alice clenched her eyes as more pain jolted through her leg.

"They put them up around town after Danielle was caught. I guess they expected you would come in your wolf form. Looks like they were right."

In the distance, Alice heard the low rumble of a truck engine and tires cutting through the dirt trails.

"Bash."

"I know, I hear them too."

"Hurry please," Alice begged listening to the sound grow closer.

"Just a few more." Before Bash could finish his sentence, Alice dropped through the air. She curled her body into a ball expecting to hit the ground hard, but when she opened her eyes, Bash's arms were snug around her.

"We don't have much time, we need to go," he said whisking her to the jeep. The headlights from the truck split the darkness that was casting long shadows around them. Bash didn't wait for Alice to buckle herself in before he jumped into the jeep and started the engine.

"They can't find you here, or they will kill you."

"I know."

"Why did you run?" Bash snapped as he slammed on the gas causing the jeep to race through the trees. "Why didn't you wait for me?"

"I had to find her."

"Don't you realize what you've done? Your little stunt just gave them the incentive to look for you. Now that they know you are still here, they will come after you."

Bash wove through the trees with his headlights still dark, refusing to give the other vehicle any further clues as to their whereabouts. Alice clung to the side handle trying not to scream as her body rocked back and forth over the rocks and fallen branches.

The little homestead came into view and Bash slammed on the brakes. The jeep slid to a stop and he jumped out. The lights from the other truck grew brighter as he pulled Alice from the passenger side and helped her into the house.

"Don't move," Bash ordered and he dropped Alice onto the bed. Her ankle dripped with blood and she nodded. Her chances of escaping were slim to none with her damaged leg and she knew her only hope was to trust Bash. Before Alice could say anything, Bash disappeared through the open door.

Alice sucked in a deep breath and held it in as her ears perked up. The rumble of the truck filled her ears and drowned the frantic beating of her heart that pounded in her head. She curled into a ball waiting for her ankle to heal. Outside Bash stood on the porch with his eyes locked on the drive.

"Hello, Ranger Bash," Derek's voice was mocking, causing the hair on Bash's neck to stand up. Bash held his position and crossed his arms waiting for Derek to make a move.

"What can I do for you?" Bash asked keeping his attention on Derek. Out of the corner of his eye he spotted a young girl in the passenger's seat of the truck.

"You can stop with the pretense. I know Alice is in there," Derek said taking a step closer before stopping. Derek sucked in a deep breath allowing the burning fragrance of Basil to consume him. He stumbled back from the stench.

"Who?" Bash scrunched his eyebrows holding his ground.

"Alice. The wolf you rescued from the trap outside of town. Hand her over. Now."

"I'm sorry, but I really don't know who you are talking about. I didn't rescue a girl, I rescued a wolf."

"Give her to me," Derek ordered. Bash laughed feeling the weight of the command roll off him like rain water. He shook his head and remained in front of the door.

"Sorry, mate, but I won't allow you to take the wolf. It was badly injured and needs a vet. I've already called Joe to come and take a look at it."

Derek whipped his head around as the light of headlights filled the dark forest road.

"I will find her," Derek hissed turning his attention back to the girl in the truck.

"Well, then go find her. Right now though, I have more pressing matters at hand." A small car pulled up beside Derek's truck. A round, heavy man opened the door and stepped out.

"Hey Joe. The wolf is inside," Bash said keeping his eyes locked on Derek. Derek glared at Bash before returning to his truck.

Joe rushed into the house leaving Bash on the porch. "Hope you find, what's her name again?" Bash called out as Derek threw the truck into reverse.

"Mark my words, Ranger, I will find her. And if it happens that she was here, you will pay."

"I doubt that."

"Bash!" Joe called from inside as Derek peeled out of his driveway. Bash exhaled and relaxed as the truck sped off back towards the main road. He turned and walked into the house. Joe sat on the couch with a smile on his face.

"You sure do like to ruffle up feathers don't ya boy?"

"Thanks for coming."

"So how about that wolf?"

Alice stepped carefully out of the bedroom with the sheets pulled around her body. Her jaw dropped as she stared at the man on the couch. Joe's eyes widened and his mouth popped open.

"Allie?" Joe whimpered. Alice's eyes flickered from the round man to Bash and back to the fat man on the couch. She shook her head as she moved in closer.

"Joe?"

"My God girl!" Joe jumped to his feet and raced over to her. In an instant, his arms were around her, lifting her up off her feet. "It's been too long. Where have you been?"

"Far away from here." Alice's voice was weak from Joe's bear hug, and he quickly released.

"Why on God's green earth did you come back?"

"The girl that was with Derek," Bash answered.

"You mean Danielle?" Joe glanced over to Bash. Both Bash and Alice nodded.

"Word around town is he is planning on turning that girl."

"When?" Alice jumped to her feet.

"Well," Joe dropped his eyes to the floor before bringing his eyes back up to Alice's face. "The transformation has already started. He bit her. Now all that's left is to wait for the new moon tomorrow night."

Alice felt her body drop to the floor. Every bit of happiness was sucked out of her as she stared at Joe.

"I'm sorry, Darling."

"No. I won't let her be tied to Derek."

"Derek's the alpha now, kid. Ever since you bailed on us, he does what he wants."

"Wait," Bash raised his hands up and shook his head. "How do you know each other? And how do you know so much about what is going on?"

Joe walked over to Alice and picked her up off the floor. He carried her to the couch and set her down gently. Sympathy filled his eyes as he stared at her. Alice nodded.

"Joe is my uncle. He was my father's brother," Alice answered dropping her head.

"I'm the one who helped her escape," Joe finished with regret filling his eyes.

"What?" Bash stepped back as if rocked by an unseen hand.

"It's a long story," Joe said with a weak smile. "But now, we need to take care of Allie."

"Alice," Bash corrected glancing at the wound on her ankle.

"I was born Allison. My family called me Allie. But after I left, I changed it to Alice," she confessed, reaching down to her ankle. The healing process had already started and her wounds were closing up around the teeth marks left by the metal contraption.

"Look, I can see that there is a lot to explain," Joe said leaning back into the soft cushions. " Bash deserves to know what he's gettin' himself into, don't you think?"

Alice nodded and nibbled on her lower lip. She sucked in a deep breath and forced herself to look at Bash.

"You might want to sit down for this," Alice whispered. Bash moved to the rocking chair and scooted beside Alice. He reached for her and set his hands on her legs.

"You can tell me anything."

Chapter 11

Alice glanced at Bash and then at Joe. Joe nodded with a small smile curling his lips. The look in his eyes gave Alice the strength she needed to continue.

"I was the first of my family's pack to be born on this land. My family came from the northern parts of Canada. But when we arrived, we assumed we were the only pack here. It didn't take long before we came across another. The red wolves that were thought to be gone, were still here. After many long scrimmages, the alpha of the red wolves came to my father and offered a treaty."

"The alpha of the red wolves had a son, and they wanted him to marry me. My father refused saying how he couldn't stand the thought of the gray wolf to be mixed with that of the red. The red wolf didn't like that and so he waged a war against our kind." Alice dropped her head letting her tears stream down her face. She sucked in a deep breath trying to hold her composure to finish the tale.

Joe reached out for her and touched her knee. Alice glanced at him and nodded.

"My father was killed by the other alpha and my mother..." Alice's voice dropped.

"Was killed as well," Joe finished. "I knew the only way to save Allie was to take her far away where they wouldn't find her. So I brought her to Seattle. Little did we know that the son of the alpha still wanted her for his own. Many years passed and we thought we were safe, but Derek found us. I left Allie alone to throw him off her trail."

"The only way for me to keep her safe was to come here and never speak to her again. So, I joined Derek's pack and convinced him that Allie was dead. Over the years, Derek's father died and I believed the feud had died with him. I was going to go and find Allie but when I heard about the girl in the forest with evidence of our kind, I had to stay. I didn't know it was Allie's friend until I overheard Derek speaking with his pack about his plans for the girl."

Apparently, Derek didn't believe Allie was dead. When he caught her smell on Danielle, all his suspicions were confirmed."

"We can't leave Danielle with Derek. You know he will do terrible things to her, once she is turned, to punish me for leaving." Alice whimpered. Joe nodded slowly keeping his eyes on the red marks on Alice's leg.

"And you can't just run into town and expect Derek to give her up. He will kill you." Bash leaned forward, his eyes filled with fear.

"I can't just sit here and let her go through with it, without knowing that Derek is evil. She doesn't know what she is getting herself into," Alice countered. Her heart broke as images of what Derek could do to Danielle filled her mind.

"Look, I'll go into town and try to get an idea of where Danielle is at," Joe offered. "Maybe even try to convince her not to do anything stupid just yet. You two need to stay here. I will come back before dusk and we will go from there."

Bash and Alice nodded as Joe rose to his feet. "Darling, walk me out will you?"

Alice shifted her weight and rose from the couch. Bash followed her moves ensuring she was capable of walking on her own. Alice smiled and patted Bash on the shoulder.

"I'm fine," she ensured him as she followed Joe out the door.

Joe paused and waited for Alice. Once she was out the door, he turned to her.

"I won't begin to ask why you came back for a human, but I get it. I do."

"Joe, don't." Alice said shaking her head and curling the sheets closer to her body.

"You know that boy in there would go through hell for you." Alice twisted her head to glance at the screen door.

"I..."

"Don't play coy. He is in love with you and you know it. But I don't think it's fair for you to bring him into your troubles. The pack doesn't bother him and he can live in safety out here alone. But with you around," Joe stopped and gritted his teeth.

"I know. But..."

"Do ya love him?" Joe stared at her and waited.

"I don't know. He is kind."

"Not all wolves are like Derek, you know that. Even Bash ain't full wolf, he loves you more than he will ever tell you. I can see it in his eyes. He will go to the ends of the earth for you. But you can't be leading him on Allie, it isn't fair."

"Then, what would you have me do? Leave him? Stay with him? What?"

Joe shook his head, "I'd have you make up your mind about him. Ever since you came into his life, he's changed. And so have you. When I left you back in the city do you remember what I told you?"

"Stick to your own kind," Alice said in hushed tones.

"He's every bit of your kind. He's strong, hard-workin' and loyal. Everything your father was. I don't doubt your father would have approved of him, if he was still around. But if you ain't willing to open yourself up to him, then you need to let him go. Derek won't hesitate to kill him. After all, he's a loner just like you and no use to the pack. Now that he knows Bash is involved with you, Derek won't hesitate to strike at him in any way possible."

Alice dropped her head letting more tears flow down her cheeks. Her heart shattered thinking of losing Bash. With her world turned upside down she nodded.

"Now stay put, for once in your life, and let me figure out what's going on in town. I'll be back later."

Joe leaned in and pecked Alice on the forehead. She lifted her head up and watched her uncle climb back into his tiny little car. She remained on the porch until the headlights had faded from her view.

The sound of the screen door opening startled Alice. She whipped her head around and stared at Bash.

"Everything okay?" he asked

Alice shook her head back and forth letting all the pain of her heart out in torrents of tears. Bash was at her side in an instant. He wrapped his arms around her tiny body and rocked her in his arms.

"It will be okay," he whispered. He stroked his hand through her hair to calm her. As his lips pressed against her forehead, she understood what Joe was saying. She knew she couldn't let Bash get any deeper into her problems.

"I have to go," Alice said quickly pushing Bash away from her.

"Joe said to stay here."

"I can't stay here. I can't put you in anymore danger. I already have Danielle to worry about and I can't lose you too."

Alice turned and stormed into the house. She dropped the sheet from around her and walked into the bedroom. Her eyes darted about the small room until they found her shirt. She moved quickly, trying to get the shirt over her head. But as she slipped her head through the opening, Bash was beside her once again.

"I can't lose you either. Haven't you figured it out by now? I'm in love with you."

"Stop, you don't know what you're saying."

"I do know what I am saying." He reached out and cupped his hand around her face. Alice squeezed her eyes shut refusing to look at him. She knew that if she did, she would lose her resolve and wouldn't be able to walk out the door.

"I get it Alice. You are scared. It seems like the world is coming down around you. But, I'm not going to leave you. I won't let you do this alone."

"Derek will kill you."

"No. He won't, I won't let him."

"Bash, please," Alice whimpered and opened her eyes to look at him. Before she could say another word, he pressed his lips to hers. His tongue parted her closed lips and slipped into her mouth.

Alice didn't stop him. Her fingers dug into back of his hair and she pulled him to her. Everything faded from her, all of her pain and her sorrow was stripped from her as Bash embraced her. She found herself at peace as she hadn't felt in years. Her body molded to Bash's as he dropped his hand down to her leg and curled it around his waist.

"I love you Alice," Bash whispered through his kiss. Alice pulled back as the pieces of her broken heart mended together. Deep within Bash's eyes were the strength she needed and the love she craved.

Alice dropped her hands to his pants and unbuckled the belt from his waistline. She leaned closer to him, fumbling with his fly until it dropped.

"Please," Alice said. "Save me."

Bash didn't need any further incentive. He grabbed Alice and hoisted her up into the air. With his arms around her he moved to the bed. The moment his knees knocked into the soft mattress he lowered her down. Refusing to let her go for even a second, he dropped down with her.

He quickly removed his pants, letting them fall to the floor next to the bed. His hands roamed over her bare body. Alice closed her eyes envisioning Bash's touch as the glue she needed to be whole once more. Every brush of his fingertips over her skin healed her in ways she never expected. Bash parted her legs and slipped between them.

"I will never hurt you," he said shifting his hips. Alice's eyes drifted to his hands as his fingers curled around the shaft of his cock. She smiled, letting her hand drift between their bodies to help him.

"I know," she said brushing the tip of her finger over the crown of his head before running over his knuckles. Bash slipped his hand out and rested on his arms as Alice rubbed the tip of his cock over her pussy lips. The moisture between her legs lathered over his flesh.

Her hips rose up to meet his, and she guided his cock into her opening. Bash exhaled as he entered her and dropped his head. Alice curled her legs around his body and rocked her hips trying to consume as much of him as she could. Each thrust grew more intense as the fluid leaked out of her and covered him.

Their bodies molded into one as the light of the moon drifted passed the window. Bash wrapped his arm under Alice's head holding her close. His thick cock penetrated her again and again. Each thrust of his hips against hers filled her with new life. With her back arched and her breasts pressed against his strong chest, Alice curled her legs around Bash's body keeping him locked to her as they moved.

The squeaky springs of the bed protested under their weight. Any other time Alice would cringe at the sound, but with Bash, it was if the bed wasn't even there. It was just him and her in this moment. All of Alice's troubles melted away. She didn't think of Danielle or Derek. All she saw was Bash and she was completely at peace with everything.

"You are amazing," Bash huffed between his thrusts.

"Do you like it?"

"God, yes. I don't ever want this to stop."

"It doesn't have to," Alice cooed running her fingers down his back. "We could stay like this forever."

"I want to," Bash panted increasing his speed. Alice kept time with Bash's movements. When his cock slipped out, she jerked her body to keep him in her. For the first time in her life, Alice felt complete. She paused and slumped down to the mattress.

"What?" Bash gasped with shock in his eyes. Alice lifted her hand up and brushed the back of her hand against his face. Her lips twitched along with her legs still clinging to Bash's waistline.

"I don't want you to get hurt," she whimpered. A smile spread across Bash's face. He slipped his cock slowly out of her body before ramming it back in. Alice gasped feeling him throbbing deep inside her.

"But?" Bash moved faster pumping his cock further into her, forcing the words out of her.

"I love you," Alice panted between gasps of air. Bash slowed his pace until he came. As the fluid was released from him, his body trembled. Alice sucked in a deep breath as he filled her up.

"That wasn't so hard now was it?" Bash teased before leaning down and pressing his lips to hers.

"I mean it though," Alice whimpered, letting her juices flow out of her body. She pushed aside the calm to stare at him in his eyes. "I can't lose you. You mean too much to me."

Bash kissed her tenderly on the cheek before lowering himself down. "You aren't going to lose me."

"But," Alice began.

"Don't ruin this. Everything will work itself out in the end. You'll see."

"How do you know?" Alice asked turning her head to the side to face Bash. He brushed his fingers over her cheek and sucked in a deep breath.

"Love like ours doesn't happen very often. I doubt the universe would be so cruel as to take it away so soon. Have a little faith, Love."

"But," Alice tried again but he pressed his finger to her lips silencing her.

"Get some sleep, will you? I'll be right here when you wake up. If you still have any doubts come morning, you can express them, then. But for now, just be here with me, like this." Bash traced the valley of her breast with his fingertips and snuggled into Alice's hair.

Alice nodded and kissed the tip of his finger before lowering his hand from her face. She let her eyes roam over the small room. The moonlight drifted into the small room and filled the space with a silver light. Alice closed her eyes and concentrated on the heat coming from Bash's body beside her. It didn't take long before sleep overtook her.

Chapter 12

"Relax," Derek said in a soothing tone stroking Danielle's hair. Her eyes flickered to the unfamiliar faces around her feeling the daggers of their gaze piercing her confidence. She had understood that becoming a wolf would affect the whole town, she didn't realize how many would come, until this very moment. She swallowed the lump that was lodged in her throat and tried to calm her nerves.

Although she had only spent a few days with Derek, she couldn't have been more certain of her decision. He was everything she had ever wanted. Handsome, fun, daring, and most importantly, a wolf. She pulled in a deep breath to solidify her resolve. Derek's lips curled up at the corners giving her chills. Something about the way he looked at her caused heat to flash through her face.

"If you don't want to do this," Derek pushed his eyebrows together, his eyes filled with concern. She understood wat the consequences would be, if she backed out now. Danielle shook her head and steadied herself in the soft-cushioned chair. Her eyes focused on the tiles lining the kitchen walls. In the corner of her eye, she noticed the crowd shifting their weight with far off gazes.

"They're bored aren't they?" Danielle whispered causing the crowd to stand straight. Derek flashed a glance to the men and woman lining the walls of his apartment.

"Don't pay any attention to them. They are only here to ensure the process is successful." Danielle bobbed her head as Alice's face drifted in and out of her mind.

"Are you sure you want this? This decision can't be undone, once I bite you."

"Do it. I offered myself to you in the truck and I am not about to back out now."

"So why is there fear in your eyes?" Derek asked moving in closer. She glanced up at him and shrugged.

"I didn't expect so many people to be witnesses, that's all."

Derek's laughter filled his living room and Danielle wondered what was so funny. She sucked in a deep breath waiting for the pain to start. But as Derek held her wrist in his hand he stepped around her to face the crowd.

"We have all seen this before. If you don't want to be here, you can go." To Danielle's surprise half the people in the room began filing out of his front door. With fewer people around her, she became more confident. A smile played on her lips as the trio of girls that had intimidated her earlier in the day filed out. She exhaled, watching them go and allowed herself to relax.

"Is that better for you?" Derek asked turning his attention back to her. She nodded. He dropped to his knees and faced her.

"This is what is going to happen," Derek started just as the door flew open. Danielle's eyes widened to see a heavy-set man enter the room. Derek hissed when he turned. He rose to his feet and brushed the back of his hand across Danielle's face before releasing her arm.

Danielle's eyes followed Derek as he walked over to the man. Her heart sputtered with confusion as she studied them. The man twitched as if he was impatient as Derek moved in closer. Danielle strained her ears trying to focus on their conversation, but with her weak human ears, she couldn't hear anything. Derek twisted his head to flash Danielle a reassuring smile before turning back to the heavy-set man.

Danielle waited with her heart pounding frantically in her chest. She could barely contain herself and twitched in her seat. The man stared at her while he spoke to Derek. Then, just as swiftly as he had come into the room, he left. Derek shook his head once before nodding to the few people remaining in the room.

For a moment Danielle almost heard Derek telling them to "go." She watched the rest of the crowd file out through the front door with the heavy set man leading the way.

"What's that all about?" Danielle asked. She couldn't hide the fear in her voice as her mind drifted to Alice.

"It seems your friend Alice is still alive. I am having her brought here to witness your transformation."

"No. I don't want her here."

Derek's smile twisted into a sinister grin. "Oh, why not? I thought you two did everything together?"

"I don't want her here."

Derek nodded, "Fair enough. Shall we continue?"

"Yes," Danielle said firmly. If Alice came, she would try to talk her out of becoming like her. Danielle forced the thought from her mind, pushing it back. Becoming a wolf was all Danielle wanted in life. After all the years she'd spent studying the creatures, to become one was more than she could have ever hoped for.

"You are going to feel the prick of my teeth cutting into you," Derek began stretching his hand out to wrap his fingers around Danielle's wrist. He traced her veins down her arm with his fingertips and stared at her.

"It won't feel like much, only a paper cut. But you will experience a burning sensation soon afterward. It will feel as if your skin is burning, but until the venom stops coursing through your entire body, it won't stop. Once the fire goes out, your next transformation will take place tomorrow night. When the stars emerge without a moon you will shift into one of us. Are you ready?"

Danielle nodded keeping her eyes locked on Derek. HIs body shimmered as he shifted into the large red wolf she had seen back in the forest. Gasping she stepped back from the mighty creature. Although she knew what she was getting herself into, she felt frightened when the wolf bared its razor-sharp teeth.

She stretched out her trembling hand. The wolf nuzzled her hand like a dog before nipping at her. The sound of the wolf's jaws clamping down startled her. Danielle pulled back expecting half her hand to be gone. When she inspected her wrist, all she saw was a few tiny punctures where the wolf had bitten her.

The wolf stepped back and shimmered once again, dropping the wolf coat to reveal the man underneath. Derek rose from the ground with his body bare. The few remaining people rushed to his side draping a robe around him. He leaned down and slipped his hand under Danielle's. His lips embraced her flesh, "Welcome to the family," he said. Danielle didn't feel anything at first. Then, slowly, a fire sparked under her skin. She retracted her hand from Derek and held it to her chest.

She glared at him trying to force the searing pain out of her body, but she knew it would do no good. Derek was right, everything burned. From her tendons to her muscles, every inch of her body smoldered with a heat too great for her to contain.

"AHHH!" Danielle cried out dropping to the floor in agony. She tried to focus on Derek, but it was no use. She couldn't see anything past her own regrets. Then just as suddenly as the heat had appeared it began to cool. First the tips of her fingers tingled, then the icy sensation washed through the rest of her.

Danielle remained on the floor begging for the pain to end. She reached up trying to grab Derek. He glanced down at her with a wicked smile and stepped away from her.

"This won't last forever," he promised kneeling inches from her reach. "And when it ends, you will have a place here with us, with me."

Tears streamed down her face as the fire burned out leaving her like the hollow husk of a person. Derek reached out for her and lifted her to her feet.

"How do you feel?" he asked draping her arm around his neck.

"Tired," she mumbled.

"I know. Let's get you down for a nap. And when you wake up, everything will be completely different for you."

"Will you be here?"

"Of course," Derek snickered. "I wouldn't leave you alone like this. There is too much that is going to happen in the next several hours and I want you to know that you are not alone."

Danielle crumbled down onto the firm mattress and snuggled into the pillows. Lights and sounds swirled around her as her ears and eyes changed. Everything about her human-self drifted into darkness. The light of dawn broke through the shadows forcing Danielle to hide her face in the pillow.

"Sleep," Derek cooed settling down next to her. He brushed the loose strands of her hair away from her face. "When you wake up, I will be here."

"Promise?" Danielle tried to speak, but even her voice was foreign to her. She shook her head burrowing it deeper into the pillow. The scratching of her hair against the pillow thundered in her new ears. Every sound echoed causing her head to pound, from Derek's drumming heart beat to the dripping of the water in the sink.

She stirred once again only causing more sounds to fill her ears. The noise was too much. She knew there was no way she would be able to sleep with all the ruckus around her. Derek sucked in a deep breath and ran his fingers through her hair.

"Try to relax, it will pass. I will teach you how to tune it all out when you wake. But you must sleep and let the transformation happen."

Danielle sucked in a deep breath trying to force everything out of her head. The more she concentrated the easier it became to fill the sound with silence. She focused on her breathing letting the sound of the air filling her lungs to push out all other sounds. Soon, she was comforted by the eerie silence and drifted to off to sleep.

* * *

The sun stretched across the blue sky. Alice curled up to Bash tracing her fingers over his smooth chest, lost in thought.

"You okay?"

"I don't know. I can't help but think of what is going to happen tonight."

"Maybe we should go now, instead of waiting for Joe to come back."

"Why? You don't trust your uncle?" Bash pulled his arm out from under Alice and propped himself up on his elbow. He stared at her with wonder and hope.

"What if something happened? After all, Derek saw him here, and he knows I am here. I don't think Joe is going to be able to help us. If you shift tonight, you aren't going to be able to help me."

"There is always a way."

"Maybe we should go now, to see what we can see. Maybe Danielle hasn't been bitten yet and we can stop her from making this decision. Maybe if she sees me, she'll change her mind."

"Alice, I will go wherever you want me to go. If you want to go to town, let's go."

"Do you mean it?" Alice didn't have to wait for him to answer. He crawled out of the bed and began dressing. Alice slipped out and dressed herself as quickly as possible.

"Are you ready?" Bash asked grabbing his keys from the side table.

"Promise me you won't do anything crazy. Derek will charge me if he sees me, and I don't want you to get in the way."

"I won't simply stand by and let you get hurt."

"I can't afford to lose you."

"You won't." Bash was at Alice's side reaching out for her. Alice stepped into his open arms letting him wrap her up into the security of his embrace. Her eyes darted to the open door of the living room. There on the dining room table, her mother's box rested untouched.

"Come on, let's go and find Danielle before the sun goes down." From the other room Bash's phone started chirping. Both Bash and Alice turned to stare at the phone.

"That might be Joe with some news," Bash said releasing Alice.

"You should answer it," she said stepping away from him. Bash went into the living room and picked up his phone. Alice moved carefully to the dining room table and sat down. With her eyes lingering on Bash, she slipped her hand over the small wooden box her father had made her mother. Relief washed over Alice as she pulled it down from the table top and into her lap.

With one flick of her wrist, the box lid popped open. Her eyes darted to the dried herbs still in the container.

"Joe said Danielle was bitten today and is resting at Derek's."

"Are you sure?" Alice's head snapped up to look at Bash. He nodded with the phone still pressed to his head.

"Joe said he saw him with Danielle earlier, along with the rest of the town. Everyone was there to bear witness. Danielle will change tonight."

"We have to get her away from Derek before she shifts. It's the only thing I can do to help her now."

Bash mumbled a few more things into the phone as Alice stared at the contents of the box. "This is all I can do now," Alice thought staring at the herbs. She slipped the lid back on the container and rose. Bash snapped the phone shut and glared at Alice.

"Derek has men all over town. We can't just barge in there, they will be waiting for you."

Alice squeezed the box in her hand and smiled. "No. That is precisely what we do."

"But you will be killed."

"Derek will want to prove to me that Danielle is now his. It's the only way for me to get close to her."

"Then what?" Bash asked stepping towards the door.

"Plan B." Alice held up the small box. Bash looked at it with wonder in his eyes.

"Just keep Derek distracted long enough for me to give her these herbs, it will slow her transformation down and maybe even halt it altogether. When Danielle doesn't shift, Derek will attack. That is when you grab Danielle and get her far away. The herbs won't last forever, but it will give us enough time to rescue her."

"You're crazy you know that?"

"Maybe, but what other choice do we have? Time is not on our side." Alice walked over to Bash and wrapped her arms around his waist.

"Trust me."

"I do. It's Derek I don't trust."

"We need to be fast. That way you can shift tonight with Danielle instead of Derek."

"Where will you be?"

"Ensuring Derek never does this to anyone else. I'm tired of hiding and running. It's time I took back what is rightfully mine. Starting with Danielle."

Chapter 13

"You go that way." Alice shifted her head and nodded, her voice dropping. She poked her head around one of the brick buildings, scanning the area for any signs of Derek or Danielle. But all she saw were the town's people carrying on about their day. She breathed a sigh of relief and pulled her head back from around the corner. Bash stood behind her keeping an eye out for any others who may be looking for them.

"You want to split up?"

"It would be better if you weren't found with me," Alice said keeping her head down. "I don't know what Derek will do to you if he finds you're helping me."

"Alice, I hate to break it to you, but he already knows. He came to my house to find you."

"But he didn't find me there. He may suspect you, but he still has no proof. Plausible deniability is still on your side." Alice glanced at Bash trying to keep her voice low. "Now go, and if you find Danielle before I do, tell her I'm here."

"Alice!" Bash's hand flew up trying to hold her back. His fingertips across her arm as she slipped around the building. She straightened her shoulders but kept her head down trying to blend in with the bystanders and shoppers. Bash held his position for a brief moment before heading out into the crowd.

"There she is!" Someone called out. Alice froze scanning the area to determine where the voice came from. But before she could make a run for it, two strong hands had clasped her arms holding her still.

"Look what the cat dragged in," the husky man chuckled picking Alice up by her arms.

"Let me go!" She screamed trying to kick and squirm her way out of his grasp. But the tighter she wiggled, the tighter his grip got.

"You got a death wish, Girlie? Keep it up and you may not make it to Derek's place. Word on the street is you are not welcome here. I have every right to do with you as I please."

Alice opened her mouth to protest, but she stopped as the man released her. Alice spun around to find Bash raising his hand up in the air before crashing it down against the man's head once more. The husky man stumbled over Alice before turning around with his arms up ready to fight.

"Take them both!" Another said as Alice and Bash found themselves surrounded. Two men stepped forward with their hands in the air ready for a fight. Bash stepped forward swinging wildly.

"Run!" Bash cried out. Alice kept her stance ready to take on anyone who came her way.

Three more men stepped up, closing in on the couple. "We are severely outnumbered," Bash mumbled over his shoulder keeping his eyes locked on the crowd.

"Remember the plan," Alice said as knuckles crashed against her cheek bone, sending her crashing to the ground. "Bash!" Alice threw her hand up reaching out for him, but the men were already on to him, kicking and punching until he dropped to the ground.

"Take that one to the jail," a thin man sneered glaring at Bash before turning his attention to Alice. "This one has a meeting with Derek."

Alice tried to reach Bash but only her fingertips brushed his as the crowd split them up. She continued to kick and scream as they forced her away from Bash.

"Alice!" Bash's voice faded as she was thrown into the back of a car. Two men climbed in next to her pushing her to the center of the backseat before a third climbed into the driver's seat. Alice kept her eyes on Bash as they dragged him down the street towards the town's police station.

"Let me go." Alice tried to wiggle out of his grasp.

"Sorry little lady, but the boss wants you."

"Do you know why? Or are you just blindly following orders?"

"You lone wolves are all the same. Spouting about how great it is to be free, but we are a pack and pack is family. Maybe one of these days you'll get that into your thick head," the man to Alice's right said staring at her. He cracked his knuckles with a spark in his eyes, daring Alice to do something.

Alice plopped back onto the seat as the car moved down the road. It didn't take long before they came to a stop in front of a small office building. Alice glanced up at the brick apartment building as the men pushed her out of the car.

"Move," they ordered shoving her up the side walk. Alice's heart drummed as she walked closer towards the door.

"This is it," she thought as the three men surrounded her like sentinels guarding a priceless artifact. She sucked in a deep breath as the door opened.

Her eyes popped open as she stared at her friend. She shook her head trying to make sense of the scene that laid out before her. Danielle stood calmly beside Derek. Derek remained seated as Alice was pushed into the room.

"Found her," the men said shoving Alice closer to Derek and Danielle.

"Danielle?" Alice stared at her friend wondering if what she saw was a mirage or her friend. Danielle smiled brightly at her and took a step forward, before Derek lifted his hand up stopping her from going further.

"As you can see Alice, Danielle is perfectly safe here with me."

"What have you done to her?" Alice asked searching for signs of Danielle's transformation. There on her left wrist, Alice spotted the two puncture marks from Derek's bite.

"I have liberated her. Come nightfall, she will be one of us."

"Danielle, you don't have to do this," Alice said stepping closer to her friend before two men stepped in front of her blocking her way.

"Alice, you don't understand, I want this."

"What?"

"I want this," Danielle said with a smile on her face. Alice watched as Danielle touched Derek's chest with her hand before glancing at him with devotion in her eyes.

"Did he tell you what it will be like? Did he mention how you won't have control of yourself?"

"You have it wrong Alice. I will have control. Derek is planning on making me his. He said that if I gave myself to him, I will be like you."

"How so?" Alice's eyebrow rose with suspicion.

"If I am the wife of the alpha, then I will be able to pick and choose when I shift. I will be just like you. In control of myself and this new nature."

Alice shook her head. "It doesn't work like that Danielle. Derek is lying to you. Please, just come with me and I will help you through this." Alice reached out for Danielle's hand. Danielle took one look at Alice and stepped back towards Derek.

"Danielle wants to be here. But you I'm afraid do not belong here."

"I have every right to be here," Alice hissed glaring at Derek.

"Actually you don't. Not anymore. But I will let you stick around to watch Danielle shift into the woman she was meant to be."

Alice dropped her head, realizing she wasn't going to win over any friends today. She stuffed her hand into her pocket letting her fingers play with the lid of the box she had concealed there.

"I'm sorry Danielle. Sorry for bringing you into this life. I never wanted this for you." Alice lifted her head to stare at her friend. "But if you would have told me that you wanted this so badly, I would have changed you myself."

"But you didn't." Derek rose to his feet, snickering. "Poor Danielle never had a chance because you kept this from her." Derek's smirk spread to a smile.

"You're right. I didn't do it because I wanted my friend to live a long and normal life. A life where the supernatural doesn't exist."

"How long are you going to deny what you are?" Derek shouted taking a step closer to Alice. Danielle reached out and tugged on his sleeve, keeping him back from Alice.

"I have never denied who I am or what I am. I just don't go about flaunting it to everyone."

"You think you are so noble being born a gray wolf. But, let me remind you that it was your tribe that came in and started the feud. If you hadn't come here..."

"But we did come and here we are. Even after you slaughtered my entire family, here we are. Derek, I didn't come here to challenge your role as alpha. I came for my friend."

"Your friend doesn't want to leave."

"I can see that. Danielle," Alice turned her attention to her friend and sucked in a deep breath. Her heart broke as the words spilled from her lips. "If this is really what you want, I will leave and never come back. But you have to understand that you can't have both worlds. You can't stay here and call yourself my friend. This change will rock you to your core and everything will be different."

Danielle paused and her eyes flashed between Derek and Alice. Danielle's heart drummed in her chest and her mind raced. "It doesn't have to be like that. Derek said that we can still be friends."

Alice shook her head. "No, either you are with him, or with me."

"I told you she would make you choose," pride dripped from Derek's lips as he spoke.

"Alice please. Try to see this from my perspective."

"No. You have made up your mind," Alice's fingers ran over the small box and paused. "But I do have something for you." Alice pulled out the box and showed it to Danielle.

"Even if you won't listen to me, at least do me one favor and take this."

Derek reached out snatching the box from Alice's outstretched hand. He pried it open and glanced inside before snapping his head back up to Alice.

"What is this?" Derek asked poking the dried herbs.

"Wolfs bane. It will ease Danielle's pain tonight when she shifts."

"Why haven't I heard of this before?" Derek snapped sniffing the box. His nose wrinkled, and he pulled back from the sickly sweet fragrance.

"Because you never listened to my father. If you had, you would have known all about it. Now please, take it. If you won't come with me, at least understand that I never wanted this life for you." Alice's eyes lingered to Danielle.

"I know," Danielle's voice was hushed. Derek nodded once and the men were at Alice's side once again, crowding her. She shoved her shoulders into them, forcing them to give her more room. They laughed at her and only closed in further.

"Alice, I want you to know that Danielle and I have come to an agreement," Derek snickered keeping his eyes locked on Alice. Alice moved uneasily, readying herself for the fight.

"Danielle has agreed to take your place by my side. For this gesture, she has asked that no harm come to you."

"You didn't." Alice's eyes flashed to Danielle. Danielle's face grew bright red as she dropped her head and took a step back.

"I assure you I'll take good care of her in your absence," Derek nodded once again and the goons surrounding Alice grabbed her by the arms. "Take care, Alice."

The men lifted Alice off her feet and escorted her out of the door. Danielle reached out for her friend but Derek raised one hand and she clamped her mouth shut.

"You promised she wouldn't be harmed," Alice heard Danielle shouting from behind the door.

"I have no intention of hurting her. The pack, on the other hand, is a different story," Derek's voice drifted away as the men threw Alice back into the car.

"Where are you taking me?" Alice demanded shrugging the men off once she hit the back seat.

"Where we can keep an eye on you," the driver answered and he started the car. Alice swallowed trying to push some moisture down her parched throat. The town flew by her as they took off down the road. For a split second she wondered where in the forest they would try to kill her. Her mind raced to the lake and then it dawned on her. They had no intention of killing her—that would be too easy. The town jail came into view and Alice sighed.

"At least I'll be with Bash," she thought as the car came to a stop. The men pushed her out, and she stumbled over the curb. With three men on her, she knew there was no way she could escape. Her only hope lay inside and her eyes darted to and fro counting the men in the building as she passed them.

It was only when she came to the long hallway that she finally breathed a sigh of relief. The harsh smell of basil filled her nose, and she knew that Bash was in there, waiting for her. Alice moved with purpose through the long hallway until she reached the back door. The man to her left pulled open the door and shoved her into the room.

"Keep a close eye on this one," he said. Alice's eyes popped open to see Joe waiting with the cell door wide open.

"With pleasure," Joe grunted grabbing Alice by her arm and forcing her into the cage. Alice opened her mouth to scream but suddenly shut it. Her eyes softened as her eyes fell on Bash in the corner of the room.

"Alice?" Bash gasped turning to face Alice. She nodded as the men piled into the room inspecting the situation.

"Hey," Alice whispered.

"Did you give it to her?"

"Derek has it. Now it's up to him to give it to her."

"What if he doesn't?"

"He will. Or he will use it himself. Either way works for us."

"Will you two keep it down," a guard huffed glaring at them.

"And if we don't," Bash challenged. Alice shook her head trying to keep Bash quiet. The man cracked his knuckles and straightened his back.

"Easy there, Sam. Derek said not to harm them," Joe said stepping between the bars and Sam. Sam grunted and shook his head.

"One of these days you won't have anyone here to stop me."

"I look forward to that day," Bash said keeping his eyes locked on Sam. Joe pushed Sam aside forcing him out of the room.

"Let me know how that feisty little thing does tonight," Joe said calling to Sam as he walked away. Joe turned to Bash and smiled, then glanced at Alice. He gave her a quick little wink as his lip curled up at the corner. Alice nodded and stepped back.

"Ready?" Alice turned to Bash.

"Ready."

Chapter 14

"Keep it down in there," the guards yelled from the other room. Alice and Bash paid no attention to their pleas as they continued to rattle the bars holding them prisoner. The crashing of metal against metal echoed through the room and resonated down the hall.

"I don't see how we are going to get out of here." Bash slumped down to his knees trying to catch his breath. His arms wobbled from the exertion of trying to bend steal with no luck.

Alice clenched her teeth, before she moved to the back of the small cage and then raced to the bars, slamming her shoulder into the cage. The metal groaned and the door rocked but didn't budge. She rubbed the pain from her shoulder and stepped back again, refusing to give up. Once more she rammed her body against the cage only to crash into it again, bruising her arm again as well.

"Alice! It's no use. We are stuck."

"Have faith," she answered. "We'll get out of here one way or another. The sun is still high in the sky which means we still have time." Alice pointed to the tiny window high above their heads. "If Derek gave Danielle the drink, then it will take an hour to kick in."

"What happens if he hasn't given it to her yet?"

"We still have time. But I am certain that he will give it to her. Danielle could never handle pain. She will be begging him for it sooner or later."

"But if he has a hold over her, he may like the idea of her in pain." Bash's words stabbed Alice. She flinched thinking of how cruel Derek could be. Memories of her family flashed into her mind. She sucked in a sharp breath envisioning Derek standing over her slain father. She shook her head and forced the thought away. Her eyes flicked to Bash and she slumped to the cold concrete floor in defeat.

"Are you two done sulking or should I come back later?" Joe poked his head around the corner with a grin stretching from ear to ear.

"What's going on?" Alice jumped to her feet with new hope swelling within her. She moved over to the door of the cage, curling her fingers around the bar. A shimmer of silver caught her attention and she noticed objects spinning around Joe's finger. The jingle of metal objects flying around Joe's finger caused her heart to swell.

"I told you I would help you didn't I?" Joe asked slipping the key into the lock. Alice smiled as the door popped open. Joe moved to Bash's cage and unlocked his door too. Alice paused to listen to the men in the other room.

"Derek is taking Danielle to the lake tonight for her to shift without interference," Joe said holding the door open wide for Bash.

"I counted five coming down here," Alice whispered as her eyes darted to Joe. He nodded in agreement.

"Sounds about right, but you gotta be careful of the big one. That one can swing like Babe Ruth."

"I'll take him," Bash said stepping out of his cell.

"Look," Joe paused and glanced over to Alice. "You are going to have to hit me hard. Make it look real and all."

"You sure you know how to throw a fight?" Alice asked with a smirk on her face. Joe chuckled and shook his head.

"Don't matter, all that matters is you getting yourself outta here. Can't stand to think what Derek will do after that girl is changed."

"Thanks Joe," Alice leaned in and wrapped her arms around him. She squeezed him tight wondering if she would ever see him again.

"Count to five before heading out the door. Then come out with guns blazing so to speak."

"If I don't get a chance to apologize later," Alice's eyes softened as she looked at her uncle.

"I know, I know, now get. You kids are running out of time."

Alice and Bash waited for Joe to leave them alone before they started counting. Bash slipped over to the opening and pressed his head against the wooden door. His eyes popped open and he stared at Alice. He lifted his hand to wave her over. Alice moved quickly next to Bash and leaned in.

Through the wooden frame she could hear each of the guys on the other side.

"Almost time gents," one said with a raspy voice.

"Looks like the alpha will be getting himself a new whore," another chimed in, causing Alice's blood to boil. Bash held out his hand and shook his head. The look in his eyes warned Alice not to move yet.

"I heard the alpha is keeping her away from the other females in town, so she'll believe she's going to be his bride."

"That dirty, slimy," Alice gritted her teeth trying to stick to the plan. But the longer she remained by the door, the more she wanted to rip every last one of them to shreds. Danielle may have made up her mind about being a wolf, but there was no way Alice was going to let her be turned into the pack's whore.

"Wait for it," Bash whispered.

"For what?"

"Listen further into the room. There are others waiting. I think there are more than five standing guard."

"I don't care. We will take them all on."

"Be smart about this," Bash warned. "We have to be quiet. We don't want the whole place coming down on us. If we do this right, we can slip out of here with no one knowing any better."

Alice sucked in a deep breath. She knew Bash was right, but she just didn't want to admit it. She nodded and listened, waiting for the opportune moment to strike.

"Wonder if the boss will let us all have a go with the new girl? After all, she ain't really one of us."

Alice had heard enough. Before Bash could calm her down, Alice ripped through her clothes and landed on all four paws. She bared her teeth at Bash and pushed through the door. Snarls and growling filled the room as Alice took charge injuring anyone who stood in her way. Bash emerged from behind the door ready to strike anyone Alice left for him.

As he moved through the hallway and headed towards the front door, he realized Alice was on a mission. She was mopping up the floor with the men leaving him with nothing to do but walk out the front door.

Alice lunged at the husky man and nipped his leg before tossing him through the wall. The man dropped like a sack of potatoes and crumbled to the floor unconscious. Once Alice was certain there was no one left to sound the alarm, she shed her wolf coat and rose up.

"You could have let me help you know," Bash said pulling a long jacket off one of the men and wrapped it around Alice's shoulders.

"Sorry," Alice said with her cheeks flushed. "I couldn't stand them talking about Danielle that way. No man has the right to take a woman without her consent and if Danielle is turned tonight with Derek by her side, then that is exactly what will happen."

"You really think Derek would share her like that?"

"I don't know, and I am not about to find out. Come on, we need to get Danielle out of here before nightfall."

Alice and Bash stepped out of the town jail and glanced up towards the sky. The soft oranges of dusk were filtering through the light blues. Alice waved Bash to follow as they slipped through the town.

"Can I ask you something?" Bash turned to Alice with wonder in his eyes. She dropped behind a dumpster and stared at him.

"What?"

"How do you do it?"

"Do what?" Alice asked as she scanned the area.

"Shift so easily? Doesn't it hurt you?"

"No. When you are born this way, it is as natural as breathing. But for those that are bitten, like you and Danielle, your bodies aren't equipped to handle the transition. That's why it hurts. Why?"

Bash shrugged as a couple walked down the street forcing Bash and Alice to lurk around the corner of the dumpster.

"You shifted so fast, and I noticed Joe wasn't among the crowd you took out back there."

"So?"

"So, what happened to him? I thought he said he wanted to make sure he wasn't blamed for our escape. But I didn't see."

"Maybe he walked out faster than we thought. He did say to count to five."

"Alice, I know he is your uncle and all, but something doesn't sit right with me."

"Bash, we don't have time to argue about my uncle. We have to get Danielle and time is not on our side." Alice pointed to the rusty orange sky.

"Danielle isn't the only one who is going to shift tonight remember? If we don't get her now, chances are she will shift with Derek and that will be the end of my friend. You heard what Derek was planning on doing with her once she changed."

Bash nodded his head and closed his mouth. Alice noticed the insecurities lurking beneath the surface, but she pushed her thoughts aside. Right now all she could think about was Danielle.

She waved to Bash and then she pulled the hood of the long jacket up over her head to cover her face. People didn't even give them a second glance. She knew they were probably used to wolves walking around with their faces covered during this time. After all, it was a new moon and many of them were too preoccupied getting settled for their own transformations to be dealing with other people's ones.

"Where does Derek live?" Bash asked keeping pace with Alice.

"A few miles away. Think you can keep up?" Bash glanced down at his hand. It rocked with small tremors but, he nodded, squeezing his hand into a tight little ball. Together, they raced down the street following the same route Alice had taken in the car. It didn't take them long to make it to the small brick apartment building. Alice paused trying to catch her breath and pointed to the building. Bash tugged on her sleeve forcing her into the alley.

"How do you want to do this?" Bash asked between gasps of air. Alice lifted one finger to him. Her face was flushed and beetroot-red. Her lungs burned for oxygen but she knew time was slipping through their fingers. She glanced at Bash. His hands trembled with each passing moment. She knew he wasn't going to last much longer.

"Do you think you can hold out for a few more minutes?" Alice asked straightening herself. Bash's head bobbed up and down despite the tremors coursing through his body.

"We need a plan," he said pulling himself together.

"I know, but we don't have time for perfection. You are going to shift soon—I can see it in your hands. If you change on me now, I won't be able to save Danielle. Please Bash, tell me you can keep it together for a few more minutes."

"I told you, I would do anything for you. Now just tell me what you want me to do and I will get it done."

Alice leaned close to him and pressed her lips to his. She cupped her hand around his face and smiled.

"I need you to surrender to Derek."

"What?!"

"Just do it. Tell him I went ballistic and feral on you or something. Make anything up, just get him out of that house."

Bash nodded. He sucked in a deep breath steadying his nerves and walked towards the front door. Alice hung back and walked around to the window. Through the thin yellow curtains, she could clearly see Danielle keeled over in pain.

"Hold on just a few minutes longer," Alice whispered to the glass. "Everything is going to be okay."

"Don't stop on my account," Bash said forcing his body to remain in control until they reached their destination.

Chapter 15

"Please," Danielle was curled up on herself as the pain ripped through her body. Every inch of her burned and seared as if she was being cooked from the inside out. She tried to push through the pain, but with each pump of her heart, a new wave of fire flushed through her. She remained curled up on the bed with her knees to her chest, writhing in pain. Every muscle in her body tensed and pulled, stretching out beyond their capacity before retracting once again.

"Derek, give me the tea," she pleaded spitting her words through her clenched teeth.

"You don't know what it will do to you. I can't risk it. Alice may be trying to poison you."

"She would never do that! Not in a million years," she spat as she glared at him. "Please, she is my friend and if you cared for me at all, you would help me through this." Danielle's voice strained as she panted forcing each word through her teeth.

The sunlight faded through the curtains of the apartment and as her body strained and pulled, she knew she was on the verge of shifting into her wolf form for the first time. Her body jerked and jolted as if struck by electricity, causing her extremities to spasm.

"I am trying to help you," Derek pleaded leaning close to Danielle. Tears streamed down her agonized face. The look in her eyes was too much for Derek. He rushed to the kitchen, pried open the box and twisted towards the cabinets. He reached for the mugs and pulled one down setting it on the counter with a thud. He pushed the valve of the faucet letting a stream of water flow down into the sink. As he pushed the cup under the running water, the beating of knuckles on the door startled him.

"GO AWAY!" Derek shouted.

"Alice has escaped," Bash called through the door.

"I don't have time for this," Derek huffed pulling the mug out of the stream of water and pulling open the microwave door. He set the timer and moved swiftly to the door, throwing it open.

"What do you want?" Derek spat trying to keep his cool. Bash glanced around Derek and saw Danielle behind him, on the bed in tears. He flashed his eyes back to Derek and swallowed hard.

"Alice, she is gone."

"Why do I care about that, now?"

"She went feral. Killed a lot of people in the jail, before bolting. She can't be allowed to roam free on the streets," Bash explained. Derek glared at him and shook his head.

"Sounds like an animal problem to me. Aren't you the park ranger? Do something about it." Derek tried to close the door on Bash, but he held it tight as more tremors rocked through his body. Derek's eyes drifted to Bash's hand, and he nodded.

"You're on the verge of shifting too, aren't you?" Derek's eyes narrowed then he twisted around to Danielle.

"Get in here," Derek said reaching out and grabbing Bash by his collar. Bash stumbled through the door as Derek held tightly to him. Derek moved towards the kitchen as the microwave beeped.

"Here's the thing," Derek started opening the microwave and pulling out the steaming mug filled with water. He glanced at the mug then back to Bash. His eyes narrowed as he spoke, "I have the tea right here. Thing is I don't know what it does. Alice gave it to Danielle. It could be poisonous, or it could actually be helpful. I am not about to let Danielle suffer any longer with this. Which is why," Derek pried open the box, took a pinch of the dried herbs and sprinkled it into the water. He glanced up to Bash with a twisted smile and pushed the mug towards Bash.

"You drink it first."

Bash glanced at the herbs mixing into the water and grabbed the glass. He lifted his head to stare at Derek.

"What's the matter? You know it's bad don't you?" Derek said leaning forward.

"Just waiting for the herbs to settle," Bash§ said calmly before grabbing the mug. The cup twitched in his hand as he brought it to his lips. With a straight face, Bash drank the contents of the mug and set the cup down.

Instantaneously his tremors stopped. He looked about the room, letting the warm liquid sooth every fiber of his being. With a smile on his face he exhaled. Derek watched with eagerness. Danielle remained on the bed twitching in agony and moaning for help.

"I don't believe it," Derek gasped. He ripped the cup off the counter and filled it with water again. Then he started the process again. The seconds on the microwave seemed to drag on forever as he waited for it to beep.

Before the timer went off, Derek pried open the microwave and sprinkled the herbs into the cup.

"Here," Derek said bringing the mug over to Danielle. "Drink as much as you want."

Bash watch Derek administer the tea to Danielle ever so carefully. Sip by sip Danielle's face eased until she was completely relaxed on the bed. Her muscles were no longer splitting and her face no longer contracting from the pain.

"I told you Alice wouldn't hurt me," Danielle said in a calm voice.

"I couldn't take that chance," Derek answered wiping the beads of sweat from Danielle's forehead. Danielle smiled weakly at him before lifting her head up to look at Bash.

"Thank you," Danielle said. Bash shook his head and shrugged.

"I didn't do anything. It was Alice. She is the one who found the herbs. But please," Bash turned his attention to Derek.

"She is out there and I need help to bring her in."

Derek turned to Danielle and stroked her hair. "Can you hold off a little while?"

"With the tea—yes. It helps. But please, don't kill my friend."

"I will do everything in my power not to hurt her, but if she has gone wild, I can't keep that promise," Derek said staring into Danielle's eyes. Bash took a step back. Everything about the way Derek cared for Danielle to the gushing looks of love and compassion startled him.

"I'll round up the others and find Alice," Derek added glancing at Bash. "I don't think you'll be much help though. We don't know how long the effects of the tea last. Just make sure Danielle gets as much as she needs. Don't let her transition before I get back," Derek ordered rising to his feet. Bash nodded as if his order would be followed.

"I'll be back soon. I think I know where she may have gone."

"Hurry back," Danielle whispered rising up to sit cross legged on the bed. Derek flashed her a smile before grabbing his cell phone and bolting to the door.

Derek turned and stared at Danielle, "Please don't go anywhere. The moment I get back we will head for the lake."

Danielle nodded as Derek opened the front door and slipped out.

Danielle flashed a smile at Bash before turning away. Bash counted in his head then scrambled to the window. With a flick of his wrist he threw open the glass pane and popped his head outside. His eyes scanned the area until he spotted Alice.

"Psst," Bash whispered. Alice turned her head and smiled to see him.

"What are you doing?" Danielle asked. Bash pulled his head back inside and turned around.

"We are getting you out of here," Bash said walking towards Danielle.

"But Derek said not to go anywhere."

"Look, I know where Alice is at. She is the one who sent me here. We have to get you out of here before Derek comes back."

"I'm not going anywhere."

"You have to. Derek is not who you think he is."

"I know exactly who Derek is and I won't leave here without him."

"You must," Bash pleaded reaching for Danielle. He wrapped his arms around her waist and threw her over his shoulder.

"Put me down!" Danielle screamed hitting Bash over his back with her fists.

"Danielle, please," Alice popped her head in through the open window and stared at her friend. Bash turned around to face the front door giving Danielle a clear view of Alice.

"What are you doing here?" Danielle gasped. "He said you were feral."

"We lied. Now come on, we need to go. The tea won't last all night and you will shift soon."

"No. I won't go."

"Danielle, you know I would never hurt you. You are my best friend. Truth be told, you would have never known about my kind if you had just listened to me and not come here. But you did. Now, please, we have to get to the lake. It is the only safe place for a new werewolf to shift."

"This is all your fault, you know that!" Danielle hissed trying to get free of Bash's grip. "If only you had just trusted me to begin with!"

"I do trust you. Just like you trust me. Only you aren't thinking clearly. The venom in your system is overpowering your common sense. But please, don't make me have to kidnap you. It would easier for all of us if you came quietly."

"I am not going anywhere!" Danielle shouted. Alice climbed up into the window and walked over to her friend.

"I hope someday you will forgive me," Alice said staring into Danielle's eyes. Danielle narrowed her gaze and her lip pulled up into a snarl.

Before Danielle could say another word, Alice lifted her hand back and let it fly through the air. Her knuckles crashed against Danielle's face knocking her out cold.

"Did you have to hit her?" Bash asked holding on to Danielle tighter to ensure she didn't fly off his shoulder.

"It was the only way she would come. Now get her outside. I stole a car. It's the blue one."

"What are you doing?" Bash asked glancing around the room as Alice moved towards the kitchen.

"Grabbing the herbs. She will need them when she comes to. Now go. We are running out of time."

Bash nodded and bolted for the front door. He propped the door open and peeked outside. With no signs of life on the street, he made a break for the blue car parked right in front of the long concrete walkway.

Alice glanced around the kitchen until she found the small wooden box. The moment her fingers grabbed it, she took off in a sprint for the front door. Her eyes widened when she saw the reds and oranges of the sunset filling the sky.

"Running out of time," she whimpered closing the door behind her. Her only hope was to get Danielle into the forest and as far away from Derek as possible.

She raced to the car and found Danielle still passed out in the back seat. Her eyes flickered to Bash. "Can you handle her if she wakes up?"

"I think so, but..." Bash lifted his hand up. Alice's eyes narrowed on his fingers as they started to tremble. The effects of the tea were fading. Alice hoped that Bash would be able to hold it off for the drive.

"Where are we going?" Bash asked as Alice slipped behind the steering wheel.

"Your place?"

"They know that's where you might take her," Bash said concern dripping from his words.

"It's the only place we have time to get to. The lake is too far and I don't think either one of you will make it. Now hold on."

Alice leaned down and played with the wires under the steering wheel. The engine came to life, and she sat back. Stealing one last glimpse at the apartments, Alice slammed her foot down on the pedal and sped off down the street. Her heart raced as she wove in and out of the traffic. She held her breath waiting for the sound of sirens as she sped through red lights and skidded around corners. Once she saw the open road spread out before her, she exhaled.

"Almost there," she said flicking her eyes to the rear-view mirror. Bash's face was scrunched up as he concentrated. Alice pulled out the box and handed it to him.

"Take a pinch of herbs and eat them," Alice ordered. Bash shook his head refusing to open his mouth to answer. Alice knew he time was short. She put the pedal to the floor and raced down the road as the reds turned to pink and the night was ready to fall.

Chapter 16

The trees surrounding the small homestead began to thin until Alice saw the cabin in the clearing. She breathed in a small sigh of relief and glanced in the rear-view mirror. In the reflection, she saw Bash holding himself and rocking back and forth in the seat trying to stop his body from trembling.

"Hold on a bit longer," she said turning the mirror down. Her eyes flashed to Danielle crumpled on Bash's lap. The girl was still knocked out and resting peacefully, but Alice didn't know for how much longer.

"We're almost there," Alice said wondering if Bash was paying any attention to her. She knew he could shift at any moment but she had no other choice but to keep going. The bumpy road tossed her about as she held onto the steering wheel and she kept her foot lodged on the gas pedal.

"Bash, if you can hear me, the moment you get out, try to cover Danielle's scent."

Through squinted eyelids Bash lifted his head and nodded. He clinched his jaw tight pushing back the tremors with all the strength he could muster. His breathing came in quick bursts and he knew the minute he stopped concentrating his wolf would break out.

Alice skidded to a stop and flew out of the driver's door. She raced to the back and pulled open the door. Danielle moaned as Alice lifted the girl out and carried her to the house. With a shaking hand, Bash reached for his door. His body ached and jerked as he tried to stand. He clung to the side of the car to hold himself steady.

"Where can we put her?" Alice asked, her eyes darting around the front of the house. With nowhere to keep a wild animal, Alice was out of options.

"In the back," Bash grunted through clenched teeth. With a trembling hand he pointed to the side of the house. Alice nodded once and hoisted her friend up to her body and dragged her to the side. Each step was a struggle as Danielle's weight increased. Alice heaved her friend closer to her, holding her steady as they moved.

"Remember that time when you got so wasted at the New Year's Party that I had to carry you like this up the stairs because the elevator was out?"

Alice tried to chuckle, but Danielle's body was changing from human to wolf and was becoming too heavy for her to carry. Alice wrapped Danielle's arm over her shoulder, refusing to give up. She kept ongoing putting one foot in front of the other until she reached the side where her eyes widened. There resting on the side of the house was a cage big enough for a moose.

"Why on earth does Bash have this?" she wondered before realizing Bash was a park ranger. It was probably used to transport animals outside of the park. Alice's heart broke as she realized the cage was the only safe place for Danielle at the moment.

"This is so much worse than that," Alice finished as she brought her friend to the side of the house and leaned her up against the siding fumbling with the locks on the cage.

"Bash!" Alice cried out. Bash hobbled over to her. Each step was a burden and Alice could see he too was having a hard time remaining human. The sight of Bash crushed Alice. He was so focused on keeping his human form that it was causing him too much pain. Alice shook her head and dropped her shoulders.

"Go," she said with pity in her voice. She knew Bash was holding on for her, but there was no more time left. The sky was darkening and Bash was losing his fight with the animal inside him.

He gave her an apologetic glance before turning and making a sprint to the safety of the trees. Alice turned to Danielle and huffed.

"Looks like it's just you and me," she said leaning down to unlock the cage door. With a rattle, the door flew open and Alice dragged her friend to the entrance.

"I hope you will forgive me for this," Alice said pushing Danielle's body into the cage and closing it up.

Danielle moaned as Alice began pushing the large cage towards the back door. She knew there was no protection from the others out in the open. With each heave, the cage shifted closer and closer to the porch. Alice's eyes flicked to the tree line and her hopes came crashing down around her.

"I can't do this," Alice panted dropping to the side of the cage.

"What's going on?" Danielle's voice was weak and distant. Alice turned her head to see her friend dripping with beads of sweat.

"You are going to shift into a wolf tonight," Alice said regretfully.

"But why am I in a cage?" Panic filled Danielle's features and she pushed her fingers through the tiny holes and grabbed the wire bars. With her head still spinning, she shook the wall. The rattling of the metal echoed in her new ears sending new waves of pain coursing through her. As the pain intensified, Danielle's anger grew into a rage.

"I had no other choice," Alice explained trying not to let her emotions get the better of her. Alice glanced at the dirty ground and pulled herself together. With a stern face, she raised her eyes back to Danielle."

"I couldn't let you shift in front of Derek. You don't know the consequences of that decision. The cage is the only safe way I know to keep you." Alice glanced over her shoulder to look up to the canopy. The soft hues of day had given way to the darker purples of twilight. "You were knocked out and the sunlight is fading fast. Please don't hate me for this."

"You put me in here?" Danielle hissed shaking the wire frame of the cage with such rage, Alice thought she might be able to snap it off. Alice gasped as Danielle's soft gray eyes shifted into bright yellow before fading back to the gray. Alice scooted away from the cage and stood up.

"I had no choice. I won't let you be bound to him. You don't know Derek like I do. He is a monster."

"You are something else you know that? You always think you know what's best for everyone. But you don't," Danielle spat her words out as the animal drew closer to the surface. "I want to be a wolf. I want to be with Derek and I don't want to see you ever again. Pray this cage keeps me contained," Danielle glared. "Because if it doesn't you'll be the first person I go after."

"You may not understand this, but I do know what you're going through. And trust me, I am doing you a favor."

"Some favor—let me out," Danielle rocked the cage bending the bars. Alice knew the wire-framed container wouldn't hold a new wolf. She stepped back and shook her head.

"I am going to leave you in here until you shift. It is the last gift I can give you."

"Gift? What gifts have you ever given me? You steal me from my home, you lie to me, you get me caught up in all this. The only person who has shown me any kindness is Derek!"

"Derek isn't who you think he is. He wants to keep you like a pet. He wanted to make sure that you shifted in front of him so that he would own you. I would never want that for you. I love you too much to stand by and watch you turn into someone's slave."

"Oh and keeping me locked up isn't a form of slavery!" Danielle's voice grew deeper and raspier as she spoke. Alice glanced up to the canopy of the trees again. The last remaining hues of the day faded and night melted over the sky.

"I love you Danielle, and maybe one of these days you will forgive me," Alice dropped her head and turned her back on Danielle. She moved around the corner of the house and leaned against the wall. Her heart shattered as Danielle screamed.

"I will kill you for this," Danielle growled. Alice's mouth dropped and she wrapped her hands around her face. It was flushed with heat and tears pooled in her eyes. The sight of Danielle trapped was more than she had ever bargained for.

"What am I doing?" Alice asked herself as she let the tears spill from her eyes. Danielle kicked and slammed her feet against the cage trying to break free, as the sun dipped below the horizon. Alice wiped away the tears and stood up.

Her ears perked up and she focused on the surrounding area. She held her breath trying to listen for any signs of Bash. Deep in the woods twigs snapped and leaves rustled. She exhaled slowly before pulling air back into her lungs. Her thoughts lingered on him, wondering if he was able to mask Danielle's scent. But with no sign of him and Danielle rattling and thrashing about her cage, Alice realized it didn't matter if the pack couldn't smell her, the noises coming from this homestead would be enough to lure them in. She pinched the bridge of her nose and closed her eyes. There was only one choice left.

Her eyes darted around the homestead searching for the basil that grew wild there. If she could pile enough around Danielle, then maybe the scent wouldn't be so strong. Alice ran about the house plucking the herbs and leaves off the bushes as she ran.

"Let me out," Danielle screamed with each pass Alice made. When Alice was finished masking the scent, she stopped in front of Danielle. The girl had dropped to the floor of the cage in pain. She curled her body up into a small ball. Alice flinched listening to her bones snapping and shifting into her wolf form.

"Don't fight it," Alice said dropping to her knees. "Let the wolf come out. If you fight it, it only makes it worse."

"What do you know?" Danielle growled through clenched teeth as her back arched from the pain before she curled up again in a ball.

"I can give you more tea if that will help, but it won't stop the transformation. It will only make you numb to it."

"No!" Danielle hissed. "This pain is all that is keeping me human. I need to feel every jolt of it."

"You are not human anymore," Alice said with guilt in her eyes. She couldn't bare the sight of her friend in so much pain.

"Please, let me make you some tea." Danielle shook and rattled the cage bending the bars until the wire-framed container no longer resembled a cage, but more a mangled and twisted basket.

Alice rose to her feet and gasped. In the distance a low howl echoed through the trees. She whipped her head around towards the sound.

"Crap," Alice said as Danielle laughed wickedly.

"What's the matter? Afraid of the big bad wolf?"

Alice turned. Her eyes narrowed and her lips pulled up at the corners. Danielle paused at her friend's menacing glare. Alice shook her head and smirked. Danielle pulled away from the cage, scooting to the corner. Alice stared at Danielle and her lip twitched. Alice released the wolf hidden within her and flashed her silver eyes before reigning the wolf back in. Danielle's mouth dropped and her eyes widened with fear.

"I am the big bad wolf," Alice said. Danielle dropped her gaze and froze with fear. She trembled and she shook her head. With the splitting pain from her human body pulling away, she rolled over and curled up into the fetal position. Alice kept her eyes on her friend as Danielle's hands shimmered and stretched revealing animal paws. Danielle opened her mouth to scream. Alice hissed at her, keeping her wolf voice stern.

"I'm sorry, but you are going to keep quiet," Alice ordered. "Company is coming and I have to prepare."

Chapter 17

Alice stepped back, scanning the tree line for Bash. Her heart raced as thoughts of the pack descending on her crushed her hopes. She knew she was seriously outnumbered and that if the wolves were on her trail, she would have no choice but to fight them. For a split second she wondered if she would be able to make a break for the trees and disappear.

However, leaving Danielle was not an option. She planted her feet into the ground. The thunder of the pack's claws digging into the dirt grew closer, and she wondered what her chances of survival were. Would she have the strength to take on all of them, if they liberated Danielle from her from the cage? Would she turn on her best friend to defend her own life? The thoughts swam in Alice's mind pulling her in all directions. She chewed on her lower lip waiting for the inevitable.

She pushed her thoughts to the back of her mind and stood ready for the wolves to descend, bracing herself as the howls grew closer and closer. Each star that appeared in the sky filled her with dread. She couldn't comprehend the number of wolves Derek had turned, but she wondered how many of the townsfolk he had ordered to come out and take back what she had stolen.

The rustle of leaves behind her stole the warmth of her blood. She jumped into the air and spun around ready to attack. Coming out of the trees with its head down and teeth bared was a massive white wolf. Alice stepped back ready for it to spring on her. To Alice's surprise, the wolf lowered its head and whimpered as it crawled to her side.

"Bash?" Alice asked glancing at the soft white fur. The wolf whimpered as it continued to inch its way closer to her. Alice flashed him a tender smile and marveled at his color.

"You're not a red wolf," she said reaching her hand out to stroke the coat of her lover. Bash rested at her feet letting her fingers run through his fur.

"How is it you're not red? I thought the white wolves had been killed off from this area?" Alice's mind raced, trying to figure out what was going on and then she heard Danielle's final cry of pain. The scream bounced off the trees filling the night with terror before fading.

"Wait here," Alice said to Bash and she raced around to the other side of the house. There in the mangled and broken cage, Danielle was no longer human. A russet brown wolf lay whimpering on its side under the broken wires.

"Oh Danielle," Alice said walking carefully towards the creature. "I am so sorry. This was the only way you wouldn't belong to him."

Alice reached for the wires and peeled them back. The wolf jerked up, teeth bared and snipped at the air between Alice's hand and the cage. Alice jerked back before Danielle nicked her with her newly sharp fangs. Alice paused to see a murderous glare in the wolf's eyes.

"You don't understand," Alice said lifting her hands up. "Derek would have stolen your very freedom. He would have kept you prisoner. But now you are free."

Carefully, Alice yanked the bars back freeing the wolf. Danielle jumped to her feet and lunged at Alice. Alice swiped her hand knocking the red wolf away from her. Danielle skidded across the dirt floor and rolled. Before Alice could take her stance, Danielle was on her feet ready to strike again.

"Danielle, I know you are in there. The wolf only has so much power over you. You have to find your human self and take charge or you will never be able to come back." Danielle thrashed her massive head about as if shooing away a bee or bad thought. She pounded the ground before returning her gaze to Alice.

"Don't," Alice warned. Danielle's claws dug into the dirt and she lunged. Before Alice had a chance for her fist to make contact with Danielle's face, the red wolf was knocked back into the trees by a white blur.

"Bash, don't hurt her!" Alice cried out but more howls ripped through the trees and Alice spotted yellow eyes staring at her through the shadows.

"Did you really think you could keep Danielle from me?"

Alice spun around on her heels to find Derek standing next to the blue car. He glanced down at his fingers picking the dirt from his nails before glancing up at her.

"You know, we almost didn't find you here. Seems that little trick with the basil works pretty well. Fortunately, when we realized that was the scent we should be looking for, it led us right to you."

Alice whipped her head around. Everywhere she looked glowing yellow eyes stared at her. She planted her feet into the ground waiting for them to attack.

"Danielle has already shifted, you are too late," Alice said with a sneer of victory. Derek shrugged his shoulders and laughed.

"Doesn't matter, my venom is coursing through her veins. She will do as I say."

"It doesn't work like that. It's not the venom that holds the wolf. It is the transformation from human to the wolf."

Derek's eyes widened as Alice spoke. He glared at her briefly before scanning the surrounding area. Alice curled her hands up into fists waiting for him to give the word for the wolves to attack.

"You're bluffing," Derek hissed taking a step closer.

"Am I? Think about it. How many of these wolves were you there for when they shifted? Three, maybe four? The reason they all follow you is because of their mates. The ones who stayed with them when they changed."

Derek glanced around the pack as it moved in closer. Each ready to strike the moment he said so. Derek smiled at Alice and shook his head.

"Doesn't matter if only one or two attack, you are outnumbered. Now give Danielle to me."

"I don't have her. She escaped."

"What do you mean she escaped?" Derek twitched his head and several wolves turned and raced back into the shadows.

"She shifted without another present. She is a lone wolf now."

"You are lying. You would never let your friend go through something like this and just leave her."

"Actually, I did. It was the only way for me to give her free choice. I could have shifted and she would be bound to me. But I didn't."

"So where is she?" Derek growled stepping closer to Alice ready to strike.

"Out there somewhere. Bash is with her."

"NO!" Derek snapped his head. Alice stepped back as the wolf split through Derek's human form. The wolf let out a long howl throwing his head up into the air. Alice sucked in a deep breath. Her heart pounded in her chest as her wolf clawed to break free.

"Face it," Alice laughed. "You lost."

Derek snipped at the space between them. From the corner of Alice's eyes she noticed the movement in the shadows. Before the wolves broke through the tree line, she shifted into her wolf self.

"If this is how you want to play—then let's play," Alice screamed in her head. The surrounding wolves charged and one by one, she sent them flying through the air as they attacked her.

She panted and huffed, forcing the pack off her flanks and dug her sharp teeth into their hides. She growled and fought as more came piling out of the trees, each ready to die for their alpha.

Alice broke through the pack and raced out into the forest. She knew they would follow. Derek would have given the order by now. She knew she wouldn't be able to keep up the fight for long. The only way to end this was to take out Derek and to make him yield to her.

"Come and get me," Alice called out in her mind. Although she knew there wasn't a single wolf that could hear her, the idea of taunting them thrilled her. With each mile she put between her and the homestead she knew she might have a chance at winning.

As she pushed herself further into the woods, she could hear the drumming of their paws scraping against the dirt path. She tried to keep up the pace making them work to reach her, but her muscles burned acid with each stride. She had to think of something.

The tree line broke and Alice found herself in a clearing. The open field was lush and green. She raced through the tall grass and flowers as she tried to figure out how to bring Derek to his knees.

"Do you remember this?" a soft gentle voice spoke in her mind. Alice shifted her head to see the glowing silhouette of her father leaning down in the field and plucking a yellow flower from the dirt. Alice tried to shake the memory out of her mind as she raced on. But the more she pushed against the thought, the more it shifted into reality.

"What is it Daddy?"

"Snapdragon. We brought them down from the north. They will protect you from your enemies," her father's voice spoke loud rumbling Alice's bones.

"Why are you telling me this?" Alice screamed in her head trying to concentrate on getting away from the wolves chasing her. "I don't have time for a stroll down memory lane right now," she huffed realizing her pace had slowed.

"Eat it, and you will be protected," her father said as he lifted his head up from the young girl and stared at the wolf racing through the patch of grass. Alice's heart sputtered.

"Do you see me?" she thought as she kept her eyes locked on her father. He nodded before fading like the memory he was. Alice shook her head and pushed herself to go faster.

She glanced over her shoulder to find the pack on her heels. "Oh crap," she thought watching one of the russet wolves spring up into the air. The wolf clamped its jaws down on her right shoulder. Alice yelped in pain, breaking her concentration.

She tumbled with the wolf still locked on her and skidded through the dirt. She rolled and clawed until her paws made contact with the wolf. With a mighty shove, Alice knocked the red wolf off her sending it crashing to the ground. She twisted and rolled to her feet ready for it to charge once again. With her eyes trained on the red wolf, she dug her claws into the dirt and paused. In the corner of her eye she spotted the yellow flower growing up to the sky.

She didn't have time to think. She opened her mouth and chomped down on the yellow flower consuming it as quickly as she could. Another wolf sprang up and crashed into her. Just before it sank its teeth into her fur, it released her and backed away. Alice rose from the ground and watched the wolf curled up in pain.

She stared at the others waiting for them to attack. The pack of wolves halted and stared at their companion writhing in pain on the ground. Alice moved forward challenging them. She glared into their eyes with her lip pulled back and snarling.

The pack stepped back away from her as she advanced.

"Thank you Daddy," Alice thought as one of the wolves moved closer to her with its head down. The young wolf yelped in agony at her feet as she passed over him. Despite the pain in her shoulder, Alice trotted through the pack of wolves. She glanced over her shoulder wondering if they would come after her, but they surrounded the young wolf trying to keep it calm, and it cried out.

A smile played in the corner of Alice's mind and she moved as fast as her pain would allow. She knew she had to get back to Derek and to take him out before he could find Danielle. She glanced up to the night sky where the stars filled the dark curtain.

"I hope you got her to the lake," Alice thought as Bash came into her mind. "It will be the safest place for her right now."

Alice pushed through the line of trees and sprinted back to the homestead. She reached the cabin and stopped. Sucking in a deep breath she pulled herself together and dropped the coat of the wolf.

"Bash?" Alice called out. Her voice echoed through the trees. In the far distance she could hear his howl coming back to her.

"Is Danielle with you? One yelp for yes—two for no," Alice screamed. Her heart raced as her lungs filled with air. There was no time for her catch her breath. If Danielle wasn't with Bash, she knew there was only one other place she would be. Alice cocked her head and listened.

Through the trees and past the cries of pain of the young wolf, Alice heard Bash's reply. Two long howls split through the forest. Alice nodded and her heart broke.

"Meet me at Derek's. This ends tonight."

Chapter 18

The soft yellow hue of the street lamp flooded around Alice as she stood on the curb, staring at the brick apartment building across the street. She sucked in a deep breath steadying her nerves. Out of the corner of her eye she spotted a shadow of a wolf racing towards her. She froze waiting to find out if it was friend or foe. Then, a flash of white drifted by her and she smiled as Bash moved like a blur. Each beat of her heart, went in time with his paws hitting the concrete. Alice smiled as her companion halted next to her.

Bash glanced up at her studying her facial expressions. He brushed his muzzle against her leg urging her to move. She pressed her lips into a tight line and turned her attention back to the apartment across the street.

"I wish you could change back to human," Alice whispered as she stroked Bash's fur. "I could really use your help."

Bash whimpered, brushing his head to her hand forcing her to pet him. She ran her fingers through his soft fur. Bash shivered under her touch and nuzzled against her giving her the courage she needed. Alice turned her head looking both ways down the street. With no signs of the pack, she moved quickly across the street and slipped into the shadows next to the building.

"Won't you come in? We have been expecting you." Alice's eyes darted to the front door. Bright light spilled out of the open door and washed over Derek. He flashed a wicked smile at Alice as his eyes narrowed in on the wolf standing beside her. Alice glanced down at Bash. She could see the hair on his neck rise and a growl ripped through his chest, filling the street with its menacing sound.

"Stay close," she said moving towards the open door.

Derek stepped inside the apartment allowing Alice to enter. Her eyes darted about the room, cautious and ready for the attack. It wasn't until they landed on the red wolf resting in the corner of the room that she froze. Alice's eyes widened and she sucked in a shallow breath—her friend was tied in the corner like a dog. Danielle lifted her massive head up and whimpered to Alice. The look in Danielle's eyes was full of sorrow and piteousness that broke Alice's heart.

"Derek, I will give you two seconds to release her." Alice turned her fury on Derek and balled her hands into little fists threatening him. Her lips pulled up and she flashed her teeth in anger, ready to shift at a moment's notice.

Derek's laughter filling the room sending chills through Alice. Bash dropped his head arched his back and growled. His growl ripped through the apartment causing Danielle to shudder and whimper. The new wolf tried to inch herself closer to them, but the chains held her in place. Bash's eyes flickered to Alice waiting for her to give him the cue to attack. Alice lifted her finger to silence him. He chomped his jaw shut and rose. His eyes lingered on the humans in the room.

"I can't let her go. She is mine now."

"She is not a pet."

Alice raised her hand and crashed it into Derek's jaw. Danielle jumped to her feet and snarled as she tested the chains that kept her locked to the corner. Alice didn't flinch. She waited for Derek to stand up straight once again before hitting him once again.

"You couldn't beat me in the forest, and you certainly aren't going to be able to now. Give it up Alice, you lost."

"As long as I have blood coursing through my veins, I will never give up. I won't stop fighting to free her."

"You don't get it do you? You think I wanted to turn her? She begged for this. She wanted to be a part of this tribe, unlike you."

"You gave me no other choice. You killed my parents. You took everything I loved away from me and you expected me to just roll over and accept your father's treaty? Grow up. This is your fault. You didn't have to take Danielle hostage. You didn't have to bite her. You had a choice, and you chose wrong!" Alice yelled allowing her wolf self to enforce her rage. Her voice dropped and rattled the glasses in the cabinets and the furniture.

Derek stepped back watching as the items on his walls rattled and then fell to the floor. Alice held her stance allowing the power to flow out of her.

"How are you doing that?" Derek asked as the furniture rumbled and shifted.

"What's the matter Derek? Aren't you the alpha? You would have this power if it flowed through your veins."

"Alice stop," Derek lifted his hands up. Alice's lips curled up at the corners as the power of the alpha surged through the apartment. It was Danielle's whimpering that caught her off guard. Alice stopped and sucked in a deep breath calming her nerves.

"Yield to me Derek and let Danielle go."

"Never." Derek growled. Alice stepped back as Derek shifted into his wolf form. Alice glared at him as he lunged towards her. Before Alice could dash her hand across Derek's face, Bash leaped forward taking the brunt force of his attack.

"Bash no!" Bash flew through the air and crashed into the wall. Alice raced to his side and dropped to her knees. She took his head into her lap, stroking his fur. His moan was weak, but it was enough to let Alice know he was still alive. She moved his head and rose to her feet. With Bash lying on the ground unconscious, Alice turned her fury on Derek.

"You're dead," Alice growled. Her body shimmered as the wolf within her scratched to the surface. Before she could unleash her full wolf, Derek was by her side. With his mouth opened wide, he chomped down on Alice's arm breaking her concentration.

Alice opened her mouth and let out a blood-curdling scream. Derek's jaw locked around her arm and yanked it. Alice flew through the air and crashed down on the counter top of the kitchen. With her head spinning, Alice wobbled to her feet. Her eyes narrowed in on Derek, waiting for him to drop like the young wolf in the forest had.

It didn't take long before Derek keeled over, writhing in pain. Alice laughed at his agony. Danielle whimpered and clawed at the carpet trying to inch closer to Derek. Alice walked over to Danielle and released her from the chains. Danielle paused to bob her head before rushing to Derek's side.

Through the pain, Derek shifted back to his human form. "What did you do to me?" he cried out.

"There are things that are only passed down from alpha to alpha. Clearly you jumped the chain."

"Take it away."

"No. You deserve this."

Derek rolled around clenching his stomach as the poison of the flower spread through his body. In his pain, he cried out, "I wasn't the one who killed your family."

Alice paused and stepped back. "Explain."

"It wasn't me. I just followed orders."

"Whose orders? Your father's?" Alice leaned in closer. She reached out with one hand and curled her fingers around Derek's throat blocking the air to his lungs. A low rumbled from the corner caught her attention and she glanced over to Bash who stirred with life.

"No," Derek gargled. "My father was killed too, and I was forced to yield or die too."

"Who?" Alice sneered crushing her fingers around his neck.

"Joe." Derek's voice was weak from the pressure of Alice's fingers lodged on his vocal cords. Alice released her hand slightly allowing him to speak.

"Joe killed them."

Alice dropped Derek and stepped back. She shook her head trying to wrap her mind around Derek's confession.

"Why do you think I came after him all those years ago? I wanted revenge. I wanted to kill him like he killed my family. He took over both tribes and stole you away."

"No," Alice shook her head in denial. Her mind raced as memories flooded her mind. Everything Joe had done since they arrived made no sense. Joe had freed her from the jail. Joe was the one who had protected her from Derek when she was younger. "You are lying to me."

"I'm not lying. Think about it. He was the one who stole you away. That kept you from taking your place as the alpha. He killed both our parents to get the title. He was the one who told me about Danielle. He told me where she would be and ordered me to shift," Derek's breath grew shallow as he spoke. Alice rose to her feet and walked over to the kitchen. She pulled open the fridge and pulled out the container of milk.

Quickly she poured a glass and brought it over to Derek. "This is will help clean the poison out, but you have to tell me everything."

Derek nodded and reached for the glass. Alice watched as he gulped down the milk and dropped it. Slowly, color started to return to his face and he sucked in a deep breath.

"Tell me everything."

"When your family came here, we all lived in peace—the red wolves and the gray in harmony. We even hunted together. Both packs worked in unison. But your uncle wanted more than just harmony. He wanted control of both tribes. He lured my parents to a field where buffalo were grazing. The plan was to bring back food for everyone." Derek paused and glanced over to Danielle. She inched her way closer to him and set her head down on his lap.

"They didn't return from the hunt. Only your uncle came back." Derek's eyes drifted to Alice. Alice's jaw dropped and shook her head.

"But why keep me alive?"

"Maybe he didn't want to kill a baby."

"No, he was waiting for a real challenge," Alice answered. Her eyes flickered around the apartment.

"Alice, I am sorry that Danielle got caught up in all this. But she really did want this life. Joe didn't want me to kill her after she videotaped us transforming. He needed her to lure you back."

"And he blamed you for it, knowing that I would see you as my enemy."

"Please, understand that I do love Danielle. There is something about her," Derek's eyes dropped to the creature resting in his lap. He stroked his hand through her fur and snuggled into her. Alice glanced at Bash who sat like a sentinel by her side. Alice flashed Bash a small smile and nodded.

"When the morning comes, and if Danielle still wants to be here, then we had better give her a safe place to stay, don't you think?"

Derek stared up at Alice and nodded. "It seems that we are working together once again."

"Derek, I thought you were my enemy for so long. I am sorry."

"Don't apologize I wouldn't have been able to tell you all of this if you hadn't broken my bonds to Joe."

Alice's eyebrows rose as she stared at him.

"What are you talking about?"

"Your alpha power, it overwrote whatever Joe did to me to keep me bound to him. You are the true alpha. Now, you have to take back your tribe from your uncle."

"I can't do this alone."

"We know," Derek glanced at Danielle and winked. Danielle lifted her head up and nodded before giving a quick yip. Alice turned to Bash and he jumped to his feet. He barked excitedly showing his support for Alice.

"It's time to put the past to rest," Alice said. "But first we are going to need an edge."

"What kind of edge?" Derek asked rising to his feet.

"One that will tip the balance of justice to our side." Alice winked and looked down at the bite mark Derek had given her. Derek's eyes widened as Danielle and Bash stepped closer.

"We have to take this to the forest. Do you know where Joe is at?"

Derek smiled and nodded. "He will go to the lake. He is waiting for us to return there with your head."

"Then we should give him what he wants," Alice smiled and a drop of blood splattered on the carpet.

Chapter 19

The stars sparkled above Alice's head and she paused to let the peace flow around her. Memories raced through her mind. When she opened her eyes, her father was before her. He smiled at her through his wrinkly eyes. The peace filled him and he turned. Behind him stood her mother and the rest of her tribe whom she had long forgotten.

"I didn't... " Alice's voice faded. She nibbled on her lower lip, keeping the tears at bay. Her father stretched out his hand and cupped her face. He brought her head up to look at him.

"But you do now," he said and the vision faded from her eyes. Alice wiped the tears away and turned to find Derek standing behind her. His eyes were wide and filled with awe. He stared at her with his mouth open.

"What?" Alice asked trying to regain herself from her vision. She smiled as Derek tried to find the words.

"You saw that didn't you?"

Derek nodded keeping his eyes on Alice.

"How?" he mumbled. Alice shrugged and shook her head.

"It comes and goes," she said as she dropped her gaze to Derek's hand. There he held several stems of the yellow flower.

"Do you think this is enough?" Derek lifted his hand and gave Alice the bouquet.

"It should be. Did you give some to Danielle and Bash?" Alice asked as Derek nodded. "Good. Now you need some too." Alice took half the bunch and pushed the flowers into her mouth. The bitter taste caused her to gag, but she knew it was their only hope in defeating Joe.

"So now what?"

"We need to get to the lake," Alice said turning her attention to Bash, who was waiting for her in the center of the field. Danielle was chasing her tail and she stopped once she snagged it. Alice and Derek laughed.

"You know what you have to do," Alice said to Derek.

"You sure about this?" he asked.

Alice swallowed hard forcing the bitter flower down her throat and nodded. She closed and waited. Derek sucked in a shallow breath, pulled his arm back and let it fly through the air.

Pain rocked through Alice before everything went black.

"Come on," Derek turned to the wolves in the field. "Let's get her to Joe before the sun comes up."

Danielle walked over Alice who laid unconscious on the ground and licked her friend's face. Alice remained still and Danielle whimpered turning her head towards Derek.

"I had to make it look real," Derek said. Danielle whimpered again pleading with her eyes. Derek shrugged. "It was her idea. Now come on, we need to get going. Remember the plan."

Bash barked and took off towards the tree line disappearing into the forest shadows. Derek leaned down and picked Alice up into his arms, as Danielle walked beside him.

"You know," Derek said glancing down to Danielle, "if we pull this off, Alice will become the new alpha. Maybe she will let you stay."

Danielle barked happily as they moved closer to the trees. Derek kept his eyes open and scanned the area as they walked. In the distance he heard the howling of the wolf pack waiting for them.

"Stay close to me," Derek warned as they reached the slope of the mountain. "I don't want you to get hurt."

Danielle growled and shook her head. She was overwhelmed with everything that had happened. Although she had wanted this life, she had also finally realized what Alice had been trying to warn her about. All her nerves and senses were heightened, but an underlying current coursed through her. One that could easily sweep her up and push her into deeper waters if she let it.

She glanced at Derek and then to Alice. Both of them loved her so much it broke her heart. She wondered if things would have been different if she had just come home when Alice had told her to. She shook the thought from her mind as they reached the peak. Her large brown eyes grew wider as she noticed the yellow eyes staring up at them.

"Stay calm," she thought swallowing her fear. She knew being a young wolf would give her more speed and power, but seeing the pack standing before her was a bit intimidating. She sucked in a deep breath and followed Derek down the slope.

Derek grunted trying to keep Alice from slipping from his arms as he moved and slid down the mountain pass. The wolves paced back and forth, before moving in closer to get a whiff of the girl in his arms. Derek came to a stop when the trees parted revealing Joe at the center of the pack.

"Well, I must say I didn't think you had it in you," Joe smiled as his eyes stared at Alice limp in Derek's arms. Derek dropped his arms letting Alice fall to the ground with a thump.

"Why? Isn't this what you ordered me to do? Take out Alice?" Derek shifted his shoulders back and looked straight ahead like a good solider would do. Joe nodded his head and glanced at the young wolf beside Derek.

"And Danielle, don't you make a lovely pet."

Danielle held her tongue despite the overwhelming urge to bite his hand. She knew the plan and kept her distance from Joe as he moved in closer. She held her breath and her eyes straight ahead mimicking Derek.

"Loyalty is everything in a pack this size," Joe said spinning on his heel. He raised his arms up and the group of wolves howled and yelped on command. "It takes a strong leader, an alpha, to keep things under control. Now that the threat has been taken care of, we truly can live in peace," Joe gloated and turned to face the placid lake.

The water rippled and lapped against the edge as the stars flickered ever brighter in the moonless sky.

"Derek," Joe glanced over his shoulder with a wicked grin. "Cut her throat and toss the body into the water. I want to ensure the safety of this tribe and our secret."

Derek glanced at Danielle and nodded. Danielle moved over to Alice and nudged her back. The light brush of Danielle's nose on Alice's skin sent chills coursing through her. Alice tried to remain still as Derek dropped to his knees.

"One," Derek tapped his foot next to Alice's face. Alice's nerves rattled. She knew she would be able to shift in a moment's notice but now that she was so close to her parents' killer, she couldn't wait another second.

"Two," Danielle brushed her nose once more to Alice's back. Alice sucked in a deep breath and before Derek could raise his hands up into the air, Alice shimmered out of her human form and rose to her feet. Her teeth bare and snipping at the air between her and Joe.

Joe's laughter filled the area as his pack growled and snarled at Alice. Alice didn't pay them any heed. She held her stance ready to rip Joe's head off as soon as he turned.

"I knew you couldn't do it," Joe said to Derek. "Did you really think I wouldn't hear the girl's heart beat drumming in my ears?"

Joe twisted his body around and before he faced Derek, he had shimmered into his wolf form. Alice lunged at Joe ripping into his flesh before he could charge Derek. Derek didn't wait for Alice's signal, he shifted and took his place beside Danielle.

Together the red wolves ensured Alice would have her fight with Joe uninterrupted. Joe lifted his head and let out a howl. The pack descended from the trees racing towards their alpha. Derek snipped and tossed those that dared to interfere off to the side, as Danielle took out those trying to hurt Derek. Together they thinned the herd of wolves coming to their alpha's aid.

Alice slammed her body against Joe's forcing him into the water. Joe twisted around causing Alice to lose her footing before crashing his head against her ribs. Alice whimpered from the blow and stumbled back. Before Alice got her paws on the ground, Joe lunged at her snipping her neck with his sharp teeth.

Alice's howl of pain rose higher than the snarls and growls of the pack. The wolves paused and turned to the battle at the mouth of the lake. Alice dropped her head as Joe sprang high into the air and came down on her back with his teeth plunging into her shoulder blade.

Once more Alice let out a howl. Bash rushed down the mountain slope pushing all others from his path as he made his way to Alice's side. With blood pouring from her shoulder and neck, Alice dropped her wolf coat and slumped to the ground.

"Is this what you wanted uncle?" Alice gasped for air as she covered her neck with her hand. The old gray wolf barked with pleasure. Alice glanced at Bash who took his place between the gray wolf and Alice.

"You thought you could steal the position of alpha, but something tells me you have underestimated me." Alice rose to her feet and dropped her hand. The wound Joe caused was already healing and closing. Alice towered over the old wolf as it snipped at the air waiting for Alice to strike.

"I am taking back this tribe," Alice glanced at the wolves around her, studying each one as she looked at them. The wolves whimpered and panted as they stumbled back from her glare. "This is my tribe," Alice said letting the full power of the alpha to escape from her lips.

As she spoke each word, the alpha command was clear. The wolf pack shook their heads confused as the trees quaked from the power Alice was unleashing.

"I don't know what this impostor told you, but hear this now. You are all free!"

Alice opened her arms up and closed her eyes. The surge of energy pulsed out of her like an earthquake rattling the ground. When she opened her eyes, the wolf pack was on their hind legs with their heads bowed. Alice flashed her eyes to Joe.

"You are not welcome here," she said. Immediately the pack turned on Joe. He shimmered into his human self and held up his hands ready to defend himself from the surrounding wolves.

"Attack her!" Joe ordered pointing at Alice, but the wolves remained focused on him. "I am the alpha," Joe coughed. Alice kept her eyes locked on him as his body began to convulse from the poison which was wreaking havoc on his body. He dropped to his knees and curled up. The water lapped around his knees as he stared into the dark reflection.

"Kill her," Joe gasped between the sharp stabs of pain.

"They aren't yours to control anymore Joe," Alice hissed kneeling beside her uncle. She dropped her hand down into the water. "You took something from them and they want it back."

"I can't give it back," Joe huffed as Bash moved in closer to Alice. Alice glanced over to Bash and shook her head. Bash paused and held his position. The moment Alice turned her attention back to Joe, he pulled his arm back and swung wide. His knuckles crashed against Alice's face sending her flying into the water.

The wolf pack growled and dug their claws into the dirt. Bash snipped at them keeping them in their place. The wolves held their position as Alice rose up from the water.

"You thought you could take me out with a flower?" Joe laughed through his pain. He rose to his feet and shook his body. "Who do you think showed your father that trick? Me." Joe hissed as he advanced towards Alice.

Alice closed her eyes and thought of her parents. Their smiles, their love, and their vengeance. She opened her eyes ready for Joe's attack. But he stood inches from her with fear dripping from his face. He stumbled back tripping over the rocks in the dark water and landing hard on his back.

"You're dead!" he screamed at the ghosts rising behind Alice. "I killed every last one of you."

"You left them here didn't you? In these waters?" Alice asked lowering her gaze.

"But how?" Joe huffed scrambling to his feet trying to slip away.

"It's an alpha thing," Alice said and nodded.

At her signal, the wolf pack descended on Joe and ripped him to shreds. Alice turned her head as his last cry faded into the night sky. When she looked back, Joe was no more. All that was left was the wolf pack.

"Those that are pure may return home and sleep. This nightmare is over. For those of you who are made, you are free to live out your lives as you see fit. But remember, the secret must be kept at all costs. You cannot let the humans know of us."

The wolves moved away from Alice and those that had the power shifted to their human forms. The crowd laughed and cheered—freed from the Joe's shackles. Alice smiled, watching the families reunite and hug one another celebrating their new found freedom. Danielle walked over to her and nudged her nose to her leg.

"If you want to stay, you can. I am not going to take that choice away from you."

Danielle turned her large head and glanced over at Derek. He dropped to his knees and shimmered letting the wolf out. Alice sighed and her heart splintered to see her best friend and her old enemy together. The red wolves turned to glance at her. She bobbed her head once, flashing them a small broke smile and watched as they disappeared into the shadows of the forest. Alice spun around filled with a bittersweet joy. But the emotions faded as she glanced around at the happy faces. It had been so long since she had had a family, and now that she did, her heart overflowed.

"Looks to me like everyone is happy you came home."

Alice turned her head to find Bash emerging from the water and walking towards her. He stood beside her with his crooked little grin. Before Alice could say a word, his arms were around her waist pulling her towards him. He stared into her eyes for a brief moment and she pulled him to her, pressing her lips to his.

As they embraced, Alice pulled back and cupped her hand around his face.

"How? You said you were bitten. Only those born this way have the ability to shift at will."

Bash smiled and brushed the wet strands of hair away from Alice's face. "Unless you are the mate of the alpha," he said with a spark in his eyes. He pulled Alice to him once again. His hands drifted to the small of her back holding her in place.

"I love you," she whispered molding her body to his.

"I know. I love you more, though."

Epilogue

The sun's rays broke through the tree line pushing the darkness back. The chirping of birds and the rustle of the leaves broke through the dreams swirling in Alice's head. She rolled over, throwing her arm across her face to shield her eyes from the intrusive light.

"Wake up sleepy head," Bash whispered in her ear. Alice stirred refusing to open her eyes. After all she had been through over the last several days—she didn't want to ruin the peacefulness shrouding her. "Come on," he cooed brushing his fingers over her spine. Alice shivered under his touch and scooted away trying to hold on to the nothingness around her.

"We got a lot of things to do today."

"Five more minutes," she mumbled trying to hold on to the dream. Bash pulled her body to his. The heat of his bear skin soothed her aching muscles. She moaned as she shifted closer to him. Everything from her neck down ached.

"If you don't want to get up, there are other things we can do," he teased letting his fingers trace over her hips.

Bash nibbled on her neck sending chills racing through her body that eased the aches. Her body shivered uncontrollably with pleasure as her body responded to his wants. His fingertips continued to race down the curves of her body igniting the passion within her. Alice's eyes fluttered open letting the blinding light of the sun in. She twisted her body around to face him and snuggled into him.

"You know," his lips brushed against the top of her head. "I don't mind staying like this forever."

"Then why are you ruining the moment," she mumbled. "Can't we just stay like this?"

"We could, but I don't think you want an audience."

Alice lifted her head up to stare into his eyes. He moved his hand over her skin until he had her face in his hands. With her favorite smile plastered on his lips, Bash leaned closer and kissed her. He parted her lips with his tongue as she reached down to cup her hand around his cock. Bash moaned as Alice's fingers tickled his manhood.

"Argh, get a room."

Alice's head jolted, and she twisted away from Bash at the sound of the familiar voice.

"Told you we had an audience," Bash teased. Alice's eyes widened with shock. There at the edge of the forest stood Danielle. Alice scrambled to her feet ignoring Bash's groans. She raced to her friend with open arms. Danielle smiled as Alice threw her arms around her squeezing her tight.

"This is kinda awkward," Danielle giggled. Alice pulled away to glance at her friend. Danielle's face turned a darker shade of red before shifting her gaze to the ground. Alice nodded and pressed her lips together and shrugged to realize Danielle wasn't accustomed to her nakedness.

"I can see now why you were never one for clothes," Danielle laughed holding Alice at arm's length.

"You'll get used to it," Alice said before pulling Danielle closer and hugging her tighter than ever. "I thought I'd lost you," Alice said trying to hold back tears of joy.

"Well, you will at least once a month," Danielle said giggling. Alice released Danielle and stepped back. Her ears perked up as the snapping of twigs startled her. She crouched ready to defend her friend. Derek emerged from the tree line and stopped short. The moment Alice saw the whites of his eyes, she stood straight and waited. When Derek didn't move, everything became clear. Alice glanced at Danielle who craned her neck to see Derek.

"He's not so bad you know," Danielle said with admiration. "Once you get to know him. A big softy really."

"I guess you found someone huh?" Alice said winking at Derek. Danielle blushed before turning her attention back to Alice.

"Looks to me like you did too." Danielle bobbed her head in Bash's direction and waved at him. Bash rose from the ground and moved over to Alice. He wrapped his arms around Alice's waist and pulled her in to his body.

"So, what happens now?" Danielle asked looking around the lake. Alice glanced at Derek and nodded with a smile. Derek didn't need to be told twice. He raced to Danielle's side and entwined his fingers into hers.

"Well, I am not going to play alpha, if that is what you all are wondering."

"But everyone in town is confused. Joe did a number on a lot of them and they are going to need help to sort everything out," Derek said turning his attention to Alice.

"That is why they will have you. My parents wanted this place to be a sanctuary for our kind. Each tribe lived in harmony with the other, before. I don't see why that can't happen now."

"But the word will get out that this territory is up for grabs," Derek said glancing at Danielle. She smiled squeezed his hand tightly.

"Well, there is one piece of land they won't get," Bash said cupping his hand around Alice's face and pulling her to his lips.

Alice pulled away from Bash and planted three small pecks on his lips before turning to Danielle. Alice winked at her with a smile.

"I don't know about you guys, but I am starving." Alice flashed a wicked grin to Bash. Danielle shook her head as the corners of her lips pulled up into a smile. "Who's up for getting something to eat?"

Bash shook his head and chuckled. He leaned down and nibbled on Alice's neck sending chills coursing through her and rekindling the passion. Danielle chuckled darkly as Derek stood confused studying the three of them.

"I don't get it," he said. Danielle turned to him with a playful spark in her eyes. She curled her arm into his and tugged.

"Come on," Danielle said.

"What?" Derek glanced at Danielle before shifting his eyes to Alice. "I'm hungry. I could eat." Alice blushed and dropped her gaze to Bash's arms enclosed around her.

"It's Alice's way of being not so subtle," Danielle explained as she led Derek back to the lake. The water shimmered and sparkled from the golden rays of light. Derek followed Danielle to the edge and stood with her.

"I thought we were getting something to eat together." Derek twisted his head around, glancing over his shoulder to spy on Alice and Bash.

"Race you to the house," Alice dropped her hand and cupped Bash's semi erection teasing him. Bash's eyes narrowed as Alice dropped to her knees and shifted into her wolf form.

"No fair, you cheated," Bash yelled as he watched Alice leaping over the fallen tree stump. He shook his head and shrugged before he shimmered out of his human form and followed Alice's trail.

Derek turned to Danielle and shook his head turning his attention back to Danielle.

"Show offs," she bellowed hoping her voice would carry through the dense forest as Bash caught up to Alice and they raced side by side.

"So, what is on your mind? You still want to get some food?" Danielle asked turning to Derek. Derek shook his head and pressed his lips to hers.

"Nope, I have other things I want to do." Derek's hands drifted down Danielle's bare body. She shivered under his touch and giggled as he tickled her.

"Here?" Danielle asked glancing around the open forest. The sun light reflected off the water turning the lake into gold.

"Why not?" Derek winked as Danielle dropped to her knees. She opened her mouth wide to receive him as her human life faded from her mind. She sucked the length of him letting his cock reach into the depths of her throat, before she pulled it out again.

With lust filled eyes she smiled up at him. "I think a girl could get used to this."

"Oh, honey, you haven't experienced anything yet," Derek said keeping his eyes locked on her as her head bobbed up and down. "I had to hold back when you were human," he panted.

"But I ain't human anymore," Danielle teased pulling his cock out of her mouth and looking up at him with her big brown eyes. A growl rose up from the depths of Derek's chest and rumbled his body. The vibration tickled Danielle's fancy making her want him even more.

Danielle smiled and wrapped her fingers around Derek's shaft bringing it back to her lips. Her lips squeezed around him as she took the length of him. Her body quivered with excitement. Moisture dripped from between her legs and all she wanted to do was attack him. With each stroke of her hand down his shaft, Derek's cock thickened. A salty bead formed on the tip of the head and Danielle licked it off with a flick of her tongue, before glancing up to him.

With a smile on his face his lips parted and his eyes rolled back.

"More," he grunted wrapping his fingers into her hair to keep her head from jerking away. The heat in Danielle's body consumed her. She let out a growl as her animal instincts took over.

The End.